To Jane
Congratulations on winning
the competition.
Hope you enjoy this
H R Kemp   23 Aug 2021

Deadly Secrets

H.R. Kemp

PAPERBACK ISBN 978-0-6487663-0-8
EPUB ISBN 978-0-6487663-1-5
MOBI ISBN 978-0-6487663-2-2

H.Schuster Publishing
PO Box 413
Glenelg, SA 5045,
Australia

'No passion so effectively robs the mind of all its powers of acting and reasoning as fear'
- Edmund Burke

'The tragedy of life is often not our failure, but rather in our complacency; not in our doing too much, but rather in our doing too little; not in our living above our ability, but rather in our living below our capacities.'
-Benjamin E Mays

Prologue

Sydney

It was hard to concentrate with the fog blanketing his brain. An indistinct barrage of accusations flew at him, throwing him off-balance. He clasped the arms of his office chair and squinted at the red, contorted face bellowing at him from across the desk as a spray of spittle pricked at his face. A laugh tickled at his throat.

Dragging himself up, he carefully moved to the front of the desk. A wave of nausea lodged in his throat along with the taste of scotch. He stumbled and stifled a curse and immediately the tic in his forehead spasmed. He yearned for peace and quiet.

'You don't deny it?' the visitor boomed.

'I don't admit or deny anything. This is progress. Sometimes there are losers, but they are…' He scrambled in the recesses of his mind for some clever, elusive words. 'Collateral damage.' He smirked with satisfaction. 'I'd have preferred not to have so many losers but…it's out of my hands.'

The visitor's response, a sarcastic laugh, surprised him.

'Collateral damage? That's what you call it?' The visitor leaned down, drawing close, and stale hot breath flooded his nostrils. 'You're a megalomaniac. You think you're untouchable. Well, you're not. I'm going to stop you.'

The pulse in his temple throbbed more insistently now and he glared at the hard-set mouth opposite, his thoughts too slippery to form a witty retort. He was bored with the bleeding hearts. They just complained endlessly. No matter what he did, there was always someone ready to criticise or disagree. It was just self-interest.

'I'm not quitting! So piss off and leave me alone.' He pulled himself up straight to glare up at the red face. 'I don't answer to you…or anyone else for that matter. People will applaud my time in office. They'll see I was revolutionary…visionary…taking this country to bigger and better things…taking it forward.' He threw his head back for emphasis and immediately regretted it.

'You're out of control. You have to be fucking stopped!'

Spittle landed on his face again and he slowly wiped it off with the back of his shaking hand. The rest of that bottle of scotch beckoned, but as he stepped forward, he stumbled and again had to grab the desk.

'Fuck off!' he slurred.

'You *will* be stopped…' the visitor murmured before lunging at him. 'I'll make you pay, you bastard.' The word 'bastard' echoed like a chant.

His chest clenched as steely hands dug into his shoulders and shook him.

He jerked back but the visitor's hands held fast. He almost laughed at the absurdity of the scuffle. Instead, he growled, 'You'll pay for this…you, you…'

He thrust forward but his assailant didn't budge. Nausea again rose in his throat but he was bound by a rough and clamp-like embrace and he choked on the bile. They tussled falling against the desk. He twisted, using what strength he could muster but couldn't break free. His smothered jabs at his opponent's belly had no impact.

'I'm not quitting,' he croaked through the acid taste.

As his visitor's grip waned, a glint of something caught the corner of his eye. Then, without warning, a sharp stab seared through his neck. He grasped at the pain, his hand touching cold metal. Sticky wetness pulsed from its base down onto his collar. His legs buckled and he slumped to the floor.

A moan and an oath, 'Oh my God,' floated through the darkness, followed by retreating footsteps and the thud of a closing door. Silence. At last, he was alone. The pounding in his ears softened, his strength oozed onto the carpet in a steady rhythm. He tried to shout but only a hoarse gurgle passed his lips. He'd get that bastard; later.

Chapter 1

The dark armoured van screeched to a halt at the corner. Its back doors swung wide and a black mass of helmeted figures spilled onto the road, quickly disappearing down a laneway. Shelley watched, fascinated, as excitement and apprehension rattled her nerves.

Ahead, a group of four *gendarmes* blocked the side street, their heads bent close in serious discussion. More riot police were strategically positioned along the street and her heart raced as a siren blared beside her. A police car raced past heading towards the square and she startled.

Nervously, Shelley lifted her hand to twist the ring on her finger but instead touched bare flesh. The divorce was final. She'd long dreamed of visiting Paris, never thinking she'd do it alone, yet here she was, leaping into the unknown.

More and more people joined her as she continued down the street. Then suddenly, she was there. The square in front of the

Hotel de Ville was huge, but the crowd was bigger. She stopped and trembled at what lay ahead. Rebelliousness had never been part of Shelley's nature and joining the protest march on the Paris G20 summit was out of character, but she had an irresistible urge to voice long-suppressed concerns. Life was too short and tenuous, and it was time Shelley started listening to her heart, and jet lag or nagging anxiety couldn't get in the way.

A motley mix of people spilled over into the lanes and onto the road. She wiped her palms on her jeans and then plunged forward past the *gendarmes.*

People dressed in stark white suits and grotesque monkey masks caught her eye. Cavorting through the crowd, they both shocked and amused onlookers and Shelley laughed at their antics.

She talked to the group of five standing next to her. Their tousled hair, dark tattoos, and excited chatter made Shelley feel older than her thirty-eight years. Her introductory language class hadn't prepared her for this fast and furious French but luckily, her stilted French was met with excellent, although heavily accented, English.

The man with a nose ring leaned forward to shout above the noise. 'You Australians are hard,' he said provocatively.

'Your mining companies rape poor countries,' the young girl with the torn T-shirt added.

'You turn asylum immigrants away,' his friend goaded.

Shelley grimaced. It was true. She'd enjoyed her job resettling asylum seekers until the new government policy had dashed all hope.

A move into policy enforcement, a harsher role, awaited her return and she didn't know how she'd cope.

'You are too close to America. You both worship money,' the first man said. 'Yes, you Australians are hard. You don't even believe in climate change.' He smiled but watched her reaction closely.

'No, it's not *all* Australians, it's only some,' she tried to explain.

'Ah, but your Prime Minister – Mr. Wrogarth isn't it? – has been voted in twice, so maybe it is many Australians.' He raised his eyebrows at her then continued, 'But, you are here. Good.'

Lost for words, Shelley looked down and shrugged. Like her friends, she'd reflected the Australian laid-back, 'she'll be right', attitude in the last few years, but she was changing.

Gradually, they drifted away to join other friends. Around her, the burgeoning crowd hummed with passionate conversations and she craved to be part of them. Waving hands and earnest but animated faces were everywhere. She'd been spellbound watching news reports with French farmers blocking highways or tipping container-loads of milk onto the lawns of some government building. Their fervour inspired her to action, although the radical elements still frightened her. Nerves danced in the pit of her stomach, crossing back and forth between courage and fear. Activists, non-activists, extremists, anarchists, people who cared, the labels blended into an amorphous mix and she struggled to separate them. Tom's voice sounded out a caution in her head, her parents lending their voices to his, as they always did, but she wasn't listening to them this time. Perhaps the news, this morning, of Ayisha's death, the tragedy of a gentle life lost too soon, fed her resolve. Ayisha was more than just work or a case. Ayisha was, had been, her greatest success, or so she'd thought. Clenching her fists, she willed the surrounding noise to drown out the negative voices in her head. She was doing this despite them, or maybe because of them. It didn't really matter which.

Shrill whistles pierced the air as the organisers rallied the crowd. Launching into stirring speeches from a makeshift podium, their amplified voices resonated around the square. The French language that usually sounded beautiful, in this setting, sounded fierce and frantic. They spoke fast, barely taking a breath between sentences, and she understood little. However, the crowd understood and erupted in unison with loud jeers, cheers, and slogans; spurring each other on. Shelley's skin broke out in goosebumps and her body trembled. The resounding chants and bursts of laughter accompanied placards rhythmically stabbed high into the air. She energetically punched her fist into the air too. Banners, with a mix of international messages, fluttered wildly. She noticed one in English: 'Forget the $, what about the sense.' Cries of 'Il faut nécessaire absolument' and 'Quelle honte' climaxed before the march set off along the Rue de Rivoli.

She was swept along as the marchers left the square and threaded through the shopping crowd along the footpaths. Shelley smiled at the man next to her as he lifted his small daughter down from his shoulders. He gently pulled her thumb from her mouth and took a firm hold of her hand. The man and his wife exchanged frowns as they wedged their small child between them. Her wide-eyed stare matched that of many older participants. The size of this crowd set Shelley's pulse racing too. The family moved to the outer edge of the square, but Shelley, despite her rising unease, moved in close to the lead group and followed the crowd. She wasn't staying on the sidelines today. Her stride lengthened and she stood tall responding to the camaraderie and sense of purpose.

Near her were young radicals in ragged clothes, studs protruding from unlikely places, matted dreadlocks, and elaborate tattoos. Their contorted faces formed fierce masks that stretched their piercings to a frightening tightness. Shelley pulled her jacket close around her and steered away from them.

The march fanned across the footpaths and spilled onto the road, splintering as shoppers pushed through. The crowds mingled, creating pockets of confusion. The heady smell of sweat tinged with whiffs of perfume stuck in her throat but she didn't mind. The mix of noise, colour, and energy brought a spring to her step. They veered across the road and brought traffic to a halt. Horns blared while fists waved from car windows accompanied by angry shouts. The mass of protesters swelled as more and more people flowed from the footpaths and the road, spilling into arcades along the Rue de Rivoli, creating more and more chaos. Shelley's heart thumped hard in her ears and her mouth was dry, but she couldn't stop smiling.

As the crowd compacted, she struggled to breathe. Her short, sharp gasps couldn't fill her lungs. Her back ached from staving off the crowd. She was locked in, being pushed forward and jostled from all sides. It was so much bigger than she had expected. Concentrating on staying in step, she still clipped people's heels and in turn, they trod on hers. There was no way out now. Her pulse quickened and she tried to force her elbows out to create some space, but her arms remained pinned to her sides. She couldn't move. Danger signals flashed in her brain. What had she been thinking?

The marchers ahead suddenly slowed, but those behind her continued to surge forward. Shrill cries of panic pierced the air as hot, sweaty bodies squashed against her. A scream stuck in her throat. Shelley was trapped. Sweat slid down between her shoulder blades and calamitous scenarios filled her mind with every step. Her heart thumped and air was squeezed from her lungs with frightening speed. Beside her stunned, wide-eyed people stared, the look of fear etched into their faces, yet they continued to push ahead. Propelled forward she collided with the people in front and she stifled a scream. It was taking all of her self-control and concentration to stay upright but she was weakening. If she fell now, she'd be trampled.

She tripped but quickly grabbed a shoulder in front, and luckily the man behind her clutched her elbow while others recoiled in self-preservation. Then suddenly the woman in front stumbled and

Shelley lost her balance. The road surface loomed before her eyes. The man beside her tripped and knocked Shelley sideways. A searing pain jabbed through her ankle as it twisted. She couldn't support herself, desperately grasping at the air, for someone, something, anything, to steady her. But all she felt was a throbbing, sliding mass of bodies slipping away from her and unbalancing her further. Images of her trampled body flashed across her eyes. She screamed as she planted her foot to regain traction. Her ankle buckled. Shelley was powerless to stop her fall.

***

Golden-framed mirrors adorned the hotel reception walls, reflecting the red velvet seats, flocked wallpaper and the flicker of passing pedestrians on the footpath outside. The parade of colourful winter coats enlivened by the sunshine disoriented Adrian momentarily. He gasped as he caught sight of the reflection of a familiar figure in a red coat, a tendril of curly blonde hair escaping from her red felt beret. Yasmine? His head snapped around, trying to catch a glimpse of the figure before she disappeared. His heart pounded. Yasmine couldn't be here in Paris? He slumped back into the cushions when he realised he was right. She wasn't here. He breathed again, but a dull ache settled in his chest.

He'd thought he was over her, but this city swirled with memories. Happy moments tumbled to the surface but brought with them flashes of a deeply buried pain. Paris would always hold both sides of that episode of his life.

Adrian heard his name and saw Jason's unruly mop of hair bobbing through the foyer. Jason was the only one of Adrian's friends who still had a mullet.

'Ready?' Jason asked.

Adrian nodded and grabbed his jacket and together they strode out of the door.

'I'm looking forward to this.' The breeze whipped hair into Jason's eyes and his toothy grin widened.

'Yeah, surprisingly, I am too.' Adrian laughed.

Joining the demonstration today buoyed him after his meeting yesterday with the human rights lawyer. It hadn't gone as planned and he'd left deflated and ready to head back home. It seemed that so many of his ambitions had petered out, in need of oxygen and a little nurturing. Before Africa, he'd had a fierce desire to right wrongs and make the world a better place. Now, Adrian laughed at his naivety; he'd had such lofty ideals. In Africa, he'd put his heart and soul into the work. He'd made a difference, but there was so much more to do. Yasmine had inspired him back then, but she had also cast the crushing blow. Her face filled his mind and again he saw the unruly hair always in her eyes and that infectious smile. He shook his head trying to cast the image out, but it wouldn't dislodge. He still didn't understand what had happened.

Today was a new day. It was time to rekindle his energy to fight for what was right. The demonstration at the G20 could bring change, and, convince politicians like James Wrogarth, the Australian Prime Minister, that their careers were on the line.

Jason's voice cut across Adrian's thoughts as he greeted a group of new friends: a young couple from South Africa dressed in all black; an Irish man wearing a silly hat that almost matched his silly grin and a couple from Sweden with red and white beanies pulled down low over their hair. Jason had branched out in the last five days, and it was a welcome boost. Turning forty had shaken him.

Just then, a friend from Adrian's past, Klaus, tapped him on the shoulder. After Africa, when Adrian had slunk back to Paris like a wounded lion, he'd met the short, wiry German. On a cold wintery night in an out-of-the-way bar, they were each seeking their own solace, hoping to mend their broken hearts and dreams, and their wounded egos. Klaus was now helping Jason with his latest project. The proposed exposé on mining activities was an odd venture for the easy-going Jason, but it was giving him a sense of purpose and Adrian crossed his fingers that Jason would finish it.

They rounded the corner and Adrian's heart skipped a beat. A huge crowd swarmed in the square. An excited buzz combined with an ear-splitting barrage of noise and chaos sent a shiver up his spine.

Klaus and the Swedish couple understood sufficient French to follow the speeches, translating what they could for Jason. Adrian understood, but only if he listened intently. The passionate speeches harangued the crowd and he cheered energetically. Beside him, Jason enthusiastically joined in too, although off cue.

They stuck together as the march began but, as they passed the Louvre, Adrian realised he, Klaus, and Jason had been separated from their other friends and were now being pulled in different directions. He turned to motion Jason to follow him but saw that he'd lost him too. Adrian recognised a mop of hair bobbing in the crowd but if it was Jason, he was already too far away, and the roaring noise made calling out pointless.

Chapter 2

Shelley screamed. She was falling.

Suddenly, a strong arm encircled her waist and pulled her upright. A firm, sweaty body pressed against her back and propelled her through the crowd. A resonant male voice shouted near her ear. Confusion, the relentless noise, and her rising nausea made it hard to concentrate and she stopped fighting. Tears of relief sprung to her eyes when Shelley saw a patch of empty space. The arm dragged her free of the crowd, pushing her towards a fountain. She was battered and bruised, and her ankle throbbed. She almost fell onto the fountain edge, the pain in her ankle matching the sharp pain in her chest as she tried to steady her breathing. Tears threatened to spill out in uncontrollable sobs, and she tensed. If she started crying now, she wouldn't stop.

The stranger's voice penetrated the noise and commotion. His breath warmed her cheek as he leaned in close. Grabbing her shoulders, he motioned for her to take deep breaths. Gulps of air became rhythmic breathing and although her heart still thumped furiously, she was safe now. After a few seconds, her trembling steadied. Again, she choked back tears, this time they were tears of relief.

Shelley balanced on the side of the fountain as the writhing mass of people, placards and banners continued up the Champs-Élysées. The noise moved on too. Up towards the Arc de Triomphe, the sun reflected from the helmets and shields of riot police and she shuddered. Things were going to get nasty. She turned to thank her rescuer and gazed into the most intense blue eyes she had ever seen.

'D'accord?' her rescuer asked.

'Merci beaucoup Monsieur,' she gasped breathlessly in reply, but then lost all ability to speak French and added clumsily, 'I don't know how to thank you.' She shrugged.

The rescuer laughed. 'You're welcome.' His Australian accent surprised her.

'You're an Aussie,' Shelley said, more a statement than a question.

'Yes, I am. You sound Aussie yourself.' His eyes sparkled with obvious delight.

'Yep, guilty as charged.'

'I'm Adrian McGrath, nice to meet you.' He bowed with a mock formality.

She found a shaky and quiet version of her voice. 'I'm Shelley Argyl...no, Ormond.' He didn't react to her stumble and she continued, 'It's nice to meet you.' She tried to strike a playful note, affecting her own mock formality as she shook his hand.

'Are you OK to stand?' he asked as a lock of dark hair fell across the frown on his forehead.

When Shelley tried to stand her left ankle gave way and his restraining hand tensed to keep her from falling. She sat back down. The swelling was visible above her shoe and a dark blue bruise was already forming. As Adrian surveyed the damage, Shelley's thoughts turned to how she'd get back to her hotel. She hadn't realised she'd given voice to her concerns.

'Come with me,' he said, putting his arm around her waist again and lifting her from the fountain edge.

Leaning on him heavily, she limped through the spill of people on the footpath around the corner and through the ragged line of security people still blocking off streets. She felt detached, hovering above the scene as though this was happening to somebody else. The stragglers of the march were still shouting slogans and chanting defiantly, generating noise that belied their small numbers. Shelley stumbled repeatedly. People tried to wedge their way between them, but she clung fiercely to Adrian.

They detoured down an alley and across to a side street where the crowds had thinned and then into an old building housing a sombre café. He manoeuvred her into a chair and she took the opportunity to study him. His nose was slightly crooked, and his dark hair and blue eyes made a striking combination. His manner was relaxed but efficient. She guessed he was about her age, maybe a little older.

He moved a chair into place so she could elevate her foot. 'That's better.'

Thoughts of her narrow escape engulfed her. A quiver started at her shoulders travelled down to her fingertips and ended at her toes. This inner earthquake threatened to take her over, muddling her thoughts and stifling her voice. She had to fight to regain control. Shelley turned her attention away from her inner turmoil into the café, onto the stranger and the serene face that could help set her equilibrium back to normal. He took off his jacket and placed it gently around her shoulders, its warmth enveloping her with a pleasing, woody scent.

'Delayed shock I suspect,' he said gently. His voice reached in and brought her thoughts back to the present as solidly as he had rescued her only moments ago. 'Now, let me have a proper look at that ankle. We need to get the swelling down.' He lifted her foot for a closer examination. His gentle touch tingled on her skin and his hands, callus-free, left sensory imprints wherever they made contact.

She slumped back in her chair. Her pulse slowed and her breathing finally returned to a regular rhythm although the touch of his hands threatened to speed her pulse again. She watched him examine her ankle and then order ice and coffees.

'Where are you from?' He leaned forward and his nearness made her hold her breath.

'Adelaide. I was born and raised there.'

His eyes widened. 'I moved there a few years ago.'

'Amazing!' This was a happy coincidence.

'I'm in Paris for a few weeks helping my mate celebrate a birthday. What about you?' He sat back as their coffees were served and she breathed more easily again.

'I'm just taking a well-earned holiday.'

The ice arrived and Adrian pulled a handkerchief from his pocket, wrapped it around a handful of ice and placed it over her swollen joint. The waiter returned bringing a small towel.

'You'll need help getting around for a few days, is there anyone you can call?' Adrian searched his pockets and pulled out a mobile phone.

Shelley shook her head. 'No, no-one. I'm travelling alone. I'll be alright. I'll just have to slow down I guess; plan for a few more coffee breaks.' She laughed, although her situation was anything but funny.

Her first full day in Paris, a dream come true and she'd jeopardised it already.

The lines between Adrian's eyebrows crinkled as he studied her face. 'Well, I don't think your ankle is seriously hurt, but you'll definitely have to take it easy. We can't tell how bad the damage is until the swelling subsides. Maybe you can get it strapped. That would help. See how you go but get it looked at if it doesn't improve in the next couple of days.'

She'd have to amend her plans, not just in Paris, but maybe for the rest of her trip. Maybe her family and Tom were right, she should have had more sense. Shelley slumped back in her seat and sighed. Her list of 'must–sees' was long and she might never come back here.

***

Back at the march, the protesters were close to their final destination. Jason's heart pounded. He couldn't stop grinning as he was swept along by the chaotic stream of people. His group of friends was spread throughout the crowd, only Klaus was still within sight. A wall of people pulsated between them, pushing them further apart. Across the waves of bobbing heads their eyes met. Klaus frowned; his expressive face readable from this distance. No need for an interpreter, Klaus was worried. Adrian was nowhere to be seen and Jason had given up trying to find him.

Ahead the marchers slowed, blocking the growing swell propelling him forward. Surrounded, he was locked in by a mass of angry protesters punching fists into the air to punctuate their shouts. The heady smell of sweat, the flash of colour and movement and the high-pitched noise sparked his adrenaline. The men and women beside him chanted, '*Action tout de suite!*' and he enthusiastically yelled his own version, 'Act now!' until he was hoarse. He laughed and joked in sign language as they stumbled along the Champs-Élysées.

Straining to see what was ahead, a glint of something in the sunlight caught his eye. Squinting against the glare, a line of helmets came into view. They stretched across the street, facing the

23

protesters. He caught glimpses of black ominous figures, a line of automatons with their shiny helmets jerking as they strained against the crowd. Their visors were pulled down low. His heart raced and his mouth turned painfully dry. He and Klaus locked eyes and a message passed between them. They had both seen the riot police. The angry shouts and chanting escalated and drowned out any attempt to communicate. Klaus gestured wildly; his arms high above his head as he pointed to the edge of the march. Jason grinned and shook his head. He was not leaving now. Klaus grimaced, gesturing more ferociously as if he could make Jason listen by sheer will. But Jason wasn't listening. He wasn't ready to leave and miss the action. Excitement clenched his stomach, churning it wildly. Compelled by the boisterous crowd, his heart pumped hard and strong. He felt alive; his every nerve tingled and bristled.

Lurching forward, Jason concentrated on keeping his balance and staying with the marchers beside him. His forehead, bathed in sweat, unleashed trickles that fell into his eyes and blurred his vision. Stumbling and tripping forward, he stole a sideways glance. Klaus had gone.

The pushing, shoving and jostling worsened as they neared the meeting venue. People scrambled, some struggled and pushed violently to get out, while others tore forward with renewed strength. A gang of protesters punched their way through, hitting him hard on the back. He stiffened, grabbing at his side. As he leaned down, he caught the flash of an iron bar as they passed.

Jason pulled himself up tall, his muscles ached but he tapped deep into his reserves and followed them. He stumbled as his shoes lost traction. The ever-increasing pressure from behind buffeted him mercilessly and he struggled to stave it off. Then he heard it. Piercing screams, so shrill, they rose above the din of the crowd. Urgent and hysterical, they demanded attention.

Something dreadful was happening up ahead.

The hysteria pumped up his adrenaline even more and he pushed to be in there, right in the middle of the action. Catching a glimpse of a water cannon threatening the protesters, his resolve wavered. His head throbbed and his body ached, sore from the pummelling it had already received. He steeled himself and charged forward. He was now close to the front of the march and to the screams. Then, there they were. The police had blockaded the street. The demonstrators were hurling themselves against the cordon of police uniforms, straining against the line and trying to breakthrough. Some protesters were trying to bail out and backed away, while marchers behind him continued to forge forward. In the chaos people punched, kicked and scratched him.

The batons flashed, beating down on the protesters within range. Their full force connected indiscriminately with outstretched hands, heads, backs or whatever happened to be in the way. The violence was met with violence. Hands from the crowd grabbed at helmets, fists beat at legs and the flash of metal bars blended in. As those behind realised what was happening the crowd split, some desperate to flee, some intent on joining the action and others frozen with horror.

Jason's stomach lurched. Sweat poured into his eyes. Around him, people were falling and in danger of being trampled. Fleetingly, he wondered if he would be next. Protesters buckled under the force of the batons and blood splattered across the crowd. Bright red drops sprayed across in front of him and he baulked. Screams pulled him from his trance. What was he doing? This was mortally dangerous, not fun. Shocked to see how far he'd come and how close he was to real danger, he pulled back.

He quickly realised he had to get out, to get away from the very violence he'd been striving to be part of. Trapped in the middle of the mayhem, blocked in on all sides, he was still being propelled towards the batons, towards the screaming, the chaos; ever faster, ever closer. Frenzied by his sudden overwhelming need to escape, he beat his fists violently, sometimes connecting with other demonstrators. He summoned all his strength to hack his way through. The screaming, writhing mass of people held him fast, blocking his escape. Hands grabbed at him, ripping his clothes and scratching his skin. He was afraid, scared that he was doomed to fall under the shower of batons. Faces around him reflected the same emotions; wide-eyed, open-mouthed, contorted features surrounded him. Swallowing down his panic, he frantically searched for an escape. Desperately pushing, hacking, beating his fists, feeling flesh tear and burst with the impact, until he felt the touch of cool air on his face. At last, he had broken through.

Exhausted and trembling, he fell into the gutter. Seeking refuge away from the rising screams, he pulled himself up and staggered into a nearby lane. Leaning against the wall for support Jason doubled over, struggling to catch his breath. He was free, he was safe and now his body began to shake uncontrollably. He slid down the wall, squatting down on his haunches to avoid falling. Relief washed over him and then a hysterical, uncontrollable laugh burst from his lungs. Echoing along the laneway and off the shop shutters, it racked his whole body. The eerie sound was disconnected from him and yet strangely a part of him. Jason laughed and laughed, relief mixed with fear and excitement, the depth of which he had never know before.

Chapter 3

Daryl rubbed his aching forehead. Travelling for work was anything but glamorous. He worked twice as hard for a demanding boss, slept half as long, and had no free time.

From his desk he watched Mark enter Wrogarth's temporary Paris office and he clenched his fists. Mark had already wormed his way in as a close confidante, much more than just the PR/Communications man his title suggested. In the process, he'd successfully sidelined Daryl.

'It's scandalous. We wouldn't let that rabble disrupt important meetings in Australia.' James Wrogarth's voice suddenly boomed from the office. 'We wouldn't let them in the country.'

Wrogarth was determined to ignore the issue of climate change for as long as possible, and Daryl thought it was a mistake. It was on the international agenda, even if the USA had pulled out, other world leaders wanted to address it.

'It's just scientific hysteria.' Wrogarth's thumped the table with his fist. 'Heavy emission targets would be the death of the Australian economy.'

Daryl stepped into the office and handed his boss a file.

'They need to smash those radicals,' Wrogarth muttered as he took the notes.

Daryl remained quiet. It was so familiar and perhaps that was the trouble. It was all too familiar to everyone including the electorate. Coming down hard on activists would have worked when Wrogarth had first won office. Back then, people had responded well to his hard-line approach, but now it wasn't working. Yet, Wrogarth, the consummate politician, wasn't listening to any advice except Mark's. Mark's arrival had been the turning point. Daryl looked up and pulled his thumbnail away from his mouth.

'What else do you need?' Daryl asked, hoping to finish quickly and get out.

Wrogarth shifted his stare to Mark, 'Where are the papers on the Middle East and on illegal immigrants?'

Mark pointed to a pile of papers on the side of the desk and Wrogarth shuffled through them until he found a small wad of notes.

'When is the forum going to deal with these bloody issues? We can't let the Middle East win too many concessions. Their oil supplies are holding us all to ransom.' He looked up at Mark, 'But not for long, eh?' he said quietly.

29

Daryl didn't understand the lopsided smile that passed between Wrogarth and Mark.

***

James Wrogarth smiled as he leaned back in his chair. The major world leaders had more than an aura of power. Their language played out like a carefully choreographed dance, sidestepping difficult issues only to surge forward when the final decision went their way. He wasn't in their league and even his attendance at these international decision-making forums didn't impress the Australian people anymore. He needed to turn the polls around before the November election.

The polls in the USA, France, and Germany punished their leaders. The Global Financial Crisis had caused havoc that left its mark and the unrest across the world was causing angst. Even the European Union was struggling to maintain its control. They were all political animals like him, and that was to his advantage. He'd survived before, he just needed something big.

Wrogarth stared at the unfamiliar view from his small office window. The Australian delegates' briefing was next. The mix of public servants and handpicked aides commanded his full concentration especially since some had well-known left leanings. That needed to be fixed.

The emphasis on climate change churned at his stomach. He'd sanctioned mining extensions and sales of coal and uranium to some of the smaller countries and it was critical for Australia to cash in on their growth. These emerging small powers were an important opportunity; climate change or not. If only he had more time.

The country's oil supply was his real concern. There was a lot riding on the expansion of his new project. The US was panicking, their fuel-guzzling ways made them vulnerable, demand was outstripping supply, and although the Middle East was publicly confident about their continuing supply, everyone knew it was drying up. Wrogarth smiled, the meeting next Friday was timely. He sat back, allowing himself a moment of daydreaming. At least the Swiss Bank account was building a healthy balance.

His mobile phone rang, startling him out of his musings. The caller's ID was blocked and guardedly he answered, 'Yes?'

'Sergei is gone and I'm in charge now,' the clipped accented voice spoke with authority. 'We meet to discuss new arrangements now.'

'Who the hell am I talking to?' Wrogarth refrained from uttering the curse that balanced on his lips. He didn't like surprises. True, they hadn't heard from Sergei for a while, but Mark was working on it.

'Call me Petro,' the deep voice turned smooth, Wrogarth could almost hear him smile. 'We are both busy people, true? So, let's get down to business, we meet —'

'Impossible!' A tic tapped a frantic rhythm on Wrogarth's temple. If Petro had taken over from Sergei, Mark would have to sort it out. Wrogarth ground his teeth; he wasn't supposed to be directly connected.

A throaty, sinister laugh filled the airwaves with fake mirth. 'OK, we play like this for now, but I contact you again very soon. Then I prove I mean business. I'm in charge now. Sergei is gone. Next time, be ready to talk.' The phone went dead, the threat left hanging in the air. Wrogarth wiped his forehead and cursed.

'Something wrong?' Daryl's voice made him jump; he hadn't seen him come in.

Wrogarth's thoughts stubbornly stayed focused on the phone call. He had to talk to Mark now. It couldn't wait.

Daryl's voice broke through. 'Can I show the delegates in now?' His tone sounded frustrated but Wrogarth didn't care.

'No, get Mark on the phone right away.'

Daryl stiffened and marched out the door. A minute later the phone call came through.

'What's up, James?' Mark asked cheerfully.

'I've had a call. Not our usual friend, someone who says he's taken over.' Wrogarth waited for the reaction but was disappointed. 'Do you know anything about this?'

'Shit!'

'Well?' He drummed his fingers on the desk in time with the pulse in his temple. This was no time for games. If Mark had known about this why hadn't he warned him? 'What's going on?'

'It's hard to explain…you said you didn't want to know the details,' Mark whined. 'I don't know what's happened to our usual contact. This new guy seems to have taken over his entire patch and he wants to run things differently.'

'So why are they phoning me? Why aren't you sorting it out?'

'He won't deal with an intermediary…He's adamant…but I'm working on it. The arrangements are secure, but at the moment we have to play by their rules, otherwise, they threaten to expose us.'

Wrogarth bolted upright. 'Us…Us…' The throbbing pulse at his temple turned his face burning hot. 'You were supposed to keep me out of it. How did they get my details?' He grabbed at his tightening chest and leaned back. 'What a stuff-up. We can't find an alternative now.'

He slammed the phone down then thumped the desk. He'd have to wait now. Playing with options in his head, Wrogarth came to a decision. He would sever this connection after the last shipments. He hadn't planned for this to continue after the election anyway.

His hands trembled as he rested them on the desk. The direct link to him was a risk he hadn't planned on. Mark was supposed to be the buffer. If anything went wrong, it would have been Mark's word against his and Mark would've shouldered the blame. No-one should've been able to prove otherwise. But now, everything had changed.

He pressed his hands down on the desk and put on his leader's mask; confident, assured and strong. Only then did he ring and ask Daryl to show the delegates in.

Chapter 4

There you are,' said Shelley relieved to see Adrian surface from the metro tunnel. 'This station had so many exits I was worried I'd taken the wrong one.'.

He put an arm under hers. It was a touch she remembered well from yesterday. She was pleased he'd suggested meeting again.

They stopped for coffee at a café across the road. The chairs at the outside tables faced the street so they could people-watch like the locals. Shelley watched the parade of French fashions, guessing the locals by the way they dressed, but Adrian's admiring glances caused her a twinge of jealousy. Fashion had never interested Shelley, not like her younger sister, Vonnie, who would have gasped at all the high-end labels. She caught sight of her practical sneakers under the table and pulled them back out of sight. Her ankle felt strong, although not totally healed

The conversation started slowly, and after exhausting the topic of Shelley's ankle, they fell into silence. Struggling to make small-talk, she felt more like a teenager than a mature woman.

Coffees finished, they wandered along the banks of the River Seine. Market stalls edged along the river, some open for business, some not. Grey flecks sparkled in the water as boats and barges created waves and frothy slipstreams across the surface. As they walked and talked, Adrian surprised her with his knowledge of the history of Paris and its architecture. His eyes burned with intensity as he told her he'd once worked for Medicins Sans Frontiére and lived in Paris for three months before going to Africa.

They arrived at the Musée d'Orsay, the first stop on her list, and took the elevator to the top, starting with the romantic artists. Shelley lingered over the vibrant and colourful paintings of Van Gogh, with their wavy brushstrokes. She was also drawn to Monet and his filtered, dreamy landscapes. Adrian laughed at her confusion between Monet and Manet. He obviously relished being both educator and guide, explaining the style and the period of the paintings while also adding interesting facts about the artists. Adrian lingered over the Renoir paintings, especially the 'young girls at the piano.' When she asked why it appealed to him, he mumbled something about his sister and moved on.

The artworks provided a perfect stage for talking about themselves, talking about what they liked and what they didn't and gradually they seemed less like strangers. The benches on the rooftop patio enticed them with views across the rooftops of Paris. The startling white cathedral, Sacre Coeur, sat high on the hillside, its spires and domes gleamed like snow in the spring sunshine.

'I haven't spent so much time indulging an interest for a long time,' Shelley said. She wanted to add how much she was enjoying his company too, but the words petered out.

'I haven't either. I'm always too busy,' Adrian said, then turning to her, 'Thank you for the opportunity.'

'It's been fun.' Her cheeks burned and Shelley cast her eyes down to study her hands. 'I'm still getting used to being on my own. My divorce has just been finalised,' she said quietly, not sure why she had told him this now.

Twelve years of marriage, a little more than a third of her life, had ended and perhaps the future held happy possibilities.

Adrian nodded, 'Break-ups can be tough. I've been through one too. Not a marriage but...'

Silence cloaked them momentarily, each struggling with what to say next. When both started to speak again at the same time, they laughed, breaking the awkward pause.

'Shall we continue?' Adrian asked.

On the lower floors, Shelley marvelled at the silhouettes in the special exhibit. Dramatic scenes danced on the walls in shadowy form. She'd never heard of their use in theatre before. She looked longingly at the stage replicas.

'I used to do some amateur theatre,' Shelley said dreamily. 'Back in my uni days.'

'Did you?'

'I only had bit parts, nothing significant. I don't think I was very good.'

Adrian smiled, 'But you enjoyed it?'

'I enjoyed being part of the team,' Shelley reminisced. Her amateur acting career had been abandoned once she and Tom married, just another casualty of her marriage. Maybe when she got back from her holiday...

They stopped at the first-floor restaurant for lunch. Shelley gaped at the opulence, the gilded mirrors, and sparkling chandeliers. She, a commoner, felt out of place in this setting fit for royalty. How odd to have such beauty in what was once a railway station. It was a magical setting for their first lunch together in Paris and over a soft red wine, Shelley relaxed.

'This has been a wonderful day. My aunt Maddie always talked lovingly of Paris, now I understand why.' Shelley sipped at her wine and glanced at the well-dressed patrons around her.

'Has your aunt visited recently?' Adrian asked.

'She died a couple of years ago. We had planned to do this together, but things always got in the way.' Shelley smiled. 'She'd be pleased that I finally made it.'

'Is that why you came to Paris?'

'Sort of. I needed a break, not only because of the divorce but also my job.'

'What do you do, Shelley?'

'I work at the Department of Immigration; in Asylum Seeker Resettlement. It's been difficult but a very rewarding job. Unfortunately, the department is being restructured and I'm being moved into a law enforcement role. Dealing with the detention of boat asylum seekers is not easy in the current political climate. Especially when I don't particularly like the government policy I'll have to administer.'

'What are your options?'

'I'm not sure. The new department head has set ideas about staff rotation and I've been told that I have no choice. Perhaps I could move out of the department but I've been there for almost fifteen years.' This was the first time Shelley had admitted the possibility of leaving to anyone, even herself, and a wedge of excitement caught in her throat. 'What about you? What do you do?'

'I'm a doctor but, I've struggled to get back into my stride. I took a job as a medical researcher at the Royal Adelaide Hospital. It's interesting, but it may be time to move back to what I love.'

Adrian explained his family wasn't from Adelaide and he'd moved there about five years ago. His undercurrent of melancholy was attractive; adding a layer of intrigue to his charm and gentleness, but something lurking behind his startling eyes disturbed Shelley. Was it a promise or a caution? She wasn't sure.

Shelley filled any lulls in conversation with talk about herself, her parents, her sister and her struggles, almost too much. She had a bad habit of revealing too much about herself too quickly, but words seemed to tumble out before she could stop them. Hopefully, she hadn't overwhelmed him.

That evening, an email from one of her staff, Maya, delivered more sad news about Ayisha's death. It looked like a suicide. Tears sprung to Shelley's eyes and Ayisha's image flashed before her. The beautiful but troubled girl had been so damaged and wounded from her life in Afghanistan and her years in detention. The angry scars on Ayisha's arms and wrists had borne testimony to her pain. She'd been a challenge, a sad young woman, who had so much before her if only she could escape her past.

They had become close and now Shelley felt the horror of her failure. She'd fooled herself that Ayisha was alright, that they had overcome the worst, but now it looked like self-delusion.

She thanked Maya for the email and prepared for bed. She couldn't shake her sadness and sense of failure. Ayisha had been special.

***

Jason stalked about his hotel room, feeling at a loose end. He'd got up late. A headache settled over his right eye, but otherwise, he was restless. He pulled on his jacket and set off, not sure where, but striding purposefully none the less. He decided to turn right this time, a route he hadn't taken before. He climbed the slope leading away from the Champs-Élysées and the regular tourist attractions. He was tempted to go back to the bar, but a strange feeling was demanding he do something new and he gave in to the impulse. The exhilaration of the demonstration was gone, leaving him feeling flat.

He crossed the street at the pedestrian crossing, smiling at the strangeness of it. In Adelaide he avoided crossings. Yet here in Paris, where the motorists practically disregarded them, sometimes only narrowly missing him, he felt more secure using them.

He noticed the tenants list of the building before him. It contained a selection of lawyers and doctors, mainly specialists with impressive letters behind their names. He thought of Adrian and his meetings with lawyers in Paris. Adrian had his causes, even if the fire in him had ebbed slightly, busily searching for justice, whatever that was. What did Jason have?

Forty years old and he still had no real direction in life. The birthday had caught him by surprise, somehow taking on a bigger meaning than he had thought it would. Strangely, it had left him introspective, searching for purpose in his life. How tiresome, why should things change because of an arbitrary number? Yet, they had changed. The project was an effort to put some energy into something worthwhile. There were serious mining issues in Australia, and they needed to be exposed, but he struggled to summon Adrian's fervour and drive. Perhaps it was all too personal. He wanted Carlew, the Australian mining magnate, to suffer, to expose that charlatan for what he was, but was that enough to write a whole book about the issues in the mining industry? Jason shrunk down into his jacket, pulling up the collar to shield his neck. He was

41

shaking even though he was protected from the wind and the sun was out.

His meeting with Klaus was organised for Friday morning and that would give him the boost he needed. Klaus was also fervent, and his search for the truth was a personal crusade. He was so like Adrian, willing to sacrifice his own lifestyle for the good of others. That wasn't Jason. He was struggling to make time for his research. There were too many distractions, the bars, the friends, the sights, exploring a new city and new people. He knew he should make the time; he'd regret missing the opportunity when he got back. With 70% of mining in Australia owned by overseas interests, he needed to use the contacts here. The emergence of AAAP interested him. They had sprung up out of nowhere and their company structure and ownership details were elusive. They were buying up other mining businesses and large tracts of land, even in Australia, so had lots of money behind them. At least that narrowed down the search for owners, not many companies had access to that kind of funds.

The top five operators in Australia had individual mines as well as joint ventures. Most also had mines internationally, but he couldn't work out how AAAP had come into the market so quietly. At a time when the biggest miner, Ortansea was pulling back, AAAP was expanding. It was complicated and Jason yawned, feeling overwhelmed just thinking about it.

He stopped at the crossroads, realising he was in the seedy Pigalle area. It looked tired in the light of day, not showy like the brochure pictures. Indeed, much of the area looked in need of a facelift; some parts needed demolition – a totally new start. The straggling line of tourists ambled along the centre pathway between the traffic lanes, avoiding the footpaths littered with billboards advertising sex shows and seedy bars. Even the photos publicly displayed at the entrances would make some blush. At night the lights disguised the dilapidated shop fronts and turned what was sordid into risqué. The tourists still flocked here at night trying to recapture the lost flamboyance of shows like the Lido and Moulin Rouge, attending overpriced shows with expensive cheap champagne and bland food. Adrian had told him not to bother with them, but Adrian lamented the passing of the days when Henri Toulouse-Lautrec and Edgar Degas sketched here. Who was he to judge? To Jason, the past held no romantic fascination, the present kept him interested enough.

Jason was tempted to slip into a cosy corner bar and nurse a cool beer along with his sullen mood. But instead, he walked on past the bars and the sex shows and up to the Sacre Coeur. Montmartre, with its cafés and street artists was a haphazard obstacle course. He followed the winding streets, ducking and weaving through the crowds of tourists and vendors and arrived at the glistening white cathedral. The view was spectacular, and he stood amongst the crowd at the guardrail, peering back towards the Champs-Élysées and Eiffel Tower.

He'd come a long way but still had further to go. He needed to set his mind to his project and stop being so easily distracted. Jason took deep breaths to fill his lungs and expel the sullenness that had settled over him today.

From here, he could see how enormous Paris was. It followed the river winding from inland to the coast. It was a working river, barges and transport boats passed regularly alongside the tourist craft. What made Paris so different from other cities Jason had visited? Was it the river, its architecture, the Eiffel Tower, Arc de Triomphe or the Champs-Élysées? It didn't seem any one thing but a combination. He stood taking it in, realising that this was the secret. It was never just one thing that made something beautiful, entrancing or evil. It was always a combination of factors.

His step had a renewed spring as he headed back down the steps, there was fresh air in his lungs, a kernel of an idea and for a while at least, a clear head.

Chapter 5

Shelley's new life called for a fresh, chic persona, and the large and glamorous department stores along Boulevard Haussmann loomed before her. Printemps screamed class. The beautiful handbags, stylish shoes, designer clothes and expensive jewellery on display threatened to blow her entire budget. The grand central atrium in Galeries Lafayette stretched up to a brightly coloured mosaic glass dome and when the sun shone, it bathed shoppers in colourful and patterned light. She perched on a stool at a café along the edge of the atrium and admired the theatre-like balconies with their golden balustrades fixed along the inner walls.

Shelley then stopped at a clothes rack to admire a blue silk dress, letting her fingers stroke the smooth fabric. She turned the price-tag and immediately let it drop. It would take her much too long to earn that kind of money. Her sister, Vonnie, would have bought one in every colour regardless of her overused credit card. Vacuous Vonnie, Tom had nicknamed her. Shelley resented the description more because of its accuracy.

She perused the sale racks instead. They satisfied her need for thrift without sacrificing the new and stylish look she craved. She bought a navy skirt; its wavy hem added a swish as she walked and a softly draped blouse that sparkled and sang with splashes of silver and pink. Four stores later, Shelley had a small collection of plastic shopping bags, a good morning's effort. Satisfied, she responded to the rumble of her stomach and left the shops in search of a late lunch.

She headed back towards the Opera Garnier area, taking photos at regular intervals to capture the typical Parisian scenes. She smiled. Editing and deleting photos were going to be time-consuming, but it would be worth it.

A grand old building across the road caught her eye. The ornate gold and black gate, with the guard in a resplendent blue uniform standing rigidly at attention, would make a great photo. Peering through the fence into the front courtyard, she recognised the Australian Prime Minister, James Wrogarth, striding towards a black limousine. He and a wolfish-looking young man with a striking combination of dark eyes and dark hair talked animatedly as they shared a joke.

As she turned to leave, she stumbled into someone standing behind her. Apologising, she looked up and straight into Adrian's familiar blue eyes. He'd been watching the courtyard too.

'Oh, fancy seeing you here.' Her heart skipped a beat as a warm smile spread across his face in recognition.

'What a pleasant surprise. What are you doing here?'

'I was on my way to find something to eat. It's the first time I've seen Wrogarth in person. He's a lot shorter in real life.'

'I wonder why he's here at the Resources Trade Centre. There were no meetings with oil and mining companies mentioned in the press.'

Shelley stood back as the car passed through the gates and Adrian turned to examine the building plaque. The darkened windows obscured the passengers and she was disappointed there'd be no opportunity for a close-up photo.

'I hope it's something positive for a change,' Shelley muttered, blushing when she noticed Adrian's head tilt her way with eyebrows arched. 'I really hate his policies…and…he's so arrogant,' she explained, hoping he wasn't a Wrogarth supporter.

'Me too,' Adrian said with a laugh. 'I'm meeting a few friends. Would you like to join us?'

***

Adrian and Shelley entered the dimly lit bar, their eyes blinking to adjust. A long-haired man was talking to a group of friends, his hands punctuating his conversation and his energy contagious to those around him. Adrian approached him, steering Shelley forward. She found herself sitting next to the expressive man who Adrian introduced as Jason, his friend and travelling partner. Jason's sparkling eyes danced, and his smile seemed to say more than just hello.

47

He leaned forward to look at Adrian. 'So, where did you two meet?'

'At the demo,' Adrian answered, smirking back at Jason before turning his attention to those beside him.

'I was obviously in the wrong place,' Jason retorted, his eyes scanning Shelley again.

Shelley was flattered, although she didn't take his banter seriously.

Adrian introduced his friend Klaus, and Mohamed, a bearded Afghani man with fierce eyes. Those Adrian didn't know introduced themselves. Jason drew her into the conversation. The tales of his travel adventures entertained and amused her. She barely recognised her frightening experience of the demonstration from his descriptions. Klaus eventually joined their conversation, only his recounting of the march was a much more serious version. It was only two days ago, and Shelley shivered again aware of how close she'd come to being seriously hurt.

Adrian was in deep conversation. She hadn't really noticed the other man during the introductions, but now, his darker complexion and mannerisms seemed familiar. He raised his eyes toward Shelley then, as their eyes met, quickly averted his gaze. That was enough to spark her memory. He was a translator at the Resettlement Branch. His name was Akbal. He was one of the caring ones, often going out of his way to help a refugee and their family. She was used to the way he wouldn't meet her eyes. Others thought he was shifty, but she knew it was a sign of respect.

'Shelley Argyl isn't it?' Akbal asked across Adrian.

'It's Ormond now,' she said quietly. 'Akbal, isn't it?'

'Yes, that's right. It took me a while to work out where I had met you before.' Akbal's face twisted into a smile.

'You two know each other?' Adrian asked.

Akbal explained and then turned to Shelley. 'I was just telling Adrian I got some bad news this morning.' He swallowed hard and then with his eyes fixed on somewhere in the vicinity of her neck, he went on, 'Have you heard...about Ayisha?'

'Yes. It's so sad.' Shelley's voice cracked.

'I know you helped her. Ayisha trusted you.' Akbal said quietly. 'She died in Sydney on Wednesday. The official position is suicide, although...there are some questions...some irregularities...'

Shelley cleared her throat. 'In Sydney? What do you mean 'irregularities'?' she asked.

'Well, it's not clear why, but the Federal Police have taken over the investigation. It sounds like it's suspicious.'

Shelley was lost for words. She would email Maya about this. It certainly was odd. Ayisha had been struggling financially, so a trip to Sydney was unusual.

'It must be serious for the Federal Police to get involved,' Shelley said, more to herself than the others.

49

'I never met her,' Adrian said softly, 'but Akbal and I were discussing her case, as a legal challenge.'

Jason nudged at Shelley. 'What's going on?' he asked, scanning all three faces.

'I'll tell you later,' Adrian said while holding Shelley's hand gently in support.

The waiter interrupted as he placed fresh drinks on the table. Mohamed pulled up a chair beside Akbal and they fell into an intense discussion, while Jason drew her back into his conversation, regaling her with his and Adrian's plan to hire a car and travel around France. Klaus was accompanying them to Normandy, both he and Adrian were interested in the battlefields and Jason's desire for party destinations had to wait.

'You could join us,' he suggested.

Shelley felt a momentary flutter of daring, but it didn't last. 'I couldn't,' she said firmly.

The urge to say yes caught her by surprise. Something gnawed at her; a restlessness to be more carefree, or at least less sensible, but she couldn't make herself take that step, especially after what had happened at the demonstration.

Adrian overheard the invitation. 'Sounds a good idea. It would be fun.'

'I couldn't,' she repeated.

Both Jason and Adrian seemed genuinely disappointed. Adrian handed her his card with his phone number just in case she changed her mind and Jason quickly scribbled his number on a napkin, thrusting it at her as a 'back-up'.

After a snack of baguettes and more drinks, members of the group started to leave. It was later than she'd realised and Adrian offered to walk Shelley back to her hotel.

Ambling along the crowded Champs-Élysées, she sunk into the evening ambience. The combination of lights, the bare trees with their tiny green buds formed a soft background for the bustle of shoppers and tourists enjoying coffee outdoors. The brightly illuminated Arc de Triomphe rose majestically at the end of the avenue and Shelley's heart fluttered as she succumbed to the aura of romance. Adrian's gentle touch warmed her skin and his nearness, and the warmth of his body unsettled her.

At the hotel, she impulsively invited him up to her room and his momentary hesitation fed her insecurities. She hadn't dated much since her marriage break-up, but it was time to move on with her life and the news of Ayisha's death, added a sense of urgency.

They squeezed into the lift, pressed together so close she felt his breath ruffle her hair. An ache fuelled by a desire to be loved, to be held and kissed overwhelmed her.

Once inside her room, Adrian wrapped his arms around her, holding her so close it took her breath away. 'Are you OK?'

His voice was husky, tender and any second thoughts melted away.

'Yes, I…' Shelley sighed as she reached up and drew his mouth down to hers.

Chapter 6

Beverley Wrogarth slowly undressed, tiredness dragging at her limbs and fingers. Her choreographed days were crammed with official events. She'd offered to stay home, thinking James would appreciate being able to concentrate on his high-powered meetings, but instead, he'd accused her of not supporting him anymore. She laughed at the irony as she slumped on the edge of the bed. She hadn't been at his side all day. He'd been too busy. His ego was running rampant, exaggerating his importance and influence, even to her. They both knew Australia wasn't really a big player on the world stage.

Her mind scanned the years they'd spent grappling their way to the top job. She'd once believed that the climb to the top would be worth the struggle. When had she stopped believing? The answer was obvious. Success wasn't what she'd expected. It hadn't made them happy or brought them closer, if anything, they'd drifted further apart. Anger licked at her raw emotions; James was so full of his rise in status. It infiltrated everything, spilling over into his relationships with the children and with her. She had earned the status too, but she was paying a heavy price while James reaped the benefits.

Bev missed her children and grandchildren more than ever. They were so busy with their own lives and their own families now; she felt like an outsider. She blamed James. She'd tried to restore family cohesion, but nothing worked, and she was running out of ideas. Her eyes tingled with unshed tears. She was losing on all fronts, being shut out by James and ignored by her family. She clenched her teeth, reining in her dark thoughts to regain control. He mustn't find her crying.

The clock registered 5.30 pm and she rushed to the closet and riffled through the gowns. The big dinner tonight included the wives and partners and she needed to impress. She lifted the red dress and swirled it in front of her. This was her favourite; it showed off her figure beautifully. Not bad for a fifty-nine-year-old. Then she remembered James had hated the colour last time she'd worn it. She hung it back in the closet and pulled out the elegant black dress. It was more refined but also sombre. Black always made her complexion look drawn and tired. She held it up to the light and tested her reflection in the mirror. He might prefer it for this formal occasion. She noticed the emerald suit, a deep tone that went well against her skin and hair. She flashed it across in front of her. It was a little old-fashioned and wasn't a favourite, despite its designer label. What would he prefer? She chewed at her top lip. His moods chopped and changed, and he was so hard to please. It hadn't always been like this. She used to feel they were a team, but not now. She couldn't risk waiting to ask him, he'd just be angry at her indecision. She pulled the black dress off the hanger and dressed hurriedly. Her fingers wouldn't obey instructions and her neck was unbelievably tense. The more she hurried the clumsier she became. She was still in the bathroom touching up the last of her make-up when James walked into the bedroom.

He was changing into his evening suit when she joined him.

'How was your day?' she asked, keeping the quiver out of her voice. She greeted him with a kiss and then watched his reaction. She could read the disappointment in his eyes.

'You know the Europeans are renowned for their fashion and elegance. Is that the best you could come up with, this black number? You look like you're in mourning.' His tone was intended to wound, and it succeeded.

Bev looked at the wardrobe and stuttered, 'I could change...the red dress...If you think it would be better.'

'No don't bother,' he said sharply over his shoulder, then turning to face her again, his eyes softened. 'I'm sorry. It's been a long day. You look fine.'

His tone was appeasing but not convincing. She bit her lip. Collecting her clutch purse and wrap she slunk out behind him.

Bev sunk back in the leather car seats and removed her shoes, quietly musing over the evening and its highlights. Content with her performance, she smiled. She'd voiced her opinions yet managed to carefully maintain the official line. She'd even enjoyed a genuine laugh or two. The evening reminded her of why she'd made all those sacrifices and stuck by James despite his missteps. This was why she had put all her efforts into James' career and put her own life on hold. She'd known he could do it.

It was the James of old there tonight, circulating, singling out individuals for a quiet word, charming and beguiling the important people and their wives. It was what he did best. He had worked the room beautifully and by the end of the evening had established good connections for later. Bev felt a sense of pride as she glanced at his profile against the night backdrop.

'I'm sorry sir but we have a change of plan.' The driver interrupted her thoughts. James grunted and the driver continued, 'Protesters have blocked the front of the hotel. Security wants our car and the escort to go straight to the secure underground car park. The other car will continue to the front of the hotel as a decoy. Your passes will give you access to your floor without having to go through the lobby.'

Bev remembered the Garundi delegation had arrived at their hotel that day. The issues brewing in that country had generated riots and violence and now it appeared the emotions were spilling over onto the international stage. She shifted in her seat. She didn't like these issues, especially when an Australian company was implicated in the controversy. James was sometimes casual about security, so she was relieved when he agreed to the change.

As they got out of the car and headed towards the lifts, a figure emerged from the shadows.

'I'm Petro,' the shadowy figure said. 'I want to speak with you.' as he spoke, Petro moved forward just enough for Bev to see his outline. The flash of a gold tooth glistened in the exit light but the faulty light bulb in the corner made it hard to distinguish his features clearly. Even so, Bev didn't like what she saw. His self-confident stance and the strange stare set her nerves on edge.

The security escort stepped forward, but James stopped him by placing himself between Petro and the others. He signalled an OK to the bodyguards. Bev stared at James demanding an explanation and moved forward to join him.

Petro turned slightly, and with an exaggerated bow said, 'Good evening, good lady.'

His gaze locked on James. Bev gave an involuntary gasp as the green exit light momentarily reflected in Petro's eyes. She cast a pleading look at James, but the gesture was wasted.

'You may as well head up. I'll be there in a minute,' James said brusquely and with the wave of a hand signalled for one of the security guards to accompany her.

She wanted to argue but knew better. What was this about? What was James up to now? The dark-haired security guard hesitated then followed Bev, while the stocky one took up a post out of earshot.

Bev hesitated as she exited the lift on their floor, dreaded indecision playing with her mind. She was startled by Daryl coming out of the adjoining room, but once she recovered her voice, she told him everything. The words rushed out in an almost incoherent tumble. Luckily, he was patient.

***

Daryl darted into the stairwell as soon as Bev and the security guard left the corridor. He raced down to the basement and took a deep breath before gently opening the door a sliver, grateful for the faulty overhead light. He slipped out of the stairwell, letting the door lock quietly behind him and took cover behind a four-wheel drive. He crept across the small, but exposed space between two smaller cars to get nearer the action. The security guard twitched and turned just as Daryl scrambled behind a small foreign car, but he was not seen. Crouching down low to peer around the back-bumper, Daryl watched the two silhouettes play charades in the corner. The security guard propped on the other side of them next to a pillar. As the silhouettes moved their hands waved in eerie patterns and they hissed and whispered. When Daryl thought it was safe, he stole forward another car width and was rewarded by a snatch of conversation.

'I just want to be sure we understand each other,' the strong, heavily accented voice said. 'I can make things uncomfortable for you, so work with me. The arrangements are in place, but I must deal direct, not through your lackeys.'

Wrogarth faced the man and his response was muffled, but Daryl thought he heard the name Mark, although he wasn't sure.

Petro laughed. 'I don't think you are in a position to bargain.'

Daryl missed Wrogarth's response, but he couldn't get any closer without being seen. His eyes scanned the dark space and a slight movement caught his attention however it was gone before he could study it. The security guard stood statue-like by the pillar, obviously, he hadn't noticed anything suspicious.

Petro's voice echoed in the car park, his throaty chuckle boomed across the open space, 'As you wish, but you and I will decide the main things together, no lackeys for that.'

Without warning, Wrogarth strode stiffly towards the security guard and together they crossed to the lift. By the time Daryl looked back, the silhouette that had been Petro had melted into the darkness. Daryl waited until everyone had gone then also used the lift. He hadn't learned much but it piqued his interest.

***

Upstairs, Bev paced the floor, flattening a track in the expensive carpet. She flew at James as soon as he returned.

'What kind of business needs to be done in a car park at night?' Her voice shrieked, unable to control its high pitch.

'None of your concern,' James said, acting cool and calm although the throbbing tic at his temple betrayed him.

Her mind jumped between possibilities and in the absence of a real explanation it conjured up its own. None were reassuring; none provided any glimmer of hope and the gloomiest options rose to the fore. The one thing she knew for sure was that this looked like trouble, just like last time. She sank into the chair as he escaped to the bathroom. She had thought he'd straightened out, put those bad years behind him, but now she wasn't so sure.

She clenched her fists tightly, pressing them against her thighs. He was jeopardising everything, what right did he have to do this? He owed her; owed her gratitude. Bev deserved to enjoy their success too, but he was always willing to risk it for more. If he got caught, they wouldn't recover this time. She trembled at the thought of what lay ahead; more covering up, more tension and more sleepless nights. She placed the fist into her mouth to stifle a scream of anger and frustration.

This time she was going to find out what he was up to.

Chapter 7

A stream of dust-speckled light broke through a slit in the curtains as Shelley woke alone. She'd had a fitful night, tossing and turning as her mind went over and over the events of the previous night. Her rational mind hadn't wanted her relationship with Adrian to become serious, not yet, but she couldn't stop worrying about what it all meant. Shelley's plan to take slow steps with any new relationship, to not rush her own feelings, had been abandoned. Her boldness made her squirm. Her emotions had taken over. Adrian's hesitation belied the desire in his kisses, but then, without explanation, he'd pulled back. She'd been left let down and worst of all, she hadn't known how to change the mood back or even if she wanted to.

In the morning light, it didn't look any more positive. She was a little relieved maybe, but also a little frightened. Shelley stretched, and a sigh wafted from her lips. She was already too intense about Adrian and she knew it was much too soon. Why couldn't she just allow this relationship to stay casual, at least for a while? She wasn't going to think about Adrian today. 'What will be, will be' she told herself as she threw back the covers and forced herself out of the warm bed.

She carefully ripped the tags off the swishy skirt and a stylish top, determined to not look like a tourist today. The jaunty scarf she'd found at a market stall added the right touch. She put on her favourite red walking shoes. They'd support her ankle more stylishly than sneakers. Catching a glimpse of herself in the long skinny mirror by the door, Shelley knew she didn't quite look like a local, but it would do.

The tiny lift shuddered down to the foyer. As she stepped out the chill of the March morning embraced her and Shelley pulled the scarf up around her neck. After a light breakfast at a small croissanterie, she meandered down the street taking in the kaleidoscope of images, distinctive Parisian architecture, and tree-lined streetscape. Confidence hung from her like an ill-fitting cape that threatened to float away with the first strong gust of wind. Luckily the air was still.

Although Paris was huge and the metro convenient, she walked, immersing herself in the experience of the city first-hand. At the Arc de Triomphe, she missed the entrance to the underground access tunnel and walked the full circle of the busy round-about. Standing in its shadow, the swirling traffic navigating six lanes made her jittery. Cars, buses and even trucks entered and exited through small gaps, weaving in and out of the flow. Amazingly, there were no accidents, although she saw plenty of near misses.

Next was the Eiffel Tower, she'd seen it from numerous vantage points around the city, above the rooftops and across the river. By the time she reached the Place de Vendome her ankle was throbbing, so she found a park bench with a view of the tower and River Seine. It was impossible to imagine the Paris landscape without the tower. She studied its lines and statuesque appeal and decided she was glad it had remained intact. The view reminded her of Adrian and his story about Gustav Eiffel and she warmed at the memory of his enthusiasm.

He was so different from the men she'd known. Tom had preferred the Australian outback and rugged country, scoffing at her desire to see Europe. His dismissive haughty voice still sounded in her ears, 'Why go overseas, Shelley when we have such great things to see and do here in Australia?' He wouldn't change his stance, not for anything, not even for her. He hadn't understood, but worst of all, he hadn't wanted to understand. It wasn't only about her desire to travel either. Why had she persevered for so long in that marriage? Although the breakdown of her marriage to Tom had left her feeling vulnerable it was the prospect of never having children that saddened her most. At thirty-eight, she was running out of time. A pulse of the usual anger mixed with sadness surfaced, and she pledged that she was not going to let thoughts of Tom spoil her time here.

She joined the crowd streaming across the bridge. Under the tower, she gazed up into the inner atrium where crisscrossed metal strips formed sturdy pillars. Foreign languages echoed around the square mingling with laughter and excited shrieks. Up at the top level, the wind tangled her hair and chilled her face as the view generated a warm glow. The ant-like Bateaux ferrying tourists along the River Seine left snail trails on the surface of the grey water. The sprawling expanse of the city spread before her, beckoning her to explore.

Once back on solid ground, Shelley caught a bus to the Latin Quarter. Marvelling at the driver's skill as he detoured into narrow roads flanked by parked cars and careless pedestrians, she delighted at the views of the back streets of Paris.

She found the Café Le Procope without difficulty. The waiter raised his eyebrows when she asked for a table for one. He placed her by the window, enabling her to study the café ambience and watch the constant stream of people outside. Presenting her with the menu, he flirted, and she flirted back, savouring it. She'd found a recommendation for this old-world café in her guidebook. First opened in 1686, the French Revolution had been plotted and given birth in this café. Shelley could almost feel the ghosts of Robespierre, Danton, and Marat drinking coffee, eating and engaging in rebellious discussions. Their portraits adorned the red and gold wallpapered walls and stared down at her. It was fitting the celebration of her new freedom would be here. The revolutionaries had paid a high price for change, but maybe freedom always came at a cost.

Shelley didn't think she could have been a revolutionary, she was too afraid of consequences. She had opted for a formless, almost benign life. She had buried her own needs under a respectable façade and settled for being a partner and supporter, not a hint of the revolutionary there. Tom demanded compliance and agreement in exchange for his love and she didn't challenge him. In the end, ironically, she had lost his love as well as herself and her dreams. Her life had almost fallen apart. She'd struggled to re-establish her own identity and sense of self; was still struggling.

Her commemorative meal was everything she had hoped for. It marked her new start, or maybe, more accurately, the ending of her old life, and it did it beautifully. She had eaten her delicious three courses ceremoniously. The *pâté* entree was delicate and flavoursome and the confit de canard tantalised her tastebuds, surprising the palate with small chards of truffle. So Parisian.

As she was leaving, she noticed two men huddled in the corner in the anteroom. Something about the man facing her looked familiar. His boyish good looks contrasted vividly with his fierce, dark eyes. His companion was a young man with wolfish features, distinctive black-rimmed glasses and an old-fashioned hat obscuring his face. He furtively stuffed an envelope into his coat pocket and as he turned their eyes met. He too seemed familiar. Where had she seen them before? Was it here in Paris? Were they guests at her hotel? Or was it from Australia? She suddenly realised she was staring and quickly looked away, rushing past them on her way out. A shiver travelled up her spine; those cold eyes staring at her. She'd read it as a warning, but of what, she didn't know.

Troubled by the faces, the elusive memory nagged at her as she walked up the street. Suddenly, she remembered. That face, the first one, it belonged to an Australian mining boss. Carlew, was it? Yes, he'd featured in the news after an environmental controversy. His vicious verbal attack on the Greens Senator after she raised allegations in parliament had caused an argument between Shelley and Tom. She'd sided with the senator, outraged that the mining boss was so callous about the oil spill. Whole communities were evacuated, suffering from a health risk that couldn't be thoroughly evaluated yet. The claim that they had used a new additive in the oil had been denied, but there were some serious questions left unanswered. She couldn't remember all the details, but she did remember that Tom had taken the mining boss's side. As always, he was on the side of commercial activity, regardless of the ethics or morality of it. That argument had given her the final piece of the jigsaw, showing her the real Tom.

Shelley tried to shake off her feeling of dread as she wandered out into the Rue de Buci. She ventured in and out of the myriad of tempting shops, buying cheeses and pâté to take back to her room. Supplementing her limited French language skills with pointing, charades and lots of smiling, she almost banished the disturbing images to the back of her mind.

Once her bags were full, she continued indulging in window shopping. Then, as she admired a stunning display of delicate pastries, she caught a reflection in the window. Light glinted from dark eyes or maybe from glasses, peering at her from across the street. The vision made her shiver. She turned, catching a sharp, quick movement out of the corner of her eye. Holding her breath, she searched the crowd, not sure what she was looking for, but searching intently anyway. There was nothing there, no-one stood out, there were no dark figures lurking in the shadows or shop doorways. Maybe the incident in the café had unsettled her more than she realised and her imagination was running wild. But she couldn't shake this feeling of being watched. Unnerved and trembling, she willed her heart to slow and her legs to beat a less hurried pace as she entered the metro.

Chapter 8

James Wrogarth stared at the copy of an Australian newspaper and smiled. The press had focused on his big meetings with world leaders while his other meetings remained unreported. He made a note to let Pierson know his journalists had the right mix.

A rap on the door drew his attention and he settled back as Mark entered the room. He motioned for him to close the door just as he heard Daryl, in the outer office, mutter, and a heavy thud as a file hit the desktop. Wrogarth smirked, Daryl was a good workhorse, but he didn't trust him to be part of these meetings.

Mark dropped a wad of papers on his desk and Wrogarth picked them up and scanned through them. The language was suitably vague, almost too vague.

'They're keen, it's obviously worth their while,' Mark said his grin widening.

'Yes, but let's not make it too easy.' Wrogarth tapped a pencil on his desktop. It was times like this he missed the cigarettes.

'What do you mean 'easy'? They want it and are willing to pay. We both get what we want.' Mark frowned.

Wrogarth laughed, these mining corporations were awash with funds and he was happy to relieve them of some. He was going to get the best deal he could. Had he overestimated Mark? He hadn't thought Mark naïve, but maybe he was getting scared.

'Well…there are huge risks involved, and I need…we need to, let's say…cover this properly. I don't want anything like the Petro episode to happen again.' Wrogarth glared at Mark.

'But this is different. It's unpopular, not illegal, at least not in Australia. A good communication strategy would probably minimise the fallout. The Pierson press will go easy on us.'

'Probably. Probably is not good enough' He threw the pencil onto the desktop, sending it skidding onto the floor.

'I haven't failed you before.' Mark leaned forward to make his point. He picked up his pen and clicked it on and off repeatedly.

'Well, that's what I expect. Screw them down more, I want their best offer and you need to set that up.' He put his hand up to stop Mark's protest. He wasn't interested. 'For the PR, you know what to do. We'll start with a hint about securing new business and stress its importance for the economy, but no details.'

Signing off on the deal before the election was poor timing, but couldn't be helped. So long as they kept the details secret, it should work. Their partners knew the sensitivities and they needed him as much as he needed them, although their handling of that dumping controversy in Africa was not reassuring.

***

A shadowy figure waited patiently by the corner, tucked back into a dim alcove away from prying eyes. He was bored and feeling the cold. The rush-hour crowds had petered out long ago, but Paris streets flowed with a constant stream of people. His eyes were fixed on the hotel entrance scrutinising each woman as she stepped out onto the street.

Beverley Wrogarth appeared at the glass doors. Declining the doorman's attempt to hail a taxi, she scanned the street several times before stepping out into the flow. She pulled the scarf tighter around her hair and face, adjusted the dark sunglasses then launched herself into the crowd, hurriedly turning the corner into the boulevard. Head bowed she kept pace with the steady crowd, and without being noticed, he moved up close behind her.

After a few twists and turns along side streets, she again scanned the street before disappearing into a small café, Le Lion d'Or. She chose a discrete and private corner booth with leather-look bench seats. The man followed, nonchalantly selecting a booth next to her. He could see her reflection in the mirror behind the bar and was close enough to hear. She checked her watch several times, slowly removed her scarf and jacket and laid them on the seat beside her. She sat wringing her hands in smooth circular patterns.

A tall man walked through the door and her face lit up. They kissed warmly and their lingering embrace spoke of a tender closeness. Once seated, they ordered coffees and leaned in close.

'William,' she said breathlessly, softly touching his cheek with the back of her hand.

William studied her. 'It's good to see you.'

'Yes.' She straightened up, pulling herself back against her seat. 'It's been too long.'

She lifted the menu, scanned it quickly and signalled the waiter.

'He's screening your calls, you know,' William said after the waiter left.

'No...I didn't know.' Her eyes widened with surprise. 'I didn't know you were going to be in Paris.'

'No.' William looked down, a slight rosy tint forming on his cheeks and he shrugged.

Their coffees arrived, halting the already stilted conversation, but after their baguettes were served, they slipped into a soft patter reminiscing and sharing personal stories. Her eyes drank him in and her hand twitched as it lay on the table, occasionally flicking up to gently straighten a wisp of his hair or to lightly touch his hand. William appeared uncomfortable with the smiling stare but did not move his hand.

The man listened while sipping his drink, he considered ordering lunch, but he was due for a break soon so didn't. He sighed, anticipating a long fruitless wait.

William quietly stirred his coffee. Finally, he looked up. 'Is he treating you any better?'

An inscrutable expression replaced the smile on Bev's face. 'I'm OK. He's under a lot of stress right now, but...' She looked away and it made the man doubt her protestations. 'He doesn't confide in me these days.'

'Any idea of what he's up to?'

'What makes you so sure he's up to something? He has big issues to worry about. The polls are giving him a hiding and he's struggling to get the support he needs.' She sounded protective, defensive even.

The stranger leaned back trying to catch every word. He studied Bev as she gingerly touched her face, he wasn't sure if it was a trick of the light, but her cheek looked darker just under her right eye.

'I know him too well to trust him...I can't believe you've stayed.'

Bev winced as her fingers brushed her right cheek. 'He needs me. I can't leave him now. I've ...We've got what we've worked for. I couldn't... I wish you would come back.' Her eyes pleaded; their fiery intensity reflected in the mirror.

'You know that's impossible.' William sat back hard against the bench adding to the finality of his words.

'I think about you a lot.' Her eyes misted.

'I know. I wish things could be different but...' His hand lingered momentarily on her shoulder and she reached up to hold it.

They sat quietly until Bev broke the spell. Looking at her watch, she gasped. They embraced and promised to meet again soon.

Leaving her untouched baguette, she collected her jacket and scarf. Again, she clasped him to her as though she didn't want to let go. Arranging her scarf once more and the glasses concealing her teary eyes, she dashed out of the door. William sighed and sat down again, slowly eating his lunch. A sullen, almost angry look replaced the gentle features that had been there before.

The man left the money for his drink on the table and casually left. He followed Bev back to the hotel, where he again slipped into the alcove. He phoned in and waited for his replacement to arrive.

Chapter 9

Adrian stared across flat green fields that abruptly ended at a jagged edge. The sheer rocky cliffs plummeted spectacularly to sandy beaches that reflected a rosy hue. After all these years it still seemed stained with the blood of the victims of the deadly Normandy landings.

The stinking, damp bunkers dotted along the cliff-tops where once soldiers had taken cover were now inhabited by stray cats. These concrete boxes were solemn sentinels of the Second World War. On his right, he caught sight of Jason in the cemetery, wandering amongst the row upon row of white headstones. Glistening in the momentary sunlight, they marked the soldiers who had not escaped these cliff-tops; captured in time, forever lost on foreign soil.

'I shouldn't have come,' Klaus said quietly, his voice low and tight.

Adrian, absorbed in his own thoughts, suddenly became aware of his friend's silence. Reluctantly pulling his thoughts back to the present he studied Klaus' preoccupied face. 'Why?'

Klaus swept his arm across the peaceful landscape. 'All this…devastation, this monument to a cruel war. It's hard to take, especially…' His voice trailed off, his words sailing out to sea on the rising wind.

'Especially?' Adrian asked hesitantly, suspecting where this conversation was going and not sure he wanted to go there.

Klaus had retreated deep inside himself again. Staring quietly, he scraped his feet over the well-maintained grass, a deep sigh emanating from his slight frame. 'This place, it's so full of disturbing images…'

'It's a disturbing place,' Adrian agreed, taking the safe option.

'Yes, and my family, my heritage…we were the enemy here…the perpetrators…' Words now failed him.

'Guilt is such a useless emotion.' It spilled out before Adrian could edit it; a thought unintentionally given a voice. He saw from Klaus' startled expression he had hit a nerve.

'Yes…but…'

Adrian reached back into his own life, propelled by the force of his own emotions, his own guilt. 'I've thought about it a lot over the years. Guilt either makes people lie to hide from their actions or creates inertia.' He watched Klaus staring vacantly into the distance. 'People wallow in it and become debilitated then they can't act.'

Adrian's voice sounded harsh, even to his own ears. He was on his soapbox again but felt powerless to stop himself. 'All that self-flagellation achieves nothing.'

'I suppose not, but –'

'You didn't do this. You weren't even born.'

'I know the logic, others would disagree.'

The wind whipped across the open fields, slapping their faces and flicking their hair as they stood in silence, together but apart. Adrian, finally lost for words, was struggling with his own emotions. He wanted to support Klaus, but was afraid. A life burdened with the loneliness of secrets had left Adrian weary. Held tight and close they formed a barrier to meaningful connections with others. It was one thing he and Jason shared.

A haunted look swept across Klaus' eyes. Slowly moving back from the edge, his quiet voice almost a whisper, 'You know, I never knew what my father did in the war.' He swallowed, turning to look at Adrian. 'I never asked. Now it's too late.' Klaus threw Adrian a weak smile.

Together they walked to the small bar in the village leaving Jason off in the distance, clambering around the battlefield.

The drab greyness of the village coerced their already sombre mood, the visual clues of life in a war zone surrounded them: an intact mortar shell embedded in the wall of a church, left there as a memorial of the suffering; bullet holes dotted buildings and walls, erosion wearing them into odd shapes but not disguising what they were. This village had once been in the centre of the battles and the evidence was everywhere.

The tired old Tabac nestled in the crossroads. Inside, the spotted mirror behind the bar reflected a few locals settled in for a drink or baguette. The bartender eyed them suspiciously, raising an eyebrow by way of asking for their order. Ordering local beers in fluent French earned them a nod. A table in the corner, away from other patrons beckoned them and there they sat engrossed in companionable silence; Adrian absorbed in his internal struggle to find the right words for the conversation he knew was coming.

Klaus beat him to it. 'This place, it provokes…uncomfortable thoughts…feelings.'

'We don't have to talk about it.' Adrian wished that it was true, he knew it wasn't.

'No.' Klaus' hands were shaking as they rested on the table.

'Sometimes it helps to talk,' Adrian offered reluctantly. Klaus was his friend; he had been there for Adrian during his time of need. Now he had to try to help.

Klaus smiled, acknowledging the hand of friendship being offered.

Adrian knew about secrets. They were tightly bound deep inside him where they were out of reach, most of the time. 'I don't usually like to talk about my family either,' he confessed. It was a bold admission; one he hadn't made for some time. An uncomfortable wetness made his shirt stick to him as the idea of dragging these unpalatable thoughts out into the light of day crossed his mind. It was much easier to focus on Klaus and his dilemma.

'Why didn't you ever talk to your father about the war?' Adrian asked.

'I don't know exactly. I'd never thought about it much when I was younger, then when I finally did…' His voice, soft and strange, was breaking up as though he was far away, his knuckles white from gripping his glass too tightly. 'Maybe I'm afraid of the answer.'

'What makes you so sure the answer would be something to fear?'

'My father was a morose man, withdrawn, broody. He never talked about his experiences. He behaved like a man with regrets, but I have no idea what those regrets were.'

'I know people whose parents went to war. None of their parents talked about their experiences much, if at all. It doesn't always mean anything,' Adrian offered but Klaus just smiled lightly, a sigh signalling he wasn't convinced, and Adrian added, 'he might have had his own bad war experiences.'

'No, I'm sure it's more than that. My mother once hinted that he wasn't proud of his role in the war. She won't discuss it nowadays; she says to leave the past in the past.'

'You're a journalist, you could find out once and for all, research his war service record, get the facts.'

'True.' Another sigh filled the space between them. 'I just worry that he did things we might all be ashamed of…and I'm afraid to find out, to know for sure.' Shaking his head solemnly, a deep frown etched his forehead forming a tortured and weary look. 'My sons.'

Adrian understood. He had lived with that strange human paradox, a burning desire to know the truth and yet, at the same time fearing it. Adrian had burst through his fear, but he was paying a high price.

'Klaus, so much of this is in the past, and none of it can be changed. What good does knowing do?'

Klaus studied Adrian. 'I know, I also ask myself this. It's not as if I could change anything even if I knew the truth, but I feel I should know what my father did. I am his flesh and blood, part of him, and I just can't ignore it.'

They temporarily retreated into their individual thoughts.

Finally, Adrian dragged his thoughts back to the bar and broke the silence. 'Maybe if we replaced the word guilt with the word responsible it would be easier. Even I can feel responsibility here.'

'How?' Klaus demanded. 'Australians fought on the right side here.'

'What happened here could happen again; elsewhere and with different perpetrators but... wars, conflicts, dictatorial leaders...cruel human behaviour... look at Iraq. Australia was not on the right side there. Look at our treatment of asylum seekers.'

Shifting in his seat abruptly, Klaus cut in, 'That may be, but for me it's personal. I'm talking about my family and what they may or may not have done.' His words strained through tight lips stretched across his teeth.

'For me too. My father...' The words lodged in his throat, unwilling to move. He'd come at this all wrong, clumsily and he had to set it right. Adrian coughed, dislodging the emotion and the words at the same time, 'Well, you know what he is.'

Klaus shrugged, 'Yes but is it the same?'

'I don't think I know everything about my father, but I probably know more than you do about yours. I suspect he's involved in ...deals...greedy, self-serving ones...he doesn't care who gets hurt...I hate to think that my father is like that and that I am related to him.'

Klaus leaned forward. 'Have you ever confronted him with what you suspect?'

'Sort of. I didn't get the answers I wanted and now he and I don't talk anymore. Maybe I will never know the truth either.' His body stiffened as he remembered the bitterness of that argument. 'You know Klaus, what I find hard is the knowledge that I hate my father. That I hate the man, who he is and what he does. You're not supposed to hate your father, are you?'

'Funny, but I didn't hate my father. I loved him, even though he was so out of reach. It's because I love him that I find it so hard to delve into what he may have done. I am not sure if he was the man I loved or if he fooled me. I just don't know.' A sad laugh escaped as he sat back against the chair. 'What about your mother?'

'She's also –'

'What a happy looking pair.' Jason appeared and threw himself into the chair across from Adrian and shot him a quizzical look.

Klaus looked guilty, as though he'd been caught in the act of something illegal, 'Just talking about families, fathers actually.'

Jason sighed loudly, 'No way. What a downer! I don't want to talk about my family, especially not my father, can we change the subject now?'

Disappointment and relief fought for control in Adrian, relief finally won.

***

Over breakfast, Klaus remained in work mode, his train to Paris and Charles De Gaul airport was leaving in an hour and he needed to focus.

'What exactly are you going to do in Africa?' Jason asked.

'My research is still in the early stages. So far it looks like much of the mining industry, including gas and oil, has been taken over by criminal elements with connections to Russia. Africa is not well regulated because they're desperate for mining dollars. I'm particularly interested in the African operations of Ortansea. Its coal seam gas extraction uses chemical fracking and they're trialling chemical additives in the process. There's some suggestion they could be an environmental and health risk.' He shook his head and tutted. 'They've done tests and reported their findings to the government, but no-one trusts them. Independent studies need to be done.'

'Have you identified any specific health issues?' Adrian asked, steering the conversation towards his area of interest.

'The main worry is environmental at this stage; the possible poisoning of aquifers and the fact it could poison whole river systems. It would be a disaster; any contamination could kill thousands.' Klaus stretched his legs out in front of him in one fluid movement. 'But there's not enough concrete evidence yet, environmental or health-related.'

'There's nothing specific to focus on?' Adrian persisted.

'Some of the tests in fracking sites in the USA show small levels of contamination in the soil and waterways, but the only health issues identified are possible triggers for cancer. It's inconclusive and could take a long time to prove a direct connection. But they're different processes to the Angolan operations. In Africa they are using a new method, relying on some 'commercial-in-confidence' chemical, so we have nothing to go on,' Klaus replied.

'When I worked in Angola a few years ago, Trisec Oil and Ortansea, all had huge exploration sites there. We suspected some of the symptoms we were treating were related to the mines but didn't have the resources to follow it up.' Adrian remembered his time in Medicins Sans Frontiére and the tension of renewed frustration spread across his shoulders.

'A preliminary environmental report by an independent source has mysteriously disappeared.' Klaus shook his head. 'Ortansea's operations are suspect. They were heavily fined by the French Government about two years ago for trying to illegally dump their waste here. They were passing it off as 'dirty water' and got caught.'

'Carlew's Trisec Oil has recently been involved in a similar issue in Africa too,' Jason added.

'Georg and Yasmine are still there…Perhaps they could provide some local knowledge or point you towards the right people.' Adrian tensed. Surprised that he'd spoken their names out loud.

Klaus raised an eyebrow. 'You still keep in touch?'

Jason eyed Adrian then took a bite of his croissant but said nothing.

'No, not really,' Adrian shrugged belying the tension weighing down his shoulders. He hadn't spoken to Yasmin since her marriage to Georg. 'I have their details and look them up on the web sometimes…occasionally.' His explanation sounded pathetic to his own ears.

'That would be great,' Klaus said watching Adrian carefully.

'I'll send you their details.' Memories intruded into Adrian's thoughts, taking him back to a place he didn't want to visit. Georg had been a dynamo, and Adrian remembered how exhausted he'd been in his first weeks there. He'd fall into bed at night, asleep almost before his head hit the pillow. Yasmine arrived three weeks later. She'd been tireless. He'd admired her stamina and her spirit. She lit up a room with her presence and he'd fallen for her. He'd thought she felt the same way…but Georg and Yasmine married a year later. Adrian still wasn't sure what had happened. He left for Paris soon after and headed home once he felt steady. He hadn't been in touch with them since then.

'How about your project, Adrian, did you have any luck?' Klaus' eyes bored into Adrian pursuing answers to questions he wasn't asking.

'Not much. I had a meeting with a human rights lawyer who had won a case against Italy. They were ordered to pay fifteen-thousand Euros compensation to each of the twenty-four African asylum seekers from the boat they'd turned back. I know it doesn't sound much, but the big win is the European Court of Human Rights finding Italy breached international law by pushing back asylum seekers at sea. It means human rights groups can challenge Australia's pushback approach.'

Klaus was deep in thought. 'OK.' He looked at his watch and added, 'I'd better go. Stay in touch.'

Klaus and Jason made sure they had each other's contact details. Now they'd connected Carlew to Ortansea they had something significant to collaborate on. Both Jason and Klaus were interested in Martin Carlew, just for very different reasons.

Chapter 10

Wrogarth stared out of the window at the familiar Sydney skyline. Taking advantage of the rare quiet moment before his first appointment he studied the view. The allusion of power and control at his meetings in France had been a strong aphrodisiac, unlike the annoyance of the political situation here at home. His stomach churned. He blamed it on jet lag, but he knew better. Wrogarth raised his fist in readiness to thump the desk but lowered it quietly. Why weren't these issues sorted out? He'd thought Tim Curleigh a reliable operator, once…that's why he was Deputy Prime Minister.

His chest tightened. Tim's inability to fix the problematic issues happened far too often and could jeopardise everything. If they won a third term Wrogarth would make the history books, and he deserved it. He would reap the benefits of all his hard work and the grovelling and bargaining he'd had to do.

There was a knock on the door and Daryl bustled into the room with an armful of files. 'James, Tim Curleigh is outside. Shall I show him in?'

He bristled at Daryl's use of his first name. He'd never noticed it before, but today it grated. As Prime Minister, he was owed respect.

'No, let him wait a while. I'm not ready.' Wrogarth casually shuffled through the papers then sat back. He was tempted to put his feet up on the desk but thought better of it. 'Give me another ten minutes. I'll buzz you.'

Daryl's raised eyebrows caught his boss's attention. He waited for the imminent comment but instead, Daryl straightened and left the room. Wrogarth smirked. Daryl had been with him long enough to know when to hold back. The man was about fifty years old now and he wondered if that explained his increasing reluctance to do what it took.

Finally, Tim was admitted. He stepped into the office wearing the frozen smile he used when he was annoyed and didn't want to show it. Wrogarth ignored his proffered hand and gestured for him to sit down. Tim's favourite suit was more crumpled than ever and the stubble on his chin gave him an air of sloppiness that had no place in politics.

'How are you, James?' Tim cleared his throat and removed the whine from his voice. 'The trip to France went well I hear.'

Wrogarth's higher chair meant he looked down on the taller man. He'd heard that Tim was counting the numbers again, and it didn't surprise him. He was the ambitious type but luckily, not courageous. Tim would lose a challenge right now but that could change if the polls didn't.

'Let's get down to business, shall we?' Wrogarth frowned as Tim shifted in his seat. 'This climate change report due next week is unacceptable.' He paused for effect. 'It's a publicly funded organisation for fuck's sake and it's arguing against government policy.' He glared at Tim adding careful emphasis to his words. 'What are you doing about it?' He sat back but maintained eye contact.

Tim's skewed smile signalled he thought this was an easy question. 'Well…the research and report pull together valid conclusions. I'm not sure what I can do about it? Their findings are consistent with other scientific research and are accepted by the international scientific community.'

'You always were naïve.' Wrogarth almost spat the words. His blood pressure was rising and the blood vessel at his temple had started pulsating. 'The CSIRO and Professor Matt Hutchinson, in particular, will fall into line, and you're going to make them. They're being provocative and I won't stand for it. They'll destabilise mining investment in this country. It's time to get tough!' His voice had risen to a menacing but controlled shout.

Tim laughed, taking Wrogarth aback. 'The mining industry can cope, I'm sure. We need to show we are listening and change our policy into line. Surely, James, you realise they are independent scientists…'

'They're fucking not. They're government-funded and that means they bloody well answer to me.' Wrogarth rose out of his seat and hurled his words across the desk. He paused, recovered his composure then added in a softer voice. 'You're weak. You're not up to the job.'

The fire in Tim's eyes told Wrogarth he had hit a nerve. 'You bas —' slipped out before Tim clenched his lips. He reeled back into his chair and glared at Wrogarth, then cleared his throat. 'It's ridiculous —' He had his temper under control, but Wrogarth didn't.

'Not enough, Tim.' Wrogarth had a sudden urge to hit him. 'All you do is talk, talk, talk. It has got us nowhere. Maybe it's time you were demoted, or better still, thrown out altogether.' He paused, noticing with satisfaction the disbelief on Tim's face. 'This is your last chance. We are going to review their funding and we'll decide how to best use public monies.' Nerves in his body twitched and he settled back to regain his composure. 'I want this fixed and if you can't…'

'You'll destroy us, you bastard, make us unelectable.'

'Just sort it out now, or else.' With that he turned to his papers and effectively dismissed Tim, who stormed out, slamming the office door behind him.

***

Wrogarth was home unusually early and had caught Bev out. She should never have taken down that family album. The baby photos, a picture of family holidays in their early years and the photos from

88

their first dates, sparked anger at what she had lost, instead of the happy reminiscences she craved.

'What's the matter?' he asked obviously not in the mood for problems.

'Nothing,' Bev said, looking away to give herself time to corral her emotions.

'Can we have one night together without an argument?' he snapped, and Bev knew it was not a request.

'It's not me,' she snapped back, unable to harness the emotions in time.

'No, of course not!' he shouted, daring her to go on, taunting her.

'Well…it's your fault…our family?' she said, rising to the bait and immediately regretting it when she saw his cold, fierce eyes staring at her. She'd wanted to say so much more but pulled back in time.

'Not again. I haven't done anything to our family. They're adults, they have lives, you just have to learn to let go.' His haggard face drooped. 'I've got bigger issues to worry about, and I've worked too hard to let you ruin it, so back off.'

He was clearly signalling an end to this conversation, but Bev had only just begun.

'You mean we worked hard. I made sacrifices too. It's my success as much as yours.' She stood firm, afraid of provoking him further but unable to let it drop.

'Oh no! You're not taking the credit. You helped, but without my hard work, we'd be nowhere. Without my schemes, my ideas and plans, we'd still be living in the suburbs.' He spat the words at her. 'Now I don't want to discuss it.' The fury in his eyes and the clenched fists were supposed to make Bev back down. It usually worked. 'William almost destroyed me and you did nothing to stop him. In fact, you supported him. It's over between him and me. It's been resolved.'

Her head jerked around, 'Nothing has been resolved, as you put it. What about what I want?'

'The choice was made a long time ago, now I don't want to discuss it anymore.' He pumped his fists in time with the vein in his temple.

Bev could see the signs and stopped herself from going on. Resentment was poisoning her. She stood trembling, despair fighting for control with hot rage. His feud with William was undermining everything. It had eaten away at their relationship, and there was no end in sight. It was a stalemate. She couldn't see a way forward and she buried her head in her hands.

Wrogarth stormed into the lounge turning on the TV to distract himself. He sat in his favourite chair and the news announcer's voice droned across the room. The minutiae of Sydney life was trotted out as groundbreaking news: a fire; a minor boating accident and a local council dispute; and James visibly relaxed as the mundane list of events droned on. The national news wasn't controversial either, allowing him to float far away into his thoughts.

Bev crept into the room, sitting in her chair on the other side of the fireplace. The upcoming current affair advertisement suddenly boomed louder than the normal program and Wrogarth sat bolt upright. Tonight, Professor Matt Hutchinson would discuss the latest findings of the CSIRO on climate change as a preview to its official release.

'How dare he?' he shouted at the screen, his face glowing bright red. 'What the hell is he doing?'

Bev startled by his outburst sat up sharply. 'What's the matter?'

'That arsehole is forcing the issue. He can't release that report until he makes the necessary changes. He thinks he can force my hand, but I'll show him. He won't get away with this. If he wants a fight, he'll get more than he bargained for.'

Bev was confused. 'He's a respected scientist and has quite a standing in his field, doesn't he?' she asked naively, not sure why this was such an issue.

Wrogarth stared at her in disbelief, 'You really don't take any interest anymore. He's undermining my position, but he'll pay if he continues with this stance.' He stormed out to the office, slamming the door behind him. Confused, she stared at the now-closed door.

A few phone calls later he emerged, looking a little calmer. Bev slunk upstairs hoping to avoid him and his mood. She was still struggling to shake off her melancholy and to constrain her growing anger. Her desire to mend the bridges in her family was futile. She was powerless. Bev climbed into bed, the weight of her sadness pulling her deeper into the mattress.

An hour later, her husband surprised her when he cursed as he stumbled at the threshold. Bev wasn't asleep and stifled the sob forming in her throat. She turned her face into the pillow to muffle the sound, but she was too late.

'Have you just been hiding?' he hissed. She knew he was waiting for her to turn around but resisted. 'I've got huge problems to deal with and you want to argue.'

She finally turned to face him; aware her red eyes would do nothing to appease him.

'Stop it, now.' His words struck her.

Bev sat up, rigid with anger. 'I know you don't care, but I do!'

The look on his face froze but the fire in his eyes burned her with his glare. He strode towards her with his fists clenched white.

Bev cringed. *When will I ever learn?*

Chapter 11

Shelley's European tour had left France behind. This afternoon was free time in Barcelona, and she joined the throng of tourists along *Las Ramblas*. Buskers performed acrobatic feats and played music and Shelley stepped in time to the rhythm. Pungent cooking smells emanating from the stalls set her stomach rumbling. Spices and barbequing meat mingled with the sweet scent of churros. Shelley lingered as the laughing crowd bustled in and out of brightly coloured market stalls. An ornate notebook attracted her attention. Its vivid red cover reminded her of Ayisha, dressed for a friend's birthday celebration. Shelley groaned. The Federal Police had pulled down a screen of secrecy over Ayisha's death and Maya hadn't shed any more light on the situation.

She veered into the maze of old town lanes, where it was quiet and cool. The noise of the happy crowd became a dull hum. She ambled down lanes twisting and curving in undisclosed patterns, widening only to narrow again into dimly lit and sinister spaces. She passed a tiny art studio shopfront and realised she'd seen this shop before. She'd been wandering in circles.

Steadying her breath, Shelley studied the map then entered a narrow lane that soon became dark and forbidding. It was strangely devoid of people. Her palms moistened and she tried to retrace her steps when a face at the corner startled her. Dark glasses seemed out of place in this dim setting and his features were familiar, but not in a good way. Beads of sweat dotted her brow and she fled down the nearest lane.

Then a strange tune wafted through the air. Racing towards the sound she almost fell into a square where people perched theatre-like on plastic seats. In front of them, children played instruments and sang sweetly out of tune and the audience applauded enthusiastically. An older woman noticed Shelley's distress, and with fluent charades, snatches of odd English words and good humour, she directed her towards the *Carrer de Ferran*. She had been close after-all.

Once safely in the busy pedestrian street, she leaned against a shop wall, taking deep breaths before scolding herself for being so easily alarmed. She followed the *Carrer de Ferran* to a large square flanked by a dark and foreboding gothic cathedral. A band of musicians, dressed in crisp white trousers and skirts, bright red tops and bandanas around their necks, stood on the steps. Instrumental warm-up sounds filled the air. The gathered crowd formed jagged circles of eight or ten and as the music started, they joined hands and gently swayed. When the tempo livened, the dance started in earnest. Bobbing and circling, hands raised then lowered, step forward then back, they performed a system of rhythmic movements. A woman collecting donations explained it was a traditional Catalonian dance. Shelley finally relaxed, swaying in time to the music and enjoying their celebration of life.

A touch on her shoulder startled her, but it was two of her tour companions, Harry and his wife. When the music stopped Harry suggested they find a café and Shelley agreed, suddenly aware she was thirsty.

'Enjoying your free time?' Harry asked as they walked along the square, his six-foot frame dwarfing his petite wife.

'I love the feel of Barcelona,' Shelley enthused, meaning every word. 'The Gaudi designs we saw this morning were fabulous.'

This morning's Barcelona city sights had introduced Shelley to Gaudi. Waves, curves and flower-like shapes of the *Sagrada Familia* and the Gaudi designed houses lodged in her memory. The flamboyance and creativity contrasted so strongly with the controlled architecture of her home environment.

'Yes, I love his designs too. Some don't, you know? I really enjoyed *Gruëll Park*,' his wife said, and Shelley agreed.

Shelley had admired the curved balconies edged mushroom-like patios that had sheltered her from the drizzle. She wished she had that kind of creativity. The kind of mind that could conjure up twisted wavy walls and strange chimney pots balanced on irregular roofs; or mask-like balconies unsuccessfully disguising windows in a curving façade. Her practical and controlled approach to life didn't fit that kind of flamboyance, but she wished it did.

They found a café with a perfect spot by the window. Both Shelley and Harry's wife ordered sangrias and Harry selected a Spanish beer, then they picked three tapas dishes to share.

'What did you do with your free time?' Shelley enquired.

'We went to the Columbus round-a-bout before doing some shopping.' Harry's wife raised a small shopping bag and smiled. 'The lovely little jewellery shops over there have affordable but unique designs. We bought presents for the girls. Just some earrings and bracelets, but now we have their gifts sorted.'

Their drinks and tapas arrived, and the tantalising smells made Shelley's stomach grumble. She nibbled on empanadas, Spanish omelettes, and meatball tapas and sipped her sangria.

'What do you do back home Shelley?' Harry's deep voice penetrated even a crowded setting.

'I'm a public servant,' she said and then in answer to Harry's raised eyebrow, 'Department of Immigration.'

She didn't like admitting where she worked, it sometimes started difficult conversations prompting people to offer their strong opinions on immigration policy and she wasn't good at deflecting them.

'I used to work for the Federal Police before I retired. I worked there for thirty-six years.' Harry's eyes fogged over. 'It was time to go.'

His wife reached across and patted his hand. 'It was hard to let go,' she said.

'Things change,' Harry continued, shaking his head, 'It wasn't so much hard to retire as to accept the direction things were taking. Maybe I was just getting old, but these bright sparks coming in kept proposing things that we knew had failed in the past, but they were the new guard…it was all getting too politicised for me anyway. It was a good time to retire.'

'I've only been there for nine years and I already feel like I've had enough.'

Their quiet laugh was more about understanding than humour.

'You're too young to feel that way,' Harry said.

Finishing his drink, Harry leaned toward Shelley and said quietly, 'I'll tell you something interesting. We must have someone important in our group.'

'What makes you think that?'

'We have an escort. Someone is watching our group. He's very discreet, but you can't fool a trained eye.' He touched the side of his nose with his forefinger. 'I saw him in Paris and then again at one of the Chateaux in the Loire Valley. I spotted him this morning too; at least I think it was him. His dark glasses are a good disguise.'

A nervous tremor travelled up her spine as they guessed at who the celebrity in their group could be. The South African or Canadian couples seemed most likely. They were the most mysterious.

Before they settled the bill, Shelley asked Harry if she could talk to him later. Ayisha crept into her thoughts and with his experience at the Federal Police, maybe he could help.

'I need some insider insight if you're willing,' she said.

Harry looked at his wife, who nodded gently.

'OK,' he agreed. His reluctance was obvious. 'We could have a drink after dinner and talk then.'

They headed towards Las Ramblas while Shelley walked towards the jewellery shops, armed with Harry's directions and recommendations.

Her nerves prickled thinking about the 'escort'. Could he have been in the old town lanes earlier? She remembered that day in Paris and the secretive transaction. Shelley dismissed the idea they were connected as too fanciful. She'd thought she'd seen the same face several times today but was she becoming paranoid?

Shelley found one of the recommended shops and scanned the window display. She scanned the faces near her before stepping over the threshold and then plunged into the joy of shopping. She returned to her hotel with two small parcels swinging by her side.

That evening, at the tour's traditional Spanish dinner, Shelley sat with some travelling companions she hadn't sat with before.

'Professor Hutchinson cancelled his attendance at the international climate change conference in Amsterdam,' The short wiry man from Sydney said.

'He'll be missed,' his wife added.

'Apparently, his son was in a serious car accident. He's in a critical condition in hospital. The police say it's suspicious,' the Sydney man continued.

Shelley had been impressed with the professor's speech on a current affairs program recently. It had drawn a connection between climate sceptics and vested interests. Her follow-up research found many sceptics – or she liked to call them – deniers, were associated with the very industries that produced the most pollution. No wonder the professor's latest studies were controversial. He'd linked mining activities with the degradation of sensitive environments.

'Man-made climate change is a big hoax,' the miner from country West Australia said firmly. 'It's time they stopped these scare campaigns.'

'There's no scare campaign, as you call it, just scientific evidence and conclusions,' the Sydney man rebutted.

As the debate continued, a veil of gloom settled over her. Facts were dismissed and replaced by beliefs and Shelley was left speechless. They believed what they wanted to believe regardless.

Once or twice she caught Harry signalling her and nodding towards someone in the dark corner. Her angle of vision kept the face obscured and she disregarded it. She didn't need her nerves on edge any more than they already were.

Later, she and Harry met in the hotel bar and Shelley explained what she knew about Ayisha's death.

'It's unusual for the department to get involved in a case like this,' Harry said, scratching his head. 'Although, there's a special unit operating in each state; they have a reputation…' He screwed up his nose and looked down at his beer. 'They're a bunch of…rogues. Who knows what they're involved in now.' He lifted his chin and Shelley noticed his eyes had turned fierce. 'It became worse once Benedict took over as head of the department. They report directly to him and there are rumours…' He straightened up, furtively glancing around the bar. 'Anyway, that's neither here nor there.'

Shelley sat quietly, she understood more than he might realise. 'There were a lot of changes made last year. Heads of departments moved and removed. Ours brought in a very strong political emphasis.' She knew she didn't have to explain, Harry was nodding in agreement.

'Yes, and it's not what it should be.'

They sat quietly for a while, nursing their drinks. Harry broke the silence first.

'I'm not sure how much I can help.' He studied her, then added, 'There is one thing…There is someone I can put you in touch with. He's a mate but, and it's a big but, you have to be very careful about any contact you make. He could get into serious trouble…and so could you.'

Shelley swallowed hard; her nerves jangled at the thought of this subterfuge.

Harry continued, 'I'll give him your details and he can get in touch with you. His codename is 'Beetle'.'

Harry took down her details and they finished their drinks in quiet contemplation.

'It's a funny old world. It's so complicated and full of too many ruthless players. I'm glad I got out.'

Shelley too wished she could get out, but she had to earn a living and support herself. It hardened her resolve to look for another job.

Back in her room, she wrote the codename in her new notebook. She shivered, thinking about how this was becoming like those spy novels she used to read.

Chapter 12

Bright sunshine, blue sky, bikini-clad girls and sand, well maybe not sand. Pebbles covered these beaches, but it was everything Jason had hoped he'd find in Nice. There was also the promise of fun. He and Adrian ambled along the beachfront, enjoying the opportunity to finally stretch their legs after their long drive. A gentle breeze swept along the Esplanade stinging them awake. The occasional brave swimmer dotted the sea close to shore. But Jason's eyes were drawn to the assortment of shapes on the beach, sprawled on sun lounges they'd paid handsomely for, in costumes designed for maximum exposure.

Oversized yachts bobbed beside small boats, gently swaying to waves generated by craft and jet skis. They admired the expensive vessel perched tall in the water, out of reach both physically and financially.

'How rich must these people be?' Jason said fighting down a twinge of envy.

'There's a price for it,' Adrian retorted.

Jason knew what he meant and nodded agreement. 'Unfortunately,' he said.

They continued along the waterfront, heading closer to the marina. A stream of lifeboats and dinghies docked at the small pier disgorging their yachting passengers for their daytime play onshore. A small dinghy drew up to the pier and a young seaman jumped out to secure it, then offered his hand to the bejewelled occupants. Fashionable Gucci sunglasses framed their faces, Louis Vuitton scarves twirled around their slender necks and impossibly pointy shoes struggled to climb between dinghy and pier. The women barely acknowledged the helping hand, chattering to each other with exaggerated hand gestures and facial expressions.

'Shopping trip?' Jason offered, as he appraised the two women clip-clopping along the pier. 'Too expensive for my taste,' he added, more as a warning to himself than anyone else.

'Definitely too high maintenance,' Adrian agreed.

Jason knew Adrian's tastes usually ran to intelligent women who had purpose and commitment. Women who shunned extravagance and overt displays of wealth, but Jason smiled; Adrian and he differed dramatically in their criteria.

They detoured to a café where they could enjoy the sun as well as enjoy the view of the marina. The short espresso was Adrian's choice now, while Jason persisted with the latte. It was a game. He was never sure what he would get since each French café varied in its interpretation of a latte according to the city or region. He was pleasantly surprised to find this one resembled an Adelaide latte and he grinned his approval.

A couple commandeered the corner table. The heavyset man, puffing loudly, fell into his chair and sent it colliding into the one behind. His slim young companion slid daintily into her seat and immediately produced a compact and dabbed at her face. An older couple joined them. Jason watched them, absorbed in the dynamics. The men shook hands, there was no kissing of cheeks, and the women's charade of affected air kisses was unconvincing. The wife sneered ever so slightly when she first spied the young woman but recovered quickly, forming her mouth into a fixed grimace to greet the first couple. She was immaculately groomed, not a hair out of place, which was hard to imagine given the breeze gently ruffling Jason's mop. A small roll of flesh around her midriff pushed her blouse forward as she settled into a seat beside the first woman, but she pulled herself upright and it faded from view.

Jason turned his attention to the man and grabbed Adrian's arm. He knew this wiry man with strong broad shoulders and a flat stomach. Martin Carlew, the Australian mining magnate who had recently bought an English soccer team and created a furore both in England and Australia. His poaching of administrative and coaching staff from the top clubs in Australia had been deeply unpopular. Jason shook his head. Public outrage was saved for sporting misdemeanours. Carlew's shoddy business deals never attracted the same level of anger. Jason knew only too well how Carlew had accumulated his wealth in such a short time. It was done by a sleight of hand, cheating lots of people, small mine owners, and big ones. He hadn't seen the wife before, she didn't feature much in the celebrity sections.

A third man joined the group. He was short and bustling with sharp features, dark glasses, and glistening dark hair. He shook hands firmly with the men and nodded at the women as they were introduced.

Adrian leaned across to Jason, 'That's Mark McCracken, Wrogarth's latest adviser,' he whispered.

Carlew signalled the waiter and they ordered. They formed a small circle, the women sat to one side as the men huddled together. Suddenly one of the men looked up, pushed his chair back and waved toward the beach. A burly, sauntering man boomed a friendly accented greeting as he approached. His eyes lingered fleetingly on Jason and Adrian. The glint of sunlight reflecting from a gold tooth momentarily distracted Jason, but he thought he saw a flicker of something akin to recognition register in the man's eyes before he returned his attention to the group. Jason didn't recognise him.

Jason searched his memory for the names of the first couple. Then he remembered. After Klaus had told him about Ortansea and its operations, he'd Googled the company and found a photo of one of the directors shaking hands to seal a leasing deal with an Australian company. A second photo had shown him and his wife at a movie premiere. The surname was Jacov. His first name was too long and foreign for Jason to remember but it started with M. Hers was Alicia. The young trophy wife of twelve months had been draped over his arm at the premiere event and had attracted much commentary.

Jason told Adrian what he'd remembered and together they tried to guess what the group was doing, especially the newcomer who seemed to be leading the discussion. Jason cursed his luck, they were too far away to hear but he couldn't move closer without attracting attention. The pointing, directing and hands flailing as the newcomer talked, intrigued Jason. He seemed to be outlining something in great detail. A burst of laughter punctuated the otherwise serious discussion.

The women fidgeted. They sat upright and angled slightly away from each other in what was very telling body language. They'd obviously run out of conversation already.

Mark McCracken was the first to leave. When he shook hands with the burly man a furtive look passed between them. When the others prepared to leave, each insisted on leaving their own tip and boisterously farewelled each other, promising to meet again tonight.

Jason caught the mention of Hôtel Taresco but he wasn't sure if they were staying there or going to meet there. He decided to check it out later. Adrian wondered out loud why Mark McCracken was there. It didn't look like a social meeting.

***

That night, Jason dragged out the most conservative clothes in his suitcase. He wouldn't really blend in but it would have to do. He couldn't bring himself to add a scarf or drape a jacket over his shoulders in that European style. His dark trousers and neat shirt, even if in need of ironing, were the best he could manage. Luckily Adrian had convinced him to pack something more formal.

He strolled towards the beachfront, joining the tourists and locals as they walked before dinner, parading their clothes and their partners along the Promenade des Anglais. He turned the corner and a grand pink building rose majestically from the opposite side of the road. The bold sign announced it was the Hôtel Taresco. The concierge cast a disapproving eye over Jason as he passed into the foyer but Jason pretended to recognise someone in the corner, waved and hurried away before he could be challenged. He peered through the dining room windows but there were few people in there. *So, it's true, only tourists eat before eight pm.* Carefully dodging guests in the foyer, he scanned the faces but they were not there. There was a bigger crowd of suited men and evening dress clad women, clustered around the edges of the bar. He avoided eye contact becoming self-conscious as people stared. He wished he blended in better.

He eventually found them in the seated area of the bar, perched in a nook in the quieter section. Jacov was talking to the tall gold-toothed man, their heads bent conspiratorially close. Jason searched for a table nearby that was not too obvious. He was retreating to the bar when he noticed the couple around the corner rising to leave. He dashed over, almost knocking over a table, and although the couple at the table beside it stared, he'd avoided attracting more attention. Another couple, who'd been walking across in a gentler fashion, looked unamused. Jason smiled but the woman just gave him an icy stare before she was led away.

Jason studied the drinks menu. This table was out of their sightline but near enough to eavesdrop. He could see their reflections on the window and hoped they wouldn't realise he was listening in. He raised the menu higher, but the two men were in such deep discussion they didn't look his way. Unfortunately, he hadn't counted on the background music. Jason cursed his luck as their voices were drowned out by the rousing classical piece.

Jason saw Martin Carlew standing in the doorway of the bar, hesitating in a pose to be noticed. He looked suave in his dinner suit and younger than Jason knew him to be. Carlew casually scanned the room then, as Jacov waved, he nodded recognition. He ordered a drink at the bar and, drink in hand, sauntered to the table. His smooth entrance brought a noticeable stiffness to the others.

The small-talk was loud enough for Jason to hear and the guffaw at the amount of time it took their wives to get ready seemed exaggerated. After more drinks were served, Carlew, Jacov, and the other man settled into a serious discussion. The music ebbed and Jason could overhear them.

'That transaction in Paris cost more than it should. It better pay off,' Carlew complained.

'Of course it'll pay off,' Jacov insisted as he glanced at the big man.

'That's good for me.' The big man smiled; his Eastern European accent made Jason listen more intently. 'It's worth it for you of course. A good deal, no?' he continued.

A waiter interrupted Jason's attempts to listen and he ordered the cheapest beer on the menu. Even that was in danger of breaking his credit card. At least it let him listen again.

Carlew sat back in the seat. 'I've got all the paperwork in order. We can finalise the structure now.'

They toasted the news with a clink of glasses and hearty congratulations. At this point, the big man scanned the room, then leaned towards Jacov.

'I've taken care of Sergei. It's going to plan.' His voice carried well despite heavy laughter from a nearby table.

'We need these shipments to get things moving. There have been too many delays,' Jacov responded.

'It's fine. Wrogarth's on edge, he'll do what needs to be done now,' the big man said with assurance.

Hearty laughter rose from their group in response.

Jason wasn't sure they'd said Wrogarth but if they had, this could be big. Jacov looked up and Jason followed his gaze to where the wives were entering. Carlew's wife walked tall, just ahead of Alicia.

The big man stood to leave and Jacov assured him 'We'll keep you informed.' Then he and Carlew stood to greet their wives, Jacov kissing her elaborately on both cheeks while the Carlews stood awkwardly and watched. They left, the Jacovs arm in arm discussing their reservation at an exclusive restaurant for dinner.

All this effort, not to mention the expensive drink and Jason wasn't sure what he had learned. He wished he knew who the big man with the gold tooth was. He seemed an important link. The company names might hold the clue, especially if he focused on European connections. The big man's accent sounded Eastern European or maybe Russian, so he'd start there. Klaus had mentioned Russian crime syndicates taking over mining corporations. He sat and finished his drink despite the pointed stares of those searching for a table.

Chapter 13

Bev sipped her coffee; her untouched toast was cold. When Wrogarth entered the room she shrank down, trying to become invisible. His sigh punctuated the crash of a chair as it scraped across the tiled floor. Instinctively, she touched the bruise on her arm. He leaned across, touching her shoulder tenderly, muttered sorry then rose and walked out. She didn't look up. She didn't want to see his usual look of remorse.

After he'd gone, she slumped over the kitchen table. Sobs shook her frame, her body convulsed with anger, fear, and sorrow. With her head propped on her folded arms, she let the tears flow. It was getting worse, not better. She was suddenly questioning if it was worth it. She'd believed that with recognition and success he would be more content. She was wrong. Her husband never seemed satisfied, his drive and ambition were stronger now than ever. She'd desired success too but the cost was proving higher than she had bargained for.

Even after all this, Bev still loved him, but she was afraid. He was distant, unreachable and so often, very angry. Once good days had outnumbered the bad, but now there were so many more bad days. Last night, like never before, she had been terrified. She winced as she moved, all the bruises ached and pain tore through her ribs. His rage had stormed out of control, the anger unleashed so violently and raw, she'd been seriously afraid for her life.

She limped back and forth relentlessly, her inner turmoil in sync with her outward dishevelment. In the morning light, despite her injuries, she started to doubt her assessment of what had happened. Maybe she was being melodramatic, she couldn't tell. Maybe if she understood what was happening, she could avoid his wrath, or somehow help him. Her limp body slumped back into the chair, no matter what she told herself, she was hurting and not just her pride.

***

Wrogarth was in the office early and Daryl knew this was never a good sign. The shrillness of the phone startled him, and he almost dropped the carefully collated pile of papers in his hand. Mark's agitated tone crackled down the line and he connected the call, then moved closer to the slightly ajar door, straining to hear.

'You let it come to this. The question is; how will you fix it?' Wrogarth sounded harsh; a tone he saved for special occasions. It must be serious. Daryl cursed not staying on the line.

A short pause, Wrogarth's breathing sounded steady but fast. 'We need October, but I won't renegotiate cost. It makes us look weak.' Daryl held his breath. Finally, Wrogarth spoke again, this time softly and more controlled. 'Maybe we should let him sweat for a while. You contact him and tell him the price is not negotiable. Do you think you can handle that without stuffing up?'

A thump boomed across the office and the snarl was unmistakably Wrogarth. 'Just do it. Let me know what happens immediately.'

Daryl stepped back towards his desk as he heard the phone slam back into its cradle. Mark was in trouble by the sound of it. He waited a moment, shuffling papers before he took them into the office.

'Hi, James. You're in early today.' He tried to sound casual. He wasn't good at these games, but he was getting plenty of practice.

Wrogarth had his back to the door, staring out of the window across the Sydney skyline. At Daryl's voice, he spun around, his mouth set in a tight line.

'Daryl, I'd like you to remember that I'm the Prime Minister. You should address me as such.'

The words stung and Daryl stepped back involuntarily. They'd been together for many years, he'd supported Wrogarth as a battling MP, and although he wouldn't have called the man a friend, he'd thought they were partners. He straightened, staring Wrogarth in the eyes.

'Yes sir, Mr Prime Minister,' he said with as much exaggerated pomp as he could muster before dropping the papers onto the desk.

'Will there be anything else…*sir*?' He hissed the sir. He didn't wait to see the reaction, just turned his back and marched out.

***

Bev's misgivings about dinner had been proven wrong. James' political allies were stuffy and tough-talking men but despite this, tonight she'd relaxed, confident her make-up hid all the traces of their argument. James was fun when he was in a good mood, losing the intensity that had lately been following him around. Maybe the drinks before everyone arrived had helped, but whatever it was, she'd enjoyed the shift. It had reminded her of old times. Again, he was the charming host, laughing, joking, even if some of his jokes made her cringe.

The guest list had surprised her. She hadn't realised his inner circle had changed so much. Tim hadn't been invited and she was surprised at the wisecrack James made during dinner that Tim was history. She liked him, even if he did covet the top job. He was more of a gentleman than the latest inner circle.

The new crowd was a strange mix. The Mining and Trade Minister was a self-made man turned politician. His off-colour jokes took some getting used to, but they were better than his self-promotion. The Immigration Minister was the quiet type. She hadn't learned much about him tonight. The Federal Police Minister, to her, looked more like a criminal than a minister for justice, law, and order.

After the last of the guests had gone, James poured another drink and settled into his easy chair. He lounged back and smiled a crooked smile at her. Bev pulled herself up slowly and announced she was off to bed, then climbed the stairs deep in thought. James was having one more for the road but that meant more than one these days.

Undressing slowly, she mused at how much she enjoyed the relaxed James. He was still the man she loved. If only she could turn him around, help him shed the anxieties that troubled him.

By the time he joined her, his breath and his gait revealed his extra scotches. His soft and tender caress took her by surprise as it roused her from her drowsiness. He wrapped his arms around Bev, and she snuggled into him, luxuriating in his warmth and the gentle touch of his fingers. He kissed her hard on the mouth, insistent and demanding. She knew this would be a drunken fumbling act of relief, but she preferred this to his anger. At least this felt a little like love. It made her tingle even if it left her unsatisfied. She treasured the intimacy and gave herself up to him.

Chapter 14

Weary, baggy eyes stared at Shelley from the tiny aeroplane bathroom mirror. The dark circles betraying her unsuccessful attempts to sleep on the long-haul flight to Melbourne. Splashing her face with water and pressing a cold cloth to her eyes, her heart sank. Her reflection confirmed it wasn't working the miracles she needed. Her pleasure at the thought of Adrian waiting at the airport evaporated with every weary sign.

Her Melbourne to Adelaide connection had been delayed and their flight was now late. She squeezed herself back into her window seat and pushed her legs as far forward as she could. It wasn't far at all. The ache in her knees and back made her feel old beyond her years. She peered out the window and saw they were coming in over Tailem Bend. A murky coloured ribbon twisting and threading its way along the green-brown landscape appeared below. The Murray River was completing its journey in South Australia too. Tiny grey threads crisscrossed the country and she recognised the local roads in miniature with ant-like cars gliding along at intervals. She sighed, relief mixed with sadness, nearly home now.

The captain's voice interrupted her thoughts, announcing the plane was starting its descent. Shelley gathered up her book and belongings, stowed them into her carry-on bag, then turned back to the window to catch a glimpse of Adelaide from the air.

As the plane dipped towards the runway the passenger next to her sat back in her seat, closed her eyes and tightly held onto the armrest. Shelley eagerly watched out of the window until they'd landed.

Walking up the ramp, Shelley spied Adrian almost immediately. Even standing towards the back of the crowd he was clearly visible. He seemed to be in deep conversation with someone, but they were obscured by the crowd. Adrian hadn't seen her yet, so she studied him, reacquainting herself with his face. She'd last seen him three weeks ago and he was paler and leaner than she remembered. She thought he looked tired. By the time she'd rounded the corner on the exit ramp, he was watching the disembarking passengers. When his eyes met hers, he smiled, and her heart flipped just like the first time she'd seen him. She forgot how bedraggled she felt as he hugged her warmly.

'How was your flight?' Adrian asked as they waited at the carousel for her bags.

'Cramped and tiring, you know…' Shelley shrugged. 'Border Force at Melbourne airport was very officious,' she added, remembering her encounter.

'Did you run foul of them?'

'Well. It's bad enough being exhausted and the long line to get baggage scanned, but having to unpack it in front of everyone, just for a small notebook. That seemed ridiculous.'

'A notebook? What was the issue?'

'Apparently, it had a strip of banana leaf stuck on its spine.' She swallowed hard, 'It's not the notebook, it's what was in it.' She didn't tell him about losing Harry's and Beetle's details though.

Waiting at the baggage carousel, Shelley felt a touch on her shoulder.

'Hi, Shelley.' The familiar face smiled shyly at her from inside her veil.

'Hi,' Shelley responded, searching for a name that wouldn't come. 'How are you?'

'I'm fine. Did you hear about…Ayisha? It was so very sad.'

Shelley nodded, remembering this young woman had been Ayisha's friend.

'I saw her before she went to Sydney. She asked if I could look after her cat, but I couldn't help her,' the young woman explained.

'Do you know why she was going to Sydney?' Shelley asked.

'It was to help her friend, Kadeen…I remember because she has the same name as my sister-in-law.'

'Do you know Kadeen? Or her other name?'

'No, I don't know her… It's terrible to think… suicide… it makes me so sad. I worry that I could have…' She lowered her head then suddenly looked up at Shelley again. 'There is something else. I almost forgot. She said what was happening to her friend was 'unspeakable'. She didn't answer me when I asked what it was. She was upset and muddled.'

Shelley didn't mention the mystery and possibility it wasn't suicide. She had to be sure first.

'Thank you for telling me. Please let me know if you think of anything else.'

The young woman nodded solemnly then turned as a friend pulled on her sleeve. They said goodbye, although Shelley still didn't know the young woman's name.

Adrian put an arm around Shelley's shoulders and gave her a light squeeze. It was a comfort but no consolation.

***

Back at her apartment, Adrian carried in her suitcase and some shopping he'd bought. Waiting for her on the kitchen bench was a note from her sister, Vonnie as a welcome home.

Adrian stowed the basics in the fridge then turned his attention to opening a bottle of wine while Shelley arranged some cheese and crackers on a plate. He presented her with a glass of wine, and they sat down.

'Welcome back,' he said as he raised his glass.

'Thank you,' Shelley raised her glass too before taking a sip.

He smiled at her. 'Is your sister older or younger?'

'She's younger.' Shelley thought about the weekend catch up being planned by her parents. 'She and I are not at all alike.'

'In what way?'

'She and mum got along better especially when I was younger. Vonnie is easier. She loves to watch reality TV, reads gossip magazines and generally lives life through celebrities. Her complaints are confined to the mortgage rate or electricity prices. And of course, she's still married to Cal.' She noticed Adrian's raised eyebrows and added, 'My mother adored Tom.' She felt her face heat up.

Adrian didn't say anything, just looked with an amused sparkle in his eyes.

'So, what have you been up to since you returned?' Shelley asked trying to deflect the topic and her own reminiscing.

'I've been busy with a series of tests for a colleague, Carla. She's collecting data on health issues in outback communities. In one of them, the children are exhibiting strange symptoms and she wanted us to look into it,' he explained as he sunk back into the sofa. 'When do you start back at work?'

'I'm back on Monday.' She tensed at the thought.

'Have you learned any more about Ayisha?'

'The last email from Maya at work said the Federal Police investigation is secret. They moved Ayisha's body to a special

Federal Police facility and didn't let the state coroner finish his autopsy. It's mysterious. I hope I can find out more when I'm back.'

'Hopefully, your department will still be in the loop.' Adrian finished his wine and took his glass to the sink. 'I'd better go. I still have some stuff to finish at the lab this afternoon, and you look like you could use a rest.' He reached across and kissed her tenderly. It caught her by surprise and was over before she could respond.

She needed to rest but she didn't really want him to go. In the end, she had no choice.

After he'd gone, Shelley poured herself another glass and turned her thoughts to the more pleasant remembrances of her holiday. At first, being a solo traveller had felt strange, but eventually, she'd relished the sense of freedom and the chance to be self-indulgent. Adrian had occasionally drifted into her thoughts as she wandered through the evocative back streets of Venice or walked in Rome at night. In Munich, stumbling upon the Hoffbrauhaus where tourists and locals laughed in friendly rivalry as they egged each other on to skol their one-litre steins of beer, the boisterous competitiveness had made her think of Adrian and Jason. The slight pang of loneliness that crossed her mood that day hadn't lasted long. She was feeling more comfortable in her own company at last.

She touched her lips where the kiss had sat so awkwardly and smiled, but she still liked the promise of the right kind of company.

***

The silver shimmer of the water dulled as the sun again hid behind the grey clouds. Jason pulled his jacket close as the gentle breeze brushed a cold hand across his face and whipped his hair up and out. Time to get it cut or maybe just a trim. Along the Semaphore coastline, a path wound through the fenced-off scrub and stretched toward the beach and its hard-packed sand. A trace of foot and paw prints wove around the threads of seaweed, concluding at a collection of shells someone had left in a neat pile.

Jason scoured the beach until he saw him. He was sitting on a beach towel, bracing himself against the now strong wind flying off the ocean. He strode over to Gary, his feet sinking into the soft sand and slipping back with each step. It took him twice as long as it should, and it was much more arduous. As he neared, he panted Gary's name. Gary raised his head and nodded.

'How are ya?' Jason breathed. He chose a small, half-buried rock beside Gary to perch on.

'Yeah, fine,' Gary said. He hadn't changed much since school, in fact, it looked like he was still wearing their old school jumper under his jacket. He had always been the quietest kid Jason knew. They had not really been friends but had some common interests in recent times. 'I checked out that company you wanted; I've printed out a bit of data for you.' Gary handed over the envelope and stared at Jason. 'So, what's it about?'

'I'm planning to write a book about Australian mining activities if I can get enough material.' Jason grinned, it sounded lame. His friends didn't believe he would ever complete a book and he wasn't that sure himself.

'You gone into journalism have ya?' Gary said and the corners of his mouth turned up in what passed for a smile for Gary.

'Nah. It's just a project,' Jason confessed. 'I'm still working at the minerals lab.'

'Trisec Oil hasn't got much material for an exposé.' Gary shook his head, 'Their black marks are pretty common knowledge.'

'Yeah, but they have some joint ventures in the pipeline that might be interesting.' Although Jason had explained what he was looking for when he'd asked for Gary's help, Gary was known to get side-tracked.

'They must have good connections because they got licences to open up mining exploration in national park areas, even in the Flinders. They're like pockmarks scattered on the landscape from what I can tell. I've listed them but without a map, it's hard to work out exactly where they are, they use some pretty funny names.'

Jason shuffled through the folder of notes. A highlighted note on one page caught his eye and he opened it up, careful to shield it from the wind.

'They've pulled up stumps though. They're connected to Ortansea with some joint ventures here and overseas, as well as a couple of other smaller overseas enterprises. Their structures are a tangled mess, very hard to work out who owns what,' Gary continued.

Jason smiled, 'I was wondering how you'd go.' He was rewarded by a sideways glance and a loud tut.

'I hadn't heard of AAAP before. They had a few gold mines but are now into oil.'

'Oil?' Jason mumbled as he read the accompanying notes.

'Yeah, it's odd. They don't have any off-shore rigs or oil rigs on land but are in the business of oil trading. The area they are mining is mainly metal ores.' Gary had turned back to the ocean and the wind carried his voice straight to Jason.

'They're buying up the old disused mines by what you have here. I thought those sites were no longer viable.' Jason read, quickly snatching at the top page before it floated away.

Gary shrugged. 'Can't say why but, yeah, they have and mostly in remote areas. Nearly all have been out of action for some time. Maybe they've developed a new process, or, have the cash to dig deeper and make them pay again. Whatever it is, they're quietly going about their business.'

Jason thanked Gary then tentatively asked him for another favour. 'I want to know who is behind Ortansea. And while you're at it, where's the money coming from for AAAP? Anything that explains what they're doing would be useful. Can you find out?' Gary's hacker skills were legendary, and he came cheap. A slab of beers was the going rate, though sometimes he got posh and asked for a bottle of scotch. He loved the thrill of the chase and getting into sites he wasn't supposed to get into.

Gary nodded, 'It'll cost ya.' He grinned then pushed himself off the beach towel. He flapped it high and the wind sent the loose sand into Jason's face.

'Steady on,' he growled through gritted teeth, but Gary just laughed and walked off.

Jason tucked the information into his inside pocket and zipped the jacket up tight. He strode off down the beach, deep in thought. Picking up the pace on the firm damp sand near the water's edge, he swung his arms until he felt the blood coursing through his veins. The activity brought with it a sense of exhilaration. He barely noticed the other walkers as he watched out for the methodical rhythm of the waves lapping near his feet. Lacy splatters of foam crowned the waves, dispersing into fragments as the waves retreated. His head felt clear, his mind working as hard as his body. He would talk to Klaus once he got his phone number again from Adrian. He hadn't seen much of Adrian since they'd been back, in fact, he hadn't seen much of any of the old gang. He had trouble trying to slip back into his old life, the bars, his regular haunts seemed dull and uninteresting and the conversations just covered the same old topics. They hadn't changed, but he had. The thought of Adrian brought Shelley's face to mind. Adrian was collecting her from the airport today. Jason wondered if he would see her again and then resolved to make sure he would. Her face held a strange allure. She was funny and warm, unlike the girls he usually met. Jason shook his head. This was all wrong. He knew Adrian was interested in Shelley and he was almost sure she liked Adrian too, but given Adrian's track record, he'd wait it out.

The dampness on his face turned cold as the wind whipped head-on. The sweatiness under his arms was not unpleasant, a sign of exerting and pushing himself, not something he did often. He found another walkway up to the road and slowed to amble back to his car. Three cars were parked near his, two were empty but a man sat reading a newspaper in the third. He looked up as Jason opened the car door and their eyes met. The man hurriedly looked away and Jason slipped into the cocoon of quiet and warmth in his car. With a turn of the ignition key, the car motor sprang to life and Jason reflected on what he was doing. He had to stay focused and get serious about his project. Hopefully, Gary would have the additional information he needed soon.

Chapter 15

Daryl perched uncomfortably on the edge of his seat, while Mark lounged back.

'What's so urgent?' James Wrogarth snarled at Mark.

'They've arrested the London terrorist and there's a link to four Australians,' Mark said.

Wrogarth tilted his head, indicating for Mark to go on.

'You know the case. Mohamed Yusuf was involved in an alleged plot to bomb the British Parliament. They think he's the mastermind and was in Paris recruiting for the Taliban. He was seen with a group of Australians there. The Federal Police have it covered.' Mark said then waited for Wrogarth to look up before he continued, 'International agencies have them under surveillance. One of them is of particular interest. He travelled to Pakistan after meeting Mohamed Yusuf.'

Daryl noted Mark's beaming face, Wrogarth, however, was inscrutable and absorbed in thought.

Wrogarth leaned forward. 'Get on with it. What are the Australian connections?'

'There were three males and a female. Akbal Hassam went to Pakistan after Paris. They lost him for about four days before he resurfaced in Islamabad. It's probably not enough time to undertake serious training, but it's suspicious. They're investigating. He was a refugee. The agency is maintaining surveillance on them and they want us to stay out of it for now. The woman is a Department of Immigration employee. The two men are...' Mark scrolled through the notes on his lap. 'Oh yes, there they are, Jason Morecroft and Adrian McGrath. They're all from Adelaide.'

He whipped four photos out of the file and placed them on the desk facing Wrogarth. The sharp intake of breath made Daryl pay attention. Mark's head jerked up. Wrogarth shuffled the photos and Daryl stretched to get a better look, but they were snatched away too quickly.

'Is something the matter?' Mark's wolfish features came alive, his fierce guarded eyes on alert.

Wrogarth paused drawing a slow long breath. 'Yes...er...no...um...What did you say their names were?' A strange smirk settled on his lips at the answer. He tapped his fingers lightly on the desk in deep thought, then continued, 'Concentrate on the main suspect. Ignore the others for now, but keep me posted of any developments. We need an arrest. I'll talk to the Minister. Daryl, organise a time tomorrow. This has to be done right. Get the special squad onto it and the Feds can take the running. Jacobs, the head of the Intelligence Agency, can liaise with the Americans, but we're going to handle this now.'

He paused and turned sharply to look out of the window. If that photo was William, it would explain Wrogarth's reaction. Mark looked confused and rifled through his notes again.

'This came through as I was coming to the meeting, I haven't had a chance to look at it yet, but it's a photo of the woman.'

As Mark placed it on the desk, his eyes widened. He was transfixed and took a moment to compose himself. Wrogarth turned back to the desk, glanced at the photo then slid it back to Mark.

'An arrest will boost our security credentials,' he urged.

Mark agreed. He scrutinised Wrogarth as intently as Daryl was watching them both. Mark rose and Daryl followed him out in silence, hoping to catch him before he fled down the corridor.

'Can I have a look at the photos?' Daryl used his smoothest voice.

'Why?' Mark leaned back and stared at Daryl, his eyes forming small slits in his angular face.

'Why not?' Daryl countered.

Mark laughed as he turned towards the corridor, 'Nah, they are 'need to know' only.'

He strode from the room, a snigger fading down the corridor as he went.

***

Wrogarth burst through the front door at home and strode straight to his study, barely noticing Bev as she came out of the lounge.

'You're home late.' She looked at her watch. 'Shall I get dinner served?'

He kept his hand on the doorknob. Reluctant to tear his mind away from his current preoccupation he hadn't heard her question. Her noisy deep breath stirred him and her look of annoyance was unmistakable.

'Er…not yet. There's some…er…things I need to do first.' Then as a concession to her questioning look, he added. 'Give me an hour?'

She walked away mumbling, just loud enough for him to hear, 'Glad I waited.'

He strode into the study and closed the door. Fumbling in his briefcase, he found the documents Mark had prepared. The first was a dossier on Petro. He'd been waiting for this. It had taken Mark too long and too much prompting to get it. It had been so much easier with Sergei. If only Mark had managed this better. He wanted to opt-out of the arrangement but couldn't now that the campaign had started.

The report confirmed Petro's takeover of Sergei's patch. Russian Cartels and rival groups were involved, and a soft whistle escaped Wrogarth's lips as he read the details. Petro was not the small-time criminal he had thought him to be, he had some very powerful

130

people behind him. Why was Petro involving himself in this deal? This business was not a big money-spinner. He wouldn't get rich from what they were paying or from the asylum seeker contributions. Petro's involvement didn't fit. Wrogarth's fingers tapped lightly on the desktop. Petro's business dealings read like a Who's Who of the underworld both in Australia and internationally, the litany of criminal enterprises such as brothels, drugs, gun-running, and people smuggling made him a dangerous connection. His few legitimate businesses laundered money through a complicated web of off-shore company structures.

Wrogarth drew a sharp breath, the air hissing through his teeth. Petro's links to Ortansea complicated the situation. How had Mark allowed them to be blindsided like this? The agreement was supposed to finish at the end of the year, but now he wasn't so sure it could. How did Petro fit into the picture? The briefing notes weren't specific. They weren't up to Mark's usual standard.

Wrogarth squirmed in his seat; he needed more space between him and Petro. Muscles in his chest tightened, squeezing the air out of his lungs and forcing him to lean forward. The risks were escalating while he had less and less control. It was getting messy.

He turned back to the report, scribbling notes in the margins in vivid red ink. The other reports highlighted issues with the mining ventures in the national parks, especially those in the Flinders Ranges. Wrogarth scowled at the usual requests for more assistance. They were always crying poor, wanting more and more concessions.

He'd have to talk to Martin Carlew, find out what was happening and check on the link to Petro. He scanned a list of possible good news stories Daryl had left for him. The third item, the Aboriginal Training Scheme being launched by Trisec Oil could provide the perfect vehicle for a private chat. He made a note for Mark to arrange it and to get Pierson's newspapers to cover it. Wrogarth chuckled. Pierson's expanding media empire covered the major newspapers around the country and most of the free to air channels and pay-TV news. Allowing the takeovers had been a stroke of genius and worth the flack. People had forgotten the controversy already and the benefits for him were clear.

That regular tic reappeared, beating a steady rhythm on his temple. Relying on favours, especially with newspaper moguls and mining magnates, was dangerous. They always wanted something in return. He crossed to the window, even Mark was an issue. He trusted the man, he had to, but he now knew too much. All the careful planning to keep himself out of these deals had come to nothing. He gazed at the lush, green garden outside forming a shadow play in the fading light. The paths and formal plantings danced in the glow from the street. The gardeners had done a good job changing the unruly mess into one of order and symmetry. How was he going to get things back to a neater and simpler format in his political life? Maybe after the election, he could start to prune back and regain control with less visibility.

The last report alerted him to journalists snooping around Ortansea and its activities in Africa. They were delving into its corporate structure and questioning Ortansea's links to activities in Australia. There had been a worrying computer breach too. He scribbled furiously in the margins, creating angry red scrawls 'make sure this goes into a dead-end'. Wrogarth's mouth twisted in distaste as he read the name of one of the journalists involved. Evans used to work for Waterman Press, and he was stubborn. Years ago, he'd tried to back Wrogarth into a corner over a development contract and almost succeeded. The Waterman group was small and independent and had so far, successfully resisted attempts to buy them off. Even Carlew had tried to buy into them, to exert control over their articles, but they'd resisted and protected their editorial commentary. He had to find another way to handle this. The other reporter was a European freelancer, not a name Wrogarth recognised and he made a note for Mark to find out more about him. So long as the Australian press were under control the rest would sort itself out.

The report on the detention centres was unremarkable, everything seemed to be going to plan. He was just about to turn to the climate change report when the knock on the door startled him. Bev's voice called through the opening door telling him dinner was ready. She'd taken his hour literally and despite wanting to finish these reports, he decided to take a break.

'OK, I'm coming,' he called. He shuffled the papers into a neat pile and put them to one side.

***

Dinner was quiet. Bev's attempts at conversation barely rallied her husband out of his self-absorption.

'Are you worried about the election?' she asked, keen to show her interest. She'd been his shoulder to lean on in the past, maybe she could be again.

'Always.'

His tone sounded gentler than usual and she relaxed.

'I thought your latest policy releases have been well received in the polls.'

'The polls go up and down, but yes, lately they're encouraging. It's still a long way to go to a certain victory, although, we haven't started our campaigns in earnest yet.'

His eyes rested gently on her face. Encouraged by his tone, Bev went on.

'I was surprised by Tim's comments that the party is backing away from the action on climate change. From what I've read, and even from our time in Paris, the Europeans have come around. It could leave us in the lurch economically if we resist the move, couldn't it.'

James sat still, staring down at his plate. His breath flowed evenly, and Bev took it as a sign he was listening.

'The electorate seems ready for some kind of action. You could develop our own strong policy on climate change to steal the opposition's thunder,' she said and relaxed back into her seat.

He raised his head and the fire in his eyes startled her.

'I don't need you to lecture me on policy.'

He pushed back his chair, threw his napkin on the table and stormed off. Bev swallowed back a retort. The carefully cultivated mood was lost. She was alone again – confused by his violent reaction.

James paced along the balcony, his favourite thinking place even though he no longer smoked. Bev rarely followed him out there especially not tonight.

She heard her husband's footsteps descend into the garden. He often wandered out there to clear his head, even in the dark. Bev stole into the study, she had a right to know what was going on, she rationalised. It was her future too.

The small desk lamp concentrated on the papers. His handwriting had deteriorated making the angry red scrawls along the margins difficult to decipher. The name Petro leaped off the page and she shivered, remembering the sinister dark shape commandeering James' attention in an underground car park in Paris. She was desperate to know what dealings James had with this man. She scanned the report, her skin prickled as though insects crawled over it.

The Climate Change paper was remarkably free of scribbles and the reference to mining activities, the professor and his study seemed odd. Mark's name popped up everywhere and confirmed he was James' right-hand man now. Suddenly she heard the door creak and she froze.

'What are you doing?' Wrogarth's cold and steely voice pierced the quiet.

'I...I...thought I'd tidy up for you.' She avoided his eyes; she wasn't good at lying.

'Oh really?' It was obvious he didn't believe her. 'Well don't. These papers are confidential. You don't come in when I'm not here.' It was an order.

Bev bristled, 'OK, but there was a time when we shared everything, we were partners.' She peered out from under her lids.

'Not anymore,' he snarled.

Outrage mixed with her pain. She yearned for their old partnership but was losing hope they could ever regain it. 'I could help, if you would let me.' She couldn't let him push her aside without a fight.

'No, it's too late for that.' Wrogarth waved his hand in dismissal.

Bev slumped, her whole body feeling heavy. When her blood again coursed through her veins, it came with anger. She stormed out of the room, shaking as she bit her lip to avoid saying anymore.

Chapter 16

The homebound crowd streamed towards the tram and bus stops along Grenfell Street. Shelley dodged and weaved through the current. Light drizzle dampened her hair making it stick to her head in an unflattering cap. She navigated along the sheltered verandas and shop fronts where possible but still got soaked. Turning into Rundle Street she scrutinised the designer shops glitzy window displays while guarding her purse. How long had they been here?

Her first week back at work and her holiday was almost a distant memory. Her heart and mind weren't letting go of that holiday feeling easily, clinging to the memories and emotions with more determination than she'd expected. Her new job was insistent, and it was only a matter of time before it would crowd out those wonderful images and take over.

Jason's invitation to dinner had surprised her but she was looking forward to the evening. Akbal would be there and she was keen to talk to him about Ayisha again. She hadn't really learned anymore so far. Adrian would be there too.

After her eyes adjusted to the dark interior of the Slug and Lettuce pub, she spotted them sitting in the comfortable lounges in front of the TV. Football played out on the big screen, but their attention was on Jason. Becoming tangled in his jacket as he tried to take it off, he almost fell. Onlookers, both friends, and strangers watched in amusement. Successfully free of his jacket and order restored, Jason spied her and smiled a warm welcome. He was now shifting his weight from one leg to the other, waiting impatiently for them to finish their greetings. Shelley sat next to Akbal, eying the space next to Adrian that Jason was blocking.

'OK, OK. Now, you'll never guess what happened in London yesterday.' Jason's twinkling eyes darted from one group member to the other as his grin widened with each sweep.

They looked at each other and shrugged in unison.

'Mohamed has been arrested.'

The news spilled from Jason's lips in a mad rush and after the last word, he stood back smug and self-satisfied. Shelley and Adrian exchanged glances not sure why Jason was so excited. Akbal looked down at the floor, eyes wide and mouth open.

Jason's eyes widened in disbelief then he continued, 'You know…Mohamed…the guy we met in Paris. You know,' he pleaded.

He watched them eagerly and Shelley suddenly felt a hard lump forming in her throat. It couldn't be.

'The picture I saw was definitely him. The darker skin, the beard, the beady eyes…' Jason's excitement spilled out unrestrained.

Shelley shivered.

'What for?' Adrian asked, a deep frown creasing his forehead.

'He's a suspected terrorist!' Jason surveyed them with a grin, 'and he's a recruiter for the Taliban.'

'No,' Adrian shook his head in disbelief.

Akbal sat forward, also shook his head then fell back into the couch making it tremble.

Jason turned to him, 'You talked to him the most. Did you …?'

Akbal's eyes were fixed on the floor seemingly unaware they were staring at him. He slowly lifted his head, his eyebrows raised in surprise.

'Me? Of course not. No…I… he…I didn't even…I can't believe it.' His eyes clouded over as he sunk back into his own thoughts again.

With shaking hands, he put down his half-finished coke. He mumbled something incoherent, gathered up his jacket abruptly then tore himself off the couch and fled out the door. Shelley broke out in goosebumps. She twisted around to watch Akbal's retreating figure and a knot formed in her stomach. Surely Akbal wouldn't knowingly be involved in something like that and yet…The television football commentary blared across their silence, its urgency and excitement pricked at her nerves, contrasting abruptly with her feelings; especially when the crowd erupted into wild cheers and screams.

Adrian's voice finally broke through the background noise. 'I didn't talk to Mohamed much…but…he didn't sound like a zealot or a recruiter for that matter.'

'I hardly spoke to him…' Shelley said.

Jason nodded. 'Akbal talked to him the most. I saw Mohamed slip him a note too. Do you think…?'

They stared at the door as though it could answer.

'No. No. That's all wrong. He would have said something.' Adrian sounded certain. 'We know him…'

Oblivious to the solemn mood, Jason ploughed on. 'The papers said Mohamed had been under surveillance for months. He's linked to an extremist organisation in London and was in Paris recruiting members for them.'

Shelley sunk further down in her seat fighting disbelief. Adrian leaned across to touch her hand gently.

'He wasn't recruiting us, that's for sure. He hasn't been proven guilty yet. They've got it wrong before. We should wait to see what happens,' Adrian said, shaking his head solemnly.

'But this sounds serious.' Shelley trembled unable to unravel the knot growing tighter in her stomach. This could seriously jeopardise her career, her reputation, even her life. And Akbal seemed to be implicated.

'All I'm saying is we have the example of Guantanamo Bay and Abu Ghraib Prison, they weren't all guilty,' Adrian insisted.

'Some of them were terrorists, even if some weren't.' Shelley countered trying to control her shaking hands.

'If he was under surveillance, does that mean they were watching us too?' Jason added. Adrian nodded, his eyes widened, 'Could be.'

'I'm not sure if I want him to be a real terrorist and be relieved that they've caught him, or for it to be a false alarm.' Shelley's drink swayed despite her firm grip and the knot in her stomach constricted further. 'It's awful either way.'

They settled back into the sofas, silence again raising the television commentary to prominence. The crowd's boos and whistles joined the commentators raised voices and this time it mirrored Shelley's mood.

'We should stay calm,' Adrian said as he looked across at Shelley. 'We know Akbal wouldn't...I'm sure his leaving so suddenly is innocent. After-all, his daughter is only three weeks old...he only just made it back to Adelaide in time.' Adrian touched Shelley's hand again, his effort to reassure her was suspiciously like an attempt to reassure himself.

'When he came back from Pakistan...' Jason's comments undid all of Adrian's good work.

The three sat in silence, each unsure of how to remove the cloud that hovered over them. She had known Akbal for two years and everything she knew about him was in direct contrast to someone who could plan or execute terrorist acts. He didn't seem like the kind of person who could kill indiscriminately or encourage others to commit suicide in the name of a cause. Yet Akbal was in the spotlight. How well did she really know him? She'd been proven wrong before.

Adrian interrupted her thoughts.

'I'll go and see him tomorrow,' Adrian said, then strode to the counter and brought back menus.

He shrugged his shoulders, 'There's nothing we can do about all this. We'll just have to watch developments.'

Jason's head drooped and his look of disappointment contrasted with Shelley's relief. They ordered food and slipped into a hesitant conversation about their respective adventures after Paris. By the time their meals arrived, they had managed to distract themselves with only the occasional slip. Shelley entertained them with stories of the characters from her tour. Jason had them laughing until their jaws ached with his imitations and tall stories. He had a treasury of funny tales at the ready. His version of their holiday exploits seemed light-years away from Adrian's serious accounts.

Jason had finally gone and Shelley sighed and leaned back into the accommodating sofa. She had been hoping for some time to talk to Adrian alone. Jason had kept ordering yet another beer and with each drink, he became more animated and intense. He chattered nonstop about the holiday, the adventures, Mohamed and Akbal while drinking faster than Shelley thought possible. No-one could interrupt, and she thought he'd never finish, that she would be going home without any time alone with Adrian.

She liked Jason. He was attractive in a quirky kind of way and he made her laugh, but he seemed young for his age. Something about him troubled her. She looked up and caught Adrian watching her. As their eyes met, she tingled.

'What are you thinking about?' His voice was a little husky and she liked its affectionate note.

'I was just thinking about Jason. He really is the life of the party...but...'

'He's a funny guy,' Adrian frowned slightly. 'Alcohol helps.'

'Mmm,' Shelley agreed. It was just another thing that made Adrian and Jason an odd match.

'Jokes are a cover.'

Now Shelley was intrigued. 'I know it's none of my business but a cover for what?'

'Life.'

Adrian's off-hand response disappointed her; from what she'd seen Jason wasn't hiding from life. His attitude was anything but that. He embraced life, taking risks and jumping into situations without thought. She shook her head and Adrian responded.

'Well, life's problems really.'

'Don't we all?'

'Turning forty has shaken him.' Adrian gazed at the noisy crowd assembling near the tables. 'And he has family problems. It's not common knowledge…his mum has a drinking problem and he and his dad are…not on good terms.'

Shelley took this sharing of confidence as a sign of closeness, even if his manner had cooled a little during this topic.

'Are they in Adelaide?' she asked.

'No, he's from Sydney. His dad is…' He swallowed and his eyes were drawn by the loud voice introducing a guest on a TV chat show. 'I guess you'd call him a self-made man. He's hard and uncompromising.'

'Isn't it interesting that even at our age our families still have so much impact on our lives. My parents live here, and I get along with them so long as I don't talk politics, children or a list of other taboo subjects.' This had become a big issue in Shelley's life too.

'They're big topics.'

They each reclined back into their respective sofas withdrawing into their own thoughts for a while.

Shelley broke the spell. 'You know, whenever my parents and I talk about current affairs we end up arguing. They love James Wrogarth, and I don't.' It wasn't just politics that Shelley found difficult. A little voice in her head insisted they loved Tom more than her. Obviously, blood wasn't always thicker than water. 'They'd freak out if they knew about Mohamed. I'm not sure I'd blame them though,' she added. Talking about their parents wasn't a good conversation piece.

Adrian moved along the sofa, edging closer to her and surveyed the people sitting nearby.

'By the way, before I forget, Akbal learned something new about Ayisha too,' he said.

'What is it?'

'Ayisha pawned a turquoise bracelet and bought a ticket to Sydney. She told her friend, that she was visiting another friend who had left Afghanistan and was now in Australia and needed help.'

Shelley knew that bracelet and she knew Ayisha wouldn't part with it lightly. It was a gift from her late mother – her only memento.

'Suicide seems such a ridiculous verdict, why go to Sydney to help a friend and then kill yourself?' Shelley could feel her own frustration and tension building again.

Adrian agreed, 'It sounds strange. Can't your department help?'

Shelley shook her head, 'It's complicated.'

She wasn't sure how to explain and wasn't sure she really wanted to, not yet anyway. She wished she could talk to Beetle or even Harry, but she had no contact details for them since they'd confiscated her diary at customs.

Adrian ordered drinks and a bowl of chips and then sat down next to her. His serious expression turned soft and his nearness and warmth reassured her.

'I wanted to talk to you about my research.' He twisted in his seat, watching her intently.

'Oh?' She was disappointed; this didn't sound personal. She felt wary, his research was close to her role at work and she didn't want it to lead to problems.

Adrian held her gaze. 'I volunteer at Amnesty International and help research human rights issues. In Africa, I saw first-hand how political systems let people down. I'm afraid of what's happening in Australia and the long-term consequences. Our attitude towards asylum seekers scares me, all that fear-mongering and misinformation. They're being used as political pawns.' A faraway look crept into his eyes. 'Wrogarth can't be allowed to get away with his vicious policy.' The raw and barely suppressed anger in his voice had come out of nowhere.

'So, what can you do?' Shelley asked, her nerves twitching.

'We need to make people see asylum seekers as human beings, not just 'illegals' or 'queue jumpers'. Any information about their treatment, the conditions or allegations of abuse, anything we can use to bring pressure on public opinion and eventually the government, will help.' He swallowed, but the hard edge remained in his voice. 'At the moment Wrogarth's propaganda dominates the press. The truth is quashed or clouded by layers of misinformation.' He ran his fingers through his hair, 'I just want to do whatever I can.'

Shelley sat quietly, absorbing what he'd said, not sure how to proceed. 'I agree, the government position on asylum seekers is harsh, but that's not the same as mistreating them. The policy seems to have the agreement of most people if the polls are anything to go by.'

Her personal feelings on this issue were complicated. Her role in administering government policy made it difficult to speak openly regardless of what she personally felt. The department had been politicised, it had instigated stronger and stronger controls over what staff could and could not say and she stuck to safe ground.

'Australia needs to stop the flow of asylum seekers by boat, even if the numbers are small. It is for their own safety too, although I agree detention is…soul-destroying…and they're there too long.'

'Shelley it's a disgrace. People use gossip and innuendo rather than facts. We have opinion passing as news and nationalism replaces reason or thought. It's especially dangerous when irrational fear is used to drive policy.' Adrian's intensity was almost frightening, and yet Shelley understood what he was saying and begrudgingly agreed. That didn't mean she could help him though.

Adrian continued, 'How can we be so afraid of that trickle of human misery, that handful of desperate refugees fleeing war-torn countries in hope of safety? Fear is being directed as hatred towards courageous people escaping injustice because they climb into rickety boats to sail across perilous seas. We should be challenging the men and women who twist and manipulate the truth in their lust for power.' Adrian raised his hand and forced a smile at Shelley. 'I'm sorry, I know I get carried away, but I have to help them if I can. The asylum seekers are being mistreated. The latest two detention centres are in some of the remotest places in Australia and there are rumours of abuse. We think illnesses are spreading through the facilities and it's being hushed up. Why isolate them out there? It doesn't even make economic sense. It's difficult to provide food and general living supplies, even medical treatment. Staffing must be an issue. What is the government hiding?'

'It's probably just about numbers. After all, they want the public to believe their policy is a successful deterrent.' The papers she'd read highlighted how this spread the costs, but she didn't believe it either, it sounded more like a justification than reason.

'The government presents the image of a 'flood' of people swarming into the country in boats. It's their way of scaring the public. Connecting it to threats to our security adds to the fear factor. So why hide them? The government wants to be seen as 'tough on illegal immigrants'. In that case, it doesn't make sense to hide them away unless…' His voice became quiet and she strained to hear him above the television. 'You know psychiatrists have identified a new kind of mental illness brought on by the very act of trying to gain asylum. What will the isolation do?'

Shelley couldn't argue. She'd seen the effects. Ayisha had been a classic example of the harm of detention.

'I don't know either. Maybe they don't want the public to know how many are still getting through. Twenty thousand doesn't sound like a lot, so there is more mileage in not having actual figures reported. Anyway, the government claims that their policy of turning back the boats is working and yet they've built two more detention centres. That wouldn't help them politically,' Shelley ventured, trying to stay on safe ground.

'Maybe.' Adrian sounded unconvinced, 'But I don't believe that's all.'

Shelley knew she should stop this conversation before it got too involved, but something in his manner sparked her curiosity. Emotions danced across his face as he spoke. He was absorbed in this cause and she admired him for it even if it frightened her.

'Building detention centres in remote locations doesn't equal mistreatment,' she offered.

'The prevalence of mental illness in these centres is disturbing and we can't get access or honest reports of the numbers. On top of that, they're not getting the care they need, either physically or mentally. Advocates are having their access blocked and delayed often on trivial grounds. So are the medics we try to get in there. They're hiding something.' He clenched and unclenched his fists. 'I have to find out what's happening in there.'

Shelley shifted in her seat. 'Working for Immigration means I have to be careful about what I say.'

'I know.' Adrian's fingers were now tightly intertwined, and his hands had stopped clenching. Shifting closer to her he added, 'I was hoping that you could help me though.'

Shelley's stomach lurched and she shook her head emphatically as she whispered, 'I can't.'

'I thought you cared. Your reaction to the news about Ayisha…it spoke volumes.' His eyes bored into her and again she moved in her seat, this time putting a little distance between them.

'I'm sworn to secrecy.' She couldn't find the words to adequately explain how seriously she took her oath. A breach would mean her job and reputation. It was a criminal offence. A breach could mean jail. 'I couldn't do anything illegal.' Her voice trembled and she licked her dry lips while watching his reaction. Of course, it wasn't strictly true, her enquiries into Ayisha's death were probably already a breach, but she hadn't revealed anything to anyone, or betrayed the confidential classification.

The struggle with her conscience was becoming complicated. She believed in the impartiality of the Public Service and the need to provide fearless advice to government, but the role of the Public Service had changed. The government had installed its own people into the top jobs, effectively shutting down any criticism. Her beliefs had never clashed with her role like this before. She was already questioning the justice of the policy she was administering but despite her own dilemma, to act was unthinkable. Her only way out was to change job and move to another department.

Adrian nodded acknowledgment and sighed. 'I know. Being a whistle-blower is tough, it costs. Those guys who exposed the arms deal lost everything. I wouldn't ask you to take that kind of risk.' He smiled, trying to ease the obvious awkwardness that had developed between them. 'I'd appreciate any help you can offer…that you're comfortable to offer.'

Her shoulders ached from the tension of holding them stiff and straight. 'This sounds very personal for you?'

'Yes.' Adrian said quietly, 'In Australia, we've become complacent. Do you think we would recognise a corrupt leader? I don't think so.' His voice broke and he stopped abruptly, breaking the spell. 'I'm sorry I don't want to frighten you. After hearing some of the dreadful stories told by asylum seekers, not just what they've fled, but also what they endure here, how can I stand by and allow this to go on? At the very least we are driving them crazy before they can find asylum and be accepted here. Ninety-nine percent prove to be legitimate refugees despite the hype, and yet we torture those fleeing torture.'

Excited screaming from the television made Shelley wince, the beaming face of a minor celebrity stared down at them, accompanied by cheers and clapping. Shelley waited for the television noise to die down before speaking. She needed to set the record straight before this went any further.

'I can't help you.' She reached out and touched his hand. 'I understand your concern. I've heard many of those stories too. I know they need help. I'm appalled about how they are dehumanised through the political debate but there are proper channels.' She shrugged but his face stayed impassive, this time not betraying his emotions or thoughts.

Adrian focused on his hands as raucous laughter from the TV set a background of mock derision at their stalemate. He finally looked up; a half-smile fixed on his lips. 'It's OK. Anything you can do is OK.'

Shelley relaxed her shoulders at last and she tilted her neck to unfreeze it. She couldn't, however, shake off the kernel of doubt nestled in the back of her mind. It cast a shadow over their blossoming relationship. She needed to proceed with care.

Chapter 17

Mark snatched the seat directly in line with Wrogarth, forcing Daryl to one side. His stare bore into Daryl whenever important matters were discussed, the resentment at Daryl's presence was undisguised. Wrogarth paced the floor in front of the window. Planning his election strategy energised him but also messed with Mark's seating plan.

'We'll hit the weaker links in the opposition. We should start with their leader, she's an easy mark. She's so long-winded we could easily create confusion about what she stands for.' He chuckled and Mark joined in with a snigger.

Daryl frowned, 'Why sink to personal smears? The public wants something to vote for.' The latest surveys showed people thought the government too negative, especially Wrogarth.

Mark shook his head slowly, 'Depends. A bit of mudslinging can help. We just need to use it carefully.'

Wrogarth nodded at Mark, but Daryl persisted. 'I think people are tired of the same old smear campaign and the bullying. The latest polls suggest people want vision, they want a leader and they are looking for the government of the day to set some direction.'

Wrogarth turned to stare out of the window before muttering, 'Don't be naïve.' He turned back to stare at Daryl. 'They say that's what they want, but they don't really. They prefer leaders to tell them what they want to hear. They want us to get on with the job so they can go on with their lives without too much disruption.' Directing his remarks now to Mark, he continued. 'What about their shadow treasurer? Fancy getting his figures wrong, we should be able to exploit that.' He shot a quick glance at Daryl with eyebrows arched, almost waiting for another interruption.

Daryl clamped his lips shut with determined self-restraint.

'We have a couple of things we could highlight as 'vision'. Turning back the boats is both practical and popular and has tapped into people's anxieties about illegals,' Mark suggested.

'Yes,' Wrogarth nodded. 'The opposition has really played into our hands on that one. Fear will always override facts.' He sat down heavily, then with a spectacular change of mood, stared pointedly at Mark.

'And I want climate change off the agenda. Both the opposition and the Greens are ganging up on us, accusing us of being out of touch and the polls suggest they're gaining momentum. Even a couple of our backbenchers are making sympathetic noises.' The hard edge in Wrogarth's voice said he was not to be trifled with. 'We need some stronger counter-arguments, and Tim Curleigh's not doing enough. We need to counter the scientific speak and we need it now.' He stared at Mark, a strange unreadable look passing between them as he said quietly, 'You also assured me the professor had been dealt with.'

'It's more difficult than I expected.'

Daryl stayed alert.

'It would be easier to prepare a policy to steal their thunder but…' Mark watched Wrogarth's reaction while pretending to shuffle through his papers but Wrogarth's scowl hurried him on. 'There is another way. Professor Hutchinson has clout – people listen to what he has to say. His linking new mining methods to climate change has hurt us, there's no doubt about that. But he's resigned from the CSIRO…' Mark shrugged. 'His leaving takes some heat off but also makes him harder to control. If we can discredit him or his research before he leaves, timing it so he can't effectively respond, we could take him out of the current arguments.' Mark grinned strangely and Daryl sat forward to make sure he heard what was coming next. 'We've come into possession of a few interesting emails and…if they became public, they could seriously damage his reputation.' Mark relaxed but his eyes remained fixed on Wrogarth.

A shiver crawled up Daryl's spine. This approach sounded familiar. What had Mark found? And, how had he found it?

'Well, well,' Wrogarth muttered, surveying his age-spotted hands as they formed a triangle on the desk before him.

'These emails raise sufficient doubts. They raise questions about his research and its accuracy. I'm sure the press would be very interested to get hold of them. Of course, it's harder for him to dispute the allegations if he's out of the country,' Mark continued, chuckling softly.

'Good. How did you...? No, don't tell me...I don't want to know.' Wrogarth's eyes swept across to Daryl for an instant. 'I look forward to reading about it.'

Daryl wanted to know but couldn't ask. He remembered a break-in at the University targeting Professor Hutchinson's office. Was this connected?

A strange compunction took hold of Daryl. He had to try even though it could cost him. An unsettling flutter in his stomach made him raise a fingernail to his lips, but he quickly dropped it. 'Acting on climate change would be better, even if Professor Hutchinson's research has some questions hanging over it. Isn't there enough scientific evidence to say we should do something? Why not set some positive policies? I know the mining lobby groups aren't keen, but surely there's a way.' He was still hopeful he could change the strategy from fear campaigns and mudslinging. He craved a visionary campaign, something that would brand Wrogarth as a true leader in his time.

'You just don't get it, do you, Daryl?' Wrogarth sounded exasperated. 'It's not a question of good policy, whether it achieves good things or has long-term benefits. Interest groups and their spin drive voter opinion. It's not about facts, but what they believe, and how they think it affects them. Even whether they're afraid of what's being proposed. Letting them vote on policy makes them think they know what's good for them.' His head shook vigorously. 'I don't want to find out which policies they like or don't like. I'm not interested in their selfish perspectives, or if they believe they will be better or worse off under this policy or that.' He lowered his voice, speaking slowly and clearly articulating each word. 'I already know what's best. That's my job. That's why I'm here. I don't need people to agree to take their medicine, so why ask them.' He directed his comments straight to Daryl. 'It's better to ramp up the emotion. People take their medicine to cure themselves of something unpleasant. Fear is the most powerful motivating emotion of all, so that's what we target. Fear of the consequences of the opposition policies; fear of how much it could cost them; fear of a lower standard of living. What option do they have but to vote for us so those things won't happen?'

'But the policies you're planning will do the same things, just in a different way. Why not let people see that they can vote for what's good for the country, not just their own selfish interests?' Daryl retorted.

The burst of laughter surprised him, both Wrogarth and Mark were enjoying the speech, but not in the way Daryl had hoped.

'Daryl, how have you survived in this business so long?' Wrogarth waved a dismissive hand at Daryl then turned towards Mark. 'Let's get on with our planning.'

Mark perched on the front of his seat and went on as though Daryl wasn't there. 'I think the campaigns we've run so far are working well, we don't want to change tack now.'

A tide of tiredness swept over Daryl; he was overcome by a profound sense of disappointment. 'But it's the lowest form of campaign, fear-mongering and playing silly childish games. You still have to develop unpopular policies and then you lose eventually anyway.'

'This is politics, all's fair…Of course, we implement unpopular policies, at the beginning of our term. We do what needs to be done in the first half of our term. At the end we do what we're doing now, add a few sweeteners. The electorate has a short memory. You know how it works.' Wrogarth's voice almost physically beat Daryl into submission.

Quiet and finally surrendering, Daryl couldn't dispute this argument, but his whole being revolted at the thought of using this strategy. He was part of it, no matter that he didn't agree. Wrogarth smiled, an indulgent smile, as though he was tolerating a wayward child.

'I can't achieve anything unless I am re-elected, so I will say or do whatever it takes. I won't get elected if I tell people unpleasant truths. They'll complain about what we do afterwards, but, since they didn't have to make the decision, it's not their fault.' Wrogarth rose to look out of the window again and an uncomfortable silence descended over the room.

Daryl could hear his own breathing, sharp bursts straining into his lungs. This was the man he had once admired, the man who had stood for something, even when he occasionally got it wrong, but Daryl saw now that his boss was a shadow of that man.

Wrogarth abruptly faced Daryl. 'If you don't or can't understand this, maybe it's time you moved on.'

This was an ultimatum. He had to decide here and now to either shut up or leave. Mark's grin burned into his neck. Daryl momentarily toyed with the notion of walking out, but his body was rooted to the seat, his legs heavy. He couldn't leave all this behind.

'Of course, I understand...' The words eluded him, stuttering to justify his staying, he needed words that would sound convincing. 'In the past, you've put forward ideas, policies, led the debate on issues...this change of tactic represents a move to...' To what? What could he say that would appease rather than inflame? The only words that kept springing to his mind were: 'grubby tactics', 'low blows'; he couldn't let them slip from his lips. 'Er...'

Both Mark and Wrogarth were watching him closely. Wrogarth had that amused look but it was a trick, Daryl knew he was not amused. Beads of sweat formed on Daryl's forehead and his palms had become clammy. 'Er...the kinds of tactics you always hated.'

Relief almost made him grin, but he reined it in before it could betray him.

There was a time when he could have spoken his mind and Wrogarth would have listened, whether he agreed or not. But now things were very different and of course, there was Mark. Wrogarth spoke first, echoing those thoughts.

'Times change, Daryl. These times call for strength and determination. I am still leading, but the tactics need to suit the times.' Rifling through the papers in front of him, Wrogarth was ready to get back to business. 'Now let's finish this.'

They turned their attention to their key tactics of mounting small battles to needle the opposition before the campaign war started in earnest. Wrogarth was in his element, he and Mark sparking off each other, producing a rapid-fire of clever one-liners that would stick in people's minds. The attack was to be shared across different fronts, capitalising on the good performers so Wrogarth wouldn't come across as totally negative. Wrogarth made it clear he thought that Tim was a weak link, his handling of the CSIRO had been a debacle, and Wrogarth and Mark agreed that Tim wasn't up to the challenge.

'We need to shove Tim under a bus,' Wrogarth laughed but his eyes said this was no joke. 'I need someone competent.' He stared at Mark. 'You're the fixer, so fix it.'

Daryl kept his head bowed. Wrogarth was manoeuvring Tim out. Tim's attempts to garner support for a leadership challenge were a well-known secret and while he probably didn't have the numbers

Wrogarth wasn't going to offer any chances. Publicly Wrogarth would point to the CSIRO issues and the need to minimise the damage but Tim was being punished for being ambitious.

'There's just one more thing, James.' Mark was biting his lower lip and Daryl went on alert again.

Mark's voice went strangely quiet, 'Since I am not handling the details, is everything going to plan with the…other matter?'

'Yes.' Wrogarth's eyes turned icy cold and he cast a sidelong look at Daryl. 'Is the campaign ready to go?'

Mark nodded.

Wrogarth rubbed his hands. 'Good, we need to reinvigorate it, remind the electorate of our strength in handling the 'attack on our borders'. The phrase rolled off his tongue as though he was savouring it. 'By the way, your media campaign has been spot-on so far. Well done.'

Mark raised his eyebrows in surprise, then puffed out his chest.

'Well, the recent terrorist attacks overseas made it easy to link our asylum seeker issues with threats to our security,' Mark said, his wolfish features looking hungrier and meaner than usual.

They both turned towards Daryl, as though suddenly remembering he was still there, and Daryl sensed a return of the previous tension. He sat quietly, trying to become invisible. He wasn't going to ask any questions although he craved to know what this was about. Wrogarth turned back to Mark again, 'However, the bleeding hearts are getting too much media coverage. Where are they getting their figures from? Do something about them.'

'They're not making enough of an impact to worry about. People are convinced asylum seekers are connected to terrorism and that belief is hard to shake now.'

'Well, I don't like it,' Wrogarth said pointedly. 'You have to come up with something to stop their momentum. What about that Australian link to the London terrorist? Can we use that?'

Mark shook his head, 'Nothing concrete yet.'

'Well, talk to Benedict.'

The meeting was finished, and Daryl rose from his chair with a niggling sense of unease. He was more out of the loop than ever. What was happening with the asylum seekers? What was the information about Prof Hutchinson? He needed to know what was going on.

At his desk in the outer room, Daryl watched Mark's retreating back, straight and stiff as he marched out of the door.

Daryl scratched his head; he couldn't do this on his own. He needed help. Searching through his personal diary he finally found the card stuck in the back, out of sight. He'd planned to throw it away; he hadn't expected to need Ralph's help again but for some reason had tucked the card into his diary. Ralph had offered his help anytime he needed it. Maybe now was the time to call in that favour.

Chapter 18

Bev weaved in and out of arcades, taking her usual precautions and wearing a disguise unaware that, she was being followed. The Pitt St mall was congested by the lunchtime rush. People pushed and shoved past her. She made her way to a small café in the Admiral's arcade. She was unlikely to run into anyone she knew here. Her usual preference had been the cafés in the Victoria building or in the rocks area, but they belonged to the carefree days before she'd become the 'First Lady'. She sighed, remembering when she could meet her friends openly, the fun shopping excursions and the camaraderie. James now vetoed her friends, making her lunch dates photo opportunities and PR events, in other words, a political asset.

She glanced back along the mall before passing through the café door, but failed to see the inconspicuous business-suited man who'd followed her. She slid into a booth in the corner and congratulated herself on successfully managing these clandestine meetings. She was settling into her seat when her lunch companion strode through the door. She thought his lined face screamed tiredness but when he saw her, his smile lit up his eyes and softened his features into the Daryl she knew. She smiled back, pleased at the transformation.

'Hi Bev,' he leaned across and gently kissed her cheek, then immediately blushed. 'Oh, pardon me, Mrs Wrogarth,' he corrected quietly but still smiling.

'Shhh,' she hissed, unused to formality from him but also frightened of being overheard. 'It's always been Bev to you.'

He relaxed into the seat beside her. 'It's an unexpected pleasure to see you.'

'I couldn't really explain over the phone,' Bev whispered. 'How much time do you have?'

'Oh, so it's not just social?' he teased, and Bev allowed herself a giggle. 'James had a meeting. He'll be back in an hour and I need to get back before him,' he added, settling back against the booth. 'So, what's this about?'

The waiter took their order, and when he left, she explained. 'I'm worried about James. I've never seen him so jumpy before. What's going on?'

Daryl shook his head. 'Have you asked him?' His eyes never left her face as he spoke. 'Of course you haven't. But you know I'm probably not the person to ask anymore. I'm just a glorified secretary now that Mark is in the office. Have you met him?'

Bev nodded remembering the wolfish face with the nasty smirk. 'I didn't like him much, he tries to be charming but he's too smarmy for me. He makes my skin crawl.' A tremor shook her as she spoke.

Daryl laughed. 'He has a PR background with media and advertising expertise but has taken over a bigger role. He's very ambitious and James trusts him.'

'How did that happen?' Bev struggled to understand when Daryl had been such an instrumental part of their success. Loyalty didn't mean much to James anymore it seemed.

'Not sure. I think my refusal to take care of that smear campaign, you know, the judge and his homosexual relationships...'

'No, I don't know.' Bev's stomach lurched. 'What smear campaign? And what did it have to do with James?'

'It's an old story now. James needed the judge on a case against Aboriginal land rights to make the 'right' decision. However, the presiding judge wouldn't play the game, refusing to be influenced, so James dug up some dirt to compromise him. He wanted it done so it couldn't be traced back to him. I refused to help; I just couldn't do it. In the end, Mark helped him, the judge stood down, and James' man stepped in. They got the result they wanted, the deepwater port went ahead and Carlew was happy.' Daryl shook his head slowly and Bev responded with her own slow and solemn head shake.

'Now, James is upset by that professor, the one putting out the report on climate change,' Bev said, preferring to focus on the present rather than the troublesome past.

'Professor Hutchinson. He's left the country, but his research results are still damaging, especially for the plans to reopen mining areas and the new technology they're using. It seems Mark and James have something that could damage Hutchinson's reputation. I don't know how they got hold of it, but I'd bet it wasn't by legitimate means.' His unfocused stare out of the window told Bev he was in turmoil.

'Is there anything else? Tell me,' Bev pleaded. She could sense his reluctance but knew there was more to tell.

'I'm not certain, but he and Mark are up to something involving asylum seekers.'

'No,' Bev exclaimed and the couple nearest them turned to stare. She shrunk down into her seat and continued in an exaggerated loud whisper. 'Why is he so intent on using the asylum seeker issue for his campaign?'

'He thinks it shows how tough he is on illegal immigrants. It gives him leverage now that the opposition is trying for a more humane angle. James is playing the fear card again and the polls are reacting favourably, just not favourably enough. It worked last time, so he reckons it will work again.' Daryl shook his head then sat back gnawing vigorously on his thumbnail. The waiter placed their sandwiches on the table, and they declined the offer to order another drink. Only three other couples sat in the café, but Daryl still continued in a hush. 'There is also something else…I'm not totally sure of the details…but it's to do with a mining consortium. He and Mark had meetings in Paris. It's very hush-hush. I don't think the cabinet even knows.' Daryl glanced around the café before leaning close to Bev. 'He gets private phone calls. I've seen the name Petro

Golgovich. I'm not sure what he has to do with James, but if he's involved it means trouble. You don't want to mess with him.'

'Petro? Is that the same man?' Bev gasped remembering the encounter in the car park in Paris. That name had been on those papers too.

Daryl nodded. 'I think so.'

'I wish I knew what to do. It looks like he's up to something again, doesn't it?' Bev suddenly felt very weary, her arms and legs ached as though she had run a marathon and she could feel her resolve to deal with this slipping.

'Don't get involved Bev. This could be dangerous.' Daryl pleaded.

They ate in silence as she tried but failed to devise her own strategy. She caught the concerned look on Daryl's face, the worry lines etching deep into his forehead.

'How are you going, Daryl? Is everything alright?' She cared about him and wasn't just shifting the conversation, although it was a relief to change focus.

'Yes, I'm Okay. I still attend the meetings and get help when I need to. I'm moving in the right direction now, thanks to you. Work and the impasse between James and me are a different story. I'm not much use to him anymore…I am not so sure I want to be either.' He moved his hand to rest on the table between them.

'Please let me know whatever you learn Daryl,' Bev pleaded.

'You shouldn't get involved. He's taking big risks and it could all come undone.' Daryl's eyes did the pleading for him this time. He then looked at his watch, shrugged his shoulders and slid out of the booth. 'It really is best if you stay out of it.' He repeated firmly. He scanned her face, his eyes resting on the bruise on her cheek. Her hand automatically flew up to cover the mark. 'Promise me, you'll take care of yourself and leave all this to others,' he repeated.

'I'm already involved, but I'll try,' Bev said to appease him even though she didn't mean it.

After he left, her mind went into overdrive trying to put the pieces together. She considered getting in touch with William; she had an emergency number for him, but, he already had such a low opinion of James, perhaps she shouldn't make it worse.

***

Daryl knew the score. Ralph Evans, the ex-journalist, had no love of Wrogarth and made sure anyone who cared to listen knew it. He didn't believe in redemption, especially not in politics. The bad pennies didn't change or clean up, they just learned to hide it better. That was his philosophy.

'So, how are you?' The chair creaked as Ralph moved his weight to face Daryl.

Daryl remembered a thinner, healthier-looking Ralph. He had not fared well after the scandal. Abandoned by his newspaper, he'd been left to fend for himself and he'd lost. Wrogarth had won that battle, but Ralph believed Wrogarth had not won the war – not yet.

Ralph was the kind of man who did his battles with words rather than fists and he could scrap with the best of them.

Ralph hunched at the bar, several chins underlining his face. Daryl hadn't seen him looking this rough before. The T-shirt dangerously stretched over his stomach fell short, exposing a hairy section of skin above his swollen belly button. He was unshaven, with dark bags under his eyes and his clothes had seen better days.

Ralph motioned to a small saloon area and carried his beer to a table in the corner away from the other patrons. Daryl took short breaths through his mouth. The combination of stale beer and industrial disinfectant was making him nauseous, and Ralph added to the heady mix with something akin to 'Eau de sweat'.

Not many patrons had ventured into the pub tonight. Weeknights were reserved for the regulars and they clung to the bar talking to the barman in bursts and occasionally to each other. Sometimes they sniggered or commented on something on the TV humming above their heads. As they drank their voices rose. Solving the world's problems, while propped in their comfortable cocoon, was thirsty work. Daryl laughed to himself. Unfortunately, no-one wrote down their offerings and their solutions were forgotten by morning. Daryl knew the game, every night, they revisited their ideas and voiced their solutions, but it was all about showing others how wise they were. This same scene was being played out in pubs across the country, by young, middle-aged or old people, mostly men, they all believed they were smarter than the people making the decisions

169

and that problems were so much easier to fix. He'd played this game too, before.

Leaving the regulars behind, Daryl edged across the brightly patterned and stained carpet. Ralph raised an eyebrow and nodded at the coke in Daryl's hand.

'Mmmm,' he muttered.

'You know how it is.' Daryl smiled and Ralph toasted him with his beer.

'So, what can I do for you? I'm sure you haven't looked me up after all this time for a social chat.' Ralph's voice was gravellier than Daryl remembered. His authoritative tone had faded to a weak undercurrent. He used to startle people with his booming voice, cutting in with a question, often catching people off guard. He'd been good at his job, but he hadn't counted on how much his unorthodox approach got people offside. They'd deserted him when the going got tough. He'd never learned how to play the game that could have saved him, and it was too late now.

'You once said if I needed anything…'

Ralph leaned back emitting a throaty, hoarse chuckle. 'I figured as much.' He looked Daryl up and down, his face blank but his stare serious. 'Depends on what it is.'

Daryl shifted in his seat trying to dislodge the guilt settling in his stomach. 'I'm still working for Wrogarth.' He waited for the reaction he knew was coming. Back then Ralph had kept Daryl's role in the leak a secret. It would have cost Daryl his job if Wrogarth had known he was Ralph's informant. That meant he owed Ralph too. He grimaced, he seemed to owe a lot of people. William had dug up the finer details of the scandal and had taken the blame for the exposé, and Daryl had let him. Wrogarth and William hadn't spoken since. He blushed at the thought of how weak he'd been. He regretted how it had turned out.

'You've stuck with that bastard? What are you thinking Daryl me boy?' He shook his head as though he couldn't believe the news. 'I thought you had more sense, but then…you never did know when to quit.' He stared straight at Daryl and smiled, 'Ah, I almost forgot, Bev' His voice had turned oily as he watched for Daryl's reaction.

Daryl respected Ralph, he was hard-hitting but fair, but Ralph who understood so much about human behaviour had never understood how it was with him and Bev. Daryl wasn't going to explain either. He was happy to let Ralph think he knew more than he did.

'She's worried too.'

Ralph lowered his head, his voice solemn now. 'She's a stayer, but she should have left him years ago.'

They sat for just a moment, Daryl puzzling over Bev's inability to leave Wrogarth. Remembering the shadow of the latest bruises his anger turned to confusion.

'OK, time to get down to business,' Daryl said matter-of-factly, the images spurring him on. 'I need to get background on Mark, an adviser at the office, find out about his connections.'

'Oh. Is he threatening your job, Daryl?' Cynicism dripped from Ralph's words.

'No nothing like that. He and Wrogarth are up to something and Mark seems to have all the right connections to get things done.' He swallowed hard. 'They can't know I'm prying.'

Ralph nodded slowly, 'As you can see, I work with limited resources…thanks to Wrogarth.'

'I'll pay expenses, plus a little extra.' Daryl offered. The fact that some of this would come out of the Wrogarth election funds made him smile.

'OK, maybe you could squeeze out more than a 'little' extra. So tell me more before I say yes or no.'

Daryl told Ralph about Mark and unloaded his many suspicions, giving him the outline on Professor Hutchinson, the damning environmental report, unusual connections with mining, terrorism suspects and the asylum seeker issue. He also told Ralph about Petro and the overheard conversations in the car park in Paris. He told him everything he thought was relevant except his suspicions about Bev. He preferred not to expose the violent life he suspected she tolerated; at least he would safeguard her privacy.

When Daryl had finished, Ralph sat back quietly, deep in thought. Daryl waited, aware of the dull, slurring chatter in the background and the quiet drone of a TV announcer.

Ralph nodded. 'Wrogarth was always a sucker for a simplistic answer to the complex questions.' His eyes sparkled as they bored into Daryl. 'Sounds like quite a story.' He swallowed noisily then coughed. 'This will be a pleasure. Can I use it? I've already been doing some work of my own, it should fit in neatly.'

Daryl shook his head, 'If it's as bad as I think it is, you can have it when I'm finished.'

Ralph smirked, 'I'm sure you won't be disappointed, it will be bad enough.'

They settled on a time for their next meeting, Daryl resigned to coming here again.

When he stepped out of the door he coughed as the fresh air hit his lungs. Despite the industrial fumes, the air was better out here than inside. His hands shook and he thrust them deep into his pockets. His heart thumped loudly in his ears and he felt nauseous. Here we go again. This time there would be no second chance. If this was as bad as he suspected and everything he had laid before Ralph made him realise it probably was, he couldn't shift the responsibility to anyone else. There was no turning back and Daryl's stomach churned as he walked away from the hotel and hailed a cab.

Chapter 19

Shelley hurried down the corridor, keeping her head down. There was one lone voice talking softly in a meeting room down the hall. She tip-toed past, then moved quickly into the open office space next to it. The partition around her old workstation would effectively conceal her from the corridor. She slid into her old chair, resisting the urge to adjust it and turned the computer on. Her old access codes on this computer should work. Her fingers swept across the keyboard while keeping alert for any noises.

Scrolling quickly through the files she found what she was looking for, the first report on Ayisha. She hurriedly scanned the information.

'They changed the verdict to accidental death,' she muttered under her breath and scanned further down.

There were no attached statements from the two witnesses or their names and details, but Hubbard Street in Sydney was where the body had been found. The original coroner's report had some interesting facts. There were a series of old injuries and Shelley's eyes misted over remembering Ayisha's bouts of self-harm. New, severe injuries indicated she'd been beaten before she fell. The extent of her injuries was consistent with a fall from three to four stories. That was all there was. There were no follow-up reports on the site.

Shelley shut down, thinking about how the girl had suffered. She had witnessed the murder of her parents before she fled Afghanistan and it had plagued her dreams. Even during the light of day episodes and moments of memory had tormented her. The therapy sessions hadn't worked yet. It was a dreadful loss; one Shelley was struggling to understand.

As she walked along the corridor Maya stepped out of the meeting room, stopped and shot Shelley a suspicious look. Shelley stopped too; not sure how she could explain being here.

Maya's eyes squinted at Shelley. 'It's a shame they're closing this section down. We did good work,' she said quietly.

Shelley agreed, then looking at her watch, gasped. She waved goodbye and sped from the area. She didn't look back.

***

Shelley basked in the vibrant colours of the central market stalls and the continuous hum of shoppers as happier memories crowded her mind. They'd been in their early twenties when they first met. Shelley had been too serious and conservative, and Kylie was the right tonic at the right time. She'd made her laugh and forget herself.

The last few years had been poorer for not having Kylie in her life. Her treasured friendships had withered from neglect. Tom hadn't liked any of Shelley's girlfriends and she'd been too compliant.

She meandered around people, dodging their shopping trolleys. Sombre black ones, bright pink polka-dotted ones; brightening the aisles like flashes of unique accessories. When she was single, Shelley had enjoyed her favourite stalls, engaging in small-talk with the stall owners, getting advice about what to buy, what was in season and how to cook a variety she'd not tried before. They had been her happiest days, before the conflicts and tussles for control.

Noting the time, she hurried to Rosita's café. The crowd overflowed, but as she turned to go, she spied a couple collecting their bags and shuffling back their chairs. She scrambled through the closely packed tables almost upending the one beside it. After apologising, she turned her attention to the newspaper on the adjacent table. The headlines read 'Climate Science Fact or Fiction' and she shook her head. Not another article about Professor Hutchinson.

Before she could flick through the paper, Kylie appeared at the doorway and she waved to get her attention. Kylie's brunette hair was a little shorter than before and she had a few more curves, but she still exuded so much energy and Shelley told her so. Her smile was infectious, and Shelley found her worries slip from her shoulders as they chatted. Kylie struggled to the counter to order their drinks and when she returned, they talked, straining to hear above the chatter and occasional raucous laughter around them.

'I hear you finally ditched that millstone, Tom,' Kylie smirked, a mischievous twinkle in her eye. 'Good on you.'

Shelley laughed. Tom's dislike of Kylie was obviously mutual.

'I finally came to my senses.' Her confidence sounded surer than she actually felt. 'What about you? Are you and Rob still together?'

Rob had been fun and easy-going and Shelley had envied Kylie her relaxed relationship.

'Rob's gone.' Kylie tugged at her sleeve to cover the tattoo on her wrist. The vivid red and blue scrolling letters that spelled out R.O.B. nestled in a heart shape. 'It's been about six months now.'

'What happened? I always thought you two were well suited.'

'He was fun, but things had to change. The relationship had to move on.' A slight tremble crept into her voice. 'Unfortunately, Rob didn't want the same things as me.'

'I had no idea, Kylie. I'm so sorry.' Shelley reached across and touched her friend's arm.

'Well, it's over now, I've moved on,' Kylie said, pulling her arm back off the table.

Shelley changed topics, leading them into a conversation about holidays and work.

'Is there anyone new in your life yet?' Kylie asked bringing the conversation back full circle to relationships.

Shelley hesitated, unsure if she was ready to talk about Adrian yet. It was so new, and although Shelley wasn't superstitious, she felt strangely reluctant to expose this beginning. Kylie's smile and gentle prodding loosened her resolve. She had never been good at keeping secrets.

'Well, yes,' she ventured, then, spurred on by Kylie's nodding and raised eyebrows. 'I met a guy at a demonstration in Paris. Can you believe it? He lives in Adelaide and his name is Adrian.' She watched a grin spread across Kylie's face and that well-known twinkle in her eyes was back. 'He and his friend Jason are really nice,' Shelley added, trying to downplay what she felt.

'In *Paris*, no less.'

They both giggled at her affected snobbish tone. Their conversation turned to Shelley's trip and the places she'd toured

'I'm impressed you did that on your own. Maybe next time we could do something together. I've never travelled beyond Asia and I'd love to see the world, but I'm not as brave as you.' Kylie said gripping Shelley's hand.

Kylie had always been the brave one, the one who took risks and challenged the boundaries, so this was great praise.

Coffees finished they pushed their way out into the market aisles. Kylie laughed when Shelley produced her shopping list. 'Old habits die hard,' she said

They sampled whatever was offered, buying as they went. Their mouths watered at the aromas from the nut stall and Shelley finally disregarded her list. Kylie was enticed by the exotic cheeses and quince paste and Shelley egged her on. Their overfull bags dragged at their arms and both were famished.

Kylie's car was close, and they unloaded their precious bounty into the boot and returned to the food court. They circled the Asian stalls several times comparing menus and selections. Shelley, struck with indecision, squeezed past the dumpling stall to check out the Indian food just one more time. As she turned, she spotted a familiar face in the line coming towards her. She leaned across and tapped him on the arm and he veered out of the line to stand beside her.

'Hello Jason,' Shelley said. 'Fancy seeing you here.'

'It's not usually my scene.' He shrugged.

'What's taking you so long?' Kylie said from behind Shelley.

Shelley introduced Kylie and Jason, noticing the amused sparkle in her friend's eyes. They stood awkwardly, being jostled by the crowd. Shelley invited Jason to join them, ignoring Kylie's frown. Jason hesitated but Shelley insisted.

Kylie selected a Thai vegetarian dish and Shelley went back to the Indian food stall. Jason joined them at their table with a combination Asian meal and after a slow start, the conversation flowed. Kylie and Jason seemed to have a lot in common. They had both grown up in the country; they both liked Coldplay and had the same favourite night club. Shelley couldn't interrupt their easy repartee and wondered if this had been such a good idea.

After finishing their dinner, Jason left, but not before arranging to catch a movie with Kylie. He kissed Shelley on both cheeks. 'A touch of Paris,' he said as he strode away.

'He's nice,' she said, almost purring. Kylie's cheeks were flushed and she wore a silly grin.

Shelley nodded; a bit surprised by Kylie's reaction but more surprised by her own. Surely she didn't feel jealous? She bit back the thought.

As they walked to the car park, her phone sounded a message from B. It puzzled her until she realised it was Beetle, the contact Harry had given her. All it said was, 'I've got news. Phone later.'

At home, she typed Hubbard Street into Google Streetmaps. Ayisha had fallen from a three or four-storey building, but there were only low-lying houses and a few derelict warehouses along there. None of the buildings had more than two stories.

Every piece of information she had gleaned so far just added to the mystery. She was more determined to find out what happened with every step. She just hoped that Maya didn't mention seeing her to anyone.

***

Adrian smiled into the phone. Klaus' enthusiasm seemed undaunted despite the hint of frustration.

'Georg and Yasmine are amazing. They work under terrible conditions and with so few resources. I'm impressed,' Klaus crowed with praise. 'Thanks for your introduction.'

'Yes, they just persevere,' Adrian admitted, his stomach churning at the mention of their names.

'They were a great help too. One of the oil companies operating in Angola is connected to that Congo scandal, so that alone was worth the visit. Ortansea are old hands, happy to supply facts about how they are good for the local economy, but they shut down when asked about environmental issues. The other company here, AAAP, is new in the area and only have storage facilities. Yet they were the most uncooperative. It was hard work.' He laughed as though he should have known this would happen.

'You didn't think it would be easy? Despite that, you got the answers you were looking for?' Adrian asked instead of the questions about Yasmine and Georg burning in his brain.

'Some of the locals were a great help. I still need more info about the new process they're using. The twenty big storage tanks make no sense. Usually, oil is pumped straight to tankers to be processed at refineries.' He sighed loudly, 'But the big issue is a new chemical Ortansea is using in their extraction process. It's a huge commercial secret.' He sniggered. 'I have my own commercial secret. The chemical comes from a Swiss laboratory and I have a contact there...' Klaus' voice petered out, tiredness edging into his tone.

'What are you going to do now?'

'I've done all I can in Angola. The African officials, especially the regional chiefs don't want anything to upset the oil companies. The jobs are critical for their economies. Of course, it's also good for them; you just have to see how they live.' Klaus' voice remained unemotional. 'Poverty and the fallout from the Angolan civil war are everywhere. Western Governments and businesses easily exploit them.'

'That lets the local chiefs off the hook. African governments and officials are supposed to be looking after the interests of their people not just looking after themselves. They allow exploitation by accepting a minimum benefit for their country while reaping maximum benefit for themselves. They could be doing so much more for their people.' Adrian vividly remembered his sense of helplessness when coming up against the corruption and the myriad of despots surfacing in the area. The areas with good governance and ethical leadership thrived while those where corruption was rife often had the worst health records.

Klaus chuckled, 'You sound just like Georg and Yasmine.'

'So, how are they?' Adrian asked stepping off his soapbox and into hot water.

'Both well but very stretched. There's been some kind of epidemic that's keeping them busy. They're having trouble identifying it, that's why Yasmine came to London with me.'

'Yasmine is in London too?' Adrian asked, trying to keep his voice even.

The line went quiet for a moment.

'She'll tell you about it herself. Yasmine is coming to Australia. She's returning to Africa via Sydney and wants to catch up with you.'

Adrian's stomach knotted; the news had unleashed inner unease rather than joy.

'I explained you're in Adelaide, but she seemed sure you would come to Sydney.' Klaus' laugh sounded more like exasperation.

He confirmed his flight details and Adrian reluctantly agreed to meet them at the airport.

'So how have you been Adrian?'

'Busy. We're a couple of staff down at the moment, so it might be difficult to get away to Sydney.' Adrian toyed with the idea of not going but he didn't want to miss seeing Klaus and he couldn't avoid Yasmine forever, or could he...? 'I'm helping a colleague'

'Ah, you and your causes. And Shelley?'

At the mention of her name, Adrian's mind switched between images of Shelley and Yasmine until they almost blended into one. He rubbed his head to ease the ache.

'We've been seeing each other...it's going...well. We're taking it slowly.' Adrian replied not sure why he'd added that last sentence.

'Good,' was all Klaus said.

Adrian hung up and memories flooded through his mind. He was going to see Yasmine again. She was supposed to be part of his history, but here she was intruding herself into his present. He'd never forgotten, even throwing himself into his work hadn't helped. And now, there was Shelley. He wondered if Yasmine had changed and if she was happy with her choice. He had no reason to think otherwise

Chapter 20

The feel of the new dress brought with it a confidence Shelley didn't often enjoy. She and Adrian were going to see one of his favourite bands, although she'd never heard of the Screaming Galahs before.

Adrian looked relaxed in dark jeans that neatly followed the contours of his athletic physique and a blue shirt that matched his eyes. Shelley grabbed a coat and scarf as they left but by the look of him, Adrian didn't feel the cold.

The crowded tiny basement venue was already abuzz when they arrived, and they squeezed past the people standing on the fringe to get to their reserved booth. The crowd was young, glittering nail polish and eyeshadow caught the flashing lights overhead and their summery clothes belied the weather outside. Shelley shed her coat and scarf, while Adrian got the drinks. Placing a glass of wine in front of Shelley he settled into the seat opposite her cradling his beer as he leaned back.

Conversation was impossible unless they shouted, and they were restricted to using an occasional burst of sign language to communicate insignificant things. Adrian's eyes darted about the scene but regularly returned to rest on her face. At times he appeared deep in thought and Shelley played with the stem of her wine glass, trying not to stare at him but unable to let her eyes wander too far.

When the band started, their loud and energetic music filled the small space with fiery lyrics and heavy rhythms. The social conscience messages threaded through their songs were Adrian's style. They sang of protest and anger and wrapped it in a rock and roll beat. He'd been right, she enjoyed them too but probably for different reasons.

It was over too soon. They strolled down Hindley Street to the car park as a strong wind whipped down the street, sweeping grit and debris along the footpath and into the gutter. The street teemed with young people on the move for their Saturday night entertainment. Shelley was mesmerised by the girls, young and deer-like, with their big hair and long legs, wearing dresses and shorts that barely covered the essentials. Stomping down the road in their impossible heels, they walked like zombies in shoes made for looking at not walking in. There at the door of the Hidden Pleasures nightclub, the line stretched down the block and around the corner. They huddled together for protection from the cold, their flimsy, strappy dresses flapping in the wind as they waited to find that special something in a sleazy nightclub. Shelley was glad she wasn't in that age group anymore and she huddled into the crook of Adrian's arm, his body warming more than her skin.

It got worse later in the evening. She'd seen them on late nights before, back then she'd disapproved, but now she felt a strange sympathy for the search playing out in front of her. Tottering down the street littered with late-night takeaway wrappers and beer containers, they fell off their heels, lunging and pitching, threatening to vomit and add to the detritus left by others. Their tousled hair and smeared make-up testified to the lack of hidden pleasures awaiting them. What really awaited was either lonely meandering with their persistent friends or a quick grapple down an alley with an equally inebriated young stud who could brag about it in the morning, if he remembered. Hindley Street was a place of promises but here dreams were broken, and lives dragged towards the gutter. Alcohol, drugs, and fumbling, unsatisfying sex-fuelled a heady mix.

Shelley watched the posturing bouncers gathered at the doorways. They added menace into the mix. Serpentco group had the contract to guard these premises. If you could call what those bouncers did guarding. That company's links to the vicious bikie gangs in town, meant competition for the contracts erupted into fighting each other for the spoils. Their preferred trade was in guns, drugs and destroyed lives, not protection.

The bikies frightened her. Fights amongst themselves wreaked casualties for the gang, but also for innocent bystanders. At times they unleashed their violence, just for fun, on a hapless patron who said or did the wrong thing. Their bleating justifications splashed across the papers as though it was the patron's fault, the young man or woman lying in a hospital fighting for their life and dignity. They'd been, drinking and spending their money in the very places that enticed them with free drinks and happy hours then spat them out when they became too much trouble. She didn't know how they'd been selected, but Serpentco also guarded the detention centres and the asylum seekers. She told Adrian of the link between Serpentco and the Detention Centres and he turned pensive.

Shelley studied the aggressive stance of the bouncer surveying the lines of young hopefuls. He and his associate strutted back and forth confidently, their bodybuilder physiques adding an air of macho threat. The insignia on the pocket of the shirt said 'Serpentco Security' but a small purple ball logo and what looked like JS was embroidered below. It was slightly different from those worn by the detention guards and Shelley wondered if they were hiding the connection.

Back at Shelley's apartment, Adrian settled into the sofa, comfortably spreading his arms across the back. He looked inviting. She offered him a drink, but Adrian just patted the seat next to him, an invitation she had no urge to resist. She nestled into the crook of his arm, leaning into him, soaking up his warmth. Edging forward in his seat, his hand reached across and turned her face towards him. His lips pressed down on hers, softly at first, like a butterfly flutter, but then increasing in pressure. A wave of pleasure engulfed Shelley, her nerve endings responded in unison. A small moan escaped her lips as he travelled down her neck. She had been waiting for this, it had been too long since she'd felt a tender touch and her body ached with a deep longing.

His hands stroked her skin, leaving a trail of raw nerve endings tantalising and stoking a flame deep inside. It was growing, fanned by his nearness, his warm breath against her neck, his gentle lips against her skin and his touch.

She reached for his hands, pulling him up and towards the bedroom. There was no resistance this time. It felt the most natural thing in the world. Slowly they fumbled with each other's buttons, deliberate movements allowing them to savour the moment until their mutual desire swept them forward into an urgency they couldn't resist.

***

Akbal stepped into the chilly night air. The meeting had ended later than he'd expected, and darkness now blanketed the scene in front of him. The Frome Street footpath was narrow, and he dodged past the straggle of people walking towards North Terrace. Turning down the crowded Rundle Street, he smiled, life in Australia was good. It didn't matter when he walked along here, it was always full of people eating in the cafés and gathering outside the movie theatres. He scanned the movie advertisements. He'd take Fatima to a French movie later in the week if they could find a babysitter.

As he squeezed between a collection of tables and chairs scattered on the footpath in front of Café Bellini, his eyes rested on a balding man clad in a dark suit. He was sitting alone nestled in behind a large group. Their eyes met briefly before the man looked away. He seemed familiar, but Akbal didn't know where from, all he knew was it was recently. He laughed, trying to dispel a sudden unease, not sure why the sighting bothered him, but the tightness in his stomach told him it did. He didn't turn to look again instead plunged down the footpath.

The meeting had left him frustrated and on edge. He'd hoped someone could help but no-one knew what had happened to his wife's uncle, Ashram. He'd left the camp and was last sighted in Indonesia. Akbal's friends were going to check with known people smugglers. A tight pain spread across Akbal's chest, he had to find Ashram before he did something rash.

Crossing East Terrace, he ventured along the edge of Rymill Park. The trees filtered the weak streetlights, their branches and leaves casting dancing shadows across his path. He pulled his jacket close around him. Off in the distance a dog barked; the loneliness of that sound belying his closeness to the city. He suddenly felt alone and very vulnerable. With his head down he quickened his step. A soft footfall and the snap of a twig made him turn sharply. Three shadowy figures stood talking near a line of parked cars, bright pinpricks of red light penetrated the darkness as they lit cigarettes. The jangle of car keys settled Akbal's nerves slightly and yet he resumed his journey with more pace and determination, suddenly feeling an urge to get home to his family quickly.

He turned into a shortcut through the park. Without warning, a hand gripped his arm and yanked him back. Before he could react Akbal's left hand was pushed up hard between his shoulder blades. Akbal cried out as a searing pain tore through his shoulder. Someone grabbed a handful of hair and tore his head back sharply, propelling him forward into the brick wall of the toilet block. Airburst from his lungs. He struggled, jerking and straining against the two pairs of hands holding him. Another pair of hands searched his pockets.

'I don't have much…just take my wallet and…don't hurt me,' he pleaded.

A punch between his shoulder blades sent him convulsing forward.

'We don't want your wallet, you bastard,' a deep voice growled into his ears.

He choked as fear erupted from the pit of his stomach. Acid burned his throat. He strained against their grip, but they held tight, their fingernails digging into his flesh. They tied thick straps around his wrists, burning his skin with every movement.

'What do you want?' he shouted as his legs threatened to buckle under him.

'We want you.'

Shivers radiated up his spine as a muffled voice behind him broke into mumbled but clipped instructions and within seconds wheels screeched to a halt beside them. A blindfold curled around his head and was tied tightly before he could move. Next, a gag snapped across his open lips, biting into his cheeks and tearing into the corners of his mouth. He tried to scream but his stifled protests resembled indistinct grunts rather than cries for help.

He stumbled as two strong arms dragged him along the uneven ground. They jerked him violently when he resisted or whenever he lost his footing. They hoisted him onto a hard, lumpy surface and he heard the slam of what sounded like a boot lid above him. The surrounding noises dulled, and hard objects dug into his back and legs. He kicked out but the twisting caused him more pain than relief. Akbal lay writhing, silently screaming. The sound of a motor being kicked into action penetrated the dark. Akbal was tossed around the object-strewn space, crashing against the sides as the car swerved away from the curb. He jerked and rocked with every violent change of direction. After what seemed an eternity the abrupt movement settled into a smooth ride, the motor became a constant hum and the road noise thumped a regular rhythm. His heart rate didn't reflect the change. His body shook uncontrollably thwarting his efforts to work his hands free. Unable to get any leverage, his mind went over and over the events. Who were these people? And what did they want from him? His rising panic dulled his ability to think and maybe act. He told himself he had to stay calm and in control, but it was taking everything he had to do it.

Chapter 21

Shelley rubbed her eyes, struggling to focus on the screen. Her thoughts stubbornly returned to Saturday night. She smiled then forced her concentration back to the accidental find on her computer. She glanced around the office and was reassured she was alone. Her staff was at a safety presentation.

This report was confidential and shouldn't be on the team's archive folder. Someone had made a mistake. A heavy feeling dragged at the pit of her stomach. Phrases like additional capacity required; new facilities now operational and need to use remote locations; all told a different story to the official version. Before she could change her mind, she clicked the print icon. She directed it to the printer in the training suite machine's area, it was discreet and had proved useful for printing staff appraisals and selection documentation in the past.

She activated her screen saver, grabbed her daily planner and walked briskly down the corridor. A burst of laughter and excited chatter greeted her as she rounded the corner. She cursed for not checking the room was clear first then strode forward. She had to get that report before anyone else saw it.

A group of new recruits gathered beside the photocopier; talking and laughing as they compiled a large bundle of papers. They turned as one to stare at Shelley. Moving quickly, she placed herself strategically between them and the printer as it whirred into action. It purred and clunked then spat out the first of the confidential pages. Shelley leaned back and snatched the documents off the tray, the paper rustled in her shaking hands. She took each page as it slid through, carefully folded it, writing innermost, and slipped it into her planner.

'I didn't know anyone used that printer,' the short, plump graduate spoke from behind Shelley's shoulder almost making her drop her folder.

'I do occasionally. So, what are you guys doing here today?' Shelley asked as casually as her croaky voice would allow. She heard another page slide from the printer and grabbed it, the confidential stamp seemed to scream from the page.

'We're doing the Illegal immigrants and the Law course,' the young woman announced, a self-important edge creeping into her voice.

Shelley thought she recognised her. It was Clarissa, such a sweet name for such an angular young woman. Her intense stare was unnerving. She was one of a new batch of recruits, mostly law graduates who were keen and smart but very raw.

'Has it been interesting?' Shelley asked.

'Yes, it's been insightful, especially the focus on interpreting the law according to its intent, rather than literally.' Clarissa's chest puffed forward as she spoke.

'How does that change what you do?'

'Well, the laws on illegal immigrants and asylum seekers were drafted as border protection and to fight terrorism. That means we should apply that government policy to the interpretation.'

Shelley frowned and asked her to clarify.

'The Public Service administers government policy, so by inference, we treat these people as illegal and possible terrorists until proven otherwise.' Clarissa raised her chin with self-satisfaction. She'd been paying attention in the course and was treating this like a test.

'So they're guilty until proven innocent, you mean?' Shelley couldn't keep the sarcasm out of her voice.

The members of the group looked at each other in surprise obviously unused to being challenged. Clarissa's eyes widened at Shelley's tone and a redheaded young man, face covered in freckles, took advantage of the pause to jump in.

'Well, of course, after all, they've come here illegally.' His tone suggested no-one could argue with that and his face twisted with a hint of contempt.

'That's not right. Did you look at our UN obligations as part of this course too?' Shelley asked, disregarding their obvious discomfort.

The redhead was about to answer when one of the business-suited girls looked at her watch and shrieked, 'We have to get back.'

The redhead shrugged and Clarissa's eyes flared at her. They conveyed either pity or scorn, Shelley wasn't sure which. The group noisily scurried back to their training room, leaving Shelley in silence except for the printer which managed one more clunk. She stood rooted to the spot. Things had changed since the new Director had come in a year ago, more than she'd realised. Her hands trembled as she turned back to check the printer one more time. Her heart skipped a beat when she saw another page perched on the tray. She scanned it and sighed in relief; it was only a list of references. She snatched it from its resting place and stuffed it into her planner.

Her legs threatened to buckle as she escaped to the women's toilets. Small beads of sweat covered her brow as she thought of what she'd just done. Locking herself in a cubicle, she sat down to compose herself. She heard the outer door creak and a burst of conversation filled the toilets. Shelley held her breath.

'You know this work really sucks,' a familiar voice said loudly. It sounded like Maya.

'Yeah, I know.' The high-pitched and nasal voice was easily recognised. Shelley often blocked her ears to concentrate when this girl was on the telephone.

'I wonder where Shelley is. I wanted to talk to her in the break. Barry told me to shred those reports. I know he's our manager, but I didn't think that was right. We're supposed to keep them for...I don't know how many, but I know we're supposed to keep them for a few years anyway. I wanted to check with her first,' Maya said.

'She's acting a bit odd lately, ever since her holiday.' This was a girl from the area next to theirs. She'd worked with Shelley in the previous section and was nice but nosey. 'I reckon she's met a man.'

They giggled.

'She's been very distracted these days; you may be right. I like her new image though,' the high-pitched voice added.

'Yeah, but she's becoming a bore, so serious, always banging on about things,' the nosey one insisted.

They giggled again.

The taps ran, splashing water into the sinks and Shelley breathed gently as they happily gossiped about another team member. They suddenly went quiet and Shelley assumed they'd noticed the closed cubicle door. She rustled some paper to confirm someone was there and was rewarded with the creak of the outer door as they left. Was she really becoming a bore? She was becoming very serious these days, worrying about events that seemed beyond her control. She stared down at the folder, hesitantly opening it to scan the incriminating document. It was all there. She didn't fully understand it, but she had a bad feeling about it. Just like her conversation with the graduates.

Although the interrogation room was bigger than his cell, he couldn't put enough space between him and his kidnappers. Akbal's face didn't hurt as much as his arms although it was only a close second. He suspected his left arm was broken, it sat at a right-angle and any movement caused a searing pain. Broad straps held him firmly against the chair and he'd lost all feeling in his other arm. Maybe that was a blessing. The small circular burns on his arms raged red and raw, and he trembled at the memory of the red-hot poker and the pain it inflicted. How could this be happening to him?

'I've told you the truth,' he shouted, his voice tearing through his already raw throat.

Three sets of cold eyes stared back at him barely visible through the slits in their balaclavas. There wasn't a hint of compassion there.

'Who are you?' Akbal screamed, his panic close to the surface.

'Never mind who we are. We want to know who you are or at least what you are.' The short man's eyes glistened in the bright low hanging light, betraying his enjoyment, 'Now, let's start at the beginning.' His soft tone was conversational, but it wasn't fooling Akbal.

The other interrogator stepped forward, his stocky build almost shaking the room. He was fat, his belly overhung his trouser belt, but he was deceptively strong. He was the one who'd broken Akbal's arm with his bare hands, just a twist and the bone snapped. Akbal winced as he approached.

'Now when did you first meet with Mohamed?' The sour smell of stale takeaway food emanated from his breath and clothes, even though it was filtered through his mask. It mingled with the smell of sweat, blood and fear and Akbal gagged.

'I met him for the first time in Paris. I've already told you.' Akbal moaned. He swallowed hard and avoided breathing too deeply. 'I didn't know him before that.'

'What were you planning with him in Paris?'

'Nothing! I told you…He gave me a contact in Pakistan to help me find my wife's uncle, Ashram.'

The interrogators shook their heads, rhythmically tensing and releasing their fists. Akbal shrank down into the seat as much as the straps would allow.

'Enough.' growled the short interrogator, 'We want the truth, not this pack of shit.'

'It is the truth,' Akbal insisted, his voice breaking uncontrollably. 'I've told you a million times, Ashram escaped Afghanistan…I thought he was in a camp in Pakistan…but …but I couldn't find him. Mohamed gave me a contact…he couldn't help.' He swallowed hard, trying unsuccessfully to steady his voice and his nerves. 'I didn't get involved with anything. You must believe me. I was just looking for Ashram.'

Close to tears, he felt a careless urge to tell them what they wanted to hear, but he fought it. Frantically he tried to rein in his emotions to garner just a little control.

The fat man suddenly roared, 'That's crap!'

The punch took Akbal unawares, his head lurched back. The taste of blood filled his mouth and his tongue scraped across a jagged piece of tooth. Spitting the blood and fragment across the floor, he crumpled with pain.

'Stop. Please…Please…I don't know anything.' Akbal cried, his voice unnaturally high-pitched.

The short interrogator's chilling laugh matched his eyes. The three of them moved away, leaving Akbal hunched forward, straining against the straps but unable to pull himself up. Sweat blurred his vision and his swollen face felt twice its normal size. In the corner, away from earshot, the interrogators plotted. One of the voices, loud and menacing rose above the others.

'It's time we taught him another lesson. I think I can loosen his tongue.'

Akbal trembled involuntarily despite the pain it caused. He pleaded, desperately trying to make them listen, trying to make them believe. Fear erupted from his stomach and smashed into the back of his throat. He gagged at the acidic fluid spilling into his mouth and burning the back of his throat. A scream, nothing like he had ever heard before, tore through the concrete cave, echoing from the walls. His body convulsed as the vomit bursting from his mouth sent him forward. The straps cut into him, wide welts adding to the symphony of pain his body was barely enduring. The arch of vomit projected forward landing at his interrogators' feet. His body shook uncontrollably as the straps yanked at the broken bones in his ribs. Emptying his stomach had unleashed the bile but had failed to expel the terror.

The interrogators nodded to each other and one muttered, 'You dirty bastard' as they stepped towards Akbal.

He struggled against his straps, ignoring the pain, desperate to escape. He didn't know how much more he could take.

'Let me go! I can't tell you anything. I've told you the truth. No matter how much you beat me, it doesn't change the truth.'

He collapsed in his chair exhausted, bleeding and spent. How could he keep fighting? His stomach lurched threatening to retch nothingness and he was convinced he was going to die. He would never see Fatima or his daughter, Sari again. Tears streamed down his face. The interrogators would not settle for anything less than their version of the 'truth'. Was he going to die rather than lie? He had left this kind of thing behind, his own father had died, tortured by the Taliban because he wouldn't submit to their rules. Afghanistan had seemed far away, until now. Was his darling Sari destined to suffer the same fate, growing up without her father to love and protect her?

A booming voice over the intercom interrupted his sobs. 'Men, we have another task for you.'

The fat interrogator stared at Akbal and smirked, 'Lucky. We'll be back to fix you, you lying bastard. We haven't even started with you yet.'

Akbal was alone in his stark grey cell slumped as much as he could, every part of him crying out in pain. His mind wouldn't concentrate and lurched from image to image interrupted by unbearable pain.

Chapter 22

Shelley's mind lingered on the briefcase and its dangerous contents. Printing the document and taking it home was a serious breach of security. If she was under surveillance it was an especially stupid act. What had she been thinking? She was getting involved in issues that were nothing to do with her and yet they were too serious to walk away from.

She shivered, remembering Jason's comments as her mind went back over the first time she'd met Mohamed. There was nothing out of the ordinary, no clues that he was a terrorist. He hadn't even seemed that intense. Yet according to press reports, the evidence against him was mounting. Akbal had spent more time with Mohamed than any of them but she couldn't believe he was involved in terrorism. Was she being naïve? Would she be able to identify a terrorist? Even the professionals struggled to do that. That's what had them all afraid, the unknown elements within. The fear also stopped them maintaining perspective. She didn't suspect Adrian or

Jason and it occurred to her that there was a kernel of prejudice in her uncertainty about Akbal.

The phone rang and jangled her nerves. She answered tentatively, still spooked by her thoughts.

'It's Beetle. Sorry I haven't called sooner.' His voice was a controlled whisper.

'I got your text, what did you find out?' Shelley was relieved to at last speak to him. It had been just one more thing on her mind lately.

'The local police found her body in Kings Cross, not Hubbard St. Apparently, the Feds changed the report after they took over.'

'I thought there was something wrong.' Shelley explained what she'd learned from the state coroner's report. 'Why would they change it?'

'I don't know, but the building in front of where she was found has a gentleman's club on both the second and third floors. That's another name for a high-class, exclusive brothel. Professional men and politicians tend to use them. It's been involved in other cases I've worked on. I'm sure we have the right spot.'

'Ayisha – in a brothel? Never,' Shelley exclaimed.

'I'm pretty sure, but I'll confirm it.' He coughed. 'Also, I'm not sure if this is connected, but a young Iranian immigrant woman died under suspicious circumstances in Brisbane a week ago. It has some similarities to this case. The Feds took that case over before the coroner could even start.'

203

'How could they be connected?'

'It's just the way the Feds are handling it. It makes me suspicious.'

Shelley told him about Ayisha's friend, Kadeen, and both agreed to try to find her. Without the last name, it wasn't easy, but Shelley would search recent immigration lists.

He swore under his breath. 'They are guarding this investigation as though it was a case of national security. Why the Feds are involved has me stumped.'

'It made me suspicious too.'

'I must go. I'll be in touch as soon as I have anything.'

Shelley hung up, her hands trembling. If she had fallen in Kings Cross, it must have something to do with her friend, Kadeen. The unspeakable dilemma could be the answer.

Instead of clearing up the mystery, the more they delved the more questions were raised. What had Ayisha got close to? Who and where was her friend, Kadeen? She ran her fingers through her hair, pulling it back hard off her face. Despite the dangers for her, she knew one thing; she was more determined than ever to find out what was going on.

Outside, the rain clouds gathering overhead brought premature darkness, interrupted only by the soft glow of the streetlights that barely lit the footpath. Shadows danced in time to the waves of wind, creating eerie patterns. Shelley sighed, unable to reconcile the disparate thoughts tying up her mind. She picked up the briefcase and removed the document. She was afraid of what she'd learn and what it might make her do. There would be no turning back.

With a cup of tea and a packet of Tim Tams, she started to read. The confidential report was a briefing from the Special Investigation Squad for the eyes of the commissioner of the Department of Immigration and the government adviser only. The eight-page report was interspersed with numerous graphs and tables. This squad, SIS as they were called, and sometimes SISSY by those who disliked their special status, consisted of five senior staff 'handpicked' from immigration. Although physically located in the Federal Police building, they reported to both departments.

The existence of Barker and Wilderness detention centres was common knowledge but to her surprise, two more centres, Red Centre and Desert Station, were in use since last year. All were in remote areas and designated secret for national security reasons. Two more were commissioned to be built after the next election. Shelley rubbed her forehead. Why were they building more? And, why were they secret?

The table on page two showed over one hundred asylum seekers had arrived in the last two months and the number of intakes had increased progressively over the last six months. They were expecting more in the coming months. Shelley reread the figures. She knew of no large transfers from any processing facility in the last year. In fact, many long-term detainees were being repatriated so the numbers should be reducing.

Shelley rummaged through her pile of unread newspapers and found an article from the previous week. It praised the government's tough stance on boat people and stated turning boats back to Indonesia over the last six months was working well. The Minister confirmed there had been no new arrivals in that time. Someone was lying. What was the government hiding? Was it just covering up the fact that their policy wasn't really working? Could that be all it was?

The document requested the urgent provision of additional services, especially English language classes. They already had them in metropolitan areas and Shelley wondered why they needed them specifically in these new centres.

The data on medical services confirmed mental health issues plagued the centres. A short paragraph dismissed the concerns, identifying the separation of families as exacerbating the situation. Mental health wasn't considered important and she thought of Adrian and the concerns he so often voiced. He saw it as a form of mistreatment that seemed to be sanctioned by the decision-makers and she agreed.

Neither SIS nor the Federal Police supported the contractor's level of control and presented a case to review Serpentco. Shelley shook her head. Amazing how their only concern was their own insufficient power and control. The contractors maintained strict secrecy over their operations and dealt directly with the Prime Minister's office. They refused to liaise with or provide briefings to the departments. The Immigration Department's role was reduced to overseeing funding matters and minor administrative issues. All requests for access or information from the department went to the government adviser, Mark McCracken. That name again. He was the go-between for everything and from what Shelley knew, Serpentco had never been overruled by the government adviser on any issue.

The report dismissed rumours of severe illnesses within the centres as greatly exaggerated. SIS had not conducted an independent review because the contractor insisted it was under control. They'd refused additional assistance and Mr McCracken had accepted their assessment, arguing for a review of the initial health checks instead.

Shelley wondered how Mr McCracken had become involved in these issues. It was unprecedented for the Prime Minister and his advisers to become directly involved. The oversight of asylum seekers had always remained with the department and they had provided updates, reports, and information as required to their minister.

A small paragraph on page five caught her eye. A small group of senior staff at the Immigration Department was protesting their inability to gain access to the centres. Shelley wanted to cheer, some of her colleagues had a conscience. But then she read their protests were being treated as insurrection and the department was urged to deal with the protesters forcefully to silence them, by whatever means were deemed necessary.

She shivered. The public generally supported the government's tough stance. What could be done? Top levels were maintaining secrecy and supported the cruelty.

To Shelley, Serpentco's high-level security was extreme. They cited a recent breach as justification, but Shelley couldn't remember any breaches. Only two preferred specialists had access, one was a psychiatrist, the other a GP. Barker and Wilderness had medical facilities with locally trained nurses and nursing aides recruited from nearby communities. SIS supported the limited access rule stating it avoided panic and hysterical newspaper reports. A side reference to Jupiter Security Company caught her eye. It was familiar but from a different context. The reference was vague, and she made a note to follow it up.

Hidden amongst the treatment figures Shelley noticed the number six with an asterisk beside it. At the bottom of the report, the asterisk was explained as 'losses'. Shelley screwed up her face. Six losses meant there had been six deaths. This table referred only to Barker. Surely six deaths deserved more of a mention than this. She clenched her fist. Why hadn't she heard about them? There was no indication of how many others were critically ill.

A list of symptoms on the last page included skin lesions and difficulty with breathing but there was no cause of death. The report suggested the asylum seekers had arrived ill and no further investigation was required. A footnote said figures for other centres would be included in the next report.

Shelley dropped the paper to her lap and stared at the curtain fluttering in the slightly open window. Her body slumped as she realised there must be more ill detainees and possibly more deaths in the other centres. What should she do with this information? Could she ignore it? She couldn't trust the system to deal with it, it had already failed. The dereliction of duties and responsibilities looked like they went right to the Prime Minister's adviser. If she shared this information with Adrian it would prove his concerns right, but then what? Was she prepared to put her life and reputation on the line meddling in something she didn't have all the facts for? A niggling voice at the back of her mind cautioned her, urged her to protect herself, telling her to not jeopardise her world for this, especially when she wasn't sure what 'this' was.

She stood up abruptly, she wanted to purge herself of responsibility. She wanted to believe it would all be alright without her having to risk anything. She searched for matches as a plan formulated in her mind. If she destroyed the report now no-one would need to know she'd seen it. She could simply tear it into shreds and end her own uncertainties forever. She could pretend she had never seen the report, had never printed it or even knew it existed. Shelley hesitated. An irritating doubt resisted her justifications. She might want to pretend she didn't know but once read, the report could not be unread, the information could not be unlearned and even if no-one else knew she'd read it, nothing she did could change the fact that she knew.

Children's high-pitched voices, squealing with delight, floated through her window. The sun was out again. On the footpath across the road, three coffee coloured children laughed and giggled as they took turns on a scooter, squealing each time one of them fell off. Their veiled mother laughed, calling after them in care-laden tones. Shelley recognised those carefree children. They belonged to a new immigrant family who'd recently settled in this street. Their tales of escape and associated traumas read like a fiction novel, except they were real. They had endured those horrors and survived to talk about it. Now they were starting a new safe life, just like the majority of the boat arrivals. Most of them were legitimate asylum seekers, after years of detention they had finally been accepted as needing protection and safety. She shuddered as she watched the joy on those young faces. These people were no different from those currently locked up in the detention centres, dying or suffering mental anguish. How could she do nothing? What kind of person would that make her?

She couldn't destroy the report while innocent people needed help. Adrian might recognise the symptoms and even if he couldn't investigate it directly, it would help him with where to look or what questions to ask. She stowed the papers back in her briefcase. She had to act, she couldn't ignore what was happening, not when it was so dire.

Jason casually dropped onto the chair just inside the double glass doors at Café Bellini. Adrian wasn't usually late, and he scanned the café to make sure he wasn't amongst the lunchtime crowd. He relaxed, prepared to wait and reached for the papers on the next table. He flicked through the pages of an old copy of the local paper and stopped abruptly at the business section. The picture showed Martin Carlew smiling smugly beside an equally smug-looking Wrogarth and a collection of small mine owners. Two Aboriginal youths wearing fluorescent vests and hard hats represented a philanthropic project. Jason scowled. Any philanthropic project involving Trisec Oil and Carlew could only be a sham.

He remembered a case a few years ago that his dad had inadvertently told him about. Three people died in that accident but the lack of training and their minimal compliance with health and safety had been successfully whitewashed. It was deemed an unfortunate accident rather than a case of neglect. Jason thumped his leg. The bottom line was always more compelling than anything else, even lives.

The positive treatment in the press surprised him. This project was probably just a cover to get access to lucrative deposits in the prohibited areas. He'd read Trisec Oil had been locking out smaller miners, denying them access through Trisec's land to their smallholdings. Access was usually taken for granted so Carlew's action was causing quite a stir. Strangely it wasn't mentioned here.

He tossed the paper onto the table beside him. That smug face burned into his brain, standing beside Carlew with his 'I'm so important' stance. His father being involved made it worse.

He'd investigate this further. Despite his keenness, after the meeting with Gary, he'd let his project slide again. He had to crank it up. His father hadn't learned his lesson after all. It was time to find out what else Gary had unearthed.

Jason scanned the current Australian Reporter instead. He didn't usually read this paper, but the headlines grabbed his attention. Unconfirmed reports said an Australian man was being held for questioning on terrorism charges in Adelaide. His name was suppressed but an anonymous source said it was linked to Mohamed Yusuf's arrest. They had met in Paris and both had travelled to Pakistan where it was alleged, they attended training camps and met with members of a terrorist group. The Federal Police and government sources wouldn't confirm or deny details. This was a routine follow-up of information provided by British investigators.

Jason's thoughts turned to Akbal. He'd been preoccupied and distant since his trip to Pakistan. Could he be involved? Did they know Akbal well enough to judge? There hadn't been anyone else from Adelaide at the Paris café, not that Jason knew. Just then he looked up to see Adrian walking into the café and waved to get his attention. Adrian nodded then stopped at the counter to order.

'I hate this lining up to order, I only have thirty minutes for lunch,' he said as he sat down, 'Next time lets go to Prego, they have table service.'

'OK,' Jason said then leaned across to show Adrian the article.

Adrian searched the page then whistled softly. 'Wow!'

'Akbal?' he asked watching Adrian with interest.

'Don't be ridiculous. There must have been thousands of Aussies in Paris when we were there.'

'The story fits. There wouldn't have been thousands of people from Adelaide who met up with Mohamed, surely?' He shrugged his shoulders, 'Have you seen Akbal lately?'

'No, I haven't.' Adrian fumbled in his pockets and then cursed softly. 'I've left my mobile at the lab.' He shook his head slowly, 'We have to check it out.'

'My phone's out of battery,' Jason said grimacing as he looked at the blank screen on his new phone.

'This could be serious. It could mean trouble for us too if they think Akbal is involved. The new laws on terrorism mean they can hold him for questioning for two weeks before they need to reveal who he is or before he can get legal representation. If Akbal is suspected, it connects us too.'

'Well, he's Muslim,' Jason offered.

'What do you mean by that?'

'I don't know. It's just that you never really know about them or their beliefs.'

213

'We know Akbal.'

'Do we? He talked to Mohamed and I saw Mohamed pass Akbal a note the day of the demonstration. And we know Akbal went to Pakistan.' Jason shifted uncomfortably in his seat, combing his fingers through his hair. 'I know Akbal is different, you've been friends for a long time, but…'

'It's not Muslims who are responsible for terrorism, its radicals. It's about power, not religion. Every terrorist group, even the IRA, does what it does for power. Religion is just a cover. It taps into belief systems and stops people thinking for themselves. The IRA no more represented all Catholics than Al-Qaeda represents all Muslims.'

Jason nodded his head. He understood what Adrian was trying to say. 'Right now, it's Muslims, radical Muslims who are the terrorists. I know Akbal doesn't fit the bill as a radical, but people have been turned before.'

'Akbal has always believed in justice and his willingness to help people work within the system means I can't believe it.' Adrian sat quietly, waiting for a response, but Jason was still unsure. He didn't know how to voice his doubts to someone as fervent as Adrian. 'Don't let the current spin make you doubt a friend. That's how they win. Akbal has always been moderate in his views. We have to fight the fear. It's fear that turns hearts to stone and kills compassion.' Adrian added.

'I guess you're right, but it's hard not to be afraid of the way the world is going. All the radical talk, the bombings of innocent people, it leaves its mark.'

'I know. History is full of religious violence. It's not just our times. Catholics murdered Jews and Muslims in the name of the faith, long before our current problems. The pope decrees women in Africa shouldn't use contraceptives thereby exposing them and their unborn children to AIDS. That's as heinous as any bomb killing innocents, those children are also innocents. I had to watch them die in the name of some arbitrary religious ruling.' Adrian's voice rose, his face flushed with anger as spittle formed on his lips.

'Soapbox!' called Jason, evoking their call sign.

Adrian shifted in his seat, took a deep breath adding, 'They're even trying to impose their religious rules on a sectarian society like Australia.' He swallowed then smiled, 'OK, that's enough, I give up.'

They sat in silence unable to start another conversation. They weren't talking about it, but they were both still thinking about it. Their coffees arrived and Adrian distractedly flicked through the paper stopping in the business section.

'Are you buying shares? Any tips?' Jason asked.

'No, Klaus mentioned Ortansea has a connection with Australia, but from what I've read they have pulled out and have concentrated their operations overseas. They seem to have shut down activities here.'

Jason nodded, 'Does he know that AAAP has been buying up the disused sites. The industry speculation is that they've come up with some new technological processes to make them viable again.'

Adrian grinned, 'I told him you were more up-to-date than me.'

Jason went on, he wanted to impress Adrian with the work he'd done so far. 'AAAP is quite new here, in fact, they haven't been around that long on the world stage either. A mate of mine is doing some searches for me. Ortansea is taking a hiding in the European courts, they were caught trying to dump hazardous materials again. They won't get a licence renewed if that goes down. I think they're shutting down all their operations. Then they can plead poor and escape paying huge compensation maybe. With the current downturn, it would be good if new technology helps to reopen those mines though.'

Adrian frowned, 'Really?'

'I know. I'm not usually a fan of the mining sector but I have a mate who was laid off from the new expansion planned up north. They cancelled the building of housing estates for their workers and he's been struggling to find other work. He's not really qualified for anything else. Although...' Jason continued while scratching his head, 'it says here they're building another deepwater port closer to the bight. I guess they must be optimistic to invest in that project. I wonder if my mate knows about that.'

They put the paper aside and made room for the focaccias the waiter brought. Adrian checked his watch and sighed.

'So, have you seen Shelley lately?' Jason asked, watching Adrian for a reaction.

'Yes...We went out to see the Screaming Galahs on Saturday night at the Cosmos Club,' Adrian confessed then catching Jason unawares. 'You like her too?'

The words landed between them, Adrian looking almost as surprised by them as Jason.

'Yes, she's nice.' Jason hesitated 'Is it...serious...between you?'

He was trying to sound casual but not so casual that Adrian would avoid answering.

'I don't know how to answer that,' Adrian said, rubbing his finger along the groove in his chin. 'We seem to click but...'

He let the sentence hang there, unfinished and Jason felt no wiser.

'You have to let someone in eventually,' Jason said quietly, not sure he wanted to push Adrian in that direction.

He knew Adrian too well, he had trouble letting relationships become serious, pulling back before they could develop. Shelley had gotten closer than any others in recent times, but...

Adrian cast a wistful look at his friend 'Yasmine is coming...with Klaus.'

'So, what does that mean?' he asked wondering what this meant for Shelley in particular.

'Not really sure.' Adrian bent his head and bit into his focaccia.

***

Back in the office, Adrian phoned Fatima. She told him Akbal had been missing since Saturday night. She'd rung hospitals and talked to the police when he hadn't come home but with no result. Her voice was high-pitched but controlled, insisting Akbal would never disappear like this. After three days her nerves were raw and she didn't know what else to do.

Adrian wasn't sure what to do either but didn't mention the newspaper report. He didn't want to add to her distress, especially if it was a false alarm. He hung up feeling particularly helpless. He dialled his friend, a tough human rights lawyer, who would have the resources and know-how to find out more.

He assured Adrian he'd follow-up through his own sources. Adrian paced the laboratory, his mind overflowing with issues. He had decisions to make but was reluctant to take the time to work through them. He went back to his desk and trawled through some human rights sites on his laptop. At least it felt like he was doing something.

He found a new site offering suggestions for dealing with government agencies and he scrolled through their recommendations. They highlighted the recent shift of responsibilities for home terrorism issues from the Intelligence Agency to the Federal Police. He hadn't heard about this. The new head of department at the IA, Jacobs, was known to follow a 'by-the-book' approach, and the authors believed he would at least use

218

the law as his department's guiding principle. People had no such faith in Benedict, the Federal Police head. Now with all internal terrorism issues under the jurisdiction of the Federal Police, the Intelligence Agency was restricted to international issues. The number of asylum seekers rated as a high-security risk had already increased, including a high number of women, and this change would probably make it worse. Human rights groups were mounting a challenge but since the ratings did not have to be justified it was an uphill battle. The Feds could legally keep asylum seekers rated as high risk, in detention, until they were cleared, meaning they could be there indefinitely. The Minister supported this approach, of course. Adrian pumped his fists; it was another hurdle. With their limited resources human rights groups had, they'd struggle to achieve anything substantial.

Chapter 23

Daryl was struck by the wide smile on Wrogarth's face.

'Good, an arrest,' his boss said, rubbing his hands together.

'Well, more under questioning. We'll drip-feed the details through the press but there's been no confession yet. I'm sure they'll get one.' Mark glanced furtively at Daryl.

'When can we officially tie it to the London arrest?'

Wrogarth's glance at Mark was the kind Daryl had seen a lot lately. They were co-conspirators and no-one else was invited in. Daryl wanted to know more but couldn't ask questions right now.

Mark thrust a copy of The Reporter onto the desk. 'Not yet. There's this…that's enough for now. An unconfirmed report gets us the right kind of publicity.'

Wrogarth bit his lip. 'Make sure the bleeding-heart lawyers can't get onto their human rights bandwagon before we have what we need. Get the minister involved. Benedict needs to move his Feds along. I'm counting on them to do whatever it takes,' he said as he reached for the spiky letter opener and twirled it dangerously in front of him.

Daryl grimaced as he saw the pointy end narrowly miss Wrogarth's cheek. A gift from his daughter, the lethal-looking item remained a useless decoration on an otherwise tidy desk.

Then, staring straight at Daryl he asked softly, 'We have two weeks before we have to advise anyone, don't we?'

Daryl nodded and Wrogarth continued, 'OK.' He pointed his finger menacingly at Mark. 'Just make sure they get something out of him fast.'

'There's some bickering about jurisdiction,' Mark hesitated briefly. 'Benedict is worried and wants confirmation that his Federal Police have the running on this. Jacobs is agitating and wants his Intelligence Agency involved. Will you deal with Jacobs or shall we get the Minister to do it?'

Wrogarth stared at a spot on the opposite wall. 'Jacobs wants in, does he?'

'Well not exactly. He just doesn't want the Federal Police to have control. You know how it is. There's no love lost between them.'

Daryl knew Mark would have liked to add an 'I told you so.' Mark had advised against Jacobs getting the top position at the Intelligence Agency, arguing he was too rule-bound. Now Mark was being proven right. Daryl had been happy to see Jacobs retained. Benedict was known to cut corners where possible. Wrogarth liked the tension between the two heads and had insisted on keeping Benedict and Jacobs in their respective roles.

Wrogarth waved his hands in the air dismissively. 'Let the minister earn his money.'

The Australian connection to the London arrest was tenuous. If there was clear evidence, why did they need a confession?

Outside Wrogarth's office, Daryl approached Mark.

'Is there new information?'

Mark's face screwed into a scowl. 'You know as much as you need to know. James wants me to look after this.'

Mark turned on his heels ready to walk out.

'So, you have evidence that the guy arrested is definitely involved? What about his friends, are we going to arrest them too?' Daryl continued, keeping his voice pliant and trying not to sound challenging, although he was.

Mark turned back and the room seemed to noticeably cool. 'They're working on it. You'll be advised if and when you need to be,' he said before striding out without a second glance.

Daryl sat down at his desk, resting his chin on his hands. A quick move on the terrorist threat would help the polls. But, with Jacobs getting testy, it could mean only one thing. The Federal Police were not playing by the book. He didn't trust Benedict, had even counselled Wrogarth against appointing him as head of the Federal

Police. But Benedict and the Minister were close, and the Minister got his first choice. Daryl's concerns had been dismissed.

His job was secure. His knowledge of the scandals, backroom deals, and shady associations during his years of service, made a threatening list. Wrogarth wouldn't fire him but still, he was being edged out more and more. Did he want to stay? He'd always believed Wrogarth's methods were for good reasons, but now he wasn't so sure. Maybe believed was too strong a word, more like hoped. He'd always known Wrogarth's character and his potential but had stayed anyway. He'd liked the cut and thrust of this job. And, to support Bev. But the time had come to review his career, especially if Mark's star continued to rise so dramatically.

***

Their first relaxed evening for some time and it took only a wrong word, a misunderstood question to set him off into a deranged rant. Bev sighed. The harmless discussion about upcoming commitments had turned into a shouting match. He read criticism into everything she said. She rubbed her shoulder and grimaced. They were becoming more frequent. Her shoulders slumped as she felt her fears closing in.

James' face registered disgust, 'I'm the Prime Minister. I have a position to protect. You're a liability. Questions! Questions! Always *questions*. You don't trust my judgement.'

'I don't know what you mean. I've stood by you, helped where I can. It's you, you just find fault all the time.' She felt a sob choking at her throat and fought it down.

'Help? Is that what you call it? You undermine and I have proof.' He glared at her with a frightening fierceness.

'I've supported you in every way I know. But instead of working with me you hide things from me.' She was being reckless to challenge him, but she couldn't stop herself.

'Did you support me when you met William? I bet you didn't. I bet you agree with him, soothe him, tell him his father is the problem, not your precious William.' He looked her up and down and smirked.

'What do you mean when I met him?' Bev gasped, he couldn't know about their meeting in Paris, could he? She'd never been good at bluffing and it wasn't working now.

'I have my sources. You of all people should know that. I'm the PM and you are the PM's wife. It's all about security.'

'How dare you?' She buckled under a tidal wave of anger. He'd been spying on her. What else did he know?

'That's not all of it, is it? You meet with my staff, well, one of my staff. What are you up to? Are you undermining me with Daryl too? Are you setting yourself in opposition to me? If so, I'm warning you, you'll pay. Disloyalty is unforgivable.' He thumped the table.

He strode to the bar and fixed himself a drink. Cradling it lovingly in his big hands as he turned to face her. James was now dangerously calm and wore an odd smirk.

'By the way, I've found him.' His voice was oily.

'Who?' Bev tensed; she'd dreaded this moment.

'You know who. Don't play games, Bev. I've found William.' A hint of menace underscored his quiet tone.

'I didn't know he was lost.' She couldn't quite manage a laugh; she'd carried her tension and wariness for too long and it was wearing her down.

'I know where he is. Aren't you going to ask me where?'

'OK, where?'

'He's been hiding in Adelaide.' He loomed over her. 'But of course you knew that, didn't you?'

Bev looked away. Her stomach knotted into a painful ball and it hurt to breathe. 'How did you find him?'

'He's involved in a terrorist plot.'

James rested his hands on the arms of her chair and leaned down close. She felt his hot breath on her face and shivered. He grabbed her chin and forced her face up. Their eyes locked. Bev recoiled, startled by their coldness. She felt his nails dig into her chin and a moist spot develop.

'I don't believe it. That's a vicious lie. William would never…'

He laughed at her.

'You can't believe anything bad about your precious son, can you?' Again, he gripped her face. His mouth formed an uncompromising slit and the vein at his temple throbbed an ominous rhythm. 'Well, he's in it up to his neck whether you believe it or not. I've got him this time.'

Drops of spittle settled on her cheeks and the smell of scotch wafted in her direction. Bev strained against his hands and he whipped her head sideways before letting it go.

'Of course, he's not as clever as he thinks. He's using an alias, did you know?'

Bev sunk down in her chair, trying to put more distance between them.

'Of course you did…not very smart using his middle name and your maiden name. Well, it's not very original, is it? And of course, now he won't have the name to protect him.'

Bev's heart raced, was he threatening William? Would he hurt him or was it just alcohol fuelling a rush of anger?

'How can you hate your own son so much?' Bev screamed.

She burst out of her chair and raced out of the room to escape upstairs. That question burned into her brain. It remained unanswered, unexplained and constantly whirled in her subconscious. It plagued her sleepless nights and her stumbling waking hours. How had this dispute with William become so out of proportion? It had a force of its own, crashing through between her and James, prying them ever further apart.

James shouted at her retreating back then scaled the stairs two at a time to reach her.

'You know why! He almost destroyed me and my career.' James' hands shook, his contorted face becoming a grotesque mask flaring an ugly red.

Ignoring the sensible voice in her head she shouted back. 'For fuck's sake, it's history! He was young and idealistic then. Why can't you forgive and forget? He's your son.'

She'd heard the list of grievances too many times. James clung to his anger and resentment, letting love and joy slip through his fingers. He stared at her with unseeing eyes; he was back there, reliving the past and unable to let it go.

'Don't you swear at me. I paid dearly. It took everything I had to get my reputation back. I grovelled and licked arses, we even moved for fuck's sake. It cost me. He showed no remorse even when he saw how serious the consequences were for us. He never apologised, in fact, he seemed glad. I can't forgive…'

Bev slumped onto the bed. She saw now, there would never be a resolution, things would never change. They couldn't talk about it. His rage and recriminations always got in the way. James would never admit that he had been wrong too. Being caught taking money from the criminal underworld and handing out favours was the problem, no matter what spin he put on the story. The electorate and the party reacted exactly how he should have expected. For James, it was William's involvement that had made it harder to bear.

James expected total loyalty and silence from his own. To this day Bev wasn't sure how James and her father had saved her husband's career; she'd thought it was finished. That episode surprised her. The lengths he was prepared to go to was further than she'd imagined. She had put it behind her, willing to go on in the hope he'd learned his lesson and in future, would be more careful. He needed to move on, but he was stuck.

'It's gone on for too long. Rage is woven into the fabric of your personality now,' she uttered, 'You can't change, can you?'

'It's not me that has to change.' He squeezed the words out through gritted teeth.

Fatigue pressed down on her. She was tired of fighting, tired of trying to make things work again. He was beyond reason, his eyes flared like a madman. He believed she was getting in the way of his quest for more power and she railed at the injustice of it. A spark, a tiny flame of anger simmered, and she finally understood. She couldn't go on this way, submitting to his physical and verbal abuse forever. With a flash of rare insight, she knew their marriage could no longer withstand the strain. She had to regain some self-respect. It was too late to win back his love; too late to win him back in any capacity at all. She knew that now. He was willing to hurt their son. His unrelenting anger at William had been the beginning of the end for them too. He associated her with what their son had done because she'd defended William and he knew, even if she hadn't said it out loud, that she agreed with his stand. James was dangerous and the cost to her personally was too high.

She faced him and summoned all her courage. 'You…you bastard. I can't go on like this anymore.' She hesitated. 'I'm leaving you,' she said quietly, watching his reaction and enjoying the surprise on his face.

His face snapped back as though she had physically slapped him. But then his face contorted, his shoulders tensed, and his fists clenched. He stepped nearer.

'Noooooo,' he roared.

His hand shot out and grabbed her arm. He wrenched her towards him. The slap forced her face sideways and she almost lost her balance. Bev shrunk back but he pulled her up again. She screamed. Bev had unleashed a frightening rage and he was out of control. The next slap struck her other cheek and she crumpled to the floor. He dragged her up, his fingers digging into her skin and she begged him to stop. But he didn't hear. His fists were clenched and the fire in his eyes sent terror to her heart. She saw the next blow coming, but she couldn't escape. She cringed, crawling back away from him, but he was on her like a flash.

Oh, please, don't let it end this way.

Chapter 24

Shelley's stomach churned. Barry's stern summons to his office had to be serious. He hadn't explained and his tone worried her although he was usually one of the easy-going managers. Her hand trembled as she knocked softly on the half-open door. She wiped her palms on her skirt before entering.

'Hi, Shelley. Close the door behind you.'

Barry looked up from his computer screen then swung his chair in a clean, smooth arc to settle at the small circular visitor's table. Shelley sat in the chair opposite him, her hands clasped in her lap and her knuckles turning white from the grip. Unhelpful thoughts whirled through her mind making her more nervous the longer she waited. Was this about the document she'd printed? Or did he know about her delving into Ayisha's death?

Barry pushed his glasses down to perch on the end of his nose. His expression was unusually stern.

'This leak to the press has caused a panic. It's definitely from our area. No-one else has access to that data.'

He peered at Shelley over the top of his reading glasses and Shelley couldn't tell if he was accusing her or not.

'You saw this morning's paper?'

Shelley shook her head, not trusting her voice.

'Luckily it didn't make front-page news, but it still has the hierarchy in turmoil. We can't let these kinds of breaches go unpunished.' He shook his head and looked down at the papers resting on the table. 'I don't know what kind of person does something like this. Giving out confidential data is illegal...the Minister's office is breathing down our necks, even the Prime Minister's office has become involved.' He shook his head as he shuffled papers. 'We have to find the culprit. Luckily it's a relatively...minor...leak at this stage.' He rearranged the papers again then swung his chair around to place them on his desk. He swung back and they sat in silence for a moment.

'I'm really disappointed in you Shelley,' he finally said grasping his reading glasses in one hand and lifting them high off his face.

'Why?' she asked, finally finding a shaky version of her voice.

She shifted in her seat avoiding eye contact as his rhythmic twirling of the reading glasses caught the corner of her vision. Fighting to resist the urge to blurt out a confession she sat rigid and unmoving. Eventually, he stopped twirling the glasses.

'I've had a complaint about you.'

'Complaint?' Her nails dug into the fleshy part of her palms but despite the pain, she couldn't release the grip.

'You were in the machine room on Monday, weren't you?'

'Well yes, I was.' Shelley wished he would get on with it. Whatever he wanted to say couldn't be any worse than this drawn-out discussion. She again considered confessing now and getting it over with, but her nerve deserted her.

'Why were you there?'

Her mind raced and his stare made it hard to think.

'I'd printed some documents to that printer, er…by mistake.' Shelley stammered then responding to his puzzled look, added. 'I use that printer for confidential reports sometimes.' She stole a look at his grave face and wasn't sure he believed her.

'What confidential reports do you need to print?'

'Well, um, I…I was…drafting some staff feedback reports, collating the previous manager's comments in preparation for the appraisals next month.' She hoped her nervousness wasn't too evident. She desperately hoped he wouldn't ask to see these appraisals.

Barry nodded, 'You're organised. My managers usually leave it to the last minute.'

He smiled and relief washed over her. She moved her hands, clamping them between her knees, while he looked at his notes.

When Barry looked up the smile had gone. 'Now, about that complaint.'

Shelley shifted in her seat again, unwilling to ask questions to hurry this along but anxiously wanting him to get to the point.

'Some of the graduates returned to their course saying you challenged what they were being taught.' He frowned, pausing to watch her. 'I know you didn't want to move into this area, and I hear you don't agree with our policies, but this is your role now. We can't have you picking a fight with the graduates to prove a point.'

'Oh.' Shelley unclasped her hands and sat up straight. Their eyes met and she held his gaze defiantly. 'Yes, I liked the area I was in and hadn't wanted to move but...here I am. What do you mean 'you hear' I don't agree with the policies? How would you hear that?'

'Oh, come on, Shelley. Some of your colleagues and I play golf, you don't make a secret of your thoughts, so let's say no more.'

'That's ridiculous. Gossip that's...'

His face darkened and the frown burrowed deeper. 'But it is true, isn't it?'

The hairs on the back of her neck stood up. Shelley wanted to go on, fight for her rights but decided it was better to focus on the complaint.

'I didn't deliberately go into the machine room to start a fight or to voice a contrary opinion. I heard the graduates talking and was surprised at how they're being taught such a politically biased method of interpreting laws, that's all.' She swallowed back the rest of the thought that laws should be interpreted according to the actual wording.

Barry squinted at Shelley 'Well, I've got bigger issues to deal with.' He swept his arm towards the papers nestled on his desk. 'So,

233

I don't want any more complaints about you to come across my desk.' He paused. 'In this area, there is no room for dissension on the policies we administer. The training is in accordance with the policies. The government monitors our performance very closely, they expect us to follow their instructions and senior management will accept no arguments.'

'But...but...' Shelley bristled, what happened to being apolitical? Were they now just mindless automatons performing their roles without thought?

'I won't hear any arguments about it, that's the way it is. In your role, you need to comply with and reinforce the management position regardless of your personal opinions. If you can't do that, then, we will review your suitability for this level.'

The threat was clear, and she gritted her teeth to keep her response from boiling over. She nodded despite her sudden awareness that he had pushed her towards actions that, prior to this meeting, would have been unthinkable. He'd challenged her to do what was right, not just to toe the line. Barry took her nod as compliance little knowing he had pushed her the other way.

'OK, now that's understood.' Barry turned back to his computer, the meeting obviously finished, and Shelley retreated into the corridor her cheeks flushed and her pulse racing.

***

Still shaking from her meeting with Barry this afternoon, Shelley sipped at her coffee and described what had happened to Adrian.

She didn't tell him about the copied file, she wasn't sure why not and the story lost a little of its impact without it. Adrian was sympathetic anyway.

His flat was smaller than hers, with views across the rusty rooftops of the east end of town. It was close to the Hutt street cafés, which made his lack of space more bearable. It was an older flat but had been renovated in a modern style. A bank of cupboards along one wall formed his kitchen and the small two-seater dining table doubled as extra bench space. His kitchen was clean but cluttered. The comfortable sofa faced the television which was tucked into a corner. Pride of place was Adrian's desk, a laptop sat on top and it was open and switched on. A kitchen chair served as his office chair. She'd have loved to peek at the bedroom, curious if he was the tidy or messy type, but the door was firmly closed.

The newly painted walls, all beige and soft hues, were given life by the artworks Adrian had neatly arranged in symmetrical patterns about the walls. Shelley enjoyed scanning the selection, recognising copies of some she had seen at the Musée d'Orsay in Paris. The sweet painting of the girls playing the piano sat beside some lesser-known artists.

'I wonder where the leaks are coming from? They seem very worried about them,' Adrian asked.

'I don't know. They haven't been groundbreaking. It's restricted information, but low-level stuff. It could be one of the junior staff.' She went through the names of her staff, considering each in turn but none seemed a likely candidate. She grimaced, remembering Barry's talk to her. 'I can't believe questioning an interpretation can get me into trouble.'

She stood up and peered out of the window. Adrian followed her and wrapped his arms around her protectively. He pulled her back to lean against him and she relaxed. Shelley snuggled into him, savouring the warmth of his body as his arms offered her reassurance. When he kissed her neck, her pulse raced. But, then, he moved back, creating a space between them, and breaking the spell.

He cleared his throat. 'I'm going to Sydney tomorrow,' he said.

Shelley detected an underlying tension. 'Oh. Is it for pleasure or work?'

The change of mood suggested there was more to this than she understood, and she regretted her choice of words.

'I'm going to a conference, but it ties in with Klaus' arrival in Sydney.' Adrian cleared his throat again and sat on the sofa. Shelley followed.

'Is he coming to Adelaide too?'

'He wasn't sure, so I'm meeting him there.' He turned towards Shelley, 'He's bringing an old friend of mine from Africa, Yasmine.'

The look on his face as he said her name made Shelley wary. This friend meant something. A cold shiver sped up her spine. He looked more uncomfortable than she'd seen before.

'I've mentioned her before, haven't I?' he added.

Shelley shook her head and he grimaced.

'We were in Angola together. We were both doctors with Medicins Sans Frontiéres. She arrived shortly after me. We became…good friends…there were four of us working there, we called ourselves The Formidable Four. Just before I left…Georg and Yasmine married…and they stayed on together.'

His unease sounded an alarm bell in her head.

Adrian got up and strode to his kitchen bench. 'Coffee or tea?' he asked, not looking at her. His tone was lighter but sounded forced.

Shelley shook her head. 'No thanks.'

She really wanted to ask more questions about Yasmine. He fumbled with the cups and coffee jar and then sat back down.

'Have you kept in touch with Georg and Yasmine since you left?' Shelley started on what she hoped was safe ground.

'No, not really. I sometimes follow their work on the web, but they're busy…' He looked up at Shelley and his smile only affected the corners of his mouth. 'I thought while I'm in Sydney I could follow-up on the coroner who first saw Ayisha. I looked it up and Dante is a University colleague of mine. He might be able to tell us more.'

His face had returned to its usual animated state and the clouds in his eyes had lifted. The discussion about Yasmine had finished, but for Shelley, it was a temporary break. They would have to continue this talk another time.

'That would be great. I only know Ayisha fell outside a brothel in King's Cross. Maybe he could tell you more. Even a cause of death would help.'

Adrian made notes then dropped his pen onto the paper and stood up. 'Given my great culinary skills, why don't we go down to the café on the corner and grab a late dinner?'

His genuine smile was back, and Shelley was relieved.

'That sounds great,' she agreed.

Tensions set aside for tonight, they walked arm in arm to the café, their conversation returning to their easy chatter and restoring a sense of closeness, if not the intimacy she craved.

Over dinner Adrian also told her his good news; there had been a victory in a court case.

'It's a damning assessment of Australia's human rights.'

His eyes sparkled as he told her Australia had been found guilty of 150 violations of international law by detaining refugees for over four years without appeal rights. 'The UN ordered the release from detention of forty-six refugees, mostly Sri Lankan Tamils. Let's see if this has an impact. The finding cites detention as inflicting serious psychological harm on detainees and this is in breach of the International Covenant on Civil and Political Rights.' His expression was animated and very appealing.

'It's a great win, even though it only applies to those people who have failed the security assessment, but we might be able to apply it more broadly,' he added.

They continued to chat easily, and Shelley was determined to not think about Yasmine and the trip to Sydney, even though it was proving very difficult.

Chapter 25

Rigid with fear, Wrogarth couldn't summon sufficient will to move. Usually so decisive, he was now frozen in space. The carefully juggled aspects of his life were falling and everything he'd worked for was crashing around him. The scene before him seemed surreal. The red smudges on the carpet and down the stairs concluded at a dark crumpled mass. His stomach knotted with a wave of panic as he remembered. Her limp and lifeless body lay in a heap at the bottom of the stairs. Finally, shock jolted him into action. He heard a quiet groan and raced down the stairs. Her pulse was barely noticeable to his trembling fingers. Not quite lifeless. Nausea surged up in his throat. There was so much blood. Its redness was bright and accusing and it was everywhere. It was splattered along the wall and on the carpet and stairs. He forced himself to look at her. The strangely twisted body was devoid of human form. The force of the fall had crushed her into a hideous crumpled doll. This couldn't be Bev.

He hesitated, momentarily unsure what he should do, then fumbling for the phone, he regained his composure. He dialled the ambulance first, then Daryl. Mark would ask too many questions. Daryl would help sort things out, he always did. Shifting his weight from foot to foot, he gave his version of events. He controlled the intense desire to babble and relieve his conscience.

'I've called the ambulance. Bev's fallen down the stairs…awful mess…I think so…her pulse is very faint though. Yes, yes, we quarrelled but…' The words spilled from his mouth in a gush filling in the questions he expected Daryl to ask.

'What she fell from the top of the stairs?' Daryl finally broke through the explanation.

'Yes, she just fell down the stairs. She'd had a couple of drinks.' Wrogarth added. It was worth a try.

The image of her battered face immediately before the fall flashed into his mind, her look of terror was imprinted on his memory.

'Where were you?'

'I was in the bedroom and rushed out when I heard her. That's enough questions! Just meet me at the bloody hospital.'

Wrogarth changed his clothes, stashing the blood-splattered shirt and trousers in a garbage bag at the back of the wardrobe. The ambulance sirens neared and flashing red and blue lights strobed through the windows as they approached the house. The paramedics rushed to Bev and Wrogarth gratefully stepped back. Their muffled

241

but urgent voices snapped out orders of action and he could tell that Bev was still alive. Eventually, they stabilised her and told him she was in critical condition. They had to get her to the hospital immediately. Wheeling her and the attached life support apparatus into the ambulance, the paramedic stood back and without thinking, Wrogarth climbed in after her. They got to the hospital quickly, but it wasn't quick enough for him. He needed to get out, get away from the evidence of what he had done.

Daryl was waiting at the hospital and guided Wrogarth into a private room. Then Wrogarth recoiled with horror seeing faint red smears still soiling his hands. Daryl helped him clean up and speaking quietly but firmly, took charge. Wrogarth felt reassured; it was the Daryl of old. Mark was on his way and Daryl assured Wrogarth they would sort out whatever needed to be done.

Wrogarth repeated his version of events. 'She fell down the stairs,' watching Daryl's face register unasked questions. 'OK…Yes, we quarrelled and I got riled. But she tripped and fell down the stairs.' His voice trembled but he felt stronger and a feeling of belligerence was taking over.

He avoided Daryl's eyes. The man understood more than he should, there was suspicion lurking there. Wrogarth clenched his lips shut. When Mark arrived, his curt tone left no doubt he was peeved that Daryl had been called first. Wrogarth turned his back on them, leaving Daryl to lead Mark to the other room to sort out the press release.

This couldn't happen again. His temper had spun out of control before, but never like this. He'd buy her flowers when she recovered. Maybe they could take a holiday after the election. Go somewhere nice, somewhere where they could relax together.

Daryl returned carrying two little white pills. He offered them to Wrogarth explaining they would help him to rest. They offered to prepare a cot next to Bev, but he insisted on taking a room next door. It was going to be a long night waiting for the surgeons' verdict.

The next morning the headlines screamed the news. Beverley Wrogarth was in the hospital in a serious condition after falling down the stairs at their home in Sydney. She was fighting for her life. They drew attention to Wrogarth's grief, describing him as the staunch and supportive devoted husband by her side.

The pills had worked well, and the next morning, Wrogarth felt refreshed. He'd recovered from the initial shock and was now back in business mode. He smiled, the press release had the right tone and he liked the way it highlighted his support. It hadn't mentioned Bev wasn't responding to treatment, something he himself didn't want to think about. This morning the doctors explained that her injuries were severe, much worse than expected from a fall and gently quizzed him about the accident. She had serious contusions on the brain and indeterminate neck injuries which could result in permanent disability. There was possible brain damage, and Wrogarth felt they were preparing him for the worst.

Today he felt stronger, able to resist the prodding and he stuck to his story, embellishing only where he felt it was useful. He was confident that Bev would confirm his version of the events when she regained consciousness.

He paced the room, reluctant to sit by her bed. He couldn't look at her. He hated being in that room, but it was expected. He couldn't sit here waiting for her response, it could take days. Wrogarth thought of the last message from Petro. The man's timing was diabolical. He swore under his breath and the nurse checking Bev's vital signs turned sharply. He ignored her; his mind securely focused on business. He needed to sort things out. He hadn't known the whole Sydney brothel story until Mark explained it to him yesterday. What a mess! Despite not wanting to be involved in details, this scenario was going too far. It was an unnecessary risk and he was angry that Mark had let it develop.

Bev's accident would wipe everything else off the front page for a while, but that might not be enough.

Daryl's voice roused him. He offered to take care of routine matters and pass everything else to Tim Curleigh. The vein in Wrogarth's temple reacted, springing into action at the very mention of the name.

'Tim is not going to take over anything.'

Wrogarth argued that he needed to get back to work. It would take his mind off Bev. But he was thwarted by Mark who advised him to stay by her side one more day.

'You could stop in at the office when there's no-one around, or better still, Daryl or I could bring you any important or urgent business at the hospital,' Mark explained, back in his element as a trusted adviser. 'You need to show the depth of your personal grief and worry. Be the caring husband. It will get the sympathy vote. But the public also wants to see that you're still on the job.'

Wrogarth felt trapped. He was pacing the floor and that was no relief at all. He wished he could be anywhere but here.

Chapter 26

Barry's eyes bored into Shelley; she hadn't expected to be in trouble again so soon. To her relief, his annoyance was not aimed at her. The section was being shut down while a high-security investigation was conducted. The leaks so far had been minor, although Shelley wondered at the response if that were true. Maybe senior management wanted the leaks plugged before they became significant.

'There's another thing.' Barry's voice was brittle, and Shelley went on alert.

'IT tells me your user ID has accessed data from Resettlement Branch.' He studied his notes then peered at her over the reading glasses perched on the tip of his nose.

Shelley shifted in her seat trying to maintain her composure.

'I haven't –,' she started to protest but Barry cut her off.

'You have. You've been looking into the new arrival files and the file of...' he looked down again, then tutted, 'Ayisha, what's her name?'

Shelley smiled shakily, the best she could do given her nervousness.

'Oh, that!' She tried to sound casual and off-hand. 'I'm sorry. I was looking up some of my old files. I'd heard Ayisha had died. I was her case-manager and I just wanted to find out what had happened.'

Barry rested against the back of his chair, his face set in a grim mask and she realised her manner hadn't had the desired effect.

'Well, you've breached your authority. You know you're not authorised to access files from your old area, you should have had your access adjusted.'

'I was just –'

'No, you can't justify this serious breach of security. Your access will be amended but this is the second time I've had to speak to you, there better not be a third.' He shook his head. 'Now, HR will escort you to your desk so you can pack up your personal things and go home.'

Shelley trembled as she reached for the door. She hesitated, undecided if she should try to put a better spin on this. His icy stare told her that was a bad idea. She muttered her goodbye and slipped quickly out of the door.

The full-scale investigation meant the Adelaide, Perth, Alice Springs, Darwin, and even South Australian regional sections were closed until further notice. Contractors would take over the other sections within the department. This was highly irregular. How could they allow a contractor to administer their own checks and make their own funding decisions?

The leaks this time were to WikiLeaks and senior managers were panicking. The UN was also adding to the government's woes and the department's legal team were under pressure to find a loophole. The Federal Police were involved, and Shelley assumed they were conducting the investigation.

***

At home Shelley paced, hugging herself in a vain attempt at reassurance. She hadn't passed on any information, yet she felt strangely complicit. A second report had mentioned the Sydney solution but mentioned it was being applied in all capital cities. Asylum seeking families were being separated. The women and children were held in inner-city centres while the men remained in remote areas. All able-bodied detainees were being sent to work to offset the costs of their detention. There was no reference to what jobs they were doing but the contractors lamented their lack of English. How had she not heard of this before?

'I guess English language classes would help them get higher-paying jobs,' she muttered.

Again, the report noted security breaches. What were they? As a result, they were rolling out security monitoring improvements at all detention centres. Strangely they were starting with the home detention facilities in the cities.

Her conversation with Beetle this morning had been interesting. The witness reports he'd tracked down placed Ayisha inside the 'gentleman's club' on the third-floor. His copies had been heavily censored, taking out both information and meaning and the most important details were missing. Why would Ayisha go into a brothel? Shelley couldn't think of a plausible answer.

The bouncer's witness statement said she had created a disturbance. He'd grabbed Ayisha's wrists, but she broke free and ran to the end of the corridor. He said she'd screamed 'I can't take it anymore,' turned and jumped out of the open window. He suggested she may have been disoriented and forgotten that she was on the third-floor. It was unbelievable. Ayisha spoke good English but always broke into her native tongue when she was under stress. She'd never have said that.

Since giving his statement, the bouncer had disappeared. Another headache formed above Shelley's right eye. They'd been more frequent lately. She yearned to talk to someone. Adrian was in Sydney and she'd tried his number twice, but he wasn't answering. She didn't know where Jason was. Kylie would be a pragmatic ear, but Shelley was reluctant to involve her. So, for now, she would have to work through this on her own, but she was stuck.

A headache continued to pulse behind her eyes, and she craved a change of scenery and some fresh air. She grabbed her car keys and next thing she knew; she was behind the steering wheel driving down Anzac Highway to Glenelg. Being a weekday, it should be quieter.

Parking in a side street, she sauntered to the beachfront, breathing deeply as she stared at the small rolling waves. In summer, she avoided Glenelg. Swimming in seawater, getting sand into everything and rubbing shoulders with the hot, lotion-covered crowds didn't appeal to her. However, a quiet, contemplative walk along the beachfront was always welcome and at this time of year, the Esplanade was the perfect setting. She turned her face towards the rays and closed her eyes to bask in the weak warmth. Around her, young mothers wheeled pushers along the Esplanade. As the scene of every-day life unfolded before her, some of her nervous energy dissipated.

The tide was out and the sand carting project was well underway. Large earth-moving machines rumbled on the beach, jerking, scraping and scooping, leaving strange patterns in the sand and interrupting her quiet contemplations. The annual attempt to combat nature's relentless tides and their redistribution of the sand between the various beaches, lasted several weeks and caused much disruption. The gigantic growling machines attracted the attention of a small cluster of preschool children, their noses pressed against the fence to watch these monsters perform their tricks while their mothers waited patiently for their interest to wane. A hint of sadness and a little envy washed over her as she watched their sweet intent faces. At thirty-eight she was running out of time.

The wheels of Shelley's mind churned, but she couldn't put the pieces together. Barry had warned her, but it had also sparked a flame of anger and with it an unusual feeling of boldness.

Restless still, she strode along the Esplanade, bursting into a brisk pace that made her heart pump faster. She couldn't escape the loop of thoughts circling through her mind. There were so many disparate issues, the terrorism shadow looming over them, the death of poor Ayisha, the strange SIS reports. She didn't understand what was happening or which to concentrate on first. She remembered again Ayisha's use of the word 'unspeakable'. What was that all about? Her mind circled through the options, lingering too long on the dark ones.

What was happening at the detention centres? The Prime Minister's office was overseeing Serpentco's operations, but information from Beetle suggested they were a law unto themselves. Perhaps this was all a distraction and she should concentrate on finding out what happened to Ayisha.

She longed to talk to Adrian but was afraid of unleashing his unstoppable fervour. There was so much about him that she admired; his gentle toughness, his caring and the way he'd devoted large parts of his life to helping others. He was the kind of man she'd thought she wanted in her life, yet doubts gnawed at her. There could be no turning back if she told him what she knew, and she was afraid of the consequences.

The Esplanade Kiosk offered a coffee break as the clouds cast her into shadow and the breeze became a cold wind. She sat outside sipping at the strong dark and hot liquid, bracing against the elements and hoping they would stimulate decisiveness. It worked. By the time she had finished her coffee she had come to a decision, it was risky, but it was the right thing to do, she was sure of it.

Back at the flat, she rummaged in her bag for the keys and then recoiled as the door creaked open; it wasn't locked. She was sure she had locked it before she'd left.

She peered through the gap and exclaimed, 'Oh my God, what's happened here?'

Items were scattered across the room. She gingerly stepped over the threshold and an indefinable odour, sour and stale, greeted her. Shelley shivered. She'd narrowly missed the intruder. In the bedroom, her clothes were spread across the floor. Cupboard doors were open, and the remaining items pushed into lumpy piles. Her mementos, gathered over a lifetime, littered the floor. She bent to pick one up, then stopped herself. The crystal bell from Switzerland lay in pieces on the floor amid the shards of the vase from Barcelona and fragments from unidentified objects that she would eventually miss.

Startled by a sound from across the room, she turned, adrenaline pumping. The lounge room curtain flapped in a burst of cold wind, catching on the bookcase beside it. She let out her held breath. A gold chain lay on the carpet in front of the open window, glistening with every flutter of the curtain. Sweat beaded her top lip and she swallowed her panic down. Shelley picked her way across the mess into her bedroom. Papers were strewn about the room; jemmy marks scarred the two-drawer filing cabinet and receipts and documents lay crisscrossed over the floor. She ran to her jewellery box, perched askew on the chest of drawers, its compartments open or missing. All her gold jewellery was gone. She searched through the pieces still spread across the drawers and tears scorched her eyes. The beautiful ruby engagement ring inherited from her grandma was gone. She gasped, so was the small gold band Aunt Maddie had given her as a present for her twenty-first birthday and the small locket she'd bought in Venice. They were all gone.

'The bastards,' she railed.

The kitchen and bathroom had signs of intrusion too. Recoiling from the chaos and resisting her desperate need to tidy up and restore order, she picked up the phone. Her hands shook as she dialled the emergency number and she gave her details, forcing her words through her constricted throat. Then standing awkwardly by the door she waited for the police to arrive, panic and anger fighting for prominence.

'Holy cow,' a voice behind her exclaimed, making her jump. 'What happened here?'

Her neighbour whistled down her ear. Shelley waved her hand across the room. 'I've been broken into.'

'Oh no,' he said, looking around Shelley's sparsely furnished flat.

'They've taken my jewellery. I'm not sure what else is missing.'

'I blame drugs, you know. Those bastards should get a job.' his outburst attracted others as they wandered up the staircase to their flats. The old lady from across the corridor, Shelley didn't even know her name, brought her a cup of tea and another neighbour offered to help to clean up once the police had finished. She thanked them as she shakily lifted the cup and spilled sweet, milky tea into the saucer. Relieved when the police finally came, she followed them inside.

She carefully scanned the mess to itemise what was missing, each sweep making her heart sink further. The police dusted for fingerprints, examined the broken front door lock and open window. The police said it was an expert job with no traces to identify the intruders. They explained there'd been a rash of burglaries lately in which mainly gold jewellery had been stolen. This robbery had the same pattern. They gave Shelley little hope of recovering any of the items. Her jewellery was sentimental, not valuable in dollar terms, but irreplaceable.

Then as Shelley scanned her bedroom, she noticed the laptop was missing. Her precious photos, emails, and documents and most of all her emails were on there. She'd backed it up last week, but a quick search revealed that her back-up drive was also missing. Her hands turned clammy. If this was just a burglary then the thieves had robbed her of memories and connections but, if this was more... She didn't want to think about that scenario. She rummaged through her handbag; she still had the USB containing some photos she'd planned to have printed.

Once the police left, she rang a locksmith and distracted herself with tidying up. She declined the offers of help from neighbours; there had been enough intrusions into her flat for one day. She phoned her mum who insisted Shelley stay with them for the night, and she agreed. The phone back on its stand, a wave of anger made her want to lash out. Instead, her eyes welled, overflowing into heavy drops and her whole body slumped onto the sofa as she sobbed.

Packing a small overnight bag, her eyes rested on the desk and her heart lurched. She hadn't noticed before, but her briefcase wasn't there. How had she not seen it was missing? She tore at the newly tidied drawers, spilling clothes back onto the floor. She searched all the likely places and then all the unlikely places. It was definitely gone. The SIS report was in that case. Shelley's whole body shook violently as she tried to order her thoughts. Who had that report now? Would they recognise its significance? Perhaps she should scour the area in case it had been dumped. Stealing the briefcase didn't match the pattern the police had described and again her head throbbed as her stomach tightened into a hard knot. How much trouble was she in now?

***

Adrian paced the international airport waiting lounge, his stomach gurgled but he suppressed his strong urge to flee. Their plane had landed but they had to clear customs and immigration first. He checked his mobile, relieved there were no more messages. Passengers pushing carts of luggage emerged from the sliding doors. The first three groups were met by friends or family and were engulfed by squeals of delight, warm hugs, and kisses. Adrian looked away. The hall filled with more happy noises as more people exited the arrival doors. Usually, the joy of reunions was a lovely experience to watch, but not this time.

He felt a light tap on his shoulder. Klaus looked tousled and tired. Behind him, a familiar face made Adrian's heart lurch. Yasmine stepped forward, her hair a little shorter than he remembered, but otherwise, she hadn't changed. That infectious smile was still there, and he couldn't take his eyes off her. She stepped forward and embraced him with a generous hug.

'You haven't changed a bit,' she gushed, holding him so close he could feel her heartbeat. 'It's been much too long.' She stepped back, keeping him at arm's length as her eyes swept over him. 'Georg sends his love.' She let him go and Adrian steadied himself.

'You look fabulous.' Adrian found his voice – a shadow of its usual timbre.

Klaus clapped them both on the back.

'Hey, what about me? Don't I look great too?' he teased as he stepped between them and walked towards the exit.

Adrian led them to the hire car. The two-bedroom apartment he'd arranged meant they were all together. There was sufficient room to meet and talk and Klaus and he could share a bedroom.

Close to Darling Harbour, Klaus and Yasmine would easily find somewhere for dinner tonight.

***

Jason downed his third beer, but it didn't feel as good as the first two. The effects were wearing off. He fumbled in his pocket, eventually pulling out his mobile. He scrolled through the contact list again, groaned then stuffed the mobile back in his pocket. It was no use, Adrian had his own troubles, and now Yasmine was here.

He watched the other patrons lounging at the bar. The man in the corner reminded him of his father, haughty and loud, the kind who liked to parade his importance and peddle his influence. Jason's thoughts turned to those uncomfortable dinner parties, their formality like an ABC period drama. His dad stiff until he'd downed a couple of drinks and the transformation to charming host began. More drinks and the bawdy joker appeared. At least he'd have the sense to stop there, whereas mum just ticked along, purring and smoothing the conversations expertly, stroking egos and oiling the wheels of business, because those dinners were always about business.

He hadn't planned to be in Sydney, but now he was here he was of little use. As always, he wanted to help but couldn't.

He took another gulp. He'd thought his life would be different by the time he got to forty. He loved his single life, not having to think about anyone else or compromise, but there was something missing.

Jason picked up the phone again, this time scrolling through to Shelley's number. Maybe it was time to confide in someone. She would listen and understand. Maybe it was time to tell her about his family.

The phone rang and rang, finally going to the answering machine before he hung up. He didn't want to ring her mobile. He didn't want to interrupt anything. Putting his phone back in his pocket he ordered another drink and tried to ignore the loud man in the corner.

Chapter 27

Muffled conversations floated down the corridor and Daryl's nerves twitched with every set of footsteps. Uncomfortably poised on the edge of the chair, he resisted the urge to pace the room. Banks of monitors beeped a steady rhythm and the oxygen machine whooshed in time, creating a strange hypnotic atmosphere in the dimly lit room. It was late, but that was why Daryl was here. Wrogarth had gone home so he had Bev to himself. Her limp body lay on the narrow hospital bed with a myriad of wires and tubes linked to life-sustaining apparatus. She hadn't woken up yet. The angry mask of dark bruises disguised her usually pretty features. Her laboured breathing as the machine forced air into her lungs was strangely reassuring. Tears pricked at his eyes. He owed so much to this woman.

It was almost twenty years ago, and yet it still felt so raw and new. The smell of hospital disinfectant conjured up vivid memories. Back then, he had fallen apart. It was not his proudest moment. Helping his wife Margaret through her illness had taken all his strength. He'd been stalwart throughout her treatment, staying positive for her sake, even though they both knew it was hopeless. He had held out despite his anxiety and despair. Without her, he had nothing left to fight for, nothing to keep going for. She had been his life.

The suddenness was a tragedy. The diagnosis, the treatment plan, all came at them with a rush. They had concentrated on each stage as it came, not daring to think beyond it or to look up and into the future. It was too frightening to contemplate the 'what ifs', so, they kept their thoughts focused on getting through the operation, then through the chemotherapy, maintaining enough strength to ignore the pain and the anger they both felt. Her death stripped him of the one good thing in his life and left him empty and lost. He drowned in the pain and then drowned in alcohol, hoping it would numb everything else. It did. Drinking could be done alone or in company. People understood that he was grieving. They tried to tell him that he should feel relief that her pain and struggle was over, but how could he when he was still struggling, still in pain. Margaret had never given up and had fought right to the end, but it wasn't enough. People said if you believed and stayed positive you could beat it, but it didn't work. The look in her eyes haunted him, as she grasped his hand and said with a weak smile, 'We'll get through this. We're young and strong.' They didn't.

She'd been young; much too young to be robbed of her future and much too young for them to treat the idea of breast cancer seriously when she first noticed a lump. Their hesitation had been fatal. Distracted by the busyness of life, they told themselves it was probably a false alarm. They were wrong. The aggressive, silent killer spread its tentacles through his beloved Margaret until it had a fatal hold. All he had was the 'what ifs?' and the 'why didn't I?' These questions plagued him. He wondered what else he should have done and had found himself lacking. If only he had been more attentive, if only he had made her seek medical advice sooner. If only was his steady diet.

Bev was almost too peaceful, and he checked her pulse. He had known Bev during his early days in personnel, although not well. It was by chance that they met again a year after Margaret died. Bev was a volunteer at the charity shop on Tuesdays and Thursdays back then.

Her friendship nurtured him like a salve to his wounds and helped him straighten out. It was a hard road, with a few backward slips, but Bev persuaded Wrogarth to give him a job as his assistant. He would never have made it without her.

Now, staring at her bruised face, he wondered, how it had come to this. Huge finger imprints spread across her neck and shoulders with broken blood vessels underneath. Bev had borne the brunt of Wrogarth's violent streak. Daryl shuddered at the scenarios playing out in his mind. She'd cover for him and Daryl could never convince her to let him help her. Maybe now she would.

The weight of what he knew was an unbearable burden. He trudged towards the lifts. On the ground floor, he stepped through the front entrance. A light touch settled on his arm, stopping him abruptly. His mind raced, thinking up credible excuses for still being here. Turning to see the face peering seriously back at him, he relaxed. William was recognisable even if he hadn't seen him for years.

'You,' Daryl said quietly.

He was taller than he remembered, despite his slumped posture.

'I want to see her…but he can't know I'm here. Can you help?'

Daryl nodded. He had to try, if only for Bev's sake. He owed them both.

He ushered William into the lift and up to the fourth floor. There they slipped soundlessly into the laundry room. William selected a clean white coat from the pile in the corner and put it on over his shirt, leaving his coat tucked behind the door.

The guard was in deep conversation at the nurse's station. He glanced up as Daryl and William approached, signalled recognition and returned to his conversation.

The nurse by Bev's side studied William suspiciously. Daryl reassured her and persuaded her to leave them alone with Bev for a while. She muttered that it was highly irregular and should have been cleared by the attending doctor, but left them to take her break. Once she was out of sight, Daryl shook William's hand and left. He wished

Bev could see that William had come to visit and hoped she'd regain at least that much consciousness.

Chapter 28

'Hi, mum.' Shelley always felt like a younger version of herself when she visited home.

'Hello dear, are you alright?' her mother said as she stepped forward, took Shelley's bag and led her inside.

'Yes, I'm fine. I was at the beach when it happened.'

'Thank God!' Her mother put the bag down beside the door. 'Did they make an awful mess?'

'Yes and no. They smashed souvenirs, threw things around and stole my jewellery.'

She walked into the lounge room and was transported back in time. The sombre decor hadn't changed in twenty years. Not even the knick-knacks or photos had changed, except for one new photo of Vonnie and Cal from their last holiday to Bali. Over the mantel was the photo of Shelley and Tom in happier days and Shelley bristled.

Consciously leaving the two recliners, she sat on the floral sofa. Shelley itemised what had been stolen as her mother tutted and gasped, especially when the heirlooms were mentioned. Mum then went to the kitchen.

'Are you on holidays again?' she asked as she returned with a cup of tea for herself and coffee for Shelley

Her mum put the tray on the coffee table and fussed with the cups and saucers.

'Yes…well…'

'You're not sick, are you?' Shelley's mum straightened, holding the cup midway between Shelley and the tray.

'No…nothing like that…I…'

'What's happened? Is something wrong?' Her hand rested at her throat melodramatically, a pose Shelley knew so well. Vonnie had missed out on that one.

'Mum, will you let me answer.' She'd been harsher than she'd intended and her mum's face registered shock. Her eyes brimmed and Shelley regretted her testiness.

'Well, I'm waiting…' Mum said, recovering quickly, but speaking through pursed lips.

'Yes, yes…' Shelley had rehearsed her explanation all the way here but now all her well-constructed sentences and phrases had vanished.

It always happened, leaving her with the clumsy utterances that always got her into trouble. Thankfully the carpet stifled her mum's tapping foot. Finally, Shelley cleared her throat and began.

'They closed our section to investigate recent leaks to the press.'

'Who would do such a thing? Tom said he'd seen some reports…'

'You're talking to Tom about me?'

'Well, he said he'd seen something in the papers and asked me about it. It worried us.' She sounded defensive but Shelley ignored it.

'You didn't bother to ask me though.' Shelley unintentionally snorted as she threw herself against the back of the sofa. 'But, you are still seeing Tom?'

'Well, he visits and –'

'I never call; I never visit.' Shelley finished for her. 'You preferred Tom's company anyway,' she went on, unwilling to let it go this time.

'What a wicked thing to say! We like Tom, but we love you.' Tears brimmed in her eyes again, this time threatening to overflow, and she swiped at them brusquely.

'You always took his side…'

These hurts had prodded Shelley over a long time. Buried deep, they'd never been given voice to her mum before. They were usually confined to her private rants, those times when Shelley stormed about her apartment, alone, upset and trying to excise these hurtful thoughts.

'What sides? There were no sides to take,' her mum insisted.

Shelley hadn't meant to argue and accuse and yet here she was again, making it worse rather than better.

'I'm sorry mum. I didn't mean to…' She slumped into the sofa. The mixture of emotions was so tangled that she couldn't identify a solitary one. She was confused, that's all she knew. But she couldn't let it go.

'When I married, you thought I'd done well and shouldn't jeopardise it. Don't get me wrong, Tom and I loved each other…once…'

She remembered when she and Tom had first met. How happy she'd been when he proposed and how happy her parents had been then too. She should have stopped talking here but she couldn't stem the flow of words. The need to explain, to be heard and understood forced her on.

'We had such plans, but everything changed. You don't know the Tom I know. One promotion after another and he became management material. He liked the status and sense of power. He toed the company line. At first, he baulked at saying things he didn't believe, but over time he got used to it. And me? I had to toe the line too. So long as I agreed with him, life was easy, and I did at first. I didn't really pay attention to how my life was changing, subtly, in small increments.'

Shelley's mum studied her hands, head bent forward, and Shelley couldn't see her face. Her breathing was steady, but she didn't utter a sound, a restraint Shelley hadn't often seen and it spurred her on.

'Our friends were his friends. Their tirades about 'showing asylum seekers they can't just come here when they want to' were cruel. I still remember one of them talking about staff cuts calling older workers who struggled with change 'deadwood'. It made me think of dad. Loyalty meant nothing, commitment or working hard all your life was just something they sneered at. They never thought in human terms.

'They sent their kids to elite schools, bought only brand names and imported flash cars and had mortgages that stretched them so far that a 0.05% increase would snap their grip. I didn't fit in. Worst of all, they read right-wing papers and believed what they wanted to, regardless of facts. If I offered facts or analysis or a sensible argument, they just sneered.'

The tensions from the last few days had wound Shelley into a tight ball and she couldn't loosen it.

'I was drowning in my life. Then I broke the surface. I took a breath and discovered there was something outside this clique and that was what I wanted.

'Tom hated my job helping asylum seekers. I couldn't believe the propaganda anymore. I realised asylum seekers were human beings just like you and me. They laugh, they cry much too often, they love their children and they dream of a safe life. They risk everything to make a better life for their children.'

Shelley sipped at her water, her throat closing in with emotion.

'I don't know much about all this,' her mother crackled, 'but those illegal immigrants are Muslim, and they are different to us…we don't want them to overrun this country…' The curl of her lip was one Shelley recognised with shock. She'd seen it in her own bathroom mirror.

'Mum, they're not illegal. They're entitled to flee from torture and rape. We get between 3,000 and 20,000 people arriving by boat in any year. It's a drop in the ocean. Italy alone can have hundreds of thousands arrive at their doorstep in a year. The vast majority arriving by boat are legitimate asylum seekers, so they're not illegal. They are in genuine need of help. We have signed international agreements saying they are entitled to do that.

'Tom didn't like my new insights either. But once I'd heard their stories, I couldn't wipe them from my memory. We argued. At first ideological arguments, not personal ones but the arguing led us there. I realised I wasn't allowed to have my own opinions, especially if they differed from his. I must have been blind! We went to Tom's favourite restaurants, overpriced ones where he would meet his friends; the cosy cafés I loved were never convenient. We went to his work functions where I had a role to play and he coached me in what subjects I could talk about, for his career of course. There was nothing of me in my life anymore.

'I struggled to work out where I stopped, and Tom started. Once the cracks on our life opened up, Tom toppled from the pedestal I'd placed him on. The crack exposed the mean-spirited, hard-liner he'd become. He tried to bring me back, first with cajoling, then with teasing and eventually with insults. Being called a bleeding-heart, emotional or irrational was not an insult if the alternative was being cold, greedy, self-centred and purely selfish.'

Her mother moved across to sit beside her, resting a light warm touch on Shelley's shoulder. Shelley looked up into tear-filled eyes and the floodgates opened. The force of emotion, the unburdening left a vulnerable self and Shelley buried her head in her mother's shoulder and cried. Not just because the experience had hurt but that it was still holding her back. She'd struggled to move on with her life or trust someone again.

They sat like this until the emotion was spent and the tears subsided. Shelley sat up, drying her eyes roughly with embarrassment. She apologised; she hadn't meant to do this.

'We didn't know…We didn't know you were so unhappy.' Her mother's voice was breaking up.

'No, I never told you. You liked Tom too much. I didn't know how to explain.'

Her mother sat silently, her lips moving in an effort to speak but not finding the words.

'Maybe he could change. He seems to miss you,' she finally said what to her mind was a consolation, but Shelley recoiled.

'I could never go back. I'm still working out who I am and who I want to be but I know I couldn't go on being what Tom wanted.' Shelley swallowed. 'Besides, he took up with Samantha so quickly, I realised she'd been in the background for a while. I just hadn't seen it.'

Her mother shifted uncomfortably in her seat and Shelley continued.

'I've made new friends and regained old ones. This is my second chance. I am rediscovering who I am, what I care about and what I stand for. I'm on the right track.'

They heard the front door, Shelley's dad popped his head around the door frame, his hair greyer than Shelley remembered, but his smile was the same.

'Oh hello, I thought that was your car.'

He was wearing crumpled bowls whites and held his hat in his hands. Placing his case and hat on the floor he wandered over and hugged Shelley. He gave her an odd look, turned to her mother, then back again, then offering to make a cup of tea or coffee he made his escape.

***

'The trip was not as useful as I hoped, but valuable anyway.' Klaus perched on the edge of the seat, leaning towards Adrian as if trying to physically extract a reaction. 'The mining companies operating over there are up to something, I just know it.' He paused briefly and frowned, 'Are you okay? You seem miles away.'

'Yes, Yes. I didn't sleep well last night, a strange bed and everything.' Adrian explained. He waved his hand dismissively, trying to make light of the issues weighing him down.

'Yasmine?' Klaus asked scanning Adrian's face and posture.

Klaus knew about Yasmine, but he didn't know everything. Adrian grunted to avoid further discussion, he'd thought about it too much already and there was so much more to think about now. 'Sorry, go on, what were you saying?'

Klaus brushed his hands through his sparse hairline. 'I checked with clinics in the area but they won't release any data, especially to someone who could jeopardise their funding.'

'What will you do now?'

'Environmental groups are lobbying the UN to force independent tests but Ortansea is blocking them, saying they must maintain commercial confidence. They argue that the government has current test results and given permission to proceed, so they're clean. The situation needs international pressure on the Angolan Government to demand proper independent testing. But the miners are very powerful.'

'Who owns Ortansea? They're multinational, aren't they? Maybe their home country could apply pressure.'

Klaus laughed, catching Adrian by surprise. Adrian had been serious.

'You remember the incident in the Congo where an Australian mining company got involved in local politics, even aiding in the massacre of local protesters. It wasn't until there was an international outcry that Australia finally applied pressure, and even then, it was pretty weak.'

'You're starting to sound as cynical as me,' Adrian said although he felt no joy about it.

'Maybe it comes with the job. Ortansea is a consortium with mainly Russian interests and some British, Australian and American involvement. I don't expect much pressure to be brought to bear. Interestingly I heard they're having financial difficulties though. Maybe the fines are having an impact. I can't find their subsidiary or joint venture details; their company structures are a nightmare.'

'Big business uses complicated interwoven structures to 'minimise' their tax,' Adrian said. His own efforts to look into the asylum seeker issues had been slowed by the many people and levels involved. The information was guarded by the company with the contract to run the detention centres. The frustration of trying to find leverage was exhausting him.

'Yes, you have to be an expert to untangle them. I'm sure there is more to the secrecy than just tax too, but they avoid questions about their profits or earnings. The commodities boom and oil shortage have been a godsend for them, prices have gone through the roof. Of course, they're worried countries will want a bigger stake, a few countries are already reviewing their tax structures.' Klaus shook his head slowly. 'You know how it is, the more money these companies make the more they want. It is never enough. Now that Ortansea is before the courts again, it's no wonder they're touchy about anyone snooping around. They're claiming this new episode of dirty water dumping is all a big mistake, but the evidence looks solid.'

'Again!'

'Yes. Ortansea's oil trading arm has been buying contaminated oil cheap from South America and Africa for years. Once clean they sell the good oil for healthy profits, or should I say unhealthy profits.' He chuckled then turned serious again. 'The Swiss chemical plant that produces their fracking chemicals is also researching improvements for the cleaning process. They're trying to make it both cheaper and less dangerous. My friend says there are serious concerns about the chemicals used in the cleaning process. She can't reveal too much, but her brother is another story. He used to work there too but left after raising his concerns. I'm trying to track him down.'

'Where is he now?'

'Unfortunately, he's in Asia somewhere. She thinks he's avoiding people. What I have so far though...' Klaus reached for his notebook, flicking pages until he found the one he wanted. 'The cleaning process is simple but very toxic. They pump in large amounts of caustic soda with a catalyst and the by-products settle on the bottom, they call them slops and from what I hear that's exactly what they are.'

'Sounds nasty.'

'It is. That's why it's been outlawed by the European Union. The black slops stink, that's how the French authorities discovered the illegal dumping. The slops could be treated to make them safe, but the process is expensive, and obviously, Ortansea think it's cheaper to be fined.' Klaus swallowed and smiled a wry smile at Adrian. 'They may discover they were wrong. What I don't understand, is how they are still buying massive amounts of dirty oil as well as extracting barrel loads from their African oil rigs and selling clean oil. I am curious about what they're doing.'

'Do they clean the oil at a specific plant? Could they be treating the slops with a new process?'

'My friend says they hadn't made any progress in developing a cheaper process and as far as she knows, no-one else has either. The lab is still producing the catalyst for the old process in the quantities Ortansea need so...' Klaus sat back, and Adrian followed.

'How toxic are the slops?' Adrian asked quietly.

'I'm not a chemist, but it might mean something to you. The slops produce hydrogen sulphide which leaks into the environment. Anyone coming into contact with it becomes seriously ill and can die. The tanker drivers used in France reported a whole series of symptoms. There's a full report on the web.'

Adrian whistled softly, 'So what are you going to do now? And why Australia?'

Klaus cast his eyes over his notes, 'Ortansea has an Australian venture. My friend has been following the money trail and has found a possible connection to Australia and Trisec Oil. Jason was going to look into Trisec Oil, so I'll talk to him too. Not sure if there is anything concrete but it's worth a look.' He grimaced, 'The money trail is the clue. They don't have a plant for the process, they use big tankers to hold the contaminated oil while they clean it and if they are using the old process, they must be paying someone to take the slops off their hands.'

'I thought Ortansea sold out of their Australian mining operations.'

'I wonder if they did or are operating under a different name or using a connected company. I'm following up every lead before I give up. The Australian market is so small it's the easiest place to investigate. My research is covering a few companies that operate in Queensland and Western Australia too. Their use of the new chemical fracking methods might provide an opportunity to get hold of their test results.' He grinned at Adrian. 'And of course, it was a chance to visit.'

'You old softie.' Adrian laughed as he stood to fix another drink.

The door burst open and Yasmine bounded into the room, hair flying and satchel swaying. She dropped her bag and threw herself into a chair. She leaned down to unfasten her shoes while still talking to them. Yasmine could never do just one thing at a time. She looked up into the faces of her friends and laughed the kind of laugh that warmed the room.

'Since you're up, any chance of a drink?' she asked. Her head tilted sweetly towards Adrian.

'Anything for you milady.' Adrian bowed in mock formality. 'We have wine, beer, some coke or sachet coffee or tea bags.'

Klaus ordered a beer, Yasmine asked for a glass of wine and Adrian grabbed himself a can of coke. Klaus sat back, a bemused look softening his features. Adrian could almost see his brain working overtime, but Klaus was a genius if he could work out what was going on.

Yasmine sipped her wine and grimaced. She placed the glass on the coffee table next to her bag.

'I've left copies of the other test results at the lab. They are doing some analysis and will have some initial results by the end of the week. If this lab can't help me, I'm not sure what to do. They were recommended by London, so they must be good.'

'What symptoms are you treating?' Adrian asked distracted by the way Yasmine's mouth moved as she spoke.

Her face transformed into the serious professional. 'On the surface, we have some kind of contact infection, but we don't know what. We haven't seen this before. The symptoms are similar to several bacterial infections we had last year but this one is resistant to everything we try. The symptoms don't make a logical pattern. Yet we've had four deaths…' She swallowed hard, a shadow descending over her eyes. 'It doesn't affect the women but has appeared in some of the children.'

Adrian watched her cross her legs, although not tall, her slender legs stretched along the edge of the chair, rocking gently with pent-up energy. Adrian's mind filled with memories and he had an urge to busy himself with distractions. Rising to make coffee, he didn't notice the look that passed between Klaus and Yasmine.

Chapter 29

Daryl spread today's newspaper in front of him. The office was quiet, with both Wrogarth and Mark at a PR function. He studied the article on page fifteen. He sighed and tapped his pencil on the desk, deep in thought. Wrogarth was becoming seriously entangled. In the past, he'd have maintained control. Daryl bit at his thumbnail. These close alliances with the mining sector were dangerous. They'd proved ruthless in the past and they hadn't changed.

The UN ruling against Australia's indefinite detention of risk-assessed refugees was another problem. Daryl laughed. The media, although not the Waterman Press, had been a co-conspirator in the fear campaign and now they were criticising government policy. The human rights groups challenge to the turn-back policy, even if it languished in the courts for years, would cause serious embarrassment. Wrogarth had emphasised its success and a 'backflip' would brand him as weak on security. Daryl chuckled. Mark would earn his money putting a new spin on it.

The last paragraph in the article carried the bold conclusion. Rogue elements within the Federal Police had taken over the administration. Only in the left-leaning Waterman Press would they go this far. An unnamed source said the Intelligence Agency was unhappy with the handling of key issues. Daryl grimaced as his teeth found the quick of his fingernail and he shook his thumb to disperse the pain. *Another leak? Wrogarth will be livid.* Nothing riled him more than leaks from within the Public Service, the Immigration Department could attest to that.

Daryl reached for Ralph's report. Craving something strong to fortify himself he got up and made a cup of tea instead. He waited for his hands to stop shaking before taking it back to his desk.

Daryl shivered as he read the detailed exposé of Mark and his family history. Ralph hadn't lost his journalist's touch. Mark's mother was related to the Russian crime boss, Petro Golgovich, and Mark had a stake in the Australian operations of the Golgovich Empire. Daryl finally understood. Ralph had evidence, some definite, some tenuous, that connected Mark to a massive crime network controlling security companies, brothels, drug and illegal gun importation and the notorious bikie gangs.

Evidence linked Mark to the pressure being applied to Professor Hutchinson earlier in the year. The professor's son had been deliberately run off the road, and the two events appeared to be linked. The investigating police officer had been removed from the case and the special unit in the Federal Police had closed the file. All research into climate change and mining environmental impacts at the CSIRO had been shut down due to 'funding cuts and shifts in priorities.' Daryl whistled softly; he hadn't realised Wrogarth had gone this far.

Daryl had assumed his boss didn't know how risky Mark's ventures were, but now he wasn't so sure. Maybe believing made it easier to stay and harder to act. How much was he prepared to overlook?

He slumped into his chair. Even the cabinet was disinclined to curb the extreme policies being put forward, each looking after his/her own career. Bev's face forced itself into his mind. He smiled as the image of a young, friendly Bev floated by, but he cringed as the image underwent a metamorphosis to become the bruised effigy he had last seen. He shuddered and closed his eyes to banish the image. His one honourable reason to stay was now gone. He hadn't been able to help her and he cursed the fool he had been. She hadn't really wanted his help, even though at the end she was afraid, she had clung to the role and sense of power too.

He clasped his head in his hands and moaned. He had failed both the women in his life. When they needed him most he'd been found deficient. Bev had needed convincing to save herself. She was more worried about Wrogarth getting caught than his doing something wrong. If Daryl was honest, he had been no better. Margie would have been ashamed. The scotch bottle on the bar in Wrogarth's office caught his eye. It beckoned him through the door. He ruffled his short hair, his heart heavy with longing and the weight of failure.

Daryl stepped slowly around the desk and moved towards the office door. His hand lingered on the doorknob, ready to push the door wide. He trembled and remained silently quivering at the door for a moment, unable to move but strangely unable to let go. A tantalising force dragged at him, pulling him into the room towards oblivion and relief. There was peace inside that room, it would shut out his thoughts and drown the suspicions creeping into his mind. Solace awaited him, all he had to do was move, 'seize the moment' as they said, take a step and drink it in. He could almost feel it, that welcome burn as it slid down his throat, the warmth as it spread from the pit of his stomach to his fingertips, the calmness blanketing his jangled nerves.

Then amongst the images floating past his eyes, there was Margie. Before he could change his mind, he slammed the door shut, turned sharply and collecting his briefcase, strode out of the office. His legs shook, twitching with every step but he also felt exhilarated, lightening his steps on the floor and lifting his head high as he passed the security desk. Margie and Bev would be proud of him and that had to count for something.

Chapter 30

Extensive television coverage of the funeral proceedings complemented the newspapers reports. Shelley couldn't escape it; the funeral was on every channel. The steady drone of TV commentators sounded closer to boredom than respectful interest. It was treated like a royal event except it was more sombre. Speculation on every aspect of the ceremony included scrutinising the mourners' outfits, highlighting VIPs and the planning involved. Almost everything was covered, except how Beverley Wrogarth had died and the cloud of suspicion hanging over the tragedy. The cameras zooming in on mourner's faces distracted Shelley. She picked at her lunch of macaroni and cheese and curled up in front of the heater, watching with part interest.

Her thoughts whirled in a never-ending circle over the same concerns. A tear sat on the corner of her eye, her revelations at her mother's had touched nerves that had been long buried. Personal and professional issues mixed together to form a cloudy soup of indecision. Her mind refused to concentrate or find answers, skimming and switching from issue to issue. Shelley immersed herself in vigorously stirring her lunch.

Maya's suspension and charge nagged at her. Discovering that one of her staff, had been the leak had stunned Shelley. Even if Maya had been more careless than vindictive, the department was going to make an example of her, and Shelley felt sad that such a talented and spirited young woman would lose so much.

The next notch in the continuous circle of tormenting thoughts was Adrian. His mood during their brief phone conversation was unusually sombre. An involuntary tremble shook her as she remembered Yasmine was in Sydney. Whenever he mentioned her name his voice became quiet and Shelley tensed. She wanted to believe Adrian's explanation of Yasmine's visit but he sounded unconvincing. Adrian hadn't told her the full story, but she knew Yasmine was part of his history and she fervently hoped it was finished history. *Why hadn't he booked a return flight?*

Singing from the funeral service rose above her thoughts. The crowded church pews were filled with dignitaries, celebrities and a few unknowns. Some mourned Beverley Wrogarth the woman, her extensive charity work made her more than just the Prime Minister's wife. Shelley didn't know much about her; she didn't read gossip magazines or the society sections of women's publications and she listened intently to the short offerings by those close to the woman.

The smaller graveside gathering was covered by the TV camera crews too. It was strange to allow the media into this private moment. James Wrogarth stood upright and staunch, but close-ups revealed a haggard visage. His daughter stood beside him. Stooped under the weight of her grief, she barely reached his shoulders. Her frailty made her look as though she would collapse at any minute. Unruly wisps of fluffy red hair stabbed out from under the small black hat, the short veil ending above her tightly held mouth. Despite their nearness, father and daughter stood apart. Shelley was reminded of her own family tensions, but even her family would put issues aside at a time like this. A thin young man fidgeting nervously on the other side was identified as her partner.

The commentary explained there were two sons and the camera scanned across and located the older brother. He stood stiffly beside his wife, his rigid face concealing his grief. His two young sons squirmed under the pressure of their parent's hands on their shoulders. The youngest, Shelley guessed he was six years old, fidgeted and kept staring at his older brother whose wide eyes darted about the crowd.

The cameras scanned the crowd searching for the younger brother, William. He hadn't been seen at family gatherings for years and the TV station had no recent photos of him. They screened two primary school photos and one of the complete family in which a young, shy but serious William partially hid behind his brother. The female commentator repeated the rumour that he and his father had not spoken since the scandal that had almost ruined James Wrogarth's career, but Shelley couldn't remember the scandal. The male commentator interrupted and moved the focus back onto the crowd. Despite sweeping back and forth across the small crowd, the cameras couldn't locate William.

James Wrogarth pulled his family to him and the cameras followed. Obediently the family huddled close although noticeably stiff and awkward. They posed as a unified group, albeit incomplete.

A wolfish man caught Shelley's eye as he walked behind a woman's exuberant black hat. The memory of a café in Paris flashed across her mind, and she was certain it was the same face. Shelley tried to find him again but the cameras had moved on. She cursed, failing to remember if he was part of the Prime Minister's entourage. He'd been behind Wrogarth but not immediately behind him. Then she remembered another sighting, with Wrogarth, at the Paris Commerce Centre with the golden gates. He'd accompanied the Prime Minister to the car that day. She had to find out who he was.

The cameras panned back to a wide-angle shot and Shelley spotted a tall figure tucked behind a cluster of mourners. A dark hat and sunglasses obscured his face and his hands were held stiffly in front with the fingers intertwined in a strangely familiar gesture. His dark, nondescript coat seemed heavy in comparison with those of other mourners. Shelley felt a hint of recognition, but again the cameras moved away too quickly. There was something about his stance, the way he held his shoulders and head.

She flicked channels impatiently searching for the same angle, but all the cameras had moved on. Then the wolfish faced man again came into the screen, guiding Wrogarth towards an awaiting camera and the commentator identified him as Mark McCracken, the Prime Minister's personal adviser and PR man.

His name was on those reports as entrusted with the updates on asylum seekers. She remembered his startled face as she witnessed him taking that envelope from Carlew, the mining boss, and was sure that meeting was surreptitious.

Shelley slowly lifted herself from the sofa. She dropped the nearly full pan in the kitchen sink and put the kettle on. The funeral had been replaced with a popular crime series and the graphic violence playing out on her screen with its copious visuals of blood and explicit aggression made her shudder. She switched it off and picked up the book she had recently bought. Like a faulty remote control, her mind kept flicking between the funeral, Mark McCracken, Ayisha, her dilemma, Adrian, Yasmine, and Jason. Shelley, putting down her unread book, resigned herself to a long and sleepless night.

Chapter 31

Shelley flicked through her wardrobe. Adrian was back. But her joy at hearing his voice quickly turned to concern upon hearing his strangely quiet mood. Only his abrupt invitation to go on a Sunday drive to Victor Harbor stopped her headache from springing into action. She breathed more easily when he mentioned Yasmine was flying back to Africa on Tuesday, although he evaded all her questions about Sydney.

The drive to Victor Harbor was a mix of sociable chat and distracted silence. Shelley quelled her nerves and stopped questioning him. They passed the McLaren Vale turn-off and she sat back watching the vineyards pass by her window. Talking to her mother about Tom had made her realise she should enjoy her freedom. Her world would not end if it didn't work out between her and Adrian.

She suddenly remembered to tell him about Mark McCracken and how he was the same man she'd seen in Paris. Adrian listened with interest, then told her about Nice. Again, he sunk back into an even deeper reflective mood. Shelley held back her questions when he apologised for not following up on the coroner but her mind created explanations in the absence of his. Busy? Preoccupied? Whatever it was, he was not willing to talk about it yet.

Despite the wintry weather they strolled across the causeway to Granite Island. The wind whipped her hair and stung her face and she struggled against its strength. Adrian grabbed her hand, his firm grip reassuring and warm. They climbed the stairs beside the café and stopped at the look-out to silently watch the waves crashing onto the rocks below. The waves swelled, gathering volume and momentum and their rhythmic but relentless force unleashed icy saltwater spray into the air. Occasional drops splattered her face and pricked at her already cold cheeks. Adrian withdrew into himself, his deep frown filling Shelley with renewed anxiety. The sea's energy and its release of ozone usually exhilarated Shelley but not today. Adrian seemed unable to tear his thoughts away from some black hole and was slipping further away.

Seagulls swooped and squawked around the grey, streaked rocks. The granite clung to the cliff edge looking ready to topple yet remarkably secure. Granite Island, with its smooth mounds of hard rock covered in red rust and yellow algae, also had patchy clumps of grass and the occasional tree, especially when sheltered from the wind.

Strolling along the clifftop, Adrian again held her hand and helped her over the rough pathway. His touch was so light that any sharp movement would split them apart. At the look-out, Adrian gently held her back to let a straggle of tourists pass. He moved in close and Shelley huddled against him, shielding from the wind. The intimacy reassured her, but she kept her emotions in check. He wrapped his arms around her, and she nestled into the warmth of his chest. His hand lifted and he turned her to face him. Without any preliminaries, his lips pressed down hard on her mouth in unexpected urgency. She tasted the hint of salt on his lips and her whole body ached as she responded with a matching passion. She closed her eyes and a low, guttural moan escaped her throat. His arms held her tightly and she lost all sense of place; all that mattered was the kiss. She was keenly aware of his racing pulse, his warmth, and his desire and it inflamed her, defeating any resolve to hold her feelings back.

Suddenly his arm jerked away, and she was spun around. She opened her eyes to see a blur of green-brown landscape flashing by, replaced by blue sky and grey sea. A rough pair of hands propelled her towards the cliff edge. She slid forward as the loose gravel shifted dangerously under her feet. Shelley reached out for something to hold but her hands found only air. There was no barrier here. Her hands flailed in jerks, grasping at fragments of dirt and stones, but there was nothing to hold her. Behind her, strange sounds mingled with her screams; thumps and smacks punctuated her calls for help and then dull and muffled groans as she fell.

Plummeting, her arms scraped on the rough edges of rock and tree roots, her jacket tore as it caught on a rock, barely impeding her fall. She clawed at the cliff face, but the smooth, hard rocks were unforgiving and sticky wetness mingled with dirt on her fingertips. The wind echoed in her ears along with her racing heartbeat.

All sounds ceased and the world went black as her head thudded against the rocks.

***

Adrian fought harder than he had ever fought in his life. His two assailants were strong and experienced, but he was desperate. He had to find Shelley, he had to help her. Taken by surprise, his reactions were slow, his brain still trying to comprehend what was happening. One minute she was there, the next she was gone. The men kept pushing and working him towards the edge. Their faces obscured by balaclavas, appropriate for the weather but obviously more appropriate for their task. He manoeuvred himself towards a small piece of the balustrade and was successfully fending off their attempts to force him toward the edge, but he was weakening. He wasn't strong enough to hold them both off and now a third had joined the scuffle. His footing slipped on the loose path and his shoes lost traction.

A shout in the distance interrupted their struggle. As his assailants looked up Adrian punched at the face of the nearest man. Pain exploded in his fist as the punch connected and he heard the assailant curse in a language he didn't understand. His partner pulled him off as he raised his fist ready to retaliate and instead, they fled up the gravel path into the low scrub. They'd disappeared before the strangers arrived. The men, cameras swinging and breathing heavily, were closely followed by their partners running awkwardly in heeled boots. They grabbed Adrian trying to make him sit and recover, but Adrian broke free, breathlessly explaining about Shelley. Peering over the side they spied her limp body sprawled across a rust-covered rock. Adrian cried out and started to climb over the edge, but the tourists held him back. They argued he would kill himself and even if he got to her, he wouldn't be able to bring her up. They persuaded him to get help. Reluctantly Adrian called emergency. The culprits had escaped but Shelley was more important.

***

Akbal shivered violently. The scabs forming on his arms testified to the passing of time, but he was alive, that was something to be grateful for. He hadn't expected to survive after those early interrogations. Strangely, his jailers had lost some of their spark and were questioning him less often now, although still with a frightening intensity. Cramped into the cell floor space, where he could only lie in the fetal position, he yearned to stretch out. His body ached, the tension in his muscles and back pulling him into a tighter curl. They had strapped his arm giving it support, although they didn't spare it during their questioning.

He twitched involuntarily and tensed even tighter as the big guard burst into the room surrounding his cell. Akbal feared him most. His laughter rang with pleasure as Akbal crawled into the far corner. Beads of sweat burst from his upper lip and stung his cuts. The sweat on his forehead threatened to form a torrent into his eyes and he shook his head to fling them off. The big guard approached the cell and Akbal cowered into the corner, trying to put as much distance between them as possible.

Unlocking the cell door, the guard lunged for Akbal; he was surprisingly agile for such a big man. As Akbal stretched sideways to avoid his grip, pain wracked his beaten body. His gasp elicited another burst of laughter from the big guard. That's when Akbal noticed the syringe tucked in the other guard's hand. His distraction allowed the big man to pounce and pin Akbal hard against the bars. The air rushed from his lungs and he became light-headed. He couldn't struggle; he was too weak. The broken and bruised parts of his body seized refusing further movement. The needle point pierced his skin sending a burning sensation coursing through his arm. The big guard released him and Akbal tried to move back instead of falling heavily to the floor. A thick fuzziness blanketed his brain, bringing with it a blissful numbness. His limbs disconnected from his will, he was unable to move except for jerky, uncontrolled twitches. Through blurred vision he watched the balaclava-clad jailers watch him. Their eyes sparkled with delight as he struggled on the ground, like a bug poisoned by fly spray. Akbal let the darkness descend, the painlessness a joy after all this time, but the faces of Fatima and Sari swam in the murky gloom before him, crying out to him as he struggled to reach them. They flew further and further away until they were out of reach and Akbal succumbed to his helplessness.

Chapter 32

Efficient bustling nurses popped in to administer salves and pills or bring tea or meals and set up a rhythm in Shelley's otherwise monotonous day. Her head was getting better but there were plenty of other pains. Her whole body still ached, and her fingers felt raw and tender. The heavy plaster cast on her right arm was impressive. Thankfully her memory was vague, and she couldn't remember her terror. One thing that lingered tenderly in her mind was the kiss.

She'd always believed she would live to a ripe old age; her ancestry had the signs of longevity. But now, the throbbing pain in her crushed right side reminded her of how close she'd come to dying. Luckily, it was only her mobile that hadn't survived the fall. Life was tenuous and she should be making the most of her time.

Despite her aches and pains, she was restless already. Newspapers and magazines couldn't distract her. The attack had been deliberate, she was certain of that, but didn't know why.

Adrian's head popped around the corner of the doorway, his sheepish, apologetic look screened by a voluptuous bouquet of flowers.

'Okay to come in?' he asked softly.

'Of course,' Shelley said, almost laughing at his tentativeness.

'I can come back if you're resting.'

'Those flowers are beautiful. One of the nurses could get a vase. I'm glad to have a visitor ...especially you.'

He seemed subdued but Shelley chose to ignore it, teasing him instead. She invited him to pull up a chair. Seeing the sparkle back in his eyes pleased her. Although the dark bags under them and the deep creases along his forehead gave him the look of someone who hadn't slept well lately.

'How are you feeling?' he asked as he drew his chair forward. 'I was really worried. You look a lot better than I'd expected.'

'Hard head,' Shelley laughed, then winced as a pain shot along her ribs. 'Actually, I am a bit sad and sorry for myself. It still hurts when I move but besides a broken rib and my broken arm...' She lifted the cast and grimaced again. 'I'm not too bad. It could have been worse. As it is, I come out tomorrow if all goes well.' She screwed up her face, 'I'm spending a couple of days at mum and dad's.'

Adrian sighed and placed his hand over hers.

'It could have been so very much worse,' he whispered.

They sat quietly for a while.

'I don't even know what happened. I thought I'd lost you.' Adrian swallowed and then composed himself, 'The police think it was a robbery.'

Shelley's mother and sister, Vonnie, bustled into the room talking before they had even come through the door. Shelley's father followed carrying a bunch of colourful flowers from the garden and a bag of grapes, while her mum thrust a box of chocolates at her. Vonnie dumped another bundle of gossip magazines on the bedside table, almost knocking the cup and saucer onto the floor. They rushed over to Shelley and cooed and fussed noisily, not even noticing Adrian.

Adrian sprung up from his chair, offering it to Shelley's mum who nodded and sat down. Shelley did the introductions; she'd hoped they'd meet under different circumstances.

Shelley's mother plied her with questions, many she couldn't answer, and some Adrian filled in the details. Vonnie sat forward eagerly responding to the exciting details with oohs and aahs. Once the short story was exhausted, Shelley watched her mother and sister fuss over this and that. Her dad and Adrian stood quietly against the wall. Shelley cast Adrian a wistful look. She desperately wanted some time alone with him, but she knew her mother was settled in for the afternoon. Vonnie fussed with the magazines, pointing out some story or other that was 'really interesting'.

Adrian muttered about getting back to work, leaned down and kissed her goodbye. Shelley whispered an invitation to please come in to visit again and he smiled.

'I'll try,' he whispered back.

The chaste kiss felt awkward in front of family and Shelley's mother managed to close her mouth in time for Adrian to say goodbye and leave. As her mother fussed with the covers, she plied Shelley with a new set of questions. Her father got a chair and sat back a little from the women. He'd found a paper and immersed himself in the sports pages.

'Tom sends his best wishes,' her mother said coyly. 'He wanted to know if he could visit,' she added in a rush.

'Really?' Shelley asked not bothering to disguise her annoyance.

Her father's head peered over the top of the paper and Vonnie sat back, arms folded across her chest and lips tightly shut.

'I don't want to see him. He should concentrate on Samantha now,' Shelley suggested glaring at her mother.

'He and Samantha have split up,' Shelley's mum continued, almost bouncing as she spoke.

'Well, I guess he'll have to work that out for himself, I don't want him to visit.'

Her mother looked away; her lips twitched, but she remained silent.

Jason couldn't believe it. The mining projects mentioned in this extract were in some of the most environmentally sensitive areas of the national park. The operations spanned miles, mining both a range of metal ores and oil. Jason whistled softly. The output data indicated they'd made a big find. He scratched his head at the mention of oil, he knew they had drilling rigs off-shore and at the Cooper Basin, but hadn't heard of any oil rigs in this area. The environmental impact statement said a sulphide compound was being used to improve the extraction 'efficiency'. He screwed up his face then wrote it down for later.

Jason reread sections to comprehend the jargon. The language was unusually vague for an official environmental impact statement. It was more like a summary than the full report the heading suggested. Gary had done well to track this documentation down. The tables and data set Jason's heart pounding. It was clear the companies had paid handsomely to ensure access to these areas. They wanted more concessions because of the cost of labour in remote areas and the high cost of supplying housing and recreational facilities formed significant restraining factors. They were reducing costs with the use of a support labour force, but Jason couldn't find an explanation of what that meant. He clenched his fist. Despite all the concessions the mining industry received, they were still crying poor. He looked for further references to the support labour force but couldn't find any. Maybe they were using people from the local Aboriginal communities.

Jason picked up the phone and dialled. He knew this number by heart even though he rarely used it.

'Yes,' a tired voice demanded.

Jason took a deep breath. 'I've just read a report on mining in the national parks, what's going on?' he asked as unwanted emotions threatened to spill over.

'What are you talking about?' The voice suddenly sounded alert.

'Those mining projects in the national parks are bigger than the public has been told. When did they get permits?'

'The national parks were opened up ages ago, can't you keep up? Why shouldn't they be? It's good for the country.'

'And for mining profits! I read the big companies are locking out the little fellas again too.' He heard a grunt on the other end of the line. 'You're letting it happen all over again?' Jason continued

'No, I'm not. I'm doing what I can.'

'Your mates don't seem to listen to you, do they?'

'Do you have something useful to talk about or shall I just hang up now?'

'I saw her. I came to Sydney.' Jason swallowed as he remembered her fragile form swallowed up in the hospital bed.

'Did she know you were there?'

'No. I didn't try to wake her.' Jason's lower lip trembled slightly but then a hot rage replaced his sorrow. 'What did you do to her?'

'Nothing! She did it all to herself.'

Jason swallowed and reined in his emotions. He hadn't phoned to hear his excuses.

Turning back to the report, he asked, 'What's a 'support labour force'?'

'What about it? Makes sense to put them to work instead of paying for them to sit around in the centres on their arses all day, complaining.' The deep chuckle reverberated down the line, he was back on safer topics. 'Speaking of sitting on your arse all day…'

'Ha! Ha! So, tell me who makes up the support labour force?'

There was a moment of silence then he heard another grunt.

'Never mind, you don't need to know.'

'If it's all above board why is it a secret?'

'You just have no idea about business, son. Grow up!'

'If you knew more about business you might still have some real clout. If you'd sat on your arse, mum could –' He was cut off by a familiar growl, although it had lost its effect on Jason.

'What do you want? Planning another exposé maybe? Something to make you rich and famous?' He laughed. Jason knew that laugh well. He'd heard it many times as he was growing up.

'I have a right to know what my *father* is up to.' He spat the word father.

'Your father isn't up to anything, I'm well clear. Anyway, you gave up the right to be involved in my life. Now you can just fuck off!'

The phone went dead. Jason punched at the air; he'd wanted more from this call. He should have kept his cool. His fingers drummed a rhythmic tap on the table to aid his thinking. He's up to something alright, Jason was sure of it. He smiled. He liked to rattle his father and show him he was still watching him. His father had let something slip through. The support labour force was drawn from people in 'centres'. Was that what he thought it meant? He picked up the phone again, found the number he wanted and pressed the call button. After the tone, he left his message.

'Hi, Klaus. Jason here. I'm sending you a scanned copy of a report, there's some interesting information about mining and oil interests in the national parks.'

He phoned Adrian and was glad he could talk to him in person. He told Adrian about the report.

'You'd be interested in the reference to a 'support labour force,' whatever that means. It seems suspicious especially when I found out they come from centres. It sounds worth investigating.'

He heard a rush of air being drawn into Adrian's lungs and waited for the response.

'Centres?' Adrian sounded distracted.

'I'll send you a copy and you can read it for yourself. Ring me afterwards so we can talk.'

Adrian grunted agreement then hung up. Jason scrolled through the report again, studying it carefully to be sure he hadn't missed anything.

A terrible thud pounded in Akbal's skull as he tried to open his eyes. Shaking with a combination of fear and cold, he tried to move but his limbs wouldn't obey instructions. Something soft stroked his face while something hard pressed into his side. He forced his eyes open and stared into the inky blackness. The sound of leaves rustling in the wind helped him recognise the soft touch on his cheek as a blade of grass. He slid his hands over his body in a slow deliberate movement. The various pains and sore patches sprang to life as his touch settled on them, but he was all there. His leaden legs pinned him to the ground and with an enormous effort and a heavy grunt he pulled himself up onto his haunches. A twinkle of light over the horizon and the gentle hum of traffic gave some clues of his whereabouts. He pushed himself up and cried out in pain as he tumbled back onto his side. A flash of images, the most vivid a fist pummelling into his face, brought him up with a gasp. He wasn't sure if it was a dream or not, but it felt very real.

Again, he tried to move and again stumbled, crying out in pain and frustration. The scrunch of gravel and footsteps scuttling towards him made him wince, unsure if he should be afraid and try to run or not. His mind was as slow as his body and the shouts were upon him before he could act. Hands pulled at him and the voices floated in indistinct mumbles as though through a tunnel. Their tugs and grasps made him cry out and then blackness overcame him.

With consciousness came further confusion. The inky blackness and hard resting place had now been replaced by a blinding bright environment and a pliable bed. An urgent siren sounded nearby and he was being gently rocked. He panicked when restraints bit into his skin as he tried to move. A memory flashed in his mind and the hairs on his arms bristled. He struggled against the straps, desperate to be free but something hard was pressed down over his mouth and a rush of cold air blew across his lips. It was strangely calming, and he succumbed to the urge to sleep.

Now Fatima's face loomed over him, a frown creasing her usually smooth forehead and tears tracing glistening trails down her cheeks. He wanted to reach up and touch her, to see if she was real but his arms stayed pinned to his side. Images from the past crowded his mind; times when he and Fatima had comforted each other, unsure if they would survive. A vision of Sari swam across the other images bringing tears to his eyes and stinging his already pain-wracked cheeks. No matter how hard he tried, he couldn't remember what had happened yesterday. Where was he? Bracing himself for the pain he turned his head inch by inch, recognising a hospital room with hissing and beeping machines and shiny tubes snaking around him. There were tubes attached to his arm and every movement was heavy and restrained. Everything hurt, but he couldn't remember why. What had happened to him? Had he been in an accident? The image of a fist racing towards his face startled him and a whimper escaped his lips. Fatima's face floated over him and he felt a gentle touch as she held his hand. She was real! She soothed him, plied him with water and urged him to rest and all the while holding on to him with all her strength.

He struggled against the need for sleep. There was something he needed to remember, something he needed to tell Fatima, but it sat, elusive at the corners of his mind, unreachable. His head ached with the strain until he could no longer resist, and he closed his eyes and drifted away.

Chapter 33

Relief washed over Shelley as she entered her small flat. There was evidence of Vonnie's cleaning. It was her kind of tidy. Shelley was grateful and she made a note to thank her.

Despite the break-in and the frightening events, Shelley still wanted her independence back. She swallowed down a kernel of fear. The recent tribulations had hardened her resolve and she was determined to not let them win, whoever they were.

She unpacked her new pay-as-you-go mobile phone and connected it to the charger. She'd heard they were more secure. She stowed her bag in the bedroom and put the kettle on. A fuss-free cup of tea was just what she needed. Vonnie had stocked the fridge and in addition to the usual staples, there were ready to eat meals and microwaveable treats. Shelley smiled. She might use them for convenience this time and Vonnie's efforts should be rewarded.

She sipped her tea, revelling in the peace and tranquillity. Questions about Ayisha rose to the surface. Since losing her phone she'd had no news. As she scanned the room, she noticed the blinking light on her answer machine. The message from Harry was two days old and it asked her to ring him as soon as possible. She rang his number on her new mobile then relaxed into an easy chair. His warm friendliness turned to concern as she explained what had happened. He warned her to be careful and reluctantly agreed to give Beetle her new number. Beetle had raised an alarm with Harry when he couldn't contact her. He had more news.

Shelley paced the lounge waiting for Beetle to call. Finally, she unpacked her bag and was sorting through her options for dinner when the phone rang.

'Hi. Harry told me what happened to you.' Beetle's raspy voice coursed down the line.

Although Shelley knew he didn't go for small-talk she launched into the long version of what had happened.

'I hadn't heard about them going after you,' he said, unaware of the cold shiver he sent up Shelley's spine.

'Harry says you have some news for me.'

'Yeah. We've managed to get a copy of the second witness' report. Her name is Didi and she was an escort at the club. That's who Ayisha had the altercation with.'

Shelley screwed up her face. Why would Ayisha go to help someone and become involved in an 'altercation'? 'Go on,' she said, hoping it would become clear.

'The report is hard to read. They didn't have an interpreter on hand and her English is basic. From what I can make out, Ayisha became hysterical after the girl came out of one of the rooms.'

'Is Didi an immigrant too? Do you know where she's from?'

'Yeah, she's Afghani. She hasn't been in the country long.'

'Did they give her full name?'

'No, they redacted the reports and key details are blacked out. The bouncer's name is blacked out too. We only know he worked for Jupiter Security Company.' Beetle was thinking out loud, not a usual occurrence.

'They're a subsidiary of Serpentco. They guard the family detention centres,' Shelley added.

'I know. Didi is in Brisbane now. I'm not sure how she got there. I'm trying to get someone to talk to her for me. I'll let you know if I'm successful.'

'OK, but this isn't getting any clearer.'

Beetle echoed Harry's warnings to be on her guard before he signed off.

Shelley sat quietly summing up what she knew so far. Ayisha had gone to a brothel; had an altercation with Didi, an escort; the bouncer had intervened; and she fled, throwing herself out of a third-floor window. On top of this, the Federal Police were obstructing the facts, tampering with the witness statements, changing the place where the body was found, taking over the post-mortem and now the witnesses had either disappeared or were being hidden. Could the Federal Police be conducting their own investigation and blocking outside interference?

Shelley went over her call with Beetle. Maybe Didi would shed light on what was going on. It gave her a trace of hopefulness. Didi being Afghani seemed a strange coincidence. Shelley slapped her thigh. According to Beetle, Didi hadn't been in Australia long but that was unlikely. There'd been no new arrivals registered for at least six months. Maybe Beetle meant she hadn't been out of detention long. Shelley's frustration made her pace the room. If only she still had access to the database, she could have checked her out. Damn this suspension.

Shelley sat back down heavily on her sofa. Didi was probably a 'working' name anyway and she didn't have her surname. Then, suddenly, it occurred to her. Could Didi be Ayisha's friend? Why hadn't she thought of that? Deedee could be short for Kadeen. It was possible. If it was Kadeen working as an escort in the brothel, it would fit Ayisha's use of the word 'unspeakable'.

Shelley was resigned to waiting for Beetle's next call for the missing bits of information, but she would think of little else until then.

When her home phone rang it startled her out of her thoughts. Adrian cut off her flood of information, interrupting her forcefully.

'Shelley, we're on the landline.'

'Ah yes,' she said, stopping midsentence.

'I want to ask a favour of you. Akbal has turned up but he's in a bad way. He can't remember what happened, but whatever it was, it was brutal. I've arranged for him to meet a lawyer although without his memory it may not help much.' He sighed loudly. 'Jason and I are picking him up from the meeting but Fatima needs help.'

'I'll help in whatever way I can.' Shelley shivered, Akbal and Fatima didn't have a family to rely on and this sounded serious.

'Are you up to it?' Adrian asked and she smiled at his concern.

'Sure. The homemade chicken soup has worked wonders.' Shelley laughed thinking about her mother's homemade chicken soup from a can.

'Good, I'll pick you up in about twenty minutes, is that OK?'

'Sure. We'll talk then,' Shelley said, feeling purposeful at last.

***

Jason worked hard to conceal his reaction, but the cold air stung his eyes, making them water. Stepping out of the grey legal offices was a shadow of the Akbal he once knew. His face, covered in bruises and healing scabs and his arm in a cast, gave him a ghostly presence as he shuffled along the portico. Hesitantly, he took each step, one at a time, until he was able to rest on the footpath. Jason was reminded of an old man, not the man of thirty-five he knew Akbal to be. He suddenly realised just how badly Akbal had been beaten and let a low whistle escape his lips. Despite his memory loss, it was clear to anyone that Akbal had been interrogated. They just didn't know by whom.

310

Jason looked down at his shoes, scanning the surrounds, anything but look at Akbal. Once he was in range, Jason reached out to offer his support and heard a sharp intake of breath as his hand touched Akbal's arm. Akbal violently jerked away, curling his small frame into a tight ball and Jason contented himself with creating an imperfect force field with his arms. He concentrated on preventing a fall but took extra care to avoid actual physical contact.

Adrian had parked at the loading zone on the corner. It had seemed a perfect spot but now Jason wasn't so sure. Akbal was so pale around the dark blotches patch-worked across his face that even that short distance might prove too far. Adrian must have seen them and thought the same. Within a few minutes, he pulled up in front of the kerb, ignoring the abuse from angry motorists as they skirted around his double parking.

Akbal grimaced as he slid into the seat. His slow deliberate movements elicited a range of different expressions, none of them good. His eyes stared into the distance, looking at no-one and nothing, his attention focused somewhere inside himself. His response to questions was short, sharp bursts of breath that sounded like grunts. He looked exhausted as though the mere effort of walking to the car had robbed him of the last of his reserves. He didn't even have sufficient energy to speak and Jason hoped fervently he had been better during the meeting with the lawyer. Adrian had worked hard to secure that appointment, time with one of Australia's legendary human rights lawyers didn't come easy.

Jason yearned to know more, but he realised they would not learn anything from Akbal right now.

As they pulled away from the kerb, Jason sent Shelley a text saying they were on their way. He shuffled in his seat, wanting to do something useful but instead silently watching Akbal sink into the upholstery. The haunted look in his eyes was also evidence of Akbal's inability to find solace in sleep. He was suffering more than just physical pain, although that seemed severe enough. The doctors were unsure if his memory of events would return in full. The only ray of hope were the flashbacks, the short bursts of unconnected memory that generated intense whimpers, shouts or even a sudden fleeing to crouch in a corner. They also added to Akbal's burden, leaving him unable to speak or explain. The doctors worried that the events being recalled were too traumatic and would be swallowed up and cocooned away from his consciousness. The other alternative was they would force themselves back into his memory and cause further damage.

By the time he and Adrian had discovered where Akbal had been found in Rymill Park, any clues had been removed. Jason clenched his fists, his short fingernails biting into his flesh. Adrian's rigid back sent the same message. This feeling of impotence was hard to bear, not something Jason had much experience with, but open displays of frustration would not help Akbal and would probably make it worse. Adrian was in assistance mode, but Jason fought his seesawing battle between anger and scepticism. If only Akbal could explain.

The drive seemed to take forever and Jason worried that the enamel on his teeth couldn't take too much more as the grinding sound from his mouth became audible. As soon as the car turned into the drive the front door sprung open. Shelley called back over her shoulder then ran to the car, Fatima followed closely on her heels. Fatima tenderly bundled Akbal out of the car. In pliant resignation to her ministrations, he stumbled inside. Fatima and Shelley steered Akbal to the bedroom and helped him onto the heavily cushioned bed.

When Fatima re-entered the lounge room, Jason explained. 'We don't know what happened with the lawyer. Did Akbal say anything to you?'

Fatima slowly shook her head, her glistening, brown eyes fixed on the overlapping fingers quivering in her lap.

'No, he's in shock I think.' A weak smile touched her lips, 'Thank you for your help, I'm glad he went to see the lawyer, he didn't want to go, you know, but...I think he did it for our daughter...'

Quietly, they left Fatima to administer love and care to her family. In the car Adrian, Shelley and Jason discussed the next step.

'This kind of torture can't be allowed to become accepted practice. Fear of terrorism can't justify this. Who is protecting the innocent?' He thumped the wheel several times making his point. Adrian was struggling with the way the world around him had changed. 'The information obtained by these methods is proven to be unreliable anyway?'

Jason agreed, but uneasiness niggled at the pit of his stomach. For him, there were still too many unanswered questions. Akbal had attracted attention, otherwise, why had he been questioned? Adrian was so sure Akbal was not linked to terrorism in any way, but Jason wondered if Adrian was just naïve. Was Adrian being blinded by his own experiences of injustice?

Shelley sat quietly, biting at her lower lip, offering the occasional support for Adrian. She remembered comments Harry had made about a rogue unit within the Federal Police. Maybe he knew something that could help them, something that could help Akbal.

***

Akbal slumped silently in his armchair, his breathing sounding loud to his own ears. The meeting with the lawyer two days ago was just a blur. His brain had shut down. The drone of the TV lulled him into a semi-conscious state where he didn't have to think or remember. A paralysis settled over him, pressing down and fixing him to his seat. His limbs felt heavy, incredibly heavy. He hated that look in Fatima's eyes, but he was powerless to appease her, to answer the silent plea. Only Sari's cries reached him, tugging at his heart and stirring him until his arms ached to hold her. But still, an invisible rope bound him to this chair, and he was powerless to break the bonds.

314

The Breakfast Show chatter assailed him. They talked about nothing, endless chatter and laughter as though nothing extraordinary had happened, as though all was right in the world. They imbued the trivial topics with an undeserved seriousness, scolding and ranting as they begged the viewers to feel anger, fear and even horror at some small story of ineptitude. This demand for emotions beat at him, but the ever decreasingly relevant programs could not make him react. The trivia helped Akbal to sink further into nothingness and drum out the nagging voices needling him. Occasionally, a flashback would burst into his thoughts: a fist pummelling his face; the pain as his arm was stretched beyond endurance; the sound of bone breaking, audible amongst his screams. His hands would fly to his ears to stifle them but opening or closing his eyes did not help, the flashbacks persisted. Mostly it was a memory of overriding fear, his fear, and his terror. He knew now what had happened but didn't dare admit it. It would take everything out of his control. There was no comfort in his refusal to confess to things he had not done, it had only been a matter of time. If he hadn't been released when he was, what would he have done or said? Did that make him a coward? Did it make him weak? Weak that he couldn't move; that he'd sunk into this self-imposed cell, isolating his thoughts and his feelings, refusing to share them or to reach out to those he loved. It was beyond his understanding and now he just didn't try anymore. He dodged memories as best he could, waiting for the haziness to dampen the intensity of the flashbacks and disperse the memories, hoping against hope that eventually it might seem like a bad dream, a nightmare from which he had awoken. But he knew it wasn't.

The TV coverage moved to images outside the studio, images of hysterical crying people sobbing into the cameras, pleading with the viewers and the journalists. Their distraught faces, tear-streaked and contorted in grief, jarred Akbal's nerves. He found a hidden reserve of energy and reached for the remote control. The image moved to a helicopter aerial view before he could press the button. The tin roofs of three large warehouses filled the screen. A circle of smaller buildings surrounded them and together they formed a large complex with tiny dots of open space. The high razor-wire fences looked like a concentration camp photo Akbal had once seen. The cameras zoomed in on five men perched on the roof. Their grey nondescript clothes, like prison garb, hung like sacks from the skinny men. Akbal eagerly searched the picture as the camera scanned across the men on the roof, then focused on the inhospitable dry earth outside the compound and the armed guards below screaming at the men. The camera zoomed in on a man gesturing wildly, shaking a fist at the helicopter. His face was an ugly mass of lines like a railway track had been grafted in place of a mouth. Akbal suddenly understood. This was a group of asylum seekers protesting their treatment. Some had sewn their lips together and climbed onto the roof to attract the attention of the press and highlight their despair. Akbal wondered at such self-mutilation, what desperation they must

316

feel to do something so drastic? The reporter's voice shouted above the helicopter noise, describing the scene in a cold relay of facts, there was no hint of empathy. Then Akbal saw him. He was at the back, almost hidden by the younger men who were jumping and shouting messages at the news crew above them.

He was here. Uncle Ashram, a skinny haggard effigy of the Ashram Akbal remembered, but there was no mistake, it was him. Akbal shouted, calling Fatima, calling out to the TV, wanting Ashram to hear too and to know he had seen him. The sound of crockery smashing on the kitchen floor resonated through the house and Fatima rushed into the room, eyes wide in fear. Staring at him, disbelief turned to questions as her eyes followed his pointing finger.

'There…there…' he shouted at her, willing her to see what he saw.

Searching the images on the screen as they pulled back from the young gesticulating man, she saw him too and tears streamed from her eyes. She clapped her hands in a childlike gesture of relief. They embraced. At first, Fatima buried herself into Akbal's chest until she felt him tense and she pulled back. Only now Akbal held her firmly, ignoring the pain. He wanted to feel her, to feel alive again, to be able to feel not just pain but also the small joys. They stared at each other, marvelling at how they had found him. Their thoughts didn't venture far from the fact he was safe and here in Australia. That was better than not knowing.

The program returned to the studio. The stern-faced presenters echoed the reporter's concerns. The inmates were ungrateful, the expense of keeping asylum seekers in detention was great and the violent, 'unnecessary' behaviour was shameful. But the words washed over Akbal and Fatima as they came to grips with what this meant.

Slowly, the realisation that the fight was now only just beginning bore down on them. Both pushed the dread down to savour the joy of discovery. They were relieved and immersed in a momentary sense of security, a respite from reality, welcome and much needed given what they had already endured. It was too much to think about what lay ahead for them or Ashram.

Chapter 34

Wrogarth resisted the urge to throw the glass at the TV screen. Instead, he slammed it down, splashing cold liquid over his hand. He wasn't going to be held to ransom by a handful of illegal immigrants. How had the press got onto this? All their careful planning was undone, his carefully stage-managed image was being undermined and right now, he couldn't afford any inconsistencies. At least the media was most interested in quick sound-bites but this sound-bite could hurt him.

He gripped his glass tightly as the screen filled with grotesque faces, their lips crudely sewn into jagged lines. The public might be persuaded it was a stunt to blackmail the government. He rolled those last words over his tongue again. They had a nice ring to them. He sank back into his leather chair suddenly feeling weary. The polls had been more encouraging lately. Some called it the sympathy vote, but he didn't care why.

Wrogarth grabbed the remote and silenced the reporter's hysterical shouting. He reached for the half-empty glass of scotch and drained it in one gulp. Smooth heat slid down his throat, calming his nerves instantly. Picking up the phone he dialled, it was time to get them off the roof and move the journalists on. His commands were met with agreement – he expected nothing less. He liked the sound of his own voice at times like this, the way 'do whatever it takes' rolled off the tongue. Shame it had to be followed with 'but be discreet'. Excitement again gripped at his nerves, he liked being in charge.

He fixed himself another scotch, surprised when the bottle drained into his glass. He must have opened it last week, not Thursday. He walked unsteadily to the door, planning to find Bev but as he clutched the handle he faltered. The funeral images flashed before his eyes, sharp contrasting flashes of memory with the centrepiece a dark, sturdy coffin and the foreboding glimpse of Bev's last resting place. The reverend had called it that to soften the impact – it hadn't worked. Wrogarth slumped back into his chair, downing the scotch in a rush. The potent liquor burned his throat, bringing tears to his eyes.

Alone in the quiet lounge room, memories crowded out his present worries. His mind filled with the image of Bev in hospital cradling their first child, a tiny red-faced newborn with a scraggly patch of dark down. Bev's face glowed with pride and happiness. There was Bev beside him on the stage, sharing the joy of his first election victory. An elegant Bev watched him being sworn in as Prime Minister the first time. His heart swelled with pride. But these happy images faded, and darker memories took their place. Now he saw the controlled but pained look when she accidentally touched a bruise or the fear in her eyes when he lost his temper. But, worst of all, the unrecognisable Bev lying at the bottom of the stairs and the broken and bruised Bev in her hospital bed. The final image of his wife resting in her coffin forced itself into his mind. Wrogarth shivered involuntarily and slurred a curse under his breath. She'd looked at peace but now he felt an unreasonable rage. He needed her, hadn't she known that? Why hadn't she held on? Why had she left him? Unsteadily he walked to the bar and rummaged underneath for a new bottle. He left the empty bottle propped on the bar and took the full one back to the chair.

The silence was stifling. The lamp beside his chair cast a faint light holding the darkness at bay. It was the same darkness that gave rise to his conscience.

***

As Daryl placed the coffee in front of Wrogarth, he noted how seedy he looked. He studied the deep lines etched into Wrogarth's face and the heavier touch of grey framing his temples. He'd aged noticeably in the two weeks since Bev's funeral. Death had finally made Wrogarth appreciate what he'd taken for granted in life – and it showed.

Wrogarth stared blankly out of the window, absorbed in private thoughts and almost unaware of Daryl's presence. He turned sharply as Mark burst into the room and closed the door noisily behind him.

'Sorry I'm late,' Mark said cheerfully, his tone a severe contrast to the atmosphere in the room.

Wrogarth waved them both to the chairs opposite the desk then pulled himself up straight and drew on a mantle of confidence. Daryl marvelled at the transformation; he'd seen Wrogarth do it before, but it still impressed him.

'OK. There are a couple of things we need to deal with. The press release on the riots worked. Do we need a follow-up?'

'Better to let it die rather than keep the discussion alive,' Mark said quietly, his eyes bright and wary.

Wrogarth narrowed his eyes at Mark and Daryl wondered if Mark was tactless or just angry.

'What happened to our terrorist arrest?' Wrogarth's stare lowered the temperature in the room.

Mark slumped slightly in his seat and Daryl went on alert. Wrogarth had spoken to both ministers this morning, so he was already informed.

'They couldn't get a confession. They bungled it. They caved in to Intelligence and Jacobs.' Mark glanced across at Daryl and grimaced.

'Can't you get anything right?' Wrogarth dramatically threw down a folio of papers onto the desk.

'The International Agencies said he was clean. His movements within Pakistan weren't suspicious. We couldn't legally hold him after that,' Mark whined.

Daryl smirked but kept his head down. Wrogarth punched the table then fastened steely eyes on Mark again.

'Jacobs has to go, voluntarily, of course.' He picked up the letter opener and pointed it menacingly at Mark. 'And, where's the dirt on Tim Curleigh? It was supposed to be front-page news.'

'It got bumped by the riot.' Mark's voice was becoming a whine.

'You're becoming a liability. You stuffed up badly with the others too. I told you to leave them alone.'

'They were told to scare them. That's all.' Mark squirmed.

'I make the bloody decisions, not you, right?' Wrogarth thumped the desk again and Mark jumped.

'But –' Mark started to protest but he looked at his boss' face and left the sentence unfinished.

The only sound in the room was Wrogarth's breathing and Daryl stayed very still to avoid becoming the focus but to no avail.

'The coroner, the one that's…investigating Bev's…death,' Wrogarth's voice faltered at Bev's name but he recovered quickly. 'Do we know him?'

The question caught Daryl off guard. He'd left the investigative process to go its course, especially once Wrogarth had given his police interview.

'He's been the coroner for about six months.' Daryl paused, desperately searching his memory for the details. 'He came highly recommended…he's very thorough…has a solid reputation.' Daryl was surprised to see Wrogarth's frown deepen as he talked.

'Can he be...well...persuaded...to get the job done...quickly? Skip the red tape?'

Wrogarth wasn't usually lost for words and was never tactful. He spun the letter opener dangerously with his fingers. A sheen of sweat on Wrogarth's forehead gleamed in the office light and Daryl couldn't decide if it was alcohol leaching out or a sign that the man was anxious.

'I've heard he's a stickler for procedure, but I don't know much more about him,' Daryl added carefully as Wrogarth twirled the letter opener even faster.

'Mmmmm.'

Wrogarth swivelled to glare out of the window. A blanket of silence again drew tightly over the room. Daryl understood more than he wanted to. Wrogarth was afraid of history, what the autopsy might reveal about him and his behaviour, not just about Bev's death.

Wrogarth turned a composed face back to them, his firm expression replacing the previously haggard look. He'd gained some unexpected resolve from beyond that window.

'Can we lean on him to hurry it along?'

The flash of coldness in Wrogarth's eyes almost gave Daryl frostbite.

'I want it resolved so it won't distract from the campaign, I don't want...rumours...unhelpful innuendo...clouding the messages we are trying to put out there,' Wrogarth said, his voice oily as he softened his demeanour despite the ice still sparkling in his eyes.

Daryl nodded. 'I'll see what I can do.'

He meant it, although he wasn't planning to make it too easy. Wrogarth dismissed them and then turned his chair back to stare out of the window.

Back at his desk, Daryl straightened paperwork while preoccupied with his thoughts. He'd helped his boss before, especially in the early days. But now he wanted the truth to be told, her life of suffering to be exposed and especially, he wanted Wrogarth to pay. He slumped down in his chair. He had lost everyone close to him. He'd also lost his own principles and ethics. He'd been too easily swayed, but it was time to take a stand.

His eyes stopped at an updated list of contact names and numbers on his desk. On impulse, he lifted the phone and dialled the first number before he could change his mind.

'Hi, it's Daryl, Daryl Mosset' He lowered his voice to a loud whisper, chastising himself for doing this at the office.

'Oh, yes.' Tim Curleigh sounded wary.

Daryl understood. His closeness to Wrogarth often put people on their guard, especially when he called unexpectedly.

'I need to talk to you in private…Wrogarth can't know I've talked to you,' he said, watching the door to Wrogarth's office.

'Right.' Curleigh registered interest.

'I need your advice,' Daryl pleaded, desperately wanting the call to end.

They set a date. It wasn't as soon as Daryl would have liked. His hand shook. Was this wise? Relief washed over him. It was the right thing to do and it was about time, he was sure of that.

Chapter 35

The cast on Shelley's arm stopped her scratching the persistent itch and she wriggled it to get some relief. Her speedy recovery had left her with only recurring headaches which were proving difficult to shake.

'A friend has managed to speak to Didi,' Beetle said.

Shelley pressed the phone firmly to her ear to catch Beetle's quiet explanation. 'Could Didi be Ayisha's friend, Kadeen?' Shelley asked.

'It's possible. She apparently knew Ayisha from Afghanistan.'

'How did she come to be working in a brothel?'

'She told Angie her family's safety is being threatened. She's terrified.'

'She has family here?' Each new piece of information seemed to make the story worse.

'She's been living in a city detention centre with her daughter while her husband is in a remote centre. They've been here about five months.' Beetle's voice sounded tired and flat.

'She can't be living in detention and work in a brothel?' Shelley made a fist and pressed it into her temple where a headache had started again.

'Exactly. It's bizarre. Club management has warned her to stay quiet and made her lie in the witness report.'

Shelley was struck speechless.

'When we asked for her full name and that of her husband and child, she fled,' Beetle added. 'I'm puzzled by what the Feds have to do with this.'

''Unspeakable' was right. Ayisha died while trying to rescue her friend who is under threat and working in a brothel while in detention. Detention means she is under the government's care.' Shelley said as she sunk into her sofa. 'How on earth could this happen?'

Beetle broke into Shelley's thoughts. 'We think there's more like her. There are regular transfers between the family detention centres and a number of gentlemen's clubs, both in Sydney and Brisbane. It could be happening elsewhere too.'

Shelley was struck speechless for a second time and Beetle continued. 'I have to get to the bottom of this. I don't know who is involved and who knows what, but I'll track them down. The Feds are complicit even if they're not responsible but surely even the rogue units wouldn't stoop this low.'

Shelley then told Beetle what she'd read in the reports and their connection to Mark McCracken at the Prime Minister's office.

'They couldn't be involved, could they?' she asked, looking for reassurance.

'Who knows how far up the chain of command it goes. The higher it goes, the harder it is to expose.'

They were both quiet for a moment before Beetle changed topic.

'Have you arranged to meet Neil?'

Shelley had been wavering about keeping the appointment but now, after what Beetle had told her, she was determined to follow through. Neil was a former guard at Barker detention centre and lived in Adelaide. Shelley planned to meet him and find out what she could about Ashram.

Shelley shivered. 'Yes, it's tomorrow night. Thank Harry for putting him in touch.'

Learning that Akbal was the Australian held for questioning for links to terrorism and seeing the state of him, had created a hardness in Shelley. Beetle's revelations now were not helping to dispel or soften that hardness.

After the call, Shelley wrapped herself in a quilt and brooded on the sofa. Finally, she struggled to bed, but sleep eluded her. Despite her exhaustion, her mind continued its endless search for a credible explanation.

***

As the days grew shorter the evenings became colder. The iciness arriving with such vengeance it kept Shelley indoors, in front of the heater, most nights. Tonight was the exception.

Shelley and Adrian stood quietly, jacket collars pulled up around their ears and scarves wrapped around their necks. The rowing clubs formed desolate shadow pictures in the dark and the Torrens River sparkled with the reflection of lights from the nearby convention centre and sports oval. They huddled, protected from the cold breeze, but still staking out the approaching path. Shelley shivered with excitement and cold.

The snap of a twig made her jump. Soft footsteps made their way towards the rendezvous point and a broad-shouldered, stocky figure appeared at the end of the pathway. His hazy features and heavy, plodding gait added to her unease. He stopped at the edge of the buildings and peered into the shadows. Shelley was suddenly frightened. How could they be sure this was Neil? Images of Granite Island and her fall held her frozen to the spot.

A movement beside her shoulder startled her. Adrian stepped forward into the dim light drawing the man's attention. The man jerked back. Clearly, he was also jumpy.

'Neil?' Adrian asked quietly

Neil nodded, wiped his hands on his jeans then presented it formally. 'Adrian?'

Shelley rallied and stepped forward too. Her legs shook so hard her movements became jerky and awkward. She introduced herself and presented her hand. Neil glanced at it, hesitating before eventually taking it in a limp handshake. They moved back into the shadows

'Thank you for coming.' Shelley found her voice but the effort of keeping her voice low made it quiver.

Neil nodded. 'Harry's a mate, that's why I'm here.'

His voice was rough with an accent Shelley didn't recognise. He cleared his throat, successfully shifting the gravel in his voice before he continued.

'You've been in the thick of things. Harry reckons they wanted that terrorism arrest bad. They were prepared to get it whatever way they could.' He sighed and shifted his weight. 'The Intelligence mob got in the way. They prefer to follow the rules. That's how come your mate got released.' He laughed using his hand to muffle the sound as it turned into a deep throaty cough. 'He's not in the clear yet though.'

'He's innocent,' Adrian protested.

'So?' Neil snorted, 'They've had all of you under surveillance since Paris. The international agencies cleared you, but the Feds have orders to keep working on it. They're desperate to get a result.'

Shelley wrapped her coat tighter.

'You're not making it any easier for yourselves. Getting caught up with asylum seeker issues.' Neil shook his head. 'It's a mess,' he muttered as he again shifted feet.

'Akbal saw his uncle on the TV footage of the riot. He's in Barker,' Shelley explained.

'Did he now? I worked there after I left the agency. It's the oldest and the easiest of all.'

'What do you mean?' Adrian asked quietly.

'It's the easiest to break out of I reckon, that's all. Not that it helps those poor bastards. They replaced the original guards with private security people in all the centres, and Barker was the first. They reinstated a mothballed centre to reactivate Barker, so its security systems are old and not as sophisticated as the others. The other centres were purpose-built, they have all the bells and whistles. They're regular Fort Knox's.'

'You worked there…' Shelley said as she rubbed her hands to release the tension and to warm them. An idea was forming, and she let her mind follow the train of thought.

'I was one of the last ones to leave.' Neil was on his own turf now. 'The contractors are a dodgy private company, Serpentco.' He stared at them through the flickering darkness. Shelley imagined she could see his eyes flare. 'They employ some dodgy-looking men. Those guards are brutal. They're vicious bullies who enjoy using force. It's sick.' Neil shuffled his feet and his voice came out in a hiss. 'I need to be careful. When the new boss and the new security firm took over, they lectured us about our rights…well, lack of rights actually. We signed contracts, secrecy contracts where we agreed not to talk to anyone about what was happening at the centre. It was overkill or so it seemed at the time. We didn't know nothing anyway. It spooked us though; I've never had to do that before.'

'Who is the new guy?' Shelley asked connecting his comments to something she'd read.

'A real cowboy. He's new at running detention centres but loves strutting around like a commandant. The old boss had years of experience and knew what he was doing. He'd been there since this government first won office. That's why it was so strange when he left. He'd been a political animal, followed directions but also stood up for what was right. He left suddenly. Now he's practically disappeared off the face of the earth.'

Shelley's joints were stiff, and she suddenly felt old and tired. Neil's tale reminded her of grumblings she'd overheard some time ago at work. The senior executive was directed to replace someone in a senior position, and they were unhappy because their objections were overruled.

'Anyway, soon after the new guy started, they started taking the illegals out for the day. There were two shifts each day and they come back dirty and buggered, but they are warned not to talk about it to anyone. They know about it if they do.' Neil sighed loudly.

'Everyone goes?' Adrian asked, a puff of steam rising from his mouth as he spoke.

'Yes, all the men and the boys old enough to stand up. There are no women and children at Barker. That's what started the riot, being separated from their families.' Neil shook his head.

'So, where are they holding their families?' Shelley knew the answer but wanted confirmation.

'Don't know. All I know is they're not going to Barker or Wilderness. It's a new policy brought in by the new boss.' Neil tutted and punctuated his sentence.

'What work are the men doing?' Shelley asked quietly.

'I'm not sure exactly but it's connected to the mines.' Neil looked around nervously as the wind rattled an empty drink can. 'The new boss had several meetings with this foreign guy. I'd seen him around and word is he is one of the mining execs. I don't know his name. He keeps a very low profile.' Neil chuckled. 'Unusual for these mining magnates.' He leaned in and lowered his voice. 'We heard on the grapevine the original boss objected to the new operational directives and liaisons.'

'I've heard the detainees are getting ill, physically and mentally.' Adrian leaned in too, this was the topic he'd been itching to ask about.

'Yeah the poor buggers are doing it tough,' Neil said harshly. 'The worst cases are sent to Wilderness; their hospital facilities are more up-to-date. But strangely, no-one comes back from there.'

'Can you remember any of the symptoms?' Adrian asked eagerly.

'Not exactly, it's just like a cold. They start sneezing and coughing, that sort of thing. Then some start to vomit and cough up blood. Doc said it wasn't contagious and they probably brought it into the country.' Neil paused. 'Although, it seems to have spread pretty well for something that's not contagious.'

'It must be depleting the workforce?' Shelley found her voice again.

'There are so many new arrivals they easily replace those that leave. Last I heard it's becoming overcrowded.'

'I heard there were deaths,' Shelley asked, aware of Adrian's sudden turn towards her as she spoke. She knew she had to tell him everything soon.

'Yeah.' Neil shuffled on the spot and lowered his head. 'They kept the numbers under wraps, so I don't know how many.'

'What was the cause of death?' Adrian asked, his voice tight and his eyes still fixed on Shelley.

'I've never seen a death certificate. I'm not even sure what happens to the bodies. I think they're shipped out at night.'

'Where are the new arrivals coming from? They've been turning back boats and the government claims there haven't been any new asylum seekers reaching us for at least six months,' Shelley asked. This question had perplexed her for some time.

'They never say, and I've never got a straight answer. One thing I know is, these guys are not transferring, they're new to Australia and haven't been in the system long.' He looked at Shelley and Adrian as though he thought they could explain. 'It's fishy.'

'Any guesses?' Shelley whispered.

'No, but the new arrivals always come at night, by truck. After a few days, they are put to work. The centre is like a labour camp, they work for the mine companies and I guess it isn't legal.'

Shelley thought about Akbal and Fatima's uncle, Ashram, locked up in Barker. They'd found out he was in the infirmary and might be transferred to Wilderness if his condition didn't improve. Being transferred meant it was probably getting serious. Neil's information made her realise that time was running out.

Neil broke her contemplation. 'They are really busting their guts.'

'Is there any way we could get in to see someone in Barker?' Shelley asked.

She felt a stir of cold air as Adrian's body jerked around to face her again. A crazy idea was formulating in Shelley's mind. She knew it was irrational and tried to dismiss it, but it nagged at her.

'You need a high clearance pass,' Neil replied

Shelley nodded; a plan taking root in her mind. 'Who would have one of those?'

'They're issued by the Feds for senior staff, medics or security people, but they're rare,' Neil said cautiously.

'Is there any way we can get back in touch with you if we need to?' Adrian asked interrupting Shelley's thoughts.

Neil laughed. 'My phone is a bit suss so the number you have is for my neighbour. I told him my phone has been playing up, so he's agreed to take important messages for me.'

They confirmed their respective details and after shaking hands, this time more firmly, Shelley and Adrian waited for Neil to leave. Dampness stiffened her bones and Shelley limped when they finally moved. They walked in silence, deep in thought. Once back on King William Street Shelley ventured her idea.

'Maybe we could get a pass somehow.'

'What good would that do? Talking to him can't help much.' Adrian watched Shelley from the corners of his eyes.

'If Barker has such old security, it's our only chance. We might even be able to get Ashram out of there.'

Adrian stopped abruptly and faced Shelley full-on, his face ablaze and stern.

'They won't just let you walk him out of there.'

'Of course not, but you heard him. Neil said security is easy there. We know Ashram is ill and we know he's so ill they're planning to send him to Wilderness. He may never get out of there alive.'

Shelley felt a sense of panic making her more determined. She felt responsible, her work and her apathy had allowed these things to happen and she wanted to put things right.

'He said easier, not easy. You don't know how serious this is. You can't break someone out of detention,' he protested strongly but then softened his tone when he saw her back stiffen. 'I can get the humanitarian groups involved.'

Adrian again walked on, crossing King William Street to the parade ground, listing the names of people who could help and the protests they could raise.

Shelley decided that doing the right thing wasn't always the right thing to do. 'It may be too late,' she whispered.

It was now or never.

Chapter 36

Shelley printed yet another copy. This one looked more authentic. She compared it to the copy Beetle had sent and grimaced. Would they get in with this? Neil had said the security was laxer at Barker but was it lax enough? She laminated both passes, one for her and one for Jason then studied them closely one more time. Fingers crossed that they would work. Shelley didn't want to think about what would happen if they didn't, although she knew she should.

She changed into jeans and a dark jumper and packed a bag. Her hands trembled slightly, and her fingers fumbled with the buttons and zips. This was it, the point of no return. So long as she thought about Ayisha, Akbal, Fatima, and Sari, she could justify their actions, at least to herself. Right now, she had to keep busy to avoid overthinking.

A light tap on the door startled her. Glancing at her watch she realised he was on time. Jason, sporting a new, short haircut, was flushed with excitement and his usual fluid movements had been replaced by a tight nervousness. His new look added maturity to his features and Shelley like it.

'All set?' he asked quietly. A grin split his face, revealing irregular teeth.

'Wow, I'm impressed. You got your hair cut.' Shelley said with a smile. Grateful he was here to help.

'Well, I thought I better look the part.'

Shelley scanned the room one more time, then picked up the bags by the door.

'We're not going for that long, are we?' Jason teased.

He took the heaviest bags from her and Shelley pulled on her coat, wrapping it tightly to stop her shivering.

The car hummed into action and they were off. Shelley could hardly believe what they were about to do, it felt like a movie in which she played a small part.

Her last conversation with Beetle spun in her mind. There was no Federal Police covert operation to smash the sex slave trade, of that he was certain. She hadn't wanted to believe it. When she blurted out what she was planning to do he'd cautioned her and tried to persuade her to leave it to the professionals. But realising how determined she was, he'd helped. She couldn't have done this without him.

Once they left the city, the occasional twinkle of light told of farmhouses set back off the road. She and Jason had entered another dimension, an eerie place where lights filtering through curtains replaced life. The faint blue sky formed a contrasting backdrop for the contorted dark limbs of gum trees reaching up in agonising pleas. Doubts surfaced instead of the confidence Shelley yearned for.

'Adrian didn't think this was a smart idea,' Jason said.

That was an understatement. Adrian had told her it was crazy, and she couldn't do it. Well, she could, and she was.

'You talked to him?' Shelley asked, annoyed at the squeak in her voice.

'You didn't?'

'No, not really.' Shelley's voice sounded small to her own ears.

'All the big changes in history happen through revolutions and rebellion.' Jason chuckled.

This was Jason's favourite view of history; you could tell from the conviction in his voice and the fire in his eyes. They both made his features more attractive.

'Maybe, but I just want to stand up for what's right before it's too late.'

Jason's dark face was silhouetted against the dark scenery flying past his window, but she could still see him smile. The dashboard lights cast a ghostly halo around him, an odd image for Jason.

Their plan was simple. Jason had arranged for a mate to take them up in a light plane to survey the area. The idea of going up in a light plane made Shelley both excited and worried. She was bemused but grateful at how Jason always seemed to have a mate to help.

341

Adrian propped at the laboratory bench avoiding thoughts about what Shelley and Jason were doing at this moment. He didn't like it but hadn't been able to dissuade them. Although he disapproved, he understood. Shelley was right to be concerned about time. He too was frustrated with official channels, the delays and lengthy paperwork.

He turned his attention to the readings as the steady line suddenly spiked. The spike was small but significant. Both Carla's soil and blood samples were showing inexplicable erratic results. He'd get Jason to run them through his equipment at the minerals laboratory when he was back. He scanned the results again and shook his head.

Picking up the phone, he dialled Carla's number. She confirmed the soil samples were from the area where the children had been playing. Adrian wrote down the description of the area, noting where it was in relation to the camp. He cursed under his breath when he realised his maps were too vague to pinpoint the location.

He logged into Google Earth. The cratered moonscape he saw didn't resemble earth. It's scarred and the pock-marked surface was interrupted by mounds of red soil laced with black veins. The area looked deserted. The wind had lifted the red topsoil and deposited it in wave patterns across the area. The sparse vegetation, more brown than green, was so scrawny and brittle it looked like it could spear a dingo or impale a human. The craters were remnants of past mining activity and as he scrolled over the area, he remembered AAAP had bought up many of the disused mines. He wondered if they had bought these. He searched for signs of recent activity but except for some tyre tracks, there was no fresh activity visible around the site.

He sent Carla an email, unwilling to disturb her a second time. Maybe she knew of recent activity in the area. The mounds were devoid of vegetation, but it was hard to tell how long ago they had been formed. The children had climbed through a fence to run, slide and ski down the mounds. Adrian scoured the images again. There was no sign of disturbance on the mounds consistent with their play. He rechecked the coordinates. It was the right area. The area was prone to sandstorms and maybe the sand had resettled. He again pondered the results from the tests, there was something familiar about the data and he stared vacantly into the fume-cupboard.

'You're working late. Haven't you got a home to go to?'

His short dark-haired colleague stood at the door, one hand resting on the frame as he leaned into the room.

'I've just been looking at some puzzling results,' Adrian admitted, 'from the Aboriginal study.'

He stretched up to look over Adrian's shoulder at the strange landscape on Google Earth. 'What's that you're looking at?'

'I'm testing some samples from that site. The kids are reacting to something. It's an old mining site but it doesn't look like there has been any activity or access to it recently.'

His colleague scratched his chin, 'No, but then these photos could have been taken some time ago. I don't know how often they're updated.'

'Of course!' His brain must be on a go-slow campaign.

'You look tired, want to join me for a bite to eat? My wife is at lectures so I'm kinda at a loose end tonight.'

Adrian laughed; his colleague had never learned to cook. His attempts were the butt of many jokes around the office. His wife steadfastly refused to do it for him when she was going out so they had a Mexican standoff and it didn't look like it was going to end anytime soon.

'Yeah sure.' Adrian surprised himself by accepting.

Carla was unlikely to reply to his email before tomorrow and he could use some time to think through the test results. He shut down the computer, put away the files and cleaned the machine, carefully stowing the samples in the locked cupboard. Turning off the lights, they strolled out to find somewhere for dinner. Adrian could almost guess where they were likely to go.

He'd guessed correctly. They'd ended up at one of the new hamburger cafés for dinner. Hamburgers were one of his colleague's weaknesses and another standoff between him and his wife. Adrian rubbed his stomach, he wished he had ordered something else. Despite his broken night's sleep, he felt fresh as he walked into the lab and greeted two other colleagues, their heads together in deep discussion over a toxicology sample in the fume-cupboard.

Carla's reply waited in his inbox and confirmed the area was full of dormant mines. She hadn't seen any signs of activity while collecting the samples. The site was owned by Trisec Oil but she thought it was either in the process of being sold or had already been sold. She didn't know who to or even why anyone would buy it. The land was unsuitable for agriculture, but she had heard a Spanish company was interested in starting up solar energy farms in this region.

None of this helped Adrian. The results indicated the children had been in contact with a potent chemical, but without knowing what the site was being used for, he couldn't narrow down his search. He played with various reports on his computer, trying to identify the options. He saw the email Yasmine had sent him and he opened it. A chart of neatly displayed data cascaded down his screen. Studying the test results data at the bottom caught his eye.

There were parallels between the data from Yasmine's African group and Carla's Aboriginal children. He checked again. There were similar symptoms, although the African group had more severe reactions, both groups had skin lesions and breathing difficulties.

He placed the results side by side and scanned the conclusions. Exposure to toxic chemicals, especially hydrogen sulphide compounds. He remembered a conversation with Klaus and reached for his phone. There was no answer, so he left a message. The results were persuasive. As he waited, he scrolled through previous internet searches, locating some promising sites when his phone rang.

'Hi Klaus, thanks for calling back. I had a question for you,' Adrian said.

'I'm just about to go into a meeting so I don't have much time, I could call you back.'

'No, it's just a quick question. Can you remember the symptoms of the truck drivers from that dumping incident in France, the one involving Ortansea?'

Klaus sighed. 'I remember there were reports of severe headaches, diarrhoea, eye damage, vomiting, difficulty breathing, skin lesions and worst of all, death. Will that do?'

'Yes, that's pretty comprehensive, thanks.'

'What's this for?' Klaus had suddenly found time to talk.

'I'm not sure about it yet, but we can talk later.'

'OK, but you have me intrigued. There's a report that lists all the symptoms, it was the Pangster or Plangery. Something like that. It's named after the man who investigated it. It's still on-line' Klaus offered helpfully.

'I think I just found it,' Adrian confirmed as he opened it and pressed print.

After they'd hung up, Adrian retrieved the printed report. He scanned the results he had for Yasmine and Carla; both sets of results indicated their patients had come in contact with the same kind of highly toxic substance. From this report, their symptoms were consistent with those of the truck drivers in France in the 'dirty water' incident. They were just different degrees of exposure but there was definitely a connection. Now he needed to find out how they had come into contact with this toxic waste.

Chapter 37

Shelley rubbed her stomach; glad it was again settled. She would have enjoyed the aerial views if it weren't for the air pockets. Their small craft pitched and bumped bringing Shelley dangerously close to being sick.

Jason and Shelley drove past Quorn, eventually turning at the dirt track leading up to the detention centre. Jason adjusted his borrowed suit and side by side they approached the checkpoint.

Neil had provided background on some of the guards. Wal was rostered on duty for today but Bert was in the guard station instead. Shelley cursed softly. Unlike Wal, he was a stickler for the rules. His missing teeth and the skull and crossbones tattoo peeping out from under his collar did nothing to steady Shelley's nerves. His manner was officious, and his authoritarian tone made it clear he was not interested in inconsequential chatter.

He held up Jason's pass, comparing the real-life Jason before him with the picture on the pass, his eyes cold and unimpressed. He noted the change in hair length, but Jason smoothly batted the concern away. Shelley pulled at her suit, it stuck to her arms and shoulders creating small circles of wetness under her armpits. Bert was delaying. For the second time, he scrunched his face searching the visitor list for their invented names. Jason feigned surprise at their names not being on the list. Shelley wished she'd sent them in sooner, but she'd wanted to avoid scrutiny or time for questions.

'I sent notice,' she said, her voice tight and unnatural.

'If your name's not on the list I can't let you in.' Bert raised an eyebrow making sure they knew he was in charge. He started to hand back the pass.

'I'm sorry, but you can't just send us away. If she has to go back without seeing Mr Al Hassan there will be hell to pay,' Jason bluffed. 'You don't want to rile the PM's department now do you?'

Bert looked up, frowning as he squinted at them. 'What do you mean the PM's department?'

Jason improvised. Shelley wasn't sure what would happen if this didn't work but she knew it wouldn't be good.

'This is hush-hush. It's a security issue.'

'What security issue?' Bert was getting jumpy. His hands twitched as he flicked at Jason's pass.

'We can't tell you everything. We just need to talk to him to check some facts.'

Beads of sweat erupted on Shelley's forehead and her antiperspirant lost its battle. Bert was in no hurry, but the twitch in his cheek showed he either believed Jason's story or at least had doubts. Shelley was trying desperately to keep her imagination in check, away from the horror scenarios threatening to unnerve her. This security company had links to bikie gangs and the guards were mostly ex-criminals. The example before them had all the hallmarks of belonging to one or other of those groups and Shelley just wanted to escape.

He flicked his hand at Shelley, indicating he wanted her pass too. With shaking hands, she scrambled in her bag, her nerves making her fumble even more. Her clumsy movements prolonged the process and earned her a rebuke.

'I'll have to get the OK,' he said looking Shelley up and down.

'If you try Matron Digby, she should be able to confirm our visit,' Shelley remembered the name Neil had given her just in time.

Bert dialled and turned away as he mumbled into the phone.

'She's on sick leave,' he said, shaking his head as he studied the list again.

Shelley gulped down her rising anxiety and shifted her weight. She frowned to look annoyed; after all, she was supposed to be on official business. She dug deep for some of her amateur acting experience and summoned the air of authority she should have if indeed she had been representing the PM's office.

'Look, I haven't got all day. I need to get back for an important meeting this afternoon,' Shelley said firmly.

Bert gave her a fiery look and scanned his list of numbers. Staring coldly in a vain attempt to invoke some authority, he backed down. Finally turning to Jason, he nodded although he maintained the frown as an admonishment.

'You'll have to wear the passes inside. You only have access to the areas I've marked here.' He handed back the passes.

'Yes sir,' Jason responded.

They passed through the first set of gates and the added security at the second row of gates without being stopped. Psychiatrists and lawyers were routinely turned away on technicalities and Shelley sighed with relief. They passed through the screening area, the guards not even interrupting their conversations long enough to search their briefcases. As they passed each station her legs trembled, anticipating being called back or challenged. It didn't happen.

Shelley followed Jason down the corridor, finally arriving at the wards. They passed a top security door marked 'Quarantine'. A guard stared at them through the glass and Shelley avoided his gaze. The sandy surface of the exercise yard was clear, and Shelley wondered where everyone was. According to the report the centre was filled to capacity and she doubted they could all be at work.

The medical staff looked more rough and ready than the hospital employees Shelley had encountered before. They were mostly nursing aides. The matron met them at the entrance explaining that Ashram was in the ward for minor ailments and grumbling about 'malingerers' tying up her precious time. Shelley asked why they had a quarantine section and the matron responded with an icy stare. She muttered 'just a precaution' then quickened her step.

In the ward, the matron accompanied them to the corner where Ashram lay. She hovered, crossing her arms and watching them closely. When Jason dismissed her with an impressive semblance of authority the matron hesitated, turned on her heels and clipped crisply out of the ward. Ashram watched the exchange from under hooded lids, impassive and alert. Shelley pulled the curtains around the bed, but the remaining gap meant the nurse's station was still visible. So was the matron who watched them suspiciously.

Shelley pulled up a chair and discretely passed a small talisman into Ashram's limp hand. Akbal said it would confirm they were friends. Ashram's fingers worked gently over the trinket and his eyes moistened.

'Akbal and Fatima told me you were here,' she whispered.

Although he'd been a translator for the Americans in Afghanistan, Shelley was unsure how familiar he was with Australian accents. She was rewarded by a flicker of understanding in his eyes, although his face remained impassive.

'I've come to help.'

Ashram nodded, so slight a movement that she almost missed it.

Talking quietly and quickly they hatched their plan, with adjustments as suggested by Ashram. He seemed almost too frail for this.

Jason moved out of the matron's sight and with a speed Shelley had not seen before, took the parcel of clothing from his briefcase, stowing it deftly under Ashram's sheets. They knew busloads of inmates departed and arrived twice a day. Although heavily guarded, the process was chaotic, and this created opportunities. The inmates discussed it in their desperate moments but fear and maybe hope held them back. They had nowhere to go.

The plan required Ashram to slip into the departure area without being noticed. The hardest part was getting through the gates. It needed split-second timing. Shelley didn't feel as confident as she should have. He didn't look strong enough although he insisted he was.

His friends could create a disturbance if he needed help but Shelley and Jason both cautioned him to not take extra risks. They couldn't help his friends and they needed his absence to go unnoticed for as long as possible.

Back at the motel, Shelley channel-surfed the TV, flicking through country stations so fast, the blips of sound and light blended into an incomprehensible composition. Her nerves wouldn't calm, and her thoughts spun in spiralling circles. The phone startled her, and she dropped the remote control. It slid across the floor sending the battery off in the opposite direction. She cursed softly then studied the display on her phone before answering it.

'Beetle,' the gruff voice announced. 'I just wanted to fill you in on the latest. We've talked to Didi again. She's scared but I've got her full name and the date she arrived. Can you get those to the right people? Some careful publicity could help but we can't jeopardise her safety.'

'So, is she Kadeen?'

'Yes, she is Ayisha's friend. She's been working at the brothel for months. She told us Ayisha tried to help her leave when the security guard interrupted. He hit Ayisha and pushed her so hard she crashed through the open window. She thought it could have been accidental.' Beetle tutted, 'Didi has been beaten and warned to keep quiet. She's taking a big risk talking to us. At the moment they're keeping her away from the brothel, but I'm not sure for how long.'

'Isn't there anything we can do to get her out of there?'

'Not yet. There are so many more like her.'

Shelley looked up as Jason sauntered into her room. She waved him to a seat.

'Do you have any contacts?' she asked, knowing Adrian would know who to go to.

Beetle was quiet for a moment. 'Yes, a lawyer mate of mine would be interested and a mate who's a journo. He'd be very interested. Now, how did you get on?'

'We did it. It's going to be tonight.' Shelley's stomach was doing backflips at the thought.

'Stay safe.'

The line went dead and Shelley put down her phone, her mind racing with options. She told Jason what Beetle had said, focusing on putting the facts in order. He whistled softly then offered to get a contact name from Adrian. Shelley longed to speak to Adrian but preferred to wait until this was over.

Chapter 38

When the matron left, Ashram slid silently from under the covers and arranged pillows into place. He didn't usually look that lumpy, but luckily, they never looked that closely. He pulled the curtains across to screen the bed. His roommate snored.

Ashram slipped across to the doorway, slinking back quickly at the sound of footsteps coming down the corridor. Sweat beaded his forehead as he pressed his hands against the door. He hadn't even made it to the toilets yet. He held his breath when the heels halted at the other side of the door. A voice murmured but he wasn't sure if she was talking to someone or to herself. He tensed his muscles to stop quivering. A soft 'damn!' preceded the heels retreat down the corridor. The swing door at the other end creaked and then slammed shut. He relaxed and furtively peeked around the corner. The corridor was clear.

Ashram crept along the lino-covered floor. At the toilet doors, he heard the hum of chatter floating from the nurses' station around the corner. It was always noisy, any time of night or day. Inside the toilets, he donned the dark pants and jumper then slid his feet back into the soft slippers. The next step was critical. He nudged the door open and savoured the handle's coolness momentarily. Stepping into the corridor he heard more voices approaching and jumped back. The quick movement made his head spin and he leaned against the wall for support. Two nursing aides stood in front of the door and Ashram clenched his teeth as he waited for their conversation to finish. They were frozen to the spot. Glancing at the clock on the wall his heart raced. If he didn't get out of here soon, he would be too late.

A call from down the corridor caught the nursing aides' attention and sent them racing towards the quarantine ward. Ashram sighed with relief but then pulled himself up. The call meant another of his friends was in deep trouble. He was remembering times he would rather forget. He had survived those times and was determined to survive again.

The door creaked and he felt a rush of cold air attack his sweat patches. He made it to the exercise yard and flattened himself against the wall. Its coolness kept him alert even if it didn't stem the flow of perspiration. Light-headed and suddenly feeling weak, he leaned heavily against the wall, thankful for its support.

This re-enactment of escape was a powerful pull to his imprisoned memories, and he fought them off. They would unnerve him, reminding him of the cost of escape; the loss of friends and relatives; and death, always death, there at the edge, awaiting a wrong move. He shuddered. He had to stay in control and not let the nerves and the memories undo him now.

A searchlight, high above him, clunked into action and the noise made him jump. It beamed down the road approaching the compound. He pressed his back more tightly against the wall and held his breath. Trucks rumbled in the distance. The bee-like drone deepened as they neared. The creaking gates as they swung slowly inwards announced they'd arrived. Once inside an overflowing cargo of humanity spilled into the yard. The refugees' voices grew louder as they emerged from the canvas-covered trays, but soon the shouting guards drowned them out. They directed the flow, casually pointing their menacing weapons at those who were not moving fast enough.

As the crowd swelled Ashram launched himself into the nearest group, mingling and hiding behind people as they filed past. He worked his way alongside one of the parked trucks. A guard ahead shouted for everyone to move forward, and without thinking, Ashram dived, propelling himself under the nearest truck. The impact winded him. His involuntary groan was luckily drowned out by the ruckus. He had to move but his body resisted. Through sheer force of will he rolled to the other side then, in one movement, he leaped up, catching a side rope, and pulled his legs up out of sight. A scuffle on the other side of the truck raised clouds of dust that threatened to make him cough and he buried his face low into his shoulder. His muscles screamed to be released but he held on as tight as he could. The shouts and screams around him became shrill and it was clear someone had been caught. Then a mechanical grumbling noise announced the gates were starting to close. He had to go now. His hands froze, paralysed with fear and indecision. He couldn't release his grip to launch himself off the side of the truck. Suddenly, he forced his hands to open and flung himself forward. He caught the gate just before it clanked shut. His jacket caught on the latch, suspending him mid-flight. The material ripped and released him with a jolt, and he stumbled through the gates. The momentum threw him forward, but Ashram managed to pull himself up without falling into the beam swiping across the front of the centre. Fierce shooting pain jabbed in his back and hamstrings, but he darted into the empty daytime guard post. There he waited, shivering with fear, emotion, and cold until the searchlight was turned off. With the extra room inside the guard post, he was able to squat on his haunches. His breathing rasped in short sharp bursts and his heart thumped furiously but his head was clearing. The searchlight sprung back into action, washing the approach road in an eerie bright light. It concentrated on one spot and his pulse quickened. Why was it taking so long? Had they discovered he was missing? Were they searching the hospital for him? His eyes stung from the salty sweat pouring down his face. Should he make a run for it or stay put? Then as quickly as they had sprung into action, the lights went out and cast him into darkness. An unnatural silence blanketed the area, the compound was finally devoid of human noise. His breathing sounded loud to his own ears and the more he tried to steady it, the worse it got. Creeping across to the shrubbery he prayed that his helpers were waiting there.

***

Shelley shivered gently, rustling the fabric of her jacket. She wished Jason was here with her, but someone had to stay with the car. She looked around with slow deliberate movements; hoping she was in the right place. The mounds all looked the same.

The inky black sky was broken by pinpricks of intense starlight scattered from horizon to horizon. At another time she would have looked for Orion or Scorpio, the only constellations she recognised, but not tonight. Instead, she watched the dark shadowy outline of the centre wall, searching for signs of people, or at least one specific person. She peered over the edge of the mound in bursts, unsure if others were able to see her or watch her in turn.

The meeting point Ashram had suggested was a natural blind spot from the guard posts on top of the walls. She counted the girders along the outer wall again just to be sure they had it right. She cursed as the moon slipped out from behind the clouds and bathed the scene before her in bright light. Just before she ducked her head back down a movement near the wall caught her eye. It wasn't time yet, the trucks hadn't arrived. When she peered over the mound again, focusing on the shadowy corner, she couldn't identify it. The concrete wall, crumbling in places, but still sturdy enough to hold its captives, was topped by a thorny crown of razor-wire. The centre

359

looked like a high-security prison. Shelley moved gently to forestall the cramp threatening to clutch her leg. Every movement, no matter how light, stirred the sandy soil and made her sink further into the dip created by her body. She trembled uncontrollably as she crouched in a hiding space barely big enough for her body. The moon again dipped behind the clouds and in the eerie silence, Shelley was acutely aware of the sounds she was generating with every breath. Her thoughts turned to how she would explain her actions if she was caught. Would her resolve still be strong in the bright daylight and the questioning of others?

Despite her attempts to stay alert, she didn't see the man until he was right in front of her. Shelley placed her own hand across her mouth trying to stifle her fear. The figure turned and crouched down; his silhouette outlined against the blue-blackness of the night. She couldn't see the stranger's features clearly, but his shape assured her it wasn't Ashram.

Her muscles tense, her nerves on edge, ready for flight, she crouched waiting for the man to move on. Shelley's legs ached as the sand trickled out from under her feet tipping her slightly off-balance.

The figure propped, waiting and watching. He seemed to be staring at her hiding place but then turned to stare at the centre walls. Finally, with a strange jerkiness, he crept on. His profile revealed a big, round man who was remarkably light on his feet. He left behind a faint whiff of a strong, bitter scent like beer and hot chips.

Shelley watched as the stranger moved towards the side gates. The silence now was broken by the occasional murmuring coming from inside the walls. A droning sound, off in the distance, told her the trucks were near. Shelley's heart pounded frantically, and her nerves tingled, setting off isolated pockets of sweat and heat that merged into trickles between her shoulder blades and formed a path into her eyes.

Without warning, the area was flooded with light and she slid back further from the edge. She stilled her nerves as best she could and waited. The trucks moved at an elephant pace, bouncing over the makeshift gravel roads. The gates rumbled open in a slow, deliberate motion, clanking and grinding a welcome to the approaching convoy. After what seemed an eternity, the gates again clanked and creaked their way back to the locked position.

Shelley watched, becoming more and more nervous as shadows sped across in front of the walls. She hoped it was a trick of the light and not more escapees. Once the tower lights extinguished and darkness again enveloped the area, she allowed the air to escape her lungs in a rush. Shuffling scurrying noises carried on the air in sporadic but regular bursts and a shape flew across the outside wall. Shelley held back. Ashram would come to her.

A soft glow emanated above the centre like a fuzzy corona. A stooped dark figure slowly edged his way around from the guard post then ran straight to the shrubs, falling into the small ditch beside her. Shelley threw a dark jacket over him, just in time, as a searchlight swung around to scan the area. Only flying insects were caught by the searching stream of light. Five times it scanned across the area, doubling back and forth in an attempt to catch people unawares. Then it too was switched off. It was a well-rehearsed routine, known well by those inside and tonight used to advantage by those outside.

Shelley moved stiffly from the hiding place, shuffling out of the shrubbery backwards then sliding down the incline. She bundled Ashram and felt his frail weight resting on her arm, his breath coming in hard bursts as they laboured through the sand.

Suddenly, a heavy weight slammed into them from behind, sending them forward onto their stomachs and knocking the breath from their lungs. The crushing weight pressed down on Shelley until grit crunched between her teeth. A bitter, strong odour, much more potent now, engulfed her. Her stomach twisted and she fought the urge to wretch.

'Shhh!' A hoarse voice hissed sharply into her ear.

Ashram started to move. A hand jutted forward and pressed him down.

'Stay still, they're coming.'

They froze, pressed hard against the cold sandy soil. Footsteps slipped and slid their way through the sand on the other side of the shrubs. Faint murmuring noises rose nearby and then the steps moved off in two different directions. One back from where they had come, the other moving towards Shelley's earlier hiding place. The footsteps became faint and Shelley relaxed.

'Beetle said you might need help,' the stranger whispered into her ear.

His breath made her feel ill all over again and she tried to break free.

'Stay still,' he commanded then whispered in her ear again as he rolled aside. 'I have a car behind that clump of trees. When it's clear, we'll run. Stay low and run quietly.'

When the man tapped her on the shoulder and whispered, 'Go!' she obeyed. Shelley lifted herself up into a crouched position. Resisting the urge to dust herself off she scurried as best she could while staying partially hidden by the shrubs. Supporting Ashram on one side while the stranger held the other, they scurried crab-like towards the dune. Then, without warning, they had to drop down flat against the sand again, crawling into shallow rocky crevices for cover. Shelley was sure her breathing was audible. The night air magnified sounds, even those from scurrying insects. Shelley, Ashram and Beetle's friend lay in the crevice waiting impatiently. Voices, like arguing, floated toward them. Finally, they stopped and were replaced by footsteps crunching back towards the centre. As soon as it was again still, Shelley forced her stiff joints towards the car, almost dragging Ashram. They flew through the doors, tumbling into the cramped space. She could barely move but they stayed low and out of sight.

Chapter 39

Light drizzle descended from the dark evening sky. Daryl's car's wipers scraped noisily across the windscreen, setting his nerves on edge. He missed the turn-off and cursed, then abruptly turned down the next street. The harsh sound of a blaring car horn followed him around the corner. Parked cars flanked both sides of this street and he circled the area three times before locating the casual hamburger place. He circled one more time before finding a parking spot.

He ran to the café, his stomach knotted painfully as he got close. He cringed as a bell clanged his arrival. The only occupant looked up from his magazine momentarily. Daryl wondered where all the people from the parked cars were. There was no-one around except for the man waiting for his takeaway and a jogger passing the doorway.

At the side of the café was an outdoor 'garden' area, sporting a few pot plants and the lone figure of Tim Curleigh in a dimly lit corner. When he saw Daryl, he stood and with the wave of a hand, guided Daryl to the seat beside him. It was a curiously overt gesture given the out-of-the-way meeting place he'd chosen.

Daryl sat down. What view there was, was obstructed by a rocky outcrop. The beach and a caravan park were beyond the rocks. In summer they'd be teeming with tourists but not at this time of year.

'Your call was a…surprise,' Tim said using his best politicians smile.

Daryl hesitated, instead of reassurance, the smile evoked a sense of dread. Was he doing the right thing? Was Tim really the right person to talk to?

Tim raised his arm flamboyantly to look at his watch. 'What advice do you need Daryl?'

The smile faded and Daryl ignored his misgivings and started to explain. 'I'm concerned about Mark and his connection to an international crime family, the Golgovich family. I suspect Wrogarth is being caught up,' he said before he could censure himself.

Tim gritted his teeth and stared out at the rocks. 'He always was that way inclined,' he muttered. When he turned towards Daryl his best smile was back. 'I'm glad you've come to me.'

He leaned forward and raised his arm. Daryl thought for a moment he was going to pat him on the head and ducked, but Tim just adjusted his jacket sleeve then coolly looked at Daryl.

'Go on. What do know specifically?'

Daryl detailed his suspicions and Tim didn't interrupt. He nodded or shook his head as appropriate and sometimes registered surprise. The words tumbled from Daryl's mouth in a rush. Once he'd started, he couldn't stop. Tim's silence egged him on and eventually he even confessed his suspicions about Bev.

'He's even trying to influence the coroner examining Bev's case,' he admitted.

'Why?'

Daryl looked down.

Tim coaxed him. 'Well?'

Daryl swallowed the lump in his throat. It was painful to say it out loud. 'He beat her.'

'Ah' Tim fell back against his chair, 'I suspected...he always was a bully.'

Daryl went silent. Tim fixed his eyes on the rocky outcrop deep in thought. His fist was clenched tight, his knuckles white with strain and a twitching muscle in his cheek was gaining speed.

'That bastard is leaking dirt about me to the press and my colleagues, trying to smear me, and all the time he's...He'll bring us all down,' he seethed. Tim's eyes burned in a controlled rage.

They sat surrounded in silence. Daryl didn't want to say anymore.

'Thank you, Daryl. Thanks for telling me. You haven't taken it to anyone else, have you?'

Daryl shook his head deciding Ralph was an insurance policy he wouldn't give up.

'Good. You don't need to worry about this anymore. Just leave it to me, I'll handle this now.'

They shook hands. 'You've done the right thing.'

Without another word, Tim strode out of the café.

Daryl waited for him to go before returning to his car. He fumbled with his keys and once inside sat quietly in the dark. His mind raced. He'd unburdened himself but didn't feel any lighter. The actions he'd set in motion were dangerous, not just to Wrogarth, but to his own career and reputation. Doubts enveloped him, like the dark clouds spreading across the sky.

Chapter 40

The hybrid vehicle silently sprang into action. It crawled in darkness from behind the shrubbery and bounced across the uneven ground. Only now did Shelley dare to look at their captor, or was he a rescuer? She still worried that it was a trap. What if they knew about Beetle and were using his codename to trick her? Crouched in the back of the car, she admonished herself for not making sure to protect Ashram. She was just a well-meaning amateur after all.

'I'm sorry I had to do that.' The stranger cut through her thoughts. 'I'm Ralph. I'm a friend of Beetle's. A journalist.'

The haggard and unshaven face before her didn't look like any journalist Shelley had ever met. Not that she'd met many.

'Why would I believe you?' she asked, finding her fighting spirit now it was too late.

'Why else would I help you?' he laughed, 'You hadn't noticed had you?'

'What?'

'The police were around tonight. They've either had a tip-off or they followed you.'

In the distance, they could see two cars parked on the side of the road and Ralph detoured into a siding. He parked well back behind a clutch of stunted trees.

'I'm just going to have a look. Wait here. Don't make a sound,' he said as he got out and leaned the door closed.

His form disappeared into the darkness and Shelley had to concentrate to stop her left leg jerking. When Ralph returned, he reported that neither car was a marked police car, but they still couldn't risk driving past. The only option was to go cross-country.

The siding opened onto a dry creek bed and using only parking lights for visibility, Ralph manoeuvred the vehicle down the narrow embankment. Shelley gripped the seat in front as they followed the bumpy rock-strewn path. Ashram groaned softly and Shelley wished they were on more even ground. A ribbon of trees and shrubs shielded them from the road, but their straggly branches couldn't hide the use of headlights. They came to a narrow passage threading under a bridge and the creek bed became rougher. Shelley imagined the gushing torrent that had formed these ruts after heavy rains and was glad the rains hadn't come yet. Ralph deftly steered the car around obstacles and brought them through to the other side, a bit shaken but safe.

The creek bed formed a junction. A narrow ditch speared off at right angles and connected back to the road while the creek meandered away in the other direction. They guessed they were past the cars so agreed to take the ditch. They climbed the steep incline which flattened out and led to the road. It was all clear.

Ralph switched on the headlights and accelerated, putting as much distance between them and the centre as he could.

'Beetle asked me to keep an eye out. He told me they're watching you,' Ralph said, turning to look back at them.

Ahead the road stretched before them like a straight flat ribbon of murky ochre winding through dusky outcrops and low-lying shrubs. Suddenly flashing red and blue lights sped towards them. Shelley and Ashram crouched down out of view as the police car whizzed past and splashed them in colour. Shelley let out her held breath when it was past them.

'It's OK. They've turned down the access road, heading towards the Centre,' Ralph said accelerating again.

Near Port Augusta, they detoured through back streets until they arrived at the other side of town. The double story Wheatsheaf Hotel was an old-style country pub, with a balcony and latticework framing the edges. Its new paint job couldn't hide the need for maintenance. Ralph pulled into the car park at the back and told them to stay put until he'd checked it was clear. The outside staircase creaked loudly as Ralph clambered to the first-floor. He disappeared through a screen door and Shelley scanned the row of dark windows until a light illuminated one then the curtains slid closed almost recreating the darkness except for a faint greenish glow. Ralph's head peered around the door and he motioned for them to follow. Shelley helped Ashram untangle himself from the car and Ralph came down to help. He and Ashram shuffled to the staircase, scaled the steps and disappeared through the screen door. Now it was Shelley's turn. She uncurled herself from the car, quietly closed the door, then raced up the stairs. The smell of stale beer and hospital-grade disinfectant assaulted her as she slipped into the corridor. She closed her mouth trying to limit the amount of smelly air she breathed in. Ralph was keeping watch at the door and beckoned her to hurry. She could hear the creak of an elevator and hurried past before the doors clanged open.

Ralph pulled a chair from under the small round table in the corner and placed it in the centre of the room for his guest. He threw himself into an armchair that groaned and wobbled in response to his weight. Shelley pulled pillows in place on the bed and Ashram collapsed into them. A scuffle of adjustments successfully propped Ashram up against the bedhead. His breath whistled laboriously from between his lips, his olive skin had taken on an ashen hue and his eyes had sunk further into his head. Shelley checked her phone and read a new text message, then dialled.

'Beetle?' she whispered into the phone, noticing Ralph's head jerk around.

'Yeah, all well?'

'Yes, we've met your friend,' she said, praying he would confirm Ralph's story.

'Good. He'll look after you. Talk later.' He hung up.

Shelley scanned the room. Its old-fashioned decor was worn and frayed, Ralph hadn't chosen anything upmarket. Ashram sighed. He was regaining his colour but his breathing still came in bursts. His eyes were closed and his mouth open. Ralph brought him a glass of water and helped him sip. He looked so frail and worn that Shelley suggested he needed to rest, but Ashram shook his head vigorously. He had to explain the things that plagued him. He became distressed at any suggestion that it should wait until morning.

'Akbal thought you were in a Pakistani refugee camp. Then he saw you on TV during the riot,' Shelley offered, aware Ralph had a pad and pencil in his hand.

'Pakistan was bad. It was dangerous. Every day I have to hide. Sometimes I cannot eat or sleep. I didn't think I could survive.' He swallowed noisily before continuing. 'I pay people to go to Indonesia, but it was worse than Pakistan. The camps are full of homeless people, all trying to escape the horror of their old lives. But in the camps, they suffer a different kind of horror.' He shuddered and closed his eyes. 'There is no way out. We are trapped there. We can't work, can't send the children to school, can't make a life there or find one somewhere else. We didn't know how long. How long would we have to wait for help or a new start?' He screwed up his face as he pulled himself up. 'I had to get out. I had to get to Akbal and Fatima.' He stared at Shelley and his tone softened, 'I was lucky.

I still had money, only a little, but enough to buy my way to Australia.'

'You paid a people smuggler to bring you?' Ralph asked and Ashram nodded.

'You should have seen the boat.' Ashram's eyes widened as though he could still see it. 'This piece of junk, I wouldn't trust it in a sheltered bay, and we were going to sail across the sea in it.' He shook his head solemnly. 'I thought we would die out there…. But we were lucky, the weather was good, it stayed calm. If it had been stormy, I don't know what would have happened to us. I cannot swim.'

His croaky voice broke and Shelley saw moisture building in his eyes. His hands shook as he lifted the glass of water to his lips and sipped.

'We cheer so loud when we see the ship. We jump around so they can see us…we are saved…our troubles are over. But we didn't know. They tell us to go back. We can't believe it. They can see our boat and still they tell us… turn around, you cannot come to Australia. They say go back to where you come from.'

Tears welled up in his eyes and threatened to overflow and he swiped at them violently.

'We go crazy…scream, we beg, and we cry… nearly tip the boat over. But the crew don't care, they turn us around.' Ashram shook his head, obviously still unable to believe what had happened. 'We have nowhere else to go. If we go back, we will be killed, tortured or put in prison. But they turn us around and follow us to make sure we go back. The cries in the boat tear at my heart. We cannot believe this is happening. A deep sadness fills us, our hearts are heavy. It was all for nothing. I was angry and afraid of what would happen to us. If I go back, I die. I can't sleep, people talk angrily, children cry, it is terrible. Then after dark, a big ship pulled up beside us. They tell us to leave our boat. They will save us. We get into the small boats and go onto the other ship.'

Ralph's eyes met Shelley's. Her surprise must have been easy to read.

'Was it the same ship again?' Shelley asked.

'No, this was a big tanker. The life jackets have the name Triton on them. They push us down into a large cabin below. They had blankets on the floor and some bread, water, and fruit waiting for us. Then they lock us in.'

Ashram pulled himself up, his arms struggling to lift his own weight. The telling of this story was noticeably tiring him but he fought off any attempts to make him rest.

'I don't know how long we are on that ship. When we get off, it is night. We don't know where we are. There are guards with guns. They make us get into trucks like the ones they use in the centre. The women and children went in one truck and the men in another. We didn't know they will take us to different places.'

Shelley's gasp made him look up, his eyes softening at her reaction.

Ashram continued, 'After a few days' rest, we had to work. We build roads and huts and even make caves and dig pits. The guards forget some of us speak English, so I know the work is for a mining company.'

'Do you know which one?' Ralph asked with pencil poised.

Ashram shook his head, 'I saw it once, the name was just letters, a lot of As.'

'AAAP?' ventured Shelley remembering something Jason had said.

Ashram shrugged then nodded slowly.

Shelley's phone rang and after checking the display, answered it.

'Are you OK? I couldn't get to you.' Jason's voice whispered down the line. 'Where are you?'

'Careful, we shouldn't —'

'It's OK. I'm using a payphone.'

'We're safe. I'll have to explain later. Are you alright?'

'They searched the car, frisked me and took me to the local police station for questioning.' Jason chuckled nervously, 'I just told them I got lost trying to find the Securion Motel. It was just the local police; they were patrolling the area.'

Shelley reassured Jason that all was well and agreed Jason should go back to the motel as though nothing had happened. They could talk soon.

Shelley studied the sunken form of Ashram. There was so much she still wanted to ask, but she was afraid it would be too taxing for him. Ralph seemed to pick up on her thoughts, suggesting Shelley return to her motel too.

'It's best if Ashram stays here,' he said.

It wasn't safe for Ashram to come back with her but how could she leave him here? Shelley couldn't think of an alternative, they hadn't planned for this eventuality so nervously she agreed.

'I'll let Akbal know you are safe.' Shelley touched Ashram's arm, but he pulled away sharply.

'No, I must tell you…there is more,' he protested loudly.

'We should wait until you've rested,' Shelley insisted.

Ashram shook his head emphatically, so Shelley sat back down and waited for him to catch his breath.

'I got sick, about two weeks ago, after the night shift.' His whole body shivered. 'That's when the tank trucks come. They carry the cargo we bury. We wear masks. It stinks.' His nose scrunched in response and he breathed in deeply. 'They pump the liquid into the pits we have dug…always at night. We place the hoses and turn taps on…we get splashed and it burns. The drivers don't come near.'

'What is it?' Ralph asked, looking up from his note-taking at last.

'They call it water, but it is the blackest 'water' I have ever seen.'

'Where are the trucks from?' Ralph sat forward; his face alight.

'I don't know but they come every two or three days.'

Ashram's body had slowly slid down and now he was uncomfortably slumped with his head wedged forward by the bedhead. He lacked the strength to pull himself up and Shelley and Ralph helped him.

'Do you have any idea what this 'water' is?' Ralph asked not looking up from his notes this time.

Shelley interrupted. 'Jason told me about cases of illegal dumping of toxic waste in Europe. They called it 'dirty water', could this be the same?'

Ashram shrugged his shoulders. 'It is strong and stinks. It makes my eyes water and burns my skin.'

'You think it made you sick?' Shelley asked not sure how this could be connected.

Ashram tugged at his sleeves revealing a pattern of sores festering on the backs of his hands and along his arms.

'This is from the splashes. Some of the others get much sicker than me. Some have died.' His voice faltered, finally exhausted by the effort of the escape and the telling.

On closer examination, the red and purple blotches were weeping. The angry sores spread up his arms like a badly executed tattoo. Ashram coughed, the rough and phlegm-laden sound tore at Shelley's heart. He had spent too much of his energy tonight, energy he needed for his recovery.

They helped him slide down into the bed and this time he submitted, laying his head back on the pillow. He closed his eyes. A blister peered out from beside his ear, she hadn't noticed that before.

Then she noticed another on the back of his neck as his frail body shook with a coughing fit.

Shelley and Ralph quietly made plans, trying not to disturb him. Jason and Shelley couldn't risk driving back to Adelaide with him, but she didn't like to leave him here. Ralph phoned a mate. His private plane could be the option they needed. He would take Ashram to Sydney, tonight, before the alarm went out. Would Ashram have the stamina? He needed medical attention, but they couldn't risk seeing a doctor here. Ralph wrote down Shelley's contact details in his journal and Shelley slid a copy into Ashram's pocket. He didn't even stir.

Overcome by uncertainty, Shelley forced herself out of the chair. She left Ashram with Ralph, hoping he was now in safe hands. He was safer with Ralph than with her and Jason. She slipped out of the door, walking briskly to the taxi rank down the road. Ralph watched from a safe distance until it carried her away.

***

'At last' Adrian muttered as he hastily scrawled down the number. He hung up the phone and immediately dialled the number he'd written down. He held his breath as the ringtone buzzed and transformed into a voice mail message. It didn't identify whose phone he was ringing but he left his message anyway.

'I hope this is the right number for Dante. This is Adrian McGrath, can you ring me back –' he could never remember his own mobile number. Shuffling through his notes, he found it in time to add to the message before it cut out.

He stalked the apartment, unable to sit, but unable to go out either. Opening the fridge door he scanned the contents then closed it again. A moment later, he reopened the door and grabbed a can of lemon squash. He glimpsed the paperwork he'd been avoiding. His brain couldn't fix on one thing at a time. It wasn't like him to procrastinate but he knew that's what he was doing.

The phone in his pocket simultaneously rang and vibrated and startled him. Fumbling as he reached for it he almost dropped the lemon squash and glass.

'Hi,' he answered hoping he'd caught the call-in time.

'Adrian?' The soft voice at the other end had a disguised quality.

'Yes, Dante?' He heard a sigh as he said the name.

'Yeah, it's me. Your message was a surprise.'

'You're a hard man to track down, I'd almost given up.' Adrian sat down at his desk and moved the pile of papers. 'What's all that about?'

'Where to start?' The short silence conveyed issues were weighing heavily on Dante. 'I'm just laying low.'

'Why?'

Dante was a good coroner, one of the best, careful and thorough. It was true people didn't always like him but that was usually those with something to hide. He got results.

'It's too complicated.'

'I need to talk to you about a case you briefly worked on. The Federal Police took it over before you finished the job.'

There was a sharp intake of breath at the other end.

'Ayisha? Why?' Dante's voice had turned hard.

'A friend of mine knew her and is trying to find out what happened.' Adrian waited but when there was no response he added, 'She wants to know the truth.'

'They took over before I could do my job. Your friend would be safer to stay out of it, that's why I'm lying low.'

'I don't understand. Why would that case make you lie low, especially if you didn't finish the job?'

'They don't like questions...challenges their authority...especially difficult questions.' Dante breathed out into the phone and a deep throaty chuckle accompanied the rest of his sentence. 'I'm on leave don't you know. They thought I needed a break; I was becoming too *involved*.'

'What's all this about?'

'I'm not sure. The Feds made sure I couldn't investigate thoroughly. You won't find my conclusion in the final notes.'

Dante sighed, Adrian could picture him removing his glasses and wiping his eyes with his thumb and forefinger, the way he always did when he was troubled.

'I couldn't get any straight answers after the Federal Police took over and of course as soon as I challenged their jurisdiction, I needed a holiday. It wasn't a request.'

Adrian explained what he and Shelley had learned so far.

'Yes. The local police reported finding the body at King's Cross but the next day the Federal Police amended the report. I questioned them. There've been other cases and I've ceased believing in their game.'

Adrian's head shot up. 'What others?'

'There have been two separate incidents involving unidentified, immigrant women. Both died under very suspicious circumstances. One could have been suicide, but the Feds swooped in and took over before we could start. My Melbourne counterpart has had one, but he won't rock the boat. I think there's been one in Brisbane since Ayisha.'

'What's going on?'

'I have no proof of anything…but…' he paused. 'I think it's connected to the sex slave trade. The Feds should be closing down those operations but given the casualty rate, they're either slow or incompetent or –'

'Could they be running a covert operation?'

'No. A new security group, with a number of government contracts, have taken over the brothels.' Dante sighed again, the sound heavier than before, 'They appear to be untouchable. The Prime Minister personally signed off on the Feds taking over Ayisha's case. He wouldn't normally get involved in something like this. I can't work out what's going on.'

'I'm thinking of coming to Sydney again soon, can we meet up?'

'It would be good to see you, but I warn you, I won't be much more help. Leave a message once you have your dates and we'll work something out.'

Adrian stowed his phone back in his pocket and stared out of the window. His pulse raced. He took out the phone again, this time dialling a number he hadn't called in a long time. The message service confirmed it was still the right number. He hesitated. He couldn't say what he wanted to in a message, the impact would be lost. He rang off without speaking. His sense of impotence added to his already building frustration.

Pacing his small flat he went over his options. His phone rang again, and this time Jason's chirpy voice greeted him. He sounded excited, full of nervous energy as he rattled off their news without much prompting. Their success was a relief but also added to Adrian's fears. His heart raced as Jason explained what had happened. Jason's enjoyment of all the intrigue was clear but Adrian tensed when he learned they were being watched. He shivered. Ralph's involvement was a complication they didn't need and would make things riskier.

The text from Shelley later that night reassured him although she sounded more formal than usual. Still, he spent a sleepless night pondering the new information and their growing dilemma. The later the hour, the more the options involved evil scenarios and conspiracies. His thoughts had a life of their own and he couldn't shut them down.

Chapter 41

Shelley hadn't slept at all. The motel bed had been soft and inviting, but unfamiliar. She'd wrestled with her quilt until it entangled her like a straitjacket. Now she and Jason sat quietly in the café. Her coffee had gone cold and her breakfast was untouched as she waited impatiently for Ralph's message. His text came just as they saw the convoy of police vehicles drive down the road towards Quorn. Ralph and Ashram were safely in Sydney. Now Shelley and Jason could leave too.

The drive home passed like a dream. Jason couldn't wipe the grin off his face, and he frowned at her tightly held frame perched in the seat beside him.

'What doesn't kill you makes you stronger,' he said light-heartedly.

She thought of Ayisha and Ashram. 'Sometimes what doesn't kill you leaves scars and makes you weaker,' she responded.

Jason gave her a sidelong glance. 'We did it.'

'It's not over yet.' Shelley shook her head. 'He's not safe, Didi isn't safe and we still don't have any answers.'

Jason turned his concentration back to the road, only a hint of his smile remained.

They arrived at her apartment too soon. She hesitated then invited Jason in, but he said he had something to follow-up. He kissed her lightly on the cheek. They'd grown closer during this adventure. Under his light-hearted demeanour, there was a kind and generous man. She couldn't have done this without him. But Shelley now had doubts that she'd done the right thing. Had she been reckless and risked lives? How could she have not acted?

She felt eyes watching her as she walked through the entrance to her building. It was probably just her nerves, but the familiarity of her apartment was not enough to steady them.

Shelley phoned Ralph remembering too late that her phone or apartment could be tapped. The risks to Ashram's life were real so she kept the conversation cryptic.

'All's well,' Ralph said quietly. 'A bit airsick, but safe.'

'What now?' she asked.

'I need a discreet doctor.'

'I might be able to help.' Shelley offered before hanging up.

Shelley dialled Adrian's number several times before finally letting it ring. She hoped he wasn't still angry and braced herself for a reaction.

'Oh, thank God! I've been worried.' He sounded relieved.

Shelley beamed. Now, even if he unleashed a rant it didn't matter.

'What happened?' he asked, 'Actually, let's meet for a coffee.'

Shelley took a circuitous route to the popular Rundle Street café and Adrian arrived at the same time. They selected a table away from others and Shelley told him about the trip.

'You took a big risk,' he said softly, shaking his head. 'I'm glad you pulled it off, but it's not over yet. There's been nothing in the news about it.'

'Maybe they don't want the public to know.' She shrugged then added, 'I need your help. Ashram needs medical treatment. Do you know a trustworthy doctor in Sydney?'

'I know someone who might be willing to help and keep it quiet.'

Adrian pulled out his phone and scrolled through his contacts. Shelley took out her phone and sent the details to Ralph in a text message.

Adrian ordered coffees then reached for her hand. 'I was surprised you would do something like that. I expect it from Jason but you…'

His blue eyes pierced her protective shield, making her soften.

'It was important,' Shelley said, although she couldn't really explain.

'You once told me you couldn't do anything illegal.'

'I didn't know then what I know now.' She felt more justified with every word.

The waiter placed coffees on the table in front of them and left. A young couple sat down at the table beside them, despite Adrian's pointed glare.

'I knew you cared but...' he said quietly, his eyes gently resting on her face.

Shelley leaned forward too. 'Let's go for a walk after our coffees,' she replied, pointing her gaze towards the table beside them.

The young couple scrolled through their smartphones, sitting back, totally absorbed. Their silence unnerved Shelley and made her suspicious. Adrian nodded agreement and they drank their coffees, trying to maintain small-talk while desperate to talk about what really mattered.

'I have some news too,' he said as they pushed their chairs back.

Adrian paid for the coffees and they joined the stream of people squeezing past the outside tables. A group of cyclists had set up their coffee break on the footpath, creating a bottleneck with their bikes and chairs. Adrian grabbed Shelley's hand and they looped out onto the busy road, narrowly missing a bike pulling into the kerb.

In the peaceful Botanic Gardens, they walked and talked, finally again relaxed in each other's company. Shelley told Adrian about Ashram's experience and the sores on his arms and neck. Adrian listened quietly, letting out a small whistle at times, but letting her finish without comment.

'That ties in with some of my test results.'

He pulled Shelley onto a seat overlooking the stream and duck pond. They watched the ducks squawk at passers-by, begging for a morsel of food despite their fat bellies.

'What test results?' she asked.

'Do you remember the Aboriginal children samples?' At Shelley's nod, he continued, 'Those results matched Yasmine's results. There are slight variations in symptoms, but essentially, they're the same. Here's where it gets interesting. It looks like all these cases are connected; the Africans Yasmine is treating; the Aboriginal children; the French truck drivers and Ashram and other asylum seekers in the remote detention centres. They have all been exposed to toxic waste. We just need to figure out how, who's responsible, and why.'

'Ashram says AAAP is involved. I don't know how they're getting away with it. He said initially they used drums and concreted the sites shut but, these days they're just dumping it and moving on.'

Shelley felt her stomach knot again.

'The Aboriginal children must have come into contact with this toxic material through the nearby disused mine.' He scratched his head, staring at the lake. 'The African example must be connected through Ortansea. They have a record of this kind of dumping, but they don't operate in Australia.'

'That points to a connection between Ortansea and AAAP doesn't it?'

'Jason and Klaus are researching that. AAAP started in the markets at the same time as Ortansea withdrew and they've bought up old Ortansea sites. There definitely must be a connection.'

'Ralph thinks this scandal goes right to the PM. I don't like Wrogarth but even I can't believe he would condone this.' Again, the vision of a Parisian Café and that shady deal surfaced in her mind. Maybe it was a pay-off. The envelope Mark McCracken had pocketed could have been a payment from Carlew, the mining boss. Maybe Mark McCracken was acting on his own without the knowledge of the Prime Minister.

'I can believe it.' Adrian clenched his fists and his face formed an angry mask. 'The evil in men never ceases to amaze me. I've seen it too often. Criminal and immoral behaviour isn't restricted to the obvious suspects. It's like cancer, living and growing in shadow, waiting for its next victim, those who are easily influenced or easily mislead.'

'But we have checks in place.'

'Propaganda has made people complacent. We think we're above this kind of thing. But real communication, talking, discussing, debating has been replaced by things like Twitter, the two-second opinion and meaningless interchanges with virtual strangers. In this environment, men like Wrogarth can get away with anything.' Adrian stood up and paced, his fists clenching and unclenching in a rhythm that matched a speeding heartbeat. 'It must be exposed. Otherwise, it could win and blur the difference between expediency and immorality.'

He stood at the tree edge; his head tilted back as though he was about to scream. His silent protest was a poignant reminder of how deeply he felt.

Shelley walked over to him. 'Ralph's been working on an article. Maybe this is what we need.'

They had swapped roles. She was counselling using legitimate channels and he was bent on action. Adrian wrapped his arm around Shelley's shoulder.

'Maybe.' He paused, took a few steps forward, then stopped again. 'But another general article won't get attention, not without hard evidence. We need that evidence.'

With these ominous words, they left the park. They weren't finished, in fact, this was only the beginning and she hoped she had the stamina and single-mindedness to see this through to the end, whatever that may be.

***

Jason registered the healthier colouring on Akbal's face. There was a visible lifting of the furrows in his brow and the crow's feet straddling his eyes formed a smile when Jason told him about Ashram's rescue. Fatima laughed, clapping her hands at the news. She anxiously clasped at Akbal and insisted they talk to Ashram right away. Jason explained as best he could, in between the interruptions, that even Jason didn't know exactly where he was. They, whoever they were, were probably watching Akbal and Fatima's house. Akbal shivered as Jason repeated it for emphasis.

Fatima skipped into the kitchen to prepare some refreshments, leaving Jason and Akbal to talk.

'I don't know much.' Jason hesitated, he wasn't good at subtlety and Shelley had warned him to be careful.

'I want to know everything,' Akbal said, shifting forward in his seat in readiness.

'Ashram is ill. It's not critical but it's serious.'

'We knew that. Detention is soul-destroying.' Akbal studied his hands in serious contemplation, perhaps remembering his own experience.

'Not just detention. He's been exposed to some toxic material,' Jason explained.

'What?'

Jason was under strict instructions from Shelley to not speculate, so he stuck to the known.

'We're not sure. I think they are working on infrastructure projects during the day but at night they're handling hazardous material.' Jason continued before Akbal could ask more questions, 'I can't say much more. I promise we'll tell you once we have something concrete. In the meantime, Ashram's whereabouts must remain secret.'

Akbal's disappointment played out on his face. He slid back in his seat and crumpled down into a small shell-like shape. Theories

390

formed on Jason's lips, but he stopped the speculations before they were voiced. Akbal nodded and smiled gently at Jason.

'Yes. It is enough that Ashram is safe because of you. Thank you and please thank Shelley for me too. I don't know how to repay you.'

'It's not over yet.' Akbal's gratitude was making Jason blush and he swiped at his overly warm cheeks. 'I'm glad we could help.'

Fatima bounced back into the room, a spring in her step carrying her lightly across the rug. They turned their attention to consuming biscuits and Jason sipped at his unusual but not unpleasant tea. The silence, interrupted only by Fatima's periodic exclamations of joy and thanks, was heavy with hope and quiet prayer. Jason tried unsuccessfully to urge caution, to make sure Fatima, in particular, understood Ashram was not yet safe and the Federal Police were looking for him. But Fatima's joy would not be deterred.

When Fatima left them to tend to Sari, Jason said goodbye. Akbal had shrunk back into his chair again, the colour had drained from his face and the furrows were back. He was again a man in need of rest and recovery. Akbal understood the severity of what was happening, he had shivered at the mention of the Federal Police and he understood all too well what would happen if Ashram was found. He was now absorbed by fresh concerns and issues, despite Fatima's optimistic outlook. It had already been a big day even though it was only lunchtime.

Chapter 42

Wrogarth touched the cool glass to his forehead, but it did nothing to dampen his rage. Where was that good-for-nothing Mark? This article was the last straw.

His personal life was being laid bare for all to read. He clenched his teeth; the reporter was using Bev's injuries to paint him as a violent fiend. It wasn't like that! These journalists oversimplified everything. He'd lashed out sometimes, but he'd been provoked. It wasn't easy being Prime Minister. The article didn't tell his part of the story. It just went on about the injuries Bev had suffered over the years. They called her a battered wife. What did that make him? How dare they do this to him!

He swallowed the contents of his glass in one gulp, but it didn't bring the effect he sought. The careful strategy, all that planning undermined. The end justified the means, he was sure of that, but they hadn't reached the end yet. They weren't even close. The public wouldn't understand.

Slowly lifting himself out of the chair, he stumbled towards the bar. Enfolding the bottle in his small hands, he started to pour another drink then, changing his mind, he carried the bottle back to his desk.

How would they fix this? He reread the paragraph detailing his past transgressions and snorted. They were dredging up everything. It painted him as dishonest and even suggested he was corrupt. He snorted again and tossed the paper down. Australians didn't mind dishonesty in politics. They accepted politicians saying whatever it took to get elected, but it had to stay covert and subtle. Howard got away with his Children Overboard scandal and even the Iraqi war. His core and non-core promises were a legend. He swiped at the paper, knocking it onto the floor.

Yesterday's episode with Daryl made him smile. The man didn't understand how useful Mark's connections were. His family was as useful as he was. Wrogarth scowled – where was Mark now when the proverbial hit the fan? Doubt leaped into his mind. Of course, Mark wasn't calling the shots, Daryl had that very wrong and he was going to make damn sure Mark knew it. At least he would when he finally saw him.

As though summoned by sheer will, Mark burst through the door. His face flushed and his dark eyes flashing.

'Finally,' roared Wrogarth, his tongue catching on his back teeth and making him slur. 'Explain to me how this got out?'

'I don't know.' Mark waved his arms, palms up in an exaggerated gesture of submission.

Wrogarth glared, curling his body in readiness to let him have it, but Mark leaned toward the desk interrupting his boss' thoughts.

'We had no idea he was looking into Bev's death or the detention centres. We had him stonewalled on the mining issues. We'll find the leaks and plug them quickly. He can't have done this without help.' Mark sat down heavily in the visitor's chair. 'Anyway, Daryl was supposed to sort out the coroner.'

'This report will kill me, kill my re-election chances. It will kill off your chances too. He doesn't need to get facts, the rumours will be enough, the mud will stick, regardless. Doubt is all that's required.'

Mark cocked his head as a look of surprise flashed across his face.

'Well, it's true,' Wrogarth shouted as he thumped the table for emphasis. 'They won't understand my reasons. They won't understand how important all this is for Australia…for the economy.'

'And for you?' Mark's voice was calm and low, the look had returned.

Wrogarth reached for his drink, almost spilling it as he brought it to his lips. Mark was supposed to be on his side.

'Of course it benefited me.' His tone was low, matching Mark's, but he wasn't sure what game they were playing. Then the injustice of it caught at his chest and he raised his voice. 'You know how important it was to get these projects off the ground, to keep Australian mining projects competitive on a world scale after the price dropped.'

He lost his train of thought, struggling to remember the point he was planning to use next. He looked up to see Mark smirking and his pulse quickened instantly. He wasn't going to be mocked by him, of all people.

'So, what are you going to do about it? Your family won't be pleased either,' Wrogarth shouted. Sparkling dots of spittle sprayed across the desk.

'I've got people on it, we'll shut him up.'

Volcanic levels of pressure built inside Wrogarth. He rose out of his seat and let a torrent of invective flow.

Once he was back under control he added calmly, 'We don't need another incident. People will get suspicious. We need to discredit him, not get heavy-handed, make it look like he has a grudge to settle, or he is in league with the opposition, make it look like an unfounded smear. We need to spin these things as innocent misrepresentations.'

Mark nodded and rose from his seat, muttering, 'That's easier said than done.' Then in a louder voice said, 'I'll get on to it, I have some ideas already. I'll see to it.'

Wrogarth lowered his voice to a menacing loud whisper, 'If I go, I'll take you and your family with me.'

Their eyes met, but it was Wrogarth who looked away first.

'You'd better clear out any documents too, make sure there's nothing that can point to either of us.' He frowned and leaned forward to emphasise his point. 'Just in case.'

'Sure,' Mark said and smirked.

Mark left Wrogarth to his solitude. He had a sudden urge to throw his glass at Mark's retreating back but resisted. Why waste good scotch?

***

The coroner's report made dry reading as Daryl sat motionless in his dreary kitchen. The official reports he'd seen so far hadn't put the case so strongly. Daryl cursed. He'd let his doubts be mollified. He should have known better, hadn't he known about the domestic violence, hadn't he seen the bruises himself? He had known all along that Bev had borne the brunt of Wrogarth's explosive temper. He himself had argued with her often enough, trying to persuade her to leave but Bev had staunchly denied what was happening. Daryl didn't understand her refusal to leave. He'd warned her that it wouldn't get better, only worse. Even he hadn't expected it to get this bad though. He'd underestimated Wrogarth's anger.

Bev was an easy target. Wrogarth had shown her his worst side. She'd seen his weaknesses but then he'd unleashed those frustrations on her too. Despite that, Bev had stayed loyal and maintained the façade.

The coronial inquest concluded Wrogarth had been responsible for her fall. The evidence pointed to her being pushed violently, sending her plummeting down the stairs. Even that could be construed as an accident but the medical report said in addition to her many old injuries, the badly mended broken bones and hairline fractures, there was evidence she had suffered severe blows to the face and upper body immediately before the fall. Daryl's hands shook as he placed the report gently onto the kitchen table. The words swam before his eyes avoiding comprehension and saving him from facing the facts too quickly.

The vision of a vibrant and confident woman sprung before his eyes. It was Bev as he first knew her. Over the years, fear and doubt took their toll and she became a shadow of the woman she had once been. He realised with surprise that he had probably been in love with her. He'd have never admitted his feelings. He'd always avoided analysing what drew him towards her, made him want to protect her, care for her in any way he could. Maybe he was naïve; she had shown him kindness, nothing more. Bev had never given him any reason to believe she felt more than friendship for him. Daryl bowed his head, his forehead almost hitting the table surface. Yet again he had failed, unable to prevent the inevitable. He moaned. He'd lived an ineffectual life. In fact, he was an ineffectual man in a world that swallowed up weak individuals and spat them into the gutter.

He bounced his head hard against the solid surface, the pain momentarily distracting him from the pain tearing at his heart. This beautiful woman, this generous soul, had been beguiled by Wrogarth's charisma and ambition. The ambition was hers too, of course, he could see that now. Daryl had to admit, she had used him to gather information thinking she could steer James in the right direction. She hadn't understood the terrible cost of staying.

Daryl could no longer lie to himself. James Wrogarth had become consumed by his need for power and was lost to it now. It was time to take a stand and move on. He had to do it now, today.

Daryl grabbed his jacket. He needed to escape the dim apartment and breathe some fresh air. His area was old and very quiet, even so, he didn't often venture out at night. He walked in the still evening air, the streetlights casting a gentle glow at intervals across his path. Cooking smells filtered from the small cottages along this street. Dinner was being prepared, children being put to bed, favourite television programs being watched. These were the components of a life that had eluded him. If Margie had lived, this could have been them. He'd have had an ordinary job, working in an office and they'd have built a home together. At the end of his day, he would enter the warm fold of a family and be surrounded by those he loved. Instead, here he was, outside, wandering the streets alone, with no-one to confide in. Slowly, his job and his association with Wrogarth and Bev had worked its magic until he didn't recognise the man he'd become. He'd been too pliable, and it had distorted him. He hadn't stood for anything and now he had nothing left to stand for.

He paused outside a small café across the road from the local hotel. Contemplating a coffee and something to eat he stared through the window. It was empty and the owner was busily cleaning the coffee machine. Restless and unwilling to turn back yet, he crossed the road. A stream of cars let loose by the traffic lights up ahead passed before him and he paused on the median strip, his mind preoccupied and in turmoil. As he stepped onto the curb, he noticed two familiar-looking figures emerge from the side door of the hotel. Tim Curleigh and Mark McCracken stopped near a car park light and continued their conversation. Daryl ducked down behind a four-wheel-drive parked on the side of the road, stooping so he could watch through the windows without being seen. As the two figures moved towards the car park, Daryl crept across to a row of trees. He tripped on a small twig and plunged forward noisily. Grabbing the nearest bush, he pulled himself in behind a thick tree trunk. Both the figures turned; Daryl could see their worried looks illuminated by the faint streetlight. A cat sprung down from a lower branch above him and scurried into the bushes with a flick of its tail and a soft meow and the figures returned to their intense discussion.

Daryl strained forward to filter out the bursts of traffic noise as the two men leaned into each other. There was a conspiratorial air about their closeness, relaxed gestures and the occasional laugh. The suggested friendliness or intimacy surprised Daryl.

'He's a fuckwit, a bloody liability. He'll bring us all down with him,' Tim Curleigh raged. 'He has to go! And by God, I'll make sure he does.'

He was loud and unrestrained, and Daryl remembered how obvious their meeting had been a week ago.

Mark's dulcet tones responded quietly, 'It's him or you now, but we can fix this. He needs to go quietly. It's up to you.'

They shook hands and walked to their respective cars. Daryl waited until both had disappeared out of sight before moving. Daryl shivered. He had trusted Tim, had believed he was a better man than Wrogarth. He bowed his head, wanting to scream in frustration but bottling it up as best he could. He couldn't believe how poor his judgement was.

Without consciously making a decision, Daryl found himself back at the office. He knew the drill, how to avoid the security cameras. He was invisible to the guards anyway, just part of the furniture. The Federal Police guards had been replaced by Serpentco and Daryl laughed at how inept they were. He passed Wrogarth's office, the light was on, but it was quiet. He crept along the corridor staying close to the wall. Slowly he opened the door to Mark's office, stepped inside and closed the door quietly behind him. Daryl's set of spare keys to the filing cabinets were an unexpected bonus. Luckily Mark didn't know about them.

Unlocking the filing cabinet, he fingered the file headings until he found what he was looking for. He sighed. There was nothing

400

useful, just copies of the general office correspondence and press releases. Daryl cursed softly, knowing Mark had kept papers for insurance. Angrily, he tore open the drawers one by one. The filing cabinet tottered under the weight of the open drawers and Daryl caught it just before it crashed forward. He grabbed at the drawers and a patch of white on the side of the middle drawer caught his eye. Tape lapped up the side and his heart skipped a beat. He patted the underside and discovered a soft, heavily taped parcel underneath. He carefully ripped it free and opened the envelope. It contained several USBs, a series of documents signed by Wrogarth and another envelope containing several small cassettes. Daryl stuffed the envelopes into the top of his trousers and flattened them up under his T-shirt. He pulled his jacket close and fled.

Chapter 43

Shelley perched on the edge of the sofa, swallowing her anxiety. Her hands, locked between her knees, had barely stopped shaking.

'I'm off to Sydney tomorrow...there's something I need to tell you.'

Adrian's hushed voice and serious demeanour frightened her. She could sense he was troubled. Was this the end of their relationship? He had been so distracted since his last visit to Sydney and Shelley's mind floated to Yasmine. Although she had never met Yasmine, she knew there had been something between her and Adrian. Was he going back to her? Was she waiting for him in Sydney? Shelley trembled, she couldn't fight their history and shared experiences and maybe it wasn't history anymore. She had hoped letting it run its course would bring Adrian back to her. Now she was afraid she'd chosen the wrong option. She avoided his eyes by studying her hands and clasping them even tighter.

'I should have told you a while ago, but...'

He faltered and she glanced up, watching him struggle with what he needed to say.

'I like you; I didn't want to admit…' Again, he left it hanging in the air like an executioner's sword, poised ready to strike.

Shelley's chest constricted as she held her emotions in check. She squirmed under his gaze and reluctantly summoned a quiet whisper.

'What is it?'

She needed to hear it for herself. Maybe she should end it first and save this torture, but she couldn't find her voice. Adrian stopped pacing and propped in the chair opposite her. Perching on the edge he mirrored her uncomfortable pose. He stared ahead and she looked away, not trusting herself to be calm. She had no claim on him however much she wanted to.

'I'm not who you think I am,' he said it quickly catching her unawares. Their eyes met as he continued, 'My real name is William Adrian Wrogarth. McGrath is my mother's maiden name.'

He sighed, seeming relieved but Shelley had been preparing for very different news and was confused.

'I'm the Prime Minister's son,' he added, his voice almost a whisper.

Relief washed over her and she laughed softly. She crumpled back into the chair and realised she'd been holding her breath. His hands moved in a hypnotic continuous rhythm massaging each other fiercely as she tried to shake her mind into action. He frowned, obviously puzzled at her reaction but he allowed her time to collect her thoughts. It was not the end of their relationship as she had anticipated, and she slowly focused on what he'd said. Questions flooded her mind, leaving her unsure of where to start.

'Let me explain,' he said as he reached out a hand to touch her but withdrew it before it made contact. Instead, they returned to the wringing and massaging they'd been so preoccupied with.

'My father and I fell out when I first started work. I came here to get away from him and his politics and decided a new identity would make it easier.'

He was trembling and studied her face intently. Shelley shook her head; this had weighed heavily on Adrian's mind and he was obviously worried about her reaction. She walked across to his chair and embraced him, hoping to reassure him of her feelings, and as she did so, suddenly understanding the full impact of the revelation.

'I'm so sorry...the reports about...your mother's death...your father...' she said quietly, holding him close.

His life, his parents, the family intrigue, it was all too large to comprehend in a single moment. She trembled to think of his suffering in silence for so long without help or support.

'She wouldn't leave him. I knew things had become worse.'

Shelley hadn't read all the reports, they'd seemed so sordid and full of innuendo, but she had heard snippets, 'You don't believe it was an accident, do you? Wrogarth said...she'd been drinking...' she suggested.

Adrian tore away from her. 'That's not true. She never got drunk. She'd have the occasional glass of wine with dinner, but she couldn't stand drunken behaviour. I know he did this. He has history.' His chin set in a hard line.

Shelley sat down again. 'Perhaps you should tell me about this from the beginning.'

His face collapsed with pain and she wanted to reach out to hold him close and comfort him. Instead, she stayed in her seat waiting for him to verbalise what he'd planned to tell her.

'It was no accident!' His voice was hoarse and tightly under control. 'He was always violent; he'd take his frustrations out on her. In the early days, he'd lash out when he drank too much…that was often enough…too often. It got worse after I left, I'm certain of it. He put mum in the hospital a couple of times. She lied about it, but I knew. When I saw her the last time, I couldn't convince her to leave…and now…it's too late.'

He thrust his head into his hands, his body shaking with emotion. When he looked up again his eyes were brimming ready to break their banks.

'I don't know why she stayed. I know she was ambitious…enjoyed the success; she'd worked hard for it too. But I don't understand why she tolerated it.' Adrian laid his head back into his hands, sighing loudly.

'You don't think she could have started using alcohol as a prop, do you?' At the violent shake of his head, Shelley hurriedly continued. 'So what do you think happened?'

'In Sydney...I went to the hospital. He didn't know.' He swallowed hard. 'Her injuries were...worse than a fall downstairs.' His voice was gaining strength as his anger grew. 'The final report is being kept under wraps. The inquest...her head injuries indicate she was badly beaten before she fell.' He straightened in his seat, composing himself before he continued, 'He thought he could get away with it because he's Prime Minister.'

'Surely the police wouldn't let someone get away with murder, even if they were the Prime Minister.' It even sounded naïve to her own ears, given what she knew about other issues.

'You believe that?' Adrian questioned, his voice hard and edgy.

Shelley watched him again pace the floor and realised the disguised and forlorn figure standing on the outskirts at the funeral had been him. She trembled at the thought of how alone he'd been then.

'Why didn't you tell me sooner?' An edge of disappointment crept into her voice despite her attempts to disguise it.

'I didn't know how. I've lived with this secret for such a long time. I hate him...I didn't want to admit I was related.'

'What happened to make you hate him so much?'

'He is a very ambitious politician. In the early days, I think he genuinely cared. We didn't always agree on what that meant for the policy or how to improve things, but he at least had some scruples. Then he got involved with property developers and a couple of big business tycoons and he started taking shortcuts. It sickened me to see what he was becoming. Then, one day I found out he'd given a business buddy the contracts to renew all the high-tech medical equipment in the major hospitals around the country. We were paying top dollar for their second-rate equipment. It was a billion-dollar scam. I blew the whistle on him, both to the press and the party machine. He lost his status in the party although grandpa helped him back. He couldn't prove it was me, but he knew. One night I got angry and admitted it. We haven't spoken since. He called in favours from his media mates and they watered down the story. At least I stopped the scheme.' Adrian swallowed hard.

'He hated bowing and scraping but he did it and worked his way back into the good books. He's still an arrogant prick, hooked on power and he has gone from bad to worse, especially as Prime Minister. Someone has to stop him.' He thumped his fist into the palm of his other hand.

Adrian's tone was harsh, and the only emotion Shelley could read was anger and a desire for revenge. He paced again, different emotions playing out across his face. They talked in bursts but then Adrian pulled her up and held her tight.

'I'm glad I have you,' he murmured it into her hair so softly she almost missed it. When he was gone, she began to doubt what she'd heard.

407

He'd declined her offer to stay saying he would be dreadful company and needed time to think. She hadn't wanted to let him go but his rejection left behind a veil of uncertainty. No, he hadn't said he was still in love with Yasmine, but she was still confused. Were they ever going to find a way to be together? Or were they destined to be just 'friends with benefits'? There hadn't been enough 'benefits' so far and Shelley wanted more, much more.

***

Jason had just put down the phone after a long talk with Klaus when Adrian rapped on his door. The forceful knock startled him. Adrian stormed in, anger and tension seeped from every pore but remained unexplained. Jason shuffled his notes into a neat pile and offered Adrian a drink. Adrian declined as he emptied his briefcase of notes and strew them across the table where Jason's had only just been.

Jason watched as Adrian collected the pieces of paperwork and sorted them, only to rearrange them over and over again. It was getting late and he wasn't sure why Adrian was here.

'It's all here. I really have him this time,' Adrian muttered waving sheets of paper as though they were empowering him.

He quoted facts and details, like a barrister presenting his findings to a jury but Jason struggled to convert them into the firm conclusions Adrian had.

'So, what are you going to do?' Jason asked.

Adrian got up from the chair and started to pace about the room. When he stopped, his fiery stare made Jason squirm.

408

'I'm not sure. I want him to know he's not going to get away with this.' He stared at the papers in his hand. 'That bastard is out of control. I'm going to make him pay.'

The threat was real, and Jason shuddered. Surely Adrian didn't believe he could personally bring his father down. This collection of facts told of sinister goings-on but they didn't conclusively link them to the Prime Minister.

'I'm going to expose him. This time I'll make it stick,' Adrian threatened.

This was no idle threat either and Jason knew Adrian well enough to know he meant everything he'd said. The emotions flashing across Adrian's face were instantly recognisable, rage, anguish, and despair, and they melded into a heady mix. Like a restless lion, he paced, roaring from time to time, punching the air occasionally to emphasise a point or to sap the nervous energy building up inside his already tense body. Ashram's story had simply added fuel to an already raging fire.

'I have to confront him,' Adrian said.

'What will that achieve?' Jason enjoyed playing devil's advocate, although this time he was interested in the answer.

'He has to be stopped,' Adrian said glaring at Jason, challenging him to dispute it.

'How can he change things now? It's gone too far.'

'He can…he can turn things around. It can be done. If he won't then…' He swallowed leaving the threat hanging.

'Then what?' Jason prompted, hoping to dissuade him and make him see sense.

'I'll bring him down.'

Adrian clenched his teeth and Jason wondered if this time Adrian had lost perspective and control. Wild threats were not his usual style.

'Wikileaks is already exposing details. We could use them instead,' Jason offered.

'It's not enough.' Adrian rasped loudly.

He paced back and forth, his incessant rhythm wearing a track on Jason's floor. Jason understood it was a matter of principle for Adrian, a matter of right and wrong. Despite all of Adrian's ranting and raving and getting on his soapbox over the years, Jason had rarely seen him so out of control. His fervour was arousing a strange feeling of solidarity. After-all his own father was part of this series of scandals. Jason had let him off the hook too easily. Wasn't he too trying to cash in on other people's misery? His compliance with Martin Carlew, his disastrous mining land deals losing everything and now, he was turning a blind eye to Jason's mother's drinking problem. Maybe he should be just as angry and confront his father before his mother succeeded in killing herself.

Both of them should challenge their fathers and make them accept responsibility for what they'd done. How could they turn a blind eye to what was going on? Jason recalled the emotion he'd felt on the Normandy beaches. People were wrong when they said the soldiers fought for the flag or some benign symbol, they had fought for a way of life and the betterment of their country. If Adrian stepped away, what would that make him? Their eyes met, Adrian's lit by an inner fire that almost emitted a tangible heat and Jason nodded.

'You're right...'

Maybe it was time he took on his own challenge and faced it with courage. They clasped each other in a stilted, masculine hug, one that friends give to express support, understanding, and agreement.

After Adrian left, Jason sat in the quiet room staring out of his window into an inky sky. So much had happened over the last three months and he wasn't sure what to think. He'd treated the issues with more respect than he usually would. They mattered and had spurred him on to meet the challenge.

He picked up his pile of notes and distractedly shuffled through them, about to put them aside when he suddenly saw it. The connection between Ortansea and AAAP, it was so obvious. Why hadn't they seen it before? He picked up the phone and dialled Klaus. It was late, but he would want to know.

Chapter 44

'Prime Minister Assassinated' the headlines screamed. No-one knew the full details. Articles cobbled together fragments of information, past tales, speculation and facts to build a picture of the events rocking Australians that morning. The police were investigating but in the absence of facts, news broadcasters competed for attention by supposing. Some fuelled hysteria with suggestions that terrorists or extremist environmentalists were responsible. Others provided endless lists of possible suspects. The formidable litany of people who preferred the Prime Minister gone, if not dead, belied their claims he was popular. Shelley was a 'Wrogarth hater' and she'd never denied it, but she had wanted him out of office, not dead.

She read and reread the articles trying to sift out the facts. A deep sense of dread sent a shiver along her spine. Until now, Australia had been safe from the extremism taking hold of the world, but not anymore. Political unrest and assassinations happened in other countries, countries where people were passionate, emotional and expressive, not in the laid-back Australia she knew, at least that's what she'd always believed. The apathy that so annoyed her, however, had also provided comfort.

Adrian was in Sydney. He had gone to confront his father and his mother's death and the story building around Ayisha and Ashram had fuelled his rising anger. But Adrian was not capable of this, he could never…could he?

Adrian wasn't answering his phone and Shelley thought of calling Jason to share her fears and uncertainties. But it didn't feel right. She needed to talk to Adrian first. Instead, she reached for her jacket, grabbed her handbag and walked outside.

She ambled to the bustling café precinct, her thoughts unravelling like a dropped ball of wool. The unseasonably warm weather had brought people out of their homes and the strange spring weather added to her sense of unreality. Noise spilled onto the footpath from the open cafés in full swing of their Saturday morning trade. People clustered in groups and extra chairs and tables formed irregular patterns in the usually orderly space. Shelley found a vacant table and ordered a strong long black. While eavesdropping, she noted how much more animated people were as they heatedly discussed the assassination.

She reached for the paper and gasped. Adrian's picture stared from the front page. It was a younger and more carefree version, but unmistakeably Adrian. The caption called him William Wrogarth and gave his alias, implying he was hiding something. He was wanted for questioning and although the carefully phrased comments by the police avoided attaching suspicion, the reporter had added his.

Shelley read it aloud, the sound as terrifying as the silent reading, but adding her voice made the words sink in. Adrian was suspected of murdering his father. The report implied William's fall out with his father meant William bore him a grudge. They skimmed over James Wrogarth's misdeeds and William's previous exposure of the scandal was not mentioned. James Wrogarth was dead and in death he was a much better person than he had ever been in life.

She trembled at the mention of William's link to a terrorist. Akbal's arrest, William's attempt to help him, his involvement in asylum seeker issues and his Paris meeting with Mohamed, the terrorist responsible for a failed attempt to bomb the London Underground, were carefully woven into a damning tapestry. It stacked up plausibly as the disgruntled son being turned by terrorists. It was a credible story and if Shelley hadn't known the real one, she might even have believed it herself.

No matter how fervent Adrian was, no matter how much he loathed his father, she could not believe he would do this. Was she being naïve, putting her faith in someone she didn't know that well? In the six months since Paris, she had changed and forged a new way of life. Adrian had helped her achieve that. He gave so much to help others. His strong feelings about his father, his mother's death and autopsy report had affected him deeply, but to do this? She refused to believe it.

Beside her, everyone had an opinion. The tall man at the table on the right ranted that 'William' must have been coaxed into murdering his father by a terrorist cell. It was William's naivety and hatred that had led him. It sounded like a TV crime series plot. The woman beside him counselled caution, arguing they should wait for more information before passing judgement. Most of those around her were content to use the scant fragments of information, gossip and innuendo to make up their minds. They were willing to be judge and jury, with some already convicting and passing sentence on 'William'.

Shelley drained her coffee and fled, venturing into a park where the solitude could help her mind to roam. The discussions in the café had raised ugly and frightening thoughts but now, in the peace and quiet, those thoughts focused. Despite her resolve, doubts crept in. Walking along the winding paths, Shelley again overheard snippets of other's conversations, a word here, a phrase there; everyone was talking about it. It wasn't the assassination that seemed to enthral them but the intrigue of a scandal with human emotions and passions. They couldn't stop trying to guess what had happened. This was a real-life murder mystery and they were all super sleuths uncovering the murderer.

It was impossible to accept the injustice of it. She clenched her fists. Once someone's name or reputation was muddied it was hard to set the record straight, even when proved innocent. The guesswork and innuendo were hurting Adrian and she hoped the police would not settle on an easy answer. Look what had happened to Akbal.

Shelley perched on a bench, trying to calm down. She was helpless to combat the heavy weight of public opinion. Public opinion, like the momentum of a lynch mob, could steamroll anyone who tried to resist. As though mirroring her mood, the rain clouds moved across and obscured the sky. Gloom enveloped her physically, mentally and emotionally. Cold shivers travelled up her spine, but she didn't care if it rained.

She sighed. It didn't seem to matter what James Wrogarth had done. Somehow, they had to shift the focus back onto the Prime Minister and the bigger story. How a Prime Minister and the government had been able to form corrupt deals and abuse asylum seekers were the big question that needed an answer. She would have to cope with the hysteria as the murder enquiry continued. Hopefully, Adrian would exit the limelight sooner rather than later. The police were seeking two other visitors to the PM's office from that night. There was one in dark clothing and a cap which obscured his face and another, who hadn't stayed long but had managed to avoid the camera eye. The police surmised he had known where the cameras were. They might occupy the public speculation too.

Her phone buzzed – a text from Adrian. It didn't explain but told her he was at the police station. Now she really did need a distraction to take her mind off Adrian and what he had or had not done.

Chapter 45

Shelley listened intently as Ralph gave his interview on TV. Scrubbed up in Ralph's version of tidy he stood erect and confident. His belly still protruded well into the space between him and the interviewer, but the shirt stayed firmly tucked. His gruff voice clearly explained his investigation with an elegance the events did not deserve. His face was serious and his voice deep and strong. It was a very different Ralph to the one she had met in Port Augusta. He skilfully avoided naming his sources. He seemed to be enjoying the attention, but Shelley watched with trepidation. She hoped this would shock people out of their complacency.

Ralph outlined the proof against James Wrogarth, identifying the extent of his corruption and that of Mark McCracken. It even shocked Shelley when she heard the full story of how widespread and deep the corruption ran.

The weight of the knowledge she, Adrian and Jason had uncovered bore down on her. A tear slid down her cheek at the mention of Ayisha and the story of her death. Thankfully Didi was now in the care of a human rights advocacy group who were working to expose Serpentco's involvement. The sensational story of asylum seekers being forced into sex slavery was finally igniting public outrage and the letters to the editor were turning. There was more sympathy for the human beings caught up in the tragedy and less condemnation of illegals.

Shelley flicked through the documents she'd rescued from the shredding frenzy at work. Some showed key people in her department had kept their suspicions to themselves. Being a whistle-blower was hard, Shelley understood, she herself had been a reluctant moral crusader. What she didn't understand was why some were still trying to cover it up and protect the government. Perhaps they were protecting their own positions and holding on to their minor power base.

The Minister for Immigration denied all knowledge and pledged to investigate. He wouldn't get away with it, she was sure. People in the department and others were, at last, speaking up. Emboldened by the public outcry, some, under the cover of 'I was just following orders', were telling what they knew and revelling in their five minutes of fame. The different voices illuminated the pieces of the intricate puzzle and formed a horrendous picture.

The Federal Police were clearly implicated, although Shelley believed it would take more than the current story to spark public protest at Akbal's treatment. There were plenty of excuses and justifications in the name of public security but now a groundswell of support had started for him. For now, Ashram remained hidden, but his legal team was planning their appeals and arguments. Adrian had been busy despite his own worries.

Shelley readied herself for the meeting and the chance to talk to Adrian in person and to share what they had learned. They should congratulate themselves on their tenacious investigations and now, more than ever needed to support each other. It was an important step to help them face what was ahead because they all knew the matter was far from finished.

***

Jason studied the list; it was obvious once the directors' names sat under one another. The four directors of Ortansea and their wives were: Milosevic and Alicia Jacov; Martin and Anna Carlew; Peter and Agnetha Jorgen; and Gustav and Petra Muncher. The names of the four wives formed the initials AAAP. It led them to the places to look and straight to the money trail. It was incredibly complex, but they had the evidence to show that Ortansea was secretly using AAAP to run illegal operations.

Jason puffed up his chest, savouring his opportunity to enlighten Klaus. The international newspapers had the story and were about to print the scandal. Not only had they exposed these companies' dealings in Australia, but Klaus had also discovered inconsistencies in their operations elsewhere. The UN was getting involved. It was a serious coup and he smiled as he and Klaus shared the news.

419

'It's been reported that Petro Golgovich is hiding in Russia,' Klaus said.

'Is there confirmation that Mark McCracken is with him?' Jason asked as he read how Mark was really Marcus Kraczynski, the nephew of Petro Golgovich.

'No. They're holding him in London.'

'I'm working on exposing Martin Carlew now. He's been hiding from the limelight and his press releases deny any association but Ralph has been a great help here.'

Jason marvelled at how the investigative skills of the general press improved as they got closer to the scandal. Each tussled for their own scoop. Spurred on by Ralph's success they delved deeper and now documents tying Carlew to Golgovich and McCracken had surfaced. The money trails tied back to Wrogarth and some of his closest allies were becoming embroiled in the scandal. The opposition revelled in the campaign, urging the immediate cancellation of the Serpentco contracts and a full investigation of their operations.

'How are you and your family now?' Klaus asked without expecting a full explanation.

'Dad's announced his retirement. His association with Carlew is under investigation. Mum has joined AA at last and has left dad.' Jason said, surprised that after forty-five years his mother had walked away and left Jason's dad broken. 'After seeing his struggle to cope

I have to admit I feel a twinge of sympathy, but only a twinge,' he said with a laugh.

Who'd have thought that was possible. He was reconciled to helping both of them, and although he didn't admit it to Klaus, he was almost looking forward to the role.

He checked his watch and gasped. He signed off his discussion with Klaus, promising to fill him in on the meeting. Klaus repeated his promise to help Jason edit his book. It took a while for Jason to recognise the feeling that came over him as a sense of confidence and anticipation. The book would happen. He was going to do it for once in his life, or maybe, just for the first time of many. He was going to complete his project. He grabbed his jacket and keys and raced out the door.

***

Daryl paced, not his normal reaction, but he had to do something to help him think. Ralph's interview had been impressive, sufficient information to convey the seriousness of the scandal but not overwhelm the public. The documents were safe.

The police hadn't made much progress so far. He cursed. William was still a person of interest but at least they were looking further. He was glad the images were indistinct. He'd forgotten about the camera by the door and apparently, so had the other visitor. He scratched his head pensively. The murder was a crime of passion and he'd had the passion that night. It scared him to think just how angry and out of control he'd been.

Tim Curleigh was now in charge, trying to shore up his position and nullify the controversy. At first, Mark had moved across to be Tim's right-hand man, but the allegations brought their plans undone. Mark fled but his escape from justice was short-lived. Tim was still trying to bluff it out. His cool, calm countenance and his resonant and strong voice only half succeeded in portraying outrage. The news broadcast showed him promising to investigate the 'rumours and innuendo'. He pledged to stamp out any wrongdoing. His attempt to force order into this time of disarray comforted those who wanted to believe the scandal was all lies but for others, it sounded hollow. Daryl shook his head as he watched that familiar hard-set mouth. Tim was not going to get away with it. Tim was going to pay the price for his deceit.

Chapter 46

Shelley huddled by the fire and crossed her fingers in a desperate attempt to summon the luck required to deliver the happy Hollywood ending she so craved.

Adrian rubbed his hands across his haggard face. He stooped before her, an invisible weight bearing down on him. Even the smile lines around his mouth seemed to have faded. He stood by the chair, his fingers intertwining and releasing in an erratic rhythm. He stared at his watch, taking time to focus on the dial and then sighed. Tonight was not the time for Jason to be late. She caught Akbal's eye and he grimaced, shrugging his shoulders in a sign of impatience. He too still showed the signs of the past months. His face had noticeably healed, but his spirit hadn't.

Carla, Adrian's colleague, and her family were on holiday and Carla had offered the house for their meeting. This lovingly restored bluestone cottage in Parkside was perfect as a warm and neutral space, away from the press and other surveillance and enabled them to talk freely.

The knock on the door announced Jason's arrival and all eyes watched him rush into the room. Shedding his jacket with a flourish he plopped himself down next to Akbal.

'Sorry, I got lost,' he said, his smile replaced by a shrug when he saw their reaction. 'It's starting to rain out there,' he said to no-one in particular.

'OK.' The tightness in Adrian's voice was a regular feature lately. He stared at Jason, who finally turned and caught Adrian's eye. Jason mumbled another apology.

Adrian let his gaze rest on each person for a moment before moving it to the next. He locked eyes with Shelley and they softened slightly. She longed to reach out and touch him or at least stand beside him, but she knew he had to do this alone.

'You all know by now, I've been keeping a secret. James Wrogarth is…was…my father.'

He scanned their faces again, searching for their reactions, but they had already been played out privately. 'I am the number one suspect for my father's murder,' he continued, looking down at his hands momentarily and when he raised his eyes there was an unmistakable fire there. He straightened his back. 'I didn't do it.'

Shelley watched the group react. They seemed reassured.

'I admit, I discovered things about my father that made me deeply ashamed. He was worse than even I suspected. We'd fallen out years ago, hadn't spoken since… except on the night that he was murdered.'

'You did see him?' Akbal asked as he slid forward in his seat.

'Yes, I did. That is me on the surveillance tape.'

'No-one would blame you,' Jason said, sitting forward. 'In fact, people should be applauding whoever did it.'

Adrian shook his head violently. 'Murder is never the answer.'

He paced then suddenly stopped and turned to the group. 'It's true I wanted to confront him. I wanted him to admit the truth. I was angry at him, angrier than I have ever been. My mother's…'

Adrian swallowed down the emotion threatening to choke him. He sat down then almost immediately got up again and paced the floor. 'I didn't get the chance. He was alive, but he was too drunk. He just slurred inane nonsense as justification and I realised I wasn't going to get anything sensible out of him. It had been a useless exercise. He was…' He clenched his fists, holding one inside the other tightly to stop it lashing out.

'Why did you call this meeting?' Jason asked and Shelley wondered if he'd been expecting Adrian's confession.

'I wanted you to know that I didn't do it. I hated him enough…but I didn't kill him.'

Adrian's eyes glistened and he grabbed a glass of water from the coffee table and the water inside became tidal.

Straightening his back, his voice gathered tone. 'I wanted to make him pay, pay for what he did to my mother, not just her death but during her life, to pay for the asylum seekers and all the dirty politics he's been involved in. Killing him would have let him off the hook. I wanted him to suffer, go to gaol, watch his reputation turn to dust, strip him of his power. He should have stayed alive to see people's disgust at how corrupt he had become.'

Shelley couldn't hold back now – she walked over and held his arm. She could hear him grit his teeth with frustration. His father had escaped justice.

The room filled with silence and finally, Adrian sat down and slumped in the chair. Jason looked at the faces around the group. He watched Shelley's face as he spoke, as though she was the barometer for his success.

'I believe you, Adrian. I never thought you were capable of murder. Is there any way we can help?'

Adrian leaned forward. 'I've got a lawyer, but I'm not sure what else I can do at this stage.'

Adrian had always been confident and decisive in helping others, he now seemed strangely uncertain about how to help himself.

Jason sat back, scratching his chin as he stared up at the ceiling. 'Have the press got all the dirt on him? Do they know everything?' he asked.

'Reports have tied him to criminal gangs, through Mark McCracken. He's the nephew of Petro Golgovich, who runs the Russian mafia. They're a sordid family and we can prove there are links between Mark and Wrogarth, but I'm not sure what else Ralph Evans has. He claims to have proof that my father masterminded the whole thing,' Adrian replied.

'Excuse me if I am a little behind in the story, but what are the corrupt deals? I know my arrest and…interrogation…were just the Feds and Wrogarth pushing their fear campaign and their war on terror. And of course, score points as tough on security,' Akbal said, studying the scars on his hands. 'You don't have to if it's too hard, but I would like to know the whole story.'

'Each of you found a piece of the puzzle,' Adrian replied, looking at the group in a request to take the burden of the telling.

Jason took up the baton. 'Wrogarth signed a deal with Ortansea to allow mining in the national parks. That in itself was a problem. The company had had so many dubious incidents in Africa and elsewhere, so they set up a dud company for its operations here, AAAP. They were not only mining for uranium, but they had also found coal seam gas too and were using fracking methods which were experimental, to say the least. They were using chemicals harmful to the environment. Even Professor Hutchinson has told his story about the pressure put on him. His son's accident wasn't an accident and has been linked back to Mark McCracken and to Wrogarth. We don't know who knew about the oil cleansing operations Ortansea was running. They were buying and extracting dirty oil internationally and from sites in the outback. It's contaminated with sulphur and needs to be cleaned before they can sell it. The cleaning process produces a toxic residue which is too expensive to treat and the Europeans were watching them for any illegal dumping because of Ortansea's last two cases, so the directors came up with a plan. AAAP took it off their hands. They took over the disused mines and then illegally buried the waste in the outback where it could take years before anyone would notice.'

Jason passed the baton to Shelley. 'They wanted cheap labour to maximise their profits and they needed employees that wouldn't talk. Wrogarth, Mark McCracken and the Ortansea directors came to an agreement. They built detention centres near the mines with the intention of using the asylum seekers as their labour force. Instead of the boats, organised by Petro, being turned back to Indonesia, as Wrogarth said they were doing, they had tankers pick them up under cover of darkness and bring them to a private port. They contracted Serpentco as their private security company and with their connection to the criminal world they were perfect for the job.'

'So, they used the asylum seekers to build the roads and prepare for legitimate mining as well as to dig the pits and dump the toxic sludge from the oil cleaning?' Akbal confirmed.

'Yes, that's why they were getting sick. I realised they were suffering from contact symptoms and they were the same as those Yasmine was treating in Africa. Ortansea were known to be dumping their waste there. When Carla noticed symptoms in the local Aboriginal kids who'd been playing in the dirt piles, I realised their symptoms were the same.' Adrian sounded calmer now, obviously concentrating on the details took his mind off his own plight.

'As if that wasn't enough, agreements with the Russian mafia meant they were also making a profit from the poor women. The

Russian mafia had arranged the arrival of boats to coincide with Wrogarth's media campaign. They used the men for the physical labour but they couldn't always guarantee they'd only have strong men. Sometimes there were women and children on board too. The women and children were sent to detention centres in the city. The older ones were used to babysit, cook and clean in the centre, while the young and strongest ones were handpicked to work in the brothels as prostitutes. They threatened them with deportation or harming their husbands or children, anything to force them to do as they were told.' Shelley said, a shiver running up her spine as she thought of what had been happening to these women and again thinking of Ayisha.

Akbal emitted an audible groan. 'That is the kind of evil we were running away from,' he whispered.

Adrian's phone rang. He glanced at the display then answered it.

'Hi. I've been trying to call you,' he said as he turned his back on the group.

Shelley watched him lean over his phone. The others talked quietly, using the interruption to clarify their understanding of the web of issues.

'You too? You didn't…'

The pain in Adrian's voice was easily identified and Shelley's heart beat faster. As his back relaxed, Shelley's own muscles responded.

'I'll find you a good lawyer. Don't say anything until he is with you.' Adrian said, clearly back in busy mode.

He hung up and immediately started punching numbers into his phone, walking out into the hall to complete his task. The group was transfixed and stared at the doorway, listening in on the mumbles from the hall without understanding anything. Shelley itched to find out what was happening but sat with her hands tucked under her legs, forcing down her curiosity. When Adrian walked back in, all eyes watched his progress and conversation ceased. Shelley couldn't hold back.

'What is it?' she asked, almost afraid of the answer.

'It's Daryl, dad's adviser. He was one of the others on the CCTV visiting dad that night. He's on his way to the police to confess,' he said then swallowed noisily. Adrian stared at his silent phone. 'He told me he didn't kill dad, although he planned to. He knows who the third visitor is, the one who murdered…dad. I'm getting Daryl a good lawyer. He'll need one because the third visitor is Tim Curleigh.'

'Who?' Jason asked staring at the others for an answer.

'Tim Curleigh, Dad's deputy,' Adrian responded. 'He's the current Prime Minister.'

'He's the one who's been saying there would be a full investigation…' Jason continued then stopped as they all nodded.

'Why would he murder Wrogarth?' Shelley asked, not sure she could handle any more shocks.

'He's been sidling up to Mc Cracken, and Dad was threatening his political career,' Adrian explained.

They sat silently. Shelley, unable to find any satisfactory words, reached out and held his hand. Adrian's body tensed, as if ready for action.

'Daryl has the documents. They prove Dad and Mark McCracken conspired with the mining companies and knew what was happening. He's sending me copies. He's already given a copy to his journo friend, Ralph.'

Shelley gasped. Ralph had friends in interesting places and she felt more confident now that the scandals would be exposed. Now they just had to work out what she and Jason would do about Ashram and their part in his escape.

Chapter 47

As Shelley and Adrian drove along King William Road a newspaper advertising board caught her eye. Tim Curleigh had been arrested last night. At last, Adrian was in the clear. Curleigh's attempts to bluster his way through in true politician style had failed, although he claimed it had been an accident. He'd been provoked and he hadn't meant to kill Wrogarth. Ralph's daily articles combined with the ad hoc confessions of bureaucrats and tell-all exposés on TV had destroyed Wrogarth's credibility along with that of a number of government ministers. Tim Curleigh had some questions to answer too.

His deep hatred for Wrogarth, their long-running feud and Wrogarth's tactics to thwart Curleigh's ambitions, were all exposed in the media. Curleigh's wife joined the chorus of voices, claiming her husband should have been Prime Minister but had waited too long. She hadn't known he had an association with McCracken. Her statements, issued from her parent's home in the Caribbean, painted a picture of Curleigh as a weak, ambitious and ruthless man.

Shelley rubbed her forehead trying to concentrate on the confrontation ahead. During the week her emotions had plummeted to new depths, only to soar in equal measure to great heights, and it had left her drained. Her stomach knotted painfully as they pulled up in front of the bungalow with the cottage garden. Adrian held her hand all the way to the front door.

Inside, the familiar worn sofa felt less familiar with Adrian sitting beside her. Her mother fussed with plates of sandwiches and cups of tea while Shelley desperately wanted her to sit down and join in the conversation. Shelley's dad was his usual self, engaging Adrian in sports talk as though he had always known him. Shelley smiled; she hadn't realised Adrian was interested in football. There was still so much to learn about him. Shelley got up and joined her mother in the kitchen.

'Well?' she said nervously.

Shelley's mother's eyes lit up as she smiled. 'I had my reservations,' she said placing more canapés on a plate. 'The newspaper reports…his history.'

Shelley's heart sank. Was it ever going to get easier? Before she could speak her mother patted her on the shoulder.

'He's not a traditional man…not like…Tom,' she added.

Shelley grimaced but suppressed the spark of anger at the mention of Tom's name. Again, before she could respond, her mother went on.

'He seems nice and most of all, he seems to care about you. You obviously care about him too.' She stood awkwardly at the kitchen bench and added quietly, 'I want you to be happy. You deserve to be.' Mother and daughter embraced.

'You've changed,' her mother said.

'Yes, I have,' Shelley answered and laughed. She didn't know if her mother approved or not, but it didn't matter.

Shelley and Adrian still had a lot to learn about each other, although they knew the important things. Her pulse quickened, the path before them would have rocky spots, he was a man of passion and, as she'd discovered, she had passions too. Thankfully she wouldn't have to battle her family along the way. No-one knew about her part in Ashram's escape, except their close friends, and hopefully, it would remain her secret. The breakout was reported as a detainee capitalising on weak security and Serpentco was taking the flack. Ralph denied knowing Ashram was a fugitive until after they had reached Sydney. His enemies would probably dispute this but it was only minor news, overshadowed by the sordid scandal unfolding in the public domain.

Shelley smiled. What lay ahead held promise, commitment, and a new life. She'd grown, no longer someone else's version of Shelley although more change was before her. This was the real new beginning. A new career, a new relationship and a new phase in the country's governance were more than enough to start with.

Acknowledgments

It has taken me many years to write this novel. It began as a concept in 2007 (although the seed was planted before then), and while I was writing I was learning. With the help of WEA courses, the Adelaide University Creative writing post graduate course and SA Writers' I learned the craft of building a story.

I want to thank the members of the Novelist Circle writers' group that are a valuable source of feedback and advice. They critiqued one chapter at a time and then, once the novel was ready, the entire novel. Special thanks to Sandra O'Grady, Steve Davey, Ros Whysall, Poppy Nwosu, Joe Wrin, Debbie Rumere, Sonya Bates and Susan Neuhaus.

Thank you also to the Inkitt community, especially authors, Greg McLaughlin, Barry Litherland, Trudy Knowles, Kelly Reigner, Dominic Breiter, Matthew Arnold Stern and Mark Mijuskovic who read and reviewed Deadly Secrets, offered comments, advice and support and encourage me still. They are a valuable boost to my confidence.

This novel is fiction but the plot began with the inevitable question of 'what if?' It is a work of imagination however, I devoured news and newspapers as research and the book, *Dirty Money: The true cost of Australia's mineral boom* by Matthew Benns helped me to refine the plot using real life events. It is worth reading.

Huge thanks to Amanda Ní Odhràin from Let's Get Booked who edited the book, designed the stunning cover and formatted the file ready for publication. She turned my manuscript into a professional looking novel.

And, last but certainly not least, thank you to my family, especially John, Michaela, Andrew and Leeann who have supported and encouraged me along the way, have been my first readers, offering their advice and critiques and shared the Inkitt version with friends to help me get reviews. I love you and appreciate your interest, unwavering support and encouragement.

I also want to thank those people not individually mentioned but who helped me along the way.

It has taken a lot of years, commitment, effort, and rewriting to get to this point and I really hope readers enjoy reading it.

ABOUT THE AUTHOR

Hi. I'm an Australian author, based in Adelaide, South Australia although I grew up just outside of Melbourne.

Deadly Secrets is the culmination of many years of learning, writing and rewriting. Besides novels I have written numerous short stories, to date three have been published.

'A Present of Presence' included in the auspicious anthology, *When Stars Will Shine* (9 Dec 2019)

'Reunited' in the *Writers' and Readers' Magazine* (Jan 2020)

'Unforgivable' in the *Writers' and Readers' Magazine* (Oct 2019).

Although I've scribbled story snippets and scenes all my life, in 2011 I got serious and successfully completed a Graduate Certificate in Creative Writing at Adelaide University. I'd taken a variety of writing courses at Writers SA and WEA before that (and still do). My original degree is a Bachelor of Science (majoring in chemistry), and my career in the public service spanned roles as diverse as management trainer, team facilitator, statistician and laboratory assistant. Writing waited until I had time, energy and brain-space, but perhaps it also helped me gather a wealth of ideas and life experience.

One of my other passions is travelling, which includes writing a travel journal and taking copious photos, some of which feature on my website linking images to scenes in the novel. I also enjoy live theatre, art and of course, reading. Most years you'll find me hanging around the Adelaide Writers' Week event in March, listening to authors speak and adding to my overflowing to-be-read pile of books.

You can register on my website and stay tuned for my second thriller coming soon, or connect with me on:

Facebook page: https://www.facebook.com/hrkemp01

Facebook: https://www.facebook.com/hr.kemp.31

Website: https://www.hrkempauthor.com

If you enjoyed this novel – and I certainly hope you did – please leave a review on Goodreads or the site where you purchased the novel. It can be short (one sentence) or longer, but please don't include any spoilers. Thank you.

Printed in Australia
AUHW020833130821
350317AU00001B/1

9 780648 766346